The Chronicle of Stolen Dreams

ALSO BY TERRY TARNOFF

The Bone Man of Benares

The Thousand Year Journey of Tobias Parker

Once Upon a Time in Goa

The Chronicle of Stolen Dreams

A Novel

Terry Tarnoff

San Francisco

ISBN 978-0-9888585-4-1

www.terrytarnoff.com

For Tina,
who came to me as if guided by some unseen hand

ACKNOWLEDGMENTS

My deepest thanks to everybody everywhere who ever encouraged me, supported me, sustained me, put up with me, and took me just seriously enough to read between the lines.

—Terry Tarnoff

The Chronicle of Stolen Dreams

Bring me all of your dreams,
You dreamers,
Bring me all of your
Heart melodies
That I may wrap them
In a blue cloud-cloth
Away from the too-rough fingers
Of the world.
—Langston Hughes

Author's Note

I awoke one night from a disturbing dream, a dream which recurred each and every night but varied just enough to keep me completely off-balance. The dream had something to do with being evicted from my cottage, the appearance of an unidentified intruder, and the fear of wandering down a long, dark alley. The images weren't particularly unusual, but they existed in a kind of void which offered no context or background information that might allow me to uncover any kind of deeper meaning. Every night it was the same thing: I'd wake up in the haze of this alternate world, I'd tell myself not to forget the details, and then I'd watch them disappear right before my eyes. I tried everything to grab hold of them, telling myself, wait, you're fully conscious, you're aware of your surroundings, yes, you're in your bed, it's the middle of the night, the dream is in your conscious mind... except that it wasn't anymore. Night after night, the dream simply faded away. On this particular night, however, there was something different. I awoke as always, but rather than seeing the usual images disappear, I saw a series of ones and zeroes that were sitting just a few inches outside my mind's eye. I can't explain how, but I simply *knew* that those ones and zeroes were digital representations of the cottage, the man, and the alley, and now *they* were disappearing, as if lines of computer code were being sucked out of my brain by a vacuum cleaner. I watched in a kind of mental paralysis as the ones and zeroes were being erased and carted away. They disappeared from the bottom up, row after row after row, like a teletype machine in reverse. Only now it wasn't just the usual mental images that were gone; now it was something more, something sinister. It was as if my innermost thoughts were being harvested, processed, and exported somewhere else. I lie there defenseless as the lines of ones and zeroes were being added up, subdivided, and repackaged into little bundles of mental energy. My dreams themselves were being stolen and there was nothing I could do about it. I was being stripped of something terribly private. This, I think, is where it all began:

Chapter 1

*"The difference between stupidity and
genius is that genius has its limits."*
—Albert Einstein

The 17th moon of Aspara disappeared behind a magnetic cloud formation as Jaxson Epsilon and his crew
of merry miscreants passed by in a blur on their way
from somewhere to somewhere else. That one planet could
have 17 moons seemed excessive and Jaxson had no idea how
they could all stay in orbit without at least a few of them
crashing into one other. It was another miracle of science
which completely escaped him, probably because he had not
the slightest aptitude for that most arcane of disciplines. As
far as Jaxson was concerned, a puppeteer could've been
dangling those moons on strings, were it not for the fact that
there were no strings in space and precious few puppeteers.

Jaxson and his crew had been on their spaceship for so
long, they barely knew what was up and what was down
anymore, not that it makes much difference when traveling
through a shapeless universe that cares not one iota for tired
concepts such as time and space. They'd been gone for two or
twenty years and had traveled eight or eighty fathoms and all
that really mattered was that they weren't there yet, "there"
being some long gone planet they were hoping to grab by the
balls and give a good shake. Earth, it was called, a strangely

guttural name that harkened back to some prehistoric, mono-syllabic time. *E-a-a-r-r-t-t-h-h*. The very name made you swallow hard.

Jaxson was bored silly. As Ship's Observer he had remark-ably little to do except to observe and report, but when staring into the endless blackness of space there wasn't all that much observation to report upon. How many ways, after all, were there to describe absolute nothingness, the infinite abyss, and the interminable void? Sixty-three, at last count, but even a master wordsmith like Jaxson was nearing his limit. Mostly he just sat there daydreaming, which is to say, he dreamt of day, those extraordinary hours of natural light that were now nothing but a faint memory. He desperately missed the subtle variations of morning sunlight, the elon-gated shadows of late afternoon, and the chiaroscuro grid of the evening landscape. Now it was nothing but sameness, the same sameness that always hung outside his observation portal like a thick black curtain.

Space is full of unimaginable sights and sounds, of ex-ploding nebulae and pulsating energy streams, but not the part of space that Jaxson and his crew were in, no, they were in a subsection of the universe known as *empty* space, an appropriately named corridor in which a big cosmic broom had swept an alleyway completely clean and left absolutely nothing, which is to say there was no matter, no anti-matter, no quasar puffs, and no squiggly shimmers. They were there because Hieronymus Wambold, their overly cautious cap-tain, had decided to play it safe and had chosen a flight plan that minimized conflict, danger, and anything of possible interest. By Wambold's thinking, to enter nothingness was to assure that nothing would go wrong, but it also made less likely the possibility that anything would go right, either, and as far as Jaxson was concerned nothing had gone right since the day they strapped him into the spaceship and said, "Have a nice day."

Not that Wambold was to be taken lightly. He was a legend in the rarified circles of astroclimatology, where a whole new temperature system had been named after him. The average temperature of space was forevermore known as −90° Wambold instead of the old +60° Witherspoon due to his discovery that ice fizzles straight into gas when looping around the planet Abkazar on the sequester equinox. Jaxson, being of unscientific mind, had no idea whether −90° Wambold meant that he should bring sun block or thermal underwear on his journey across the skies, so he brought both his thermies *and* his string lace T-shirt, just in case. That was a long, long time ago. Jaxson, Wambold, and five other crew members had set off on a grand experiment to the far reaches of the universe where they were to test a theoretical proposition on some human guinea pigs called "Earthlings." If it worked, they'd be heroes back home. If it didn't, they might not even be able to *get* back home. It was, therefore, with a combination of exuberance and trepidation that Jaxson flashed their headlights at the first spaceship they passed, just like they used to do in the old days.

"Hey, Jaxson, what was that all about?" said Captain Wambold, jerking his brittle body into what was clearly marked as Jaxson's personal space of the spaceship.

"Nothing."

"Nothing? I don't think that was nothing. Did someone tell you to flash our beams like that?"

"No, not really."

"*Not really.* Hmm. So what you did was not nothing. It was something. Would you agree with that?"

"I suppose so. Technically."

"*Technically.* I see. And the something you did, did it occur to you that it was completely outside your jurisdiction as Ship Observer, that there are inherent dangers in abrogating the chain of command, and that nowhere in your job description is there any mention whatsoever of your taking a proactive role in the running, maintaining, and functioning of this vehicle?"

"Hey, I flashed the headlights. That's all I did. It wasn't a big deal. I just did it."

Wambold stared at Jaxson a moment too long, then leaned back into his pod chair. "I shall duly make note of the incident in our logs."

"Fine."

"As you were."

As I was? said Jaxson to himself. *Isn't this guy wound a little too tight? Okay, then, where was I?* Jaxson thanked his lucky stars that at least there were other crew members onboard to share this excursion to the other side of oblivion. Not that he really believed in lucky stars, but the idea of giving mystical significance to big balls of compressed gas helped pass the time. He loved imagining that some obscure constellation could be the personification of health, wealth, and happiness, not just the random accumulation of hydrogen and helium. As for the crew, they were their own random masses of obscure elements that provoked their own mysteries. Strange how often he viewed the stars in terms of exotic, vibrant personalities while seeing his crewmates as mostly inert chemicals.

Inert or not, those six co-inhabitants in space were all he had to keep from going completely crazy, so he welcomed them with broad pen strokes and an open heart. Not that his attempts at brotherhood and fraternity were well-received or even returned. It was a serious bunch he was thrown in with, a group of specialists more renowned for their scientific achievements than for their life skills and Jaxson's injections of levity usually floated right over their heads. Take for example, Chief Engineer Westinghouse Teller, a remorseless misanthrope who was unsympathetic to any kind of frivolity in even the best of times. Teller was in charge of the mechanical operations of the spacecraft, a run-of-the-mill Pulsar 7 that had been demothballed and put into emergency service. The Pulsar 7 was a proletarian vehicle guaranteed to get its passengers where they were going but lacking any frills that might set their hearts aflutter. It was part of Reverie Energy's new austerity program that placed efficiency above extravagance and Teller was the perfect face of austerity run amok. He'd heard somewhere that "less is more" and took it to heart, not realizing that less is more only on the rare occasions when excess isn't vastly preferable. Teller made sure there was less of everything onboard—less space, less food, less relaxation, less entertainment, less conversation—and had succeeded in creating a catatonic atmosphere that perfectly mirrored the abject landscape outside.

"Hey, Teller," said Jaxson, leaning over to the rigidly straight visage seated at the next observation post, "did you hear the one about the mechanical engineer who walks into a bar with a frog on his head?"

"Not now, Jaxson, I'm busy."

Teller was always too busy, as far as Jaxson was concerned. That was the problem with him and the rest of the crew and the entire flight. Everyone was too busy to laugh or joke around or kick back and enjoy the scenery of which, of course, there was none. "So the bartender says, 'Hey, what's that?'"

"Did you hear me, Jaxson?"

"To which the frog replies, 'I don't know. It started out as a wart on my ass and then *this* happened.'"

"Jaxson!"

You're a real dickhead, Teller, Jaxson wanted to say. "Sorry to bother you, Teller," Jaxson said.

The crew's legacy was in Jaxson's hands and he took pains to present his compatriots in the best possible light, light, of course, being a relative term extracted from their collective memories since none of them had seen any light since the day of their departure. Ah, the glorious day of departure! It had been a bright early morning, the sun had risen over the horizon, and little waves of heat radiated off the tarmac. "God speed," said the controller at Countdown Central and off they went, five-four-three-two-one, into the not-so-great beyond.

Here's a little experiment, wrote Jaxson in his log. *Tie a blindfold around your eyes. Place your head inside a thick, corrugated, cardboard box. Tape the box closed. Place a heavy-duty, triple-ply plastic bag around the cardboard box and tie it tight. Open your refrigerator door and remove the light bulb at the rear of the unit. Push yourself all the way inside the refrigerator and close the door. Set the temperature gauge at zero. Sit there until you lose all sense of time. That's what it's like to travel through space.*

Jaxson's log was full of personal reminiscences, opinions, and fantasies that had no real place in a journal of serious scientific inquiry. He was interested in the big picture, not the nuts and bolts of its construction, and his log was veritably bursting at the seams with overblown, grandiloquent observations. One can arbitrarily open to any page of his journal, where the fractured tone of his account becomes apparent. Throw the pages into the air and rearrange them in any order, it doesn't really matter. This is not science writ large, it is barely science at all. Dip into the stew anywhere and spoon out a paragraph, this one, for example, from page 12 of his log:

Time. Who the hell knows what time is in outer space? When everything is circling everything else, there's no way to measure the passage of, well, whatever that thing is that appears to be passing, so there's no real way to tell you how long we were up in that spaceship, if up even makes any sense when there's no down, other than to say the stubble on my chin appeared to be getting longer every time I ran my fingers through my beard, which, due to my somewhat nervous nature, was pretty much always. With no sunrise and no sunset to help count off some arbitrary calendar, the whole journey was an exploration of nothingness through the dark space of timelessness unrelieved by any sense of camaraderie or joy.

Such was the nature of Jaxson's log. Where circumstances called out for scientific explication, he responded with autobiography. Where protocol demanded precision, he provided poetry. That a sci-phobe such as Jaxson would find himself front and center on an expedition of monumental importance was no small irony, one which he took delight in recounting to anyone who would listen. How many times, after all, could one report on the temperature variables of the sleeping pods, the barometric pressure of the reserve module, and humidity levels of the supply port? The old ships had cinemas, galleries, and exotic food courts. What Jaxson would've given to review a mouthwatering Baked Pulasky or critique a pre-Abolistic cloisonné vase or declaim upon the use of handheld cameras in taut Halverian thrillers! His creative side was veritably bursting from forced confinement.

My soul screams out into the night, release me, oh great incandescent puppeteer, let me soar headlong into the great unknown waves of heat and light, let the wind baffle me to and fro, let me set sail upon a sea of pure elemental energy, let me expose my innermost desires, my yearnings, my untamed madness, my insatiable lust, let me twist and turn in the firmament, carom and cruise the nine corners of the golden sphere...

Such ramblings indicated that Jaxson was quite possibly losing it, although what *it* was wasn't entirely obvious since the whole crew had become noticeably disoriented. It was as if they were piloting an intergalactic mental clinic into the craziest part of the universe and *they* were the patients. If one were to believe *Dr. Efron's Encyclopedia of Spaceborne Disease*, they were becoming too disoriented to properly evaluate the extreme risks to the physiological and psychological well-being of their team. Jaxson, for one, would've jumped at his own shadow if he even *had* a shadow anymore, but that, like everything else in this damned darkness, had been stripped away from him. To act the fool in a mental ward just might be the definition of sanity, if one were to stretch a point, and Jaxson was, if nothing else, not above stretching a point. "I'm so bored, I'm gonna blow my brains out!" he screamed at Navigation Officer Algonquin Raleigh as he came running into Raleigh's bunk-down area holding a Commander Singh ray gun to his head.

Raleigh was of a preternaturally stoic nature, a strange fellow who'd entered a transcendental meditative state at take-off and had barely said a word since. Raleigh had a look that told you everything and nothing at the same time. You could read whatever you wanted into his expression, whether agreement or disapproval, support or opposition. He blinked his eyes open, took a quick read of the situation, and gave Jaxson's shoulders two quick shakes. "He who despairs shall know despair," he said with a faraway voice.

It was a sentiment Jaxson could hardly argue with—why would anyone want to?—but it did give him pause enough to reconsider his imminent demise. What was wrong with him? Why was he threatening to kill himself? Wasn't he overreacting to the situation which, when you get right down to it, wasn't really a situation at all but more of a condition? "Thanks, Raleigh, I owe you one."

"Turn off the lights when you leave," said Raleigh as he nodded off to what Jaxson hoped was a better place.

Jaxson headed down to the spa, a crummy closet crammed into the underbelly of the engine room where Reverie Energy had begrudgingly provided a couple spoon-fuls of sand, a patch of mud, and a steam pipe that intermittently released some odiferous vapors. Jaxson hoped to catch sight of Behavioral Scientist Marta No Last Names Please, who was the love of his life and was absolutely oozing sex appeal, while trying to avoid Molecular Biochemist Marta No Last Name Requested, who was simply oozing. Marta-1 was a one-of-a-kind beauty, a one-in-a-million genius, a once-in-a-lifetime potential birthing partner, whereas Marta-2 was 2-little-2-late, and the less said the better. Now, what were the odds that a company like Reverie Energy would have two women named Marta on the payroll? Marta, after all, was hardly a common name. And what were the odds that of all the hundreds of scientists working for Reverie Energy, these two Martas would be thrown together on the same high-profile project, the very same project Jaxson was loosely observing, even though his observations were so loose as to nearly slip off his lips like an oil slick?

Jaxson peeked into the closet, waited a moment for the steam to clear, and came face to face with a multitude of naked breasts. His remarkably good fortune turned instantly into a cacophony of high, piercing shrieks that erupted from every corner of the room. He felt a kick to his knee, a punch to his midsection, and a loufa to his face as he clawed his way out to the safety of a desolate hallway. Hitting on Marta-1 was becoming a problem that Jaxson hadn't anticipated. He'd assumed that being locked up in a confined space would make the courting ritual a snap, but he was being thwarted at every step, either by circumstance, happenstance, or Marta-1 herself. He'd figured it would only be a matter of time before Marta-1 saw his charms and fell helplessly under the sway of his hypnotic personality, but after a number of failed attempts at rendezvous, he began to question if being locked up in that tiny space was in fact having just the opposite of the intended effect. It appeared that Marta-1 was either experiencing deep space claustrophobia, or, worse, was having some kind of allergic reaction to him personally, which resulted in her making a quick retreat whenever he came close. "Eew," she'd say to Jaxson upon his approach, which sounded a lot like "you" but wasn't.

"It's not like you're going to catch something from me," he'd say as she'd hurry off scratching the small red welts that invariably arose on her neck and upper arms. He was sure she had a minor case of space hives and not the more serious Jaxsonitis that previous girlfriends had contracted after the third or fourth date.

The fact is, Jaxson had never really fit in anywhere and he seemed destined to play out all of his old behavior patterns: The loner. The joker. The wise guy. Even in the darkest, deepest space he couldn't stop himself. He approached Data Transfer Officer Oblivia Mendelssohn, whose blank expression reminded him of a blackboard that had been permanently erased. Oblivia lived in another dimension ruled by other laws of physics and other conceptions of reality. She wasn't really a person in the way people had come to know each other: she was more the echo of a person, a silhouette, a shimmer, a reflection. Oblivia had the "special powers" of an idiot savant without the benefit of a recognizable personality. "Hey, Oblivia, would you like to say something into the microphone?" said Jaxson, shoving his tape recorder into her face.

Oblivia mimed a response that might have meant yes, no, or maybe.

"C'mon, don't be shy. Give the good folks back home some insight into the mind of a medium."

Oblivia reached out, took Jaxson's arm, placed her finger on the inside of his wrist, and took his pulse. What this meant was anyone's guess, like maybe it was the way savants communicated with run-of-the-mill space explorers. Maybe she was reading his blood flow the way some people read the bumps on your head. Who knew with Oblivia? Anything was possible and everything was impossible, all at the same time.

As night led into more night and promised nothing but still more night ahead, Jaxson felt like he was at a dress rehearsal for his own funeral. In a desperate attempt to relieve the boredom, he walked over to the communication station and turned on the microphone: "Ladies and gentlemen, I would like to announce that I am taking over all operations of this spacecraft and will hereafter be acting as your captain. I will inform you as to our new set of destination coordinates as soon as I have recast the charts."

Captain Wambold rustled himself out of his control chamber, walked sprightly across the bridge, and jabbed a compass point into Jaxson's chest: "Jaxson, if you don't stop screwing around, I'll put your ass in a sling and drag you behind the exhaust valves for the rest of the trip."

"Ladies and gentlemen," said Jaxson, flicking on the microphone again, "it has come to my attention that Captain Wambold has graciously agreed to remain in charge after all. Please disregard that last announcement."

Spoken like a real reporter. Which, after all was said and done, was Jaxson's actual role as Ship Observer. The fact that he barely knew what the mission was about was beginning to wear on him. He even wondered sometimes if he was being kept in the dark intentionally. Captain Wambold avoided him at every opportunity, Chief Engineer Teller never gave him a straight answer, and the rest of the crew were each their own mysteries. All he was asking for was the straight scoop right out of any reporter's handbook: Who? What? When? Where? Why? Five simple questions to which he had not a single answer. All he really knew was that Reverie Energy was all about, well, energy, and that Obsidia, Jaxson's home planet, was running out of it. Fast.

It was the age-old story: planet develops beyond its means, planet seeks quick fix, planet blows up. It had happened time and again and there was little reason to expect Obsidia to have learned any more from history than all the other balls of dead gas floating around out there. Maybe that's just the nature of life: you arise out of the muck, you have your moment in the sun, you get buried in the trash heap of history. Who knows what it's all about?

Jaxson had five simple questions. Who's behind this mission? What is the purpose of the journey? When do we arrive? Where are we going? Why are we going there? He had no idea whom to ask or what to ask. He was incapable of manipulating emotions to his advantage, to engender pity or passion, to elicit favor or support. He walked on eggshells and skated on thin ice, a man tortured by his own metaphors. He was, quite simply, lost.

Except for his harmonica. Put a harmonica in Jaxson's hands and he could bring anyone to tears in 12 bars flat, 24 max. It was his saving grace, the one thing he could rely on in an emergency situation to pull him through. It's what he was facing right at that moment, an entire crew coming at him with pitchforks and steak knives. He pulled out his diatonic Blues Harp in the Key of D and stopped them right in their tracks. He warbled a note from the lower registers and bounced it from the bunk support to the observatory tower to the escape hatch.

"Oh, my God, that's the most beautiful thing I ever heard," said Marta-2, falling to her knees and breaking into choking, sobbing tears. Oblivia and Marta-1 tried to comfort her while Wambold, Teller, and Raleigh stood there with their hands in their pockets. Jaxson did a run up and down the scales and let the notes drift down the chamber like misty clouds on a foggy mountaintop. Everything was cool again, at least for the moment, and everyone slowly went back to their stations.

Everyone except Marta-2, that is. She lingered a few moments longer, just in case Jaxson played another tune. "It's a long night's journey to day," she said as she stared out at the eternal, endless darkness of outer space. Jaxson stood there a moment, catching her gaze and feeling a weight on his shoulders. He put his harmonica back into his pocket, turned, and walked off down a cold and lonely corridor.

Chapter 2

*"If you got something you don't want other
people to know, keep it in your pocket."*
—Muddy Waters

Nick Blake stood onstage a chicken shack juke joint, his hands cupped around his harmonica and a Shure Bullet Microphone, and let out a low, plaintive wail that echoed off the walls, reverberated off the juke box, and bounced right out the door onto Indiana Avenue. Little Walter had stood on that stage, and Sonny Boy Williamson too, and their sweat and tears and alcohol breath had fused right into the plywood floor that creaked every time Nick tapped his foot to the heavy 4/4 beat. A young guy named Muddy Waters held down the rhythm with his electrified steel string guitar and his buddy Willie Dixon helped out on stand-up bass while a succession of drummers took their turns adding embellishments that were too long, too loud, and too much on top of the beat. "Let it swizzle," said Waters to the brush man who nodded knowingly but didn't understand a word. "Ain't arithmetic we cooking up, let it ride." It was Monday night at the Flame Club and anybody sober enough to make it up to the stage could blow a few bars or pound out a few beats before Muddy gave them the hook and brought down the curtain on their musical aspirations. Waters had come up from Mississippi a year or two before, along with a bunch of Delta sharecroppers who figured they'd try their luck up north in the cold and snow. A million soldiers were just back from Europe and it seemed like everyone was moving, from south to north, from east to west, from here to there, most of them with no idea what they were doing, but celebrating the fact that they hadn't left their arms and legs in the foxholes of Italy. That's who Nick was, a guy from an inconsequential town in an unimportant state who just happened to fall in with some black soldiers outside Abbruzzi who taught him to play harmonica and drink wine from a jug. It seemed only natural when his unit shipped out that he'd drift to Chicago and hook up with some of those country cats who figured out you could add electricity to your guitar and piano and suddenly those Delta blues started ringing out like the car horns and ambulances on North Clark Street. It was Waters who started it, this guy with the big voice and the electric blues guitar, but it wasn't long before Sonny Boy Williamson figured out that if you could electrify your strings you could drop a microphone onto your harmonica and that was pretty much that. Even a white boy from nowhere special could see the advantages of a modest harmonica suddenly blasting out like 16 saxophones.

Nick took a 12-bar solo, weaving in and out between Willie's thump-a-thump and Muddy's minor seventh thrillorations. Nick started in the lower register, bent a couple of notes down around his knees, then pulled them up into a tight little package of staccato bursts that punched out against the thick night air. He repeated a riff, then repeated it again, then, just for the hell of it, he repeated it *again,* and the drummer looked up to see if he had missed a change, or if the guy had completely lost count, or if maybe he'd just plain run out of ideas, but Nick's repetitive riff *was* the idea— over and over he played it, changing only slightly the pitch and timbre until it finally drilled itself right into the head, pulling at the nodes and synapses of the brain and snapping them back like strands of thick licorice. Muddy played a quick unison riff on guitar, then Willie joined in, and then the three of them hit the notes all at once and their feet moved forward together in a little subliminal strut which announced *the groove was on.* Muddy ran his fingers over an imaginary wave, then looked over and fanned Nick with his hand like to cool him down and said: "You play black." Nick took that as a compliment of the highest order since when he played it made him feel unlike anything else and took him to a place where his brain emptied out and something automatic took over. Sometimes he listened to himself play as if he were sitting in the audience, wondering with everyone else what would come next. Maybe the microphone did that. It took the notes and spun them into an old Fender Champion amp that creaked and groaned and distorted the overtones into some kind of crazy steam engine that flew down the tracks, letting off sparks and crackles while threatening to jump right off the rails. He dug deeper and pulled a B_b out of the lower register that broke some sad sister's heart and Willie looked over at Muddy and said: "The bomb."

The song ended and Nick stepped down off the stage. He limped unsteadily over to the bar where a line of short-skirted B-girls was ready to pounce on unsuspecting strangers to buy them a drink. That's what the very first girl said to him before Nick could even settle onto his bar stool. "Hey, mister, buy me a drink?" asked Esmeralda Kurlansky with a half-Jewish, half-Gypsy accent that was both charming and grating at the same time. Esmeralda had black, curly hair from her Jewish side and blacker, curlier hair from her Gypsy side and put together her hair was blacker than black—it was ebony dipped in tar washed in coal. Her eyes were just as black as her hair only they shone like black star sapphires: six points of light that pulled you right in and left you helpless and flailing and weak in the knees. That's how Nick felt right at that moment—helpless and flailing and weak in the knees—not to mention just a little jizzy in the head. "Yeah, sure, make it a double," he said, staring into her undeniably splendid punim.

"That was the most beautiful thing I ever heard," she said, staring into his eyes. That may not have been the absolute truth but it wasn't a total fabrication either and with Esmeralda half a truth was better than no truth at all. She wiped away a tear that rose out of the creaky corners of her heart and struggled with all her might not to collapse straight into his arms.

"Nick's the name," he said, reaching out for her hand.

"Esmeralda Kurlansky, but don't hold that against me. I don't believe I've seen you around this establishment before."

"I'm new in town."

"Is that right? Where from?"

"Wisconsin, originally."

"You don't say," said Esmeralda, trying to feign interest. "I've never been in that neck of the woods."

"It's just up the road. Seventy miles as the crow flies."

Esmeralda knocked back her double. "Is that right? I always liked crows. You say they got crows in Wisconsin?"

"Crows galore."

Esmeralda leaned a little closer and lowered her voice, as if to let him in on a secret. "You gotta respect crows. It's like they're always planning something behind your back, looking for an angle."

"I know just what you mean," said Nick, having no idea what she meant. He was staring into her eyes, lured inside those corneas that led a thousand miles down the road. Esmeralda was on a roll now, something about crows and angles, but he was lost on a one-way highway that led deep inside her cortex and offered no way out.

"No, you give a crow an inch, he'll take a mile," she continued. "You gotta admire that in a bird." Her words fluttered into his consciousness over the pounding jukebox and the echoing clang of shot glasses on the bar. "Buy me another?"

"Yeah, sure, why not?"

Esmeralda probably could've given him 50 good reasons why not, but that wasn't in her job description. She had a quota, he had a few bucks, and everything was sweet as molasses. They talked a little more about crows, segued somehow or other to nylons, then moved on to black silk lace, skin tight skirts, and high-heeled shoes. Esmeralda wasn't a hooker—not in the strictest sense of the word—and she knew how to say no, but she also knew how to say yes when the opportunity presented itself and Nick was, if not a real catch, at least not to be thrown back into the lake without further examination. "So, first time in Chicago you say? What brings a handsome guy like you to a place like this?"

"Music, mostly. I heard about this bar all the way back in Italy."

"Italy, huh?" Esmeralda leaned back and ran through the angles. No way this guy was actually *from* Italy, not with that Midwestern accent, which left only one possibility: he was an ex-soldier. That explained the limp. He probably got his knee blown off in Italy. It was just her luck to have landed one of those sad-sack GI mackerels. Any minute now he'd be flopping around and gasping for air. Better to cut him loose now before her Jewish side brought out the chicken soup. "Well, thanks for the drink, buddy."

As Esmeralda turned away, Muddy shuffled off the stage with a grin as wide as the Mississippi River. In the neon light of the Pabst Blue Ribbon sign, his sharkskin suit was positively aglow. "Who taught you to play like that?" he asked Nick.

"Couple of guys from the 92nd—"

"The Infantry Division? The Negro unit?"

"Yeah, the Negro unit."

Willie, always a step or two behind his quick-footed guitarist, propped his bass against the wall, then stepped down off the stage and made his way toward the bar. Muddy grabbed his beefy shoulder. "Willie, this boy been consorting with Negroes."

"I figured he didn't fall outta some polka band."

Esmeralda sat there half-listening, as if to make sure she didn't miss anything. Muddy didn't talk to just anybody—that much she knew—and she was curious what all the mumbling and grumbling was about. She pretended to be preoccupied with a spot on the wall up near the ceiling, but after Muddy, Nick and Willie shared a hearty laugh, she felt herself on the outside of the action, which didn't sit well. Esmeralda elbowed her way in—quite literally—angling her elbow between Muddy's and Willie's so that it looked like she was about to referee an arm-wresting contest. "Evening, boys," she said.

"Es," said Muddy with a certain lack of conviction. He turned back to Nick. "Now, as I was saying—"

"McKinley," said Esmeralda to Muddy, "why don't you tell Nick here how you got your name."

"Not now, Es, 'nother time."

Esmeralda didn't take rejection well. As far as she was concerned, she was back in the conversation, like it or not. "McKinley Morganfield, that's his real name," she said, just in case Muddy had any idea of running off on some tangent that might not include her. "Now, how we got from McKinley Morganfield to Muddy Waters, that's a story."

"Sure," said Nick, "I'd like to hear it."

"Okay, Es, you win," said Muddy, giving up any idea of keeping Esmeralda out of the loop. He ran a comb through his slicked-back hair, glanced at himself in the mirror behind the bar, and ran down the rundown. "One day I's messing around out back near the river and I took to caking up my face with some of that Mississippi mud. Some'un came by and had himself a good laugh. Mud Morganfield, he called me. Since I was but five or six, they took to calling me Muddy, and then I came to be known as Muddy Water, on account of the river, and then somebody pluralized it and it began to stick."

"*Pluralized* it," said Esmeralda.

"That's right. Muddy Waters. Got me a whole waterway," said Muddy.

"And not two bits to get across the bridge," said Willie, with a good-natured jab.

Muddy shot him a look, then laughed it off. "So, tell me," he said, turning back to Nick, "what you doing Wednesday?"

"Pretty much the same thing I'm doing Tuesday."

"What say you drop by the club about nine. Maybe we'll try a few numbers."

"Sure, I suppose I could—"

Esmeralda's palm began to itch almost imperceptibly. Her fingers rubbed against each other as if they were counting money. "What did you say the rate was, Muddy? I don't think I quite caught that."

"Es, what this got to do with you?"

"I'm Nick's manager." she said

"Manager?" said Muddy, trying to keep a straight face. "Since when you enter that line of speculation?"

"Ever since Nick here signed me up. Isn't that right, Nick?"

Nick got caught up inside Esmeralda's deep Gypsy gaze and nodded despite himself. "That's right."

"Okay, okay," said Muddy. "Standard rate."

"With double on Sunday."

"Now, Es—"

"Just asking what's right, Muddy."

Muddy rolled his eyes and shook hands with Nick. "Wednesday at nine. Don't be late."

"No, sir, Mr. Morganfield," said Nick, "I'll be right on time." And that's how Nick Blake found himself playing with a real live Chicago Blues Band six nights a week and twice on Sunday.

Time, like a crow with its tail on fire, flies quickly. The next thing Nick knew he was living in Esmeralda's crummy coldwater flat, his GI pension had run out, and she was promising to give up the curvy life and get herself hooked up straight. Alcohol will do that, get you so delusional you think you can stop drinking, but her nice Jewish half battled her wild Gypsy half to a draw and she teetered somewhere in that Sephardic netherworld where the slightest push could send her off the edge. Esmeralda was plenty familiar with the edge, having walked a very fine line for several years now. Three years to be exact, when her most recent problem in a lifetime full of trouble began on the very same barstool in front of the very same bar. As she would so concisely recall it, her unfortunate tumble was initiated by a customer who proposed that they retire to the back seat of his De Soto for a quick around the world. When she replied that, what, did he think she was some two-bit whore, he inquired exactly how many bits would be required, and when she said, more than you make, buddy, he decided that was more than enough to qualify as a Class A felony—he was, after all, an undercover cop—the result of which was Esmeralda being hauled off to the local precinct station where, as was too often the case, her mouth did the talking. She faced the prospect of 180 days in the Joliet State Penitentiary—all because of a completely misconstrued sexual favor which, after all, could've been resolved quietly in the back room of the police station—but 180 days or $1000 was the choice, neither of which Esmeralda had to spare, so she called Mister Montgomery, owner of the Flame Club, and said that if he'd loan her the grand she'd be indebted to him for life, not realizing, of course, that if he loaned her a grand she'd be indebted to him for life.

Esmeralda wound up working the place every single night and twice on Sunday, barely managing to put a dent in the principal, not to mention the interest. She wasn't about to let Nick in on her little secret, of course, so her little indiscretion with the law got put through the washer and came out all clean and fluffy, to wit, she claimed she had borrowed the money from Montgomery because her mother needed an operation, to which Nick responded, come on, Esmeralda, that's the oldest one in the books, but Esmeralda held her ground and insisted that her mother, in fact, really *did* need an operation, and her merely being a good daughter is what had led her to an interminable sentence on that stool at the godforsaken Flame Club. Which, of course, rankled Nick to no end.

Nick hadn't had a good night's sleep in two years, ever since the day his army unit got bogged down on an Italian hillside. Something happened to him out there in the mud and the rain—something that left him not fully whole as a person—and he replayed it in his dreams night after night. Having experienced his own hell, he was determined to get Esmeralda out of Montgomery's hellhole once and for all. Montgomery was, as Esmeralda liked to say in her broken Yiddish, a real gonif, but in a rare moment of weakness he dug deep and uncovered a soft, mushy spot mid-chest that might've signaled heart disease, tuberculosis, or pleurisy, but which he misdiagnosed as compassion. He agreed to a trial period in which Nick would take over Esmeralda's shift—not at the bar, of course, but on stage—so that Esmeralda could be free to pursue a more honorable line of employment. If nothing else, Montgomery figured that putting a white guy in the band might bring in a few more paying customers and give the joint a little class.

Esmeralda was home now, pretending to be good, and Nick was at the club, tapping his Doc Martins on the plywood. Three months had passed, the band was tight, and Nick fit right in. He added trills and ululations to Muddy's howls and growls, then flew off to the outer edges of a bluesy, jazzy, Gypsy stew which threatened to boil right over. He never could really explain what he was playing, but he liked

to say it made him feel strangely crowlike. That was fine—
crowlike?—but the fascination of a mixed race band proved
to be less than expected since Muddy was still the focus of
the show and the idea of Nick backing up a black man didn't
really seem so strange after all. It was all pretty ho-hum as far
as the audience was concerned and the crowds were neither
larger nor smaller than before.

Willie segued into an A-minor boogie, thwapping the
strings with his signature full, fat sound. This was Nick's
bread and butter, two minor chords for him to riff on without thinking about breaks and changes. He started simply,
repeating three notes again and again, but he began changing them subtly as he bent the reeds a little farther each time
and finally he took a note down an entire half-tone, caressed
it for two full beats, then sling-shotted it right up the scale.
The melody soared and flitted and flew right through the
ceiling and Nick was carried along for the ride—his mind
was blank and he was just listening to the wind blowing
through the air, he was floating above Halsted Avenue on the
far South Side, he was dipping into the waves of Lake Michigan, he was gliding over the upper deck of Wrigley Field, he
was circling the peak of the Masonic Temple, he was flutter-
ing above the broad boulevards of the North Shore, he was
zooming over the concourse of Arlington Racetrack, he was
hovering along the sheer walls of the Board of Trade Building, he was ascending the heights of Barrington Hills, he was
flapping along the Fox River Valley, he was crossing Lincoln
Park in a Gypsy caravan—

The set ended and Nick stepped down off the stage. He
was still buzzing in that half-conscious zone where his
thoughts lapped up inside his head in little waves, where he
floated more than walked, where he kept moving to the beat
even if the music had stopped five verses ago. Before he got
to the bar, he felt a pair of hands on his shoulders and turned
to see a couple of dopey, goner white guys staring at him in

the shadows. "You got your wail on tonight, Nick," said the taller of the two. "You must be feeling it real deep in the gut."

Nick tried his best Robert Mitchum deadpan, but his jaw tightened just enough to belie any attempt at coolness. He glanced at the two of them and nodded imperceptibly. "Ray... Dirk..."

"Now, me, I got nothing but a burning sensation down there," said Ray, an oafish lout with a frying pan face. "Burns like a son of a bitch."

"I keep telling him he should have it looked at," said Dirk, a thick-waisted kielbasa of a man. "It could be an ulcer. Or worse."

"What's worse than an ulcer?" said Ray. "Isn't an ulcer bad enough?"

"I'm just saying."

Nick stood there wordlessly, not wanting to get involved. Ray looked up and down the bar, then leaned over to him. "Where's that lush of a girlfriend of yours?"

"Esmeralda doesn't work here anymore. You know that."

"Oh, yeah, right. You still trying to make an honest woman out of her, Nick?"

"Something like that."

"Gotta hand it to you. You're a real Father Flanagan. But there's the little issue of an outstanding debt she owes the boss. Eight hundred, is that right, Dirk?"

"Eight and change," said Dirk.

"That's right," said Ray, grimacing as he ran his hand over his stomach. "Eight and change. Mr. Montgomery wants it back."

"Montgomery and I have a deal. Every week I pay him back a little off the principle and a little off the interest—"

"Yeah, yeah, I know. The thing is, her working the club was one thing, what with the money coming in in dribs and drabs, but at least he got some face time with her at the bar, could keep tabs on her and all. But this deal you got worked out, paying him back from these gigs of yours, it's gonna take ten years and that don't cut it anymore. So Friday night, Esmeralda's back on the barstool, understood? And if Montgomery wants some action, well, I'd suggest you just look the other way."

"I'm afraid I can't do that, Ray. We made an agreement. Every Sunday he gets—"

"Yeah, yeah, 20 bucks. Thing is, Mr. Montgomery wants more now. He wants 50 now, is that right, Dirk?"

"Fifty and change."

"I don't even make that much."

"I know, Nick. That's why we'll see Esmeralda Friday night."

Nick flinched slightly. "I'll go see Montgomery," he said. "We'll straighten this out."

"Forget about it," said Dirk. "It's already decided. We got the word from on high."

"No, no, if I just talk to him—"

"No time. Tonight he's ringside at the fight, tomorrow is poker night, Thursday's something or other—"

Ray kept looking around the club, first at the band, then at the bar, then at the customers. Finally, he leaned in just inches from Nick's face. "Consider yourself lucky that Mr. Montgomery went along as far as he did. He's a trusting guy. Me, I'd think twice about extending credit to a guy who consorts with Negroes, Jews, and Gypsies. What is it, Nick, the food? The pussy? Gotta be something special to make a man turn on himself like that."

"You wouldn't understand, Ray," said Nick, pushing him back with the tips of his fingers.

"No, I guess I wouldn't," said Ray, crunching his knuckles and pounding his fist into his palm.

Willie and Muddy passed by on their way to the bar. The air was so heavy, they could cut it with a swizzle stick. "Everything all right, Nick?" said Willie.

"Yeah, Willie, it's fine."

They lingered a moment, checking out the vibe, then moved on. As soon as they left, Ray delivered an ultimatum: "Friday, Nick. Friday."

Nick didn't need to hear the "or else." He could guess well enough. He stared into Ray's opaque eyes, saw Dirk hovering in the background, and walked straight out the door to Indiana Avenue. It was quiet outside. A slight breeze from the lake blew some wispy clouds off to the horizon, leaving a sky dotted with stars. Nick looked up and counted the constellations—Taurus, Aries, the Dippers Big and Little, the Ursas Major and Minor—and wondered what life was like on other planets. Were there blues bands and B-girls and bars that stayed open late into the night? Was there injustice and prejudice and some poor guy somewhere struggling to do what's right? He buttoned up his coat, turned down a side street, and got lost in the shadows.

Chapter 3

"Don't start me to talkin,
I'll tell everything I know."
—Sonny Boy Williamson

Sonny Boy Williamson's new 78 seeped out of a record store on North Avenue. It sounded good, a raw piece of music that hadn't been watered down too much in the studio. Sonny Boy Williamson, Memphis Minnie, and Big Bill Broonzy were all laying down tracks in the studio and their new kind of electrified blues was making waves all over town. Their sounds could be heard as far away as Detroit, St. Louis, and New York, but Chicago was the center of the heat, first on the South Side, then in Old Town, and finally right up to the border of the western suburbs. Silvio's, Gatewood's Tavern, Curley's, Checkerboard Lounge, the 708 Club, the Avenue Lounge, Club Zanzibar, Smitty's, and the Flame Club were jumping every night, especially when Muddy Waters was onstage—Muddy and Willie Dixon on bass, Sunnyland Slim on piano, Elgin Evans on drums, and the white kid, Nick Blake, on harmonica. A couple of top dogs over at Chess Records had talked to Muddy about pressing his new *I Can't Be Satisfied* and maybe putting *I Feel Like Going Home* on the B side, but who knew with these guys? Talk was cheap in Chicago and recording contracts even cheaper. As for Nick, the best he could hope for was 50 bucks as a sideman and those 50 bucks would leave him a cool $750 short of paying off Esmeralda's debt. $750 might as well have been $7500 or $75,000 as far as Nick was concerned.

He stood outside the record store on an early afternoon, leaning against a cold brick wall, listening to the music, trying to figure out what he was going to do. After getting the bad news from Ray and Dirk, he'd been unable to bring himself to tell Esmeralda that she'd have to go back to work again. Not that she'd mind so much, no, Esmeralda was comfortable enough on a bar stool, sipping a drink and shooting the breeze. She didn't even have a drinking problem in the strictest sense of the word—Jews were seldom alcoholics and her Gypsy blood was already 90 Proof—but Nick couldn't stand the idea of looking down from the stage and seeing some stranger with his hand halfway up her skirt. He glanced across the street at the marquee of an old movie palace that had been closed down now for years. A tattered movie poster hung behind the door advertising Claude Rains in *The Return of the Invisible Man*. That's who Nick wished he could be at that moment—the Invisible Man—a bandaged up cipher who could just disappear into the woodwork and never be seen again. Flesh and blood life was too damned complicated.

Nick walked the streets, running through the angles, making plans, breaking plans, and making plans again. He'd rob a bank. He'd break into the Museum of Natural History and make off with the valuables. He'd shoplift 800 records from the music store and sell them on Maxwell Street. He'd get a dozen crows to peck out Dirk's eyes and Ray's ulcer. He'd become a song and dance man on the old vaudeville circuit and gain sympathy for his bum leg. As one terrible idea gave birth to another, Nick rolled up his collar against the stiff Chicago wind and aimlessly walked the shadowy streets of Old Town.

There are shadows cast by the sun and shadows cast by the moon and shadows cast by streetlights, and then there are shadows in the hallway of a third-story walkup cast by God-knows-what. They're just there—day and night, summer and winter—they just sit there as if painted on the walls. Esmeralda hated those shadows and avoided the hallway whenever possible, making her a virtual prisoner in her own home. She was firmly ensconced in her crummy little apartment when there was a knock on the door, and then another. Esmeralda finally opened it a crack and looked at some guy wearing a dark gray suit and a green tie. "Esmeralda Kurlansky?" he said.

"What if I am?" she said, duly suspicious of strangers who asked too many questions. This guy in the suit was already one over the limit.

"I'm from Greenberg, Greenberg, and O'Shaughnessy," he said.

Esmeralda didn't like the sound of it and immediately tried to close the door, but the guy was quick as a rabbit and slipped his foot inside before she could get it shut.

"This won't take a minute," he said. "Can I come in?"

"You got a warrant?"

"No-no, it's nothing like that," he said, slipping his foot a little farther inside the doorway. "You know, you're not easy to find. I've been all over the north side, the south side, and all the way down to Joliet."

"I left that burg a long time ago, before it could sink its teeth into my neck," said Esmeralda. "Now, which collection agency did you say you were from?"

"Greenberg, Greenberg, and O'Shaughnessy, but we're not a collection agency, we're a law firm."

Esmeralda turned a paler shade of dark. "I don't know what this is all about but I can tell you right now that whatever it is I had nothing to do with it. You're wasting your time, if you catch my drift."

"Yes, well, be that as it may, I'm wondering if you know of

a certain Abraham Irving Kurlansky?"

"Never heard of him."

"I'm not surprised. He's a distant relative on your father's side, a cousin three or four times removed. Your father never spoke of him?"

"My father never spoke of anyone. He left when I was two years old." Esmeralda turned, spat three times on the floor, and delivered a terse invocation. "The gonif."

"I'm very sorry to inform you that your cousin Abe passed away a few months ago. Quietly and in his sleep, if I remember correctly."

"Like I said, the Kurlanskys weren't big talkers."

"The trustees of his estate were assigned the dispensation of assets—"

"English, mister, okay?"

"—and after a thorough review of potential claimants, it has been determined that you are his one and only surviving heir."

Esmeralda blinked twice and opened the door a bit farther. "You don't say."

"Now, I should warn you that your cousin wasn't a rich man, not by the strictest standards, but he did leave a bank account with, let's see, $957.78, and a modest parcel of land covering five acres just outside the town of Petaluma."

"Peta-what?"

"Petaluma. It's 30 or 40 miles north of San Francisco."

"California?"

"Yes, California."

Esmeralda crossed her arms and looked deeply into the eyes of the mysterious stranger at the door. "So what's the rub?"

"There is no rub. The money's yours. The land, too. You'll be liable for the usual state and federal inheritance taxes, several transference fees, and you'll need to have several documents notarized at your earliest convenience, which, I might add, can be taken care of at the offices of Greenberg,

Greenberg, and O'Shaughnessy if you wish to engage us as your representatives."

"Which one are you?"

"Me?"

"Greenberg, Greenberg, or O'Shaughnessy?"

"I'm Whitley. I'm just an associate there."

Esmeralda crossed and uncrossed her arms several times as she went through all the angles. Money. For her. To spend. On stuff. "So you're telling me you're giving me 950-something dollars just for looking pretty?"

"I should think the land would be worth a good deal more than that, but yes, the $957.78 is available to you at any time."

A rush of blood shot up Esmeralda's spinal column and she yanked open the door so wide she nearly pulled it off its hinges. "Come in, come in, Mr. Whitley. Don't be a stranger. Nothing to be afraid of in here but me. Where do I sign?"

Whitley stepped inside and glanced around. The apartment looked like a flea market of the deranged. There was junk everywhere, including but not limited to clothes, tools, pots and pans, automobile parts, armoires, Chinese lacquer tables, kachina dolls, costume jewelry, cardboard suitcases, and a collection of kosher pickle jars. Whitley's lawyerly eyes took in the room as if it were a crime scene, which, by any measure of good housekeeping, it was. With exaggerated caution, he stepped over what appeared to be a half-opened parachute and paged through a sheaf of documents. "If you'll just put your Jane Hancock next to the indicated boxes, we can proceed."

"Proceed away," said Esmeralda, her eyes blinking like a slot machine gone wild as she scribbled her signature next to a bunch of exes. "Get you a drink?"

"I'm afraid I don't drink during working hours."

"That's funny, I used to do nothing *but* drink during working hours. Of course, that was in the old days. Before I retired."

"Oh, when was that?"

"About five minutes ago," said Esmeralda with a throaty laugh. "Now, this property you were telling me about, I don't suppose they've got anything worth drilling for on that land?"

"What, like oil? I'm afraid not. Have you ever heard of Petaluma Crude?"

"Peta-whocha whatcha?"

"Exactly. No, I'm afraid the oil fields and gold mines are quite some distance from Petaluma."

"Well, what then?" said Esmeralda, wracking her brains. What was California known for? Artichokes? Almonds? Fiesta dinnerware? "Wait a minute," she said. "Didn't they discover wine out there in California? Sure, that must be it. Why, they've got wine dripping off the vines!"

"I think there would need to be some grapes involved."

"Hell, I've got friends over on Wells Street who'll pay up to 50 cents a bottle."

"I'm sure you do, Miss Kurlansky."

Esmeralda tried to envision herself in the fields of California: Getting up early. Working late. Getting dirt on her forehead. She needed a rest just thinking about it. "Tell you what, Mr. Whitley, double up on the cash and the farm is yours."

"I'm afraid I can't do that. I am, however, authorized to present you with a company check in the amount of the inheritance."

Esmeralda froze Whitley with a stare. "Uh-uh. I only take cash, buddy."

Whitley rubbed his forehead, trying to avert what was quickly becoming a grand mal headache. "You seem, um, rather suspicious, Miss Kurlansky, if I may say so."

"You can say anything you want, but nobody's playing me for a fool."

"In that case, we could go to the bank and redeem the funds, if you insist."

"I insist," said Esmeralda as she rummaged through a mess on a counter. She finally found a couple of shot glasses, cleaned off the smudges with her sleeve, and poured two stiff drinks. "C'mon, I won't tell."

"Well, I suppose there's no harm," said Whitley as he raised his glass in a toast.

"To Greenberg, Greenberg, and O'Shaughnessy," said Esmeralda, clinking glasses. "The best damn lawyers in town!"

The wind kicked up, died down, and kicked up again. The sun set, the moon rose, and a few clouds rolled in off the lake. Nick glanced up from behind some bushes and made sure the coast was clear. Funny expression, that, considering he was a thousand miles from any coast, be it Atlantic, Pacific, Gulf, or otherwise. Chicago really couldn't be considered to have a coastline, even though Lake Michigan was a significant body of water, so the idea of the coast being clear was not technically true. Not that it mattered one little bit, especially not now, this was no time for semantics, not when Nick was—how do they say it?—casing a joint. He was new to this line of work and entirely unsure of himself. For example, that window leading to the basement, the one he'd been staring at for at least 30 minutes, do you kick it in with your foot or smash it with your fist or crack it with a rock? Shouldn't there be a manual for such a thing? Couldn't he *write* such a manual, get an advance of, say, $800, and be done with the whole thing?

Nick returned to reality and pushed a big pane of glass that refused to budge. He tapped it a little harder, then gave it a solid rap which caused the entire thing to fly out of its frame and crash to the floor below. A dog barked in the distance. A light snapped on across the street. A squirrel rustled in a tree. Nick waited breathlessly, made sure that no one saw him, then slipped through the window and shimmied down a pipe that ran along the basement wall. He jumped the last few feet and managed to land directly on the broken window, which loudly cracked into another dozen shards of glass. The dog barked more urgently. A few more lights snapped on. The squirrel kicked an acorn out of its nest, ricocheted it off the bark of the tree, and bounced it right against the upper window of Mister Montgomery's three story suburban home.

If Nick had ever thought of pursuing a career as a second-story man, he gave up on the idea right then and there. But the second story was exactly where he was headed, an idea which came to him in a moment of breathtaking wrong-headedness. That's what desperation will get you, a desperation brought about by having fallen in love with a high-strung, hot-blooded girlfriend whose combination of flaws, faults, and confabulations left his head spinning. Nick couldn't face going home empty-handed, so instead he decided to play Russian Roulette with his own brain and see what dribbled out. He put six ideas into a hat, spun them around like the chamber of a gun, and came up with the altogether insane idea of robbing Montgomery's Tuesday night poker game. As ideas go, it was as solid as jello.

Mister Montgomery was at that very moment staring into a nice pot of cash while holding the crummiest hand he'd been dealt all evening. He considered bailing out but folding wasn't his style, since it connoted a certain liliness of the liver, leaving bluffing as the only sensible option. Bluffing was his specialty. Bluffing was its own special joy, since to win with nothing at all was far more rewarding than winning with a full house. "I'll see you and raise 200," he said with calm confidence as he pushed two crisp bills into the pot, then leaned back and ran his puffy fingers along the collar of his silk shirt. Montgomery liked the look and feel of silk, the way it glistened under the artificial light, the way it caressed his body and evened out some of the excess folds of his skin.

A knock-off Tiffany lamp hung over the center of the table, casting a dull glow over the room and washing out the colors, giving a black and white hue to the proceedings. A street light from outside shone through the slatted blinds and left a crisscross of shadows across the walls, the table, and the faces of the assembled players. "Okay, Mister," said Brian Conroy, a hefty, shapeless man built like a garbage can, "I got two kings showing that tell me to just sit tight."

"That's why they call it poker," said Mister. Everyone nodded, even though not one of them had any idea why they or anyone else called it poker. They could've called it knockwurst for all they knew. Mister was Montgomery's real and legal first name, an appellation given him by his mother in honor of a casual evening she spent with some guy or other whom she referred to as Mister This or Mister That. He'd been called Mister ever since he was a baby, a name which could've scarred a lesser child, but it gave Mr. Mister Montgomery a sense of entitlement that prepared him for what was sure to be a life at the top of some heap or another. The heap he was presently lording it over was his weekly gathering of crooked bankers, sleazy aldermen, and corrupt cops. They were all part of an Irish mafia that liked to think they ran the city, even if all they ran was the crumbs that the *real* mafia left for them under the carpet.

"I'm in," said Fabian Patrick, a red-faced schmoozer with close-cropped hair and nervous lips.

"You gotta pay to play," said Mister, eliciting another round of nods. No one thought to object to the fact that, of *course* you've got to pay to play, that's the point of the game. Montgomery's poker room was a converted dining room which had a door in front that led to a vestibule where Ray and Dirk stood guard over the proceedings and a back door that led to the kitchen and bathroom. It was all for show, a ruse to give the veneer of respectability to a man whose various businesses dealt with the downer side of dirty. There was the retread tire business, the senior citizens' retirement home business, the hazardous waste removal business, the inner city real estate business, the unlicensed taxi cab business, and the race-based music club business. That's where Nick came in.

And that's where Nick *came in,* bursting through the back door with his hands shoved into his coat pockets, both fingers blazing. His face was wrapped in bandages, his coat was up around his neck, and a porkpie hat hung low over his forehead, giving a kind of cool, jazzy look to his Invisible Man get-up. "I'll take that," he said, pointing to the $1000 ante that was growing whiskers in the middle of the table. His heart was pounding so hard, it almost popped the blood vessels in his ears.

The five men dropped their poker faces as soon as they saw what was happening. "What's going on here?" said Judge McTeague. "Is this some kind of shakedown?"

Nick slipped a satchel from under his jacket, dropped it on the table, and motioned for Montgomery to ante up. "Easy there," said Montgomery as he reached for the money with one hand and a buzzer beneath the table with the other. "No need to do anything rash," he said as he silently gave the button one short and three long squeezes.

"C'mon, c'mon," whispered Nick.

Montgomery counted out the money from the pot and dropped it into the satchel, taking his own sweet time. "That's almost a grand you've got there," he said. "You sure you know what you're doing, buddy?"

Nick wasn't sure at all what he was doing but this was no time for second guessing. He grabbed the satchel, backed away from the table, and smashed right into a door that swung open from the vestibule. Ray and Dirk entered with a tray of drinks, popcorn and mixed nuts, and a platter of cheese and salami. Ray, Dirk, Nick, the tray, the platter, and the satchel all came together as if by a force of gravity, then spun apart with a centrifugal force that tossed the whole mess into the air. Dirk was sure he'd seen a ghost and turned whiter than Nick's bandages. Ray was a bit quicker on the uptake and reached for his gun, but then the popcorn started falling out of the air, and the nuts too, and the money, oh yes, the money, which Montgomery sucked into his coat like a vacuum cleaner. "One short buzz and three long is *not* the signal for snacks," he growled at Ray and Dirk. "There's a goddamn robbery going on!"

"Don't worry, boss, we're on it!" said Ray, struggling to get his fingers around the gun.

Now, Nick might've been guilty of extremely bad planning and even worse execution but he wasn't so delusional as not to realize when the jig was up, and this jig was as up as it gets—up, up, and away—and that's where he headed, up the hallway, up the stairs, and away through an open window, bullets flying, doors slamming, curses echoing through the air.

"Get that son-of-a-bitch!" yelled Montgomery.

Ray went right, Dirk went left, and Nick flopped headlong into the bushes, where he held his breath and resisted the impulse to howl like a wounded hyena. Even the foxholes of Italy made more sense to him than the trimmed hedges of Chicago. In the foxholes of Abbruzzi you could get a good night's sleep and a hot cup of coffee. Here, you could get ten years for robbing a crook. Twenty minutes later, the coast was clear. Which was an odd expression, Nick reminded himself, especially way out here in the middle of nowhere. Where'd they think he was, on the Costa del Sol?

At the very same moment, on the other side of town, Esmeralda's money, all $957.78 of it, went from a bank teller's hands to Whitley's hands to her hands in what quite possibly was the land speed record for negotiable currency exchange.

Esmeralda kept her eyes on everybody's fingers but her own, which was an oversight of the most serious nature, since she was not to be trusted with any amount of money that didn't clink when it fell into her purse. If there was any question to this hypothesis, it was immediately refuted when Esmeralda jumped into a taxi outside the bank and got no more than seven blocks before coming upon a car dealership that was positively festive with balloons, streamers, and flashing lights. There she spotted a maroon Hudson Commodore convertible that perfectly accented her turquoise headscarf and fuchsia Bolero jacket. Matches like that only come along once in a lifetime, she reasoned, and from that moment on her experience on Auto Row took on an almost mystical quality. There was the front man to deal with, a guy with boogie-woogie eyes and a seersucker suit that crackled when he spoke, then the lot manager, a white-haired magician whose office was in the shape of a pentagram and smelled of frankincense, and eventually a man they called the closer, a hypnotic fellow who arrived in a puff of smoke and departed by magic carpet. This was a stacked deck by anyone's measure, but Esmeralda was a high-flying crow who knew a thing or two herself about obfuscation, misdirection, and outright bamboozlement. By the time the negotiations were over it was debatable as to who exactly had the upper hand. Between the salesmen's mangling of the numbers and Esmeralda's mangling of the language, it was hard to say if she was buying a car or selling a weekend at Lake Geneva. Her hocus-pocus and their sleight-of-hand got all jumbled up in a knot Houdini couldn't have escaped from. When it was all over, the automobile dealership wound up with all of Esmeralda's big bills and most of the smaller ones, too, but she drove off in a vehicle that seemed to be worth a fair amount more than she paid, considering it was a brand new car, unless, of course, it wasn't. This was no time to quibble.

"Where's Nick?" said Esmeralda as she burst through the flimsy pinewood doors of the Flame Club. She was excited and agitated, excited because she had news of the utmost importance to tell Nick, and agitated because he was nowhere to be found. The stage was bare, the tables were empty, and only a smattering of customers was at the bar. She made a bee line for her old stool where, as luck would have it, Muddy was nursing a Pabst Blue Ribbon. Esmeralda shot him a look as if he'd trespassed on hallowed ground. Muddy wisely slipped over to the next stool while the slipping was still good.

"Nick who?" he said, messing already with his long-time sparring partner.

"I suppose I could be looking for Czar Nicholas or Nicholas Nickleby or Jolly Old St. Nick, but they wouldn't be sharing the stage with the mighty Muddy Waters, would they?"

"Now, Es, don't get me started."

Esmeralda snuggled her tush onto the cracked red vinyl stool and slipped her elbow into a well-worn groove on the bar. "How long do I know you now, Muddy? A year? Two?"

"Something like that."

"Two years and not one straight answer. Why do you think that is?"

"Just messin' with you, Es, you know how it is."

"You see, now Willie, Willie I can talk to, you ask Willie a simple question, you get an actual answer."

"Too bad Willie ain't here."

"Yeah, too bad."

"Tell you what, Es, just for old time's sake I'm gonna tell you everything I know. You ready?"

"The suspense is killing me."

"Here it is. Ain't seen Nick all day."

Esmeralda showed no reaction whatsoever. To react was to lose the battle, and the idea of losing to Muddy was worse than any news he might impart. "Now, was that so hard?" she said.

"It wasn't easy."

They stared at each other for a good long moment, then leaned back and had a good laugh. "I've missed you, McKinley."

"You, too. Since you been gone, place been much too quiet."

Esmeralda caught the eye of the bartender and motioned him over. "Sal, pour my friend Muddy here a drink. Pour everyone a drink."

"Ooo-eee," said Muddy. "Miss Es settin'em up and knock-in'em down. What happen, your horse come in?"

"You might say that," she said, playing it close to her vest. "Now, listen. I've been looking for Nick for hours. Sure he wasn't in?"

"Not since yesterday."

Esmeralda tapped her fingers on the bar, then caressed a glass of bourbon that was just sitting there all kind of lonely. "Tell me something, Muddy, what do you know about wine?"

"Wine? I'm from Mississippi. I don't know nothin' about wine. I know about chickens. Hell, I can tell you pretty much anything you want to know about chickens."

"What could I possibly want to know about chickens?"

Muddy leaned back on his stool and got a faraway look in his eyes. "Well, for example, everybody always asking, what come first, the chicken or the egg." He held out two empty hands, palms up, as if weighing a heavy issue. All he needed was baggy overalls and a piece of straw between his teeth to look like a Delta sharecropper. "But they asking the wrong question."

"Okay, I'll bite. What's the *right* question?"

"The right question is, what come first, the wing or the thigh? The cornmeal batter or the hot sauce? The fricassee or the jambalaya?"

Esmeralda stared at him, knocked back her drink, and slid off the stool. "Muddy, if you see Nick, you tell him to head home, okay?"

"You know I will," he said, sincere as a bluesman on his wedding day.

Esmeralda took one last look at her old stool at the Flame Club, sighed wistfully, and headed back into the cool Chicago night.

The side streets of Old Town twisted into the side streets of the Near North Side which opened up upon the side streets of Sheridan Park which curlicued into the side streets of the South Side which came to an abrupt end on a little dead-end cul-de-sac where Nick slipped his key into the lock and gently turned the mechanism. Somewhere around a quarter of the way around, the tumbler clunked more than clicked and the door silently opened. It was dark inside, as it should be at 2 A.M., with the hum of the refrigerator laying down a nice 4/4 beat over the saxophoning wind that was creaking in off the lake. Before Nick got halfway into the room, the light snapped on.

"Don't take off your coat," said Esmeralda. She was sitting at the kitchen table, wearing black leather driving gloves and a scarf around her head.

"What's this?" said Nick, not sure what to make of her strange ensemble. It was an odd bedtime get-up, even for Esmeralda.

"Come with me," she said, leading him back out the door. He followed her into the hallway, where the ever-present shadows cast what looked like prison bars on the wall, then headed down three flights of stairs to the sidewalk outside. "What if I told you that car over there had deep pile carpeting?" she said, pointing to the Hudson convertible parked at the curb.

"I suppose I'd ask you what deep pile carpeting is."

"What if I told you it had arm rests, twin air-horns, ashtrays, windshield wipers, stop lights, a locking glove box, and sealed beam headlights?"

"Listen, it's real late—"

"What if I told you it had a radio built right into the dash-board?"

"Es, have you been drinking? Didn't we have an agreement about that?"

"What if I told you that Hudson Commodore was ours?"

"I'd say you'd better give it back before the owner's body washes up onshore."

Esmeralda twirled in a circle and flashed the biggest Gypsy smile this side of the Romanian Steppes. "Nick, the most incredible thing happened. I inherited some money. And some land. In California."

Nick couldn't figure if Esmeralda was messing with his mind or if she was dead drunk. They usually came hand in hand. Still, she was never known to lie straight to his face, which made her crazy pronouncement all the more intriguing. "How much money?" he said with due skepticism.

"$957.78."

Nick could tell that Esmeralda was telling the truth—who makes up a number like that?—but it all seemed too good to be true. Could it really that be an act of divine intervention was going to get Montgomery off their backs once and for all? Was there really a God after all? But then he glanced back at the brand new Hudson and felt a little hiccup in his brain. "Esmeralda. That car. It must've cost—"

"$900 flat. I got a deal."

"Wait a minute," said Nick, experiencing a sudden agnostic re-conversion. "You spent all the money on a car?"

"No, Nick, you're not listening. I spent $900 on the car. The rest I spent buying everybody drinks at the Flame Club."

"You spent all the money on a car instead of paying back Montgomery?" he shouted. "Are you completely crazy?"

Esmeralda just shook her head. Sometimes she pitied Nick. He was a smart enough guy, and a hell of a harmonica player, and plenty handsome too. But he thought small. It was probably that Wisconsin upbringing. She spoke to him slowly, as if to a child. "Nick, what do you think we'd be doing after paying back Montgomery? You'd still be playing in the club, I'd still be living in that dump upstairs, and those godforsaken shadows would still be plastered on the hallway walls. No, Nickie, this is our chance for a new start. California, here we come!"

"California? What do you know about California? We won't get ten miles before Montgomery puts out the word on us."

Esmeralda opened the front door and slipped behind the steering wheel. "Wrong, sweetheart. By the time Montgomery realizes we're gone, we're gonna be gone. What's he going to do, send out a fleet of taxis after us?"

"I don't think you understand—"

Esmeralda leaned over the dashboard, turned a few knobs, and twisted some dials. Sonny Boy Williamson's *Shake the Boogie* came on the radio. "This is no time to be playing it straight. Now, are you coming or not?"

Nick listened to the soulful harmonica and melted on the spot. "Jesus, Esmeralda, you know I'm coming. Let me get my stuff."

"It's already in the trunk," she said, flashing him a quick smile. Nick rolled his eyes, then slid onto the passenger seat, leaned back, and took a whiff of the delicious leathery smell. Esmeralda cushioned her tush onto the soft foam rubber seat and turned the radio all the way up. Fifty thousand watts of power blasted in from outer space as she pulled out onto the road, took a hard left on Michigan Avenue, took another left on Grand Avenue, and headed west. West, to where the sun shines day and night. West, to where the air is sprinkled with honeysuckle and jasmine. West, to where the wine grows on trees.

Chapter 4

*"Much energy is lost in fanciful
dreams that never bear fruit."*
—High Eagle

Fifty thousand watts of power is a significant amount, even in outer space. It's enough to blast through clouds, the inner atmosphere, the outer atmosphere, and a couple of atmospheres that don't even have names. Then it just keeps on going, piercing through globular clusters, galactic halos, and expansive magnetic fields. The universe is made up of billions of galaxies, each of which has billions of planets, and when you add them all up you get so many billions there isn't an abacus this side of the Mezo Zonalities to count them. Not that anybody is using an abacus these days, but there was one in the Museum of the Ancient World on Obsidia and a couple more, rumor had it, on Earth, that long gone planet on the other side of wherever. It was one of the countless similarities of these two sibling planets which had been separated at birth and then gone their own separate, if similar, ways. They each had abaci, octopi, and platypi, not to mention tropical climate zones, polar ice caps, and mountains that rose to the sky. Earth and Obsidia had so much in common they were classified as sister planets in *Crowley's Book of Celestial Amazements*, two worlds that were identical in almost every way, minus the fact that the birth pangs of the universe had pushed Obsidia farther along the space-time continuum, leaving Earth a couple of hundred years behind in the dust. It was that dust the Pulsar-7 was traversing in order for a group of seven explorers to visit their long-lost relatives and see what life was like among the primitives. This was a risky proposition, given that the odds that Obsidia and Earth would be virtually identical to one another were about one in a hundred billion. On the other hand, that just happened to be the approximate number of planets in the universe known to host viable life forms, so it wasn't really a miracle at all that two identical places would co-exist. The miracle would be if they *didn't*. A hundred billion planets, you figure a few of them are going to be alike.

A lonely harmonica reverberated off the metal underpinnings of the observation chamber. As the Pulsar-7 shot farther into space, there was precious little for Jaxson to do except watch and wait. Night stretched on into more night, which stretched on into still more night, which, as far as he could tell, was never going to end. It was an endless universe they were traversing and the joke, if you could call it that, was on them. They were just going to keep going and going until they ran out of gas, and then they'd keep going anyway since you don't really need gas when you're hurtling through nothingness.

Not that the Pulsar-7 ran on gas. That was just an expression from the old days that Jaxson liked to plug into his log. A literary device, he called it. The Pulsar-7, like pretty much everything on Obsidia, ran on freeze-dried fusion pellets, a source of energy that had served the home planet well for over a century. All good things, unfortunately, have a way of coming to an end, and those little green pellets were slipping into extinction at breakneck speed. Hence, this journey across the heavens.

Everybody else had plenty to keep them busy. Captain

Wambold was constantly noodling around with his computers, checking coordinates, meteor storm reports, and galactic disturbances. Confident though he was to be careening through empty space, he didn't want to run into some uncharted spaceberg in the middle of nowhere and have to put out a Mayday to an unlistening universe. Chief Engineer Teller was his usual difficult self, running from this critical job to that urgent issue to this pressing problem, all of which, as far as anyone could tell, was a big ruse to make himself seem more important than he really was, which was not at all. Teller's main job was to keep busy looking busy, which, if nothing else, kept him too busy to realize how little he was actually doing. Navigational Officer Raleigh was in his transcendental state pretending, for all anyone knew, that he wasn't even there. Maybe Raleigh had it all figured out, that since there was no there there, he was better off being somewhere else, even if there was no there there either. Data Transfer Officer Oblivia was in her own particular far outer space, which had nothing to do with the fact that she was on an endless journey to nowhere. Oblivia had been in eternal orbit from the minute she was born, her brain pan having been skewed sideways at birth, thus leaving her with loose nodules. Behavioral Scientist Marta-1 and Molecular Biochemist Marta-2 were the only ones who seemed to be doing anything that really mattered. They were conducting a series of experiments with light sources, mirrors, gamma rays and combustion waves that left the rest of the crew pretty much lost in the ozone which, given that they were in outer space, was lost indeed.

Jaxson was left to his own devices, always a dangerous proposition. After a quick jaunt around the circular air vent track, a dozen isometric resistance thrusts against the meteor wall, and some zero gravity push-ups, he was back to staring into black space. He took increasing refuge in his log, not only to keep from going completely crazy, but in order to

recount to anyone who might be listening what it was like to
be trapped in his own imagination. After a dozen entries, he
had exhausted the dictionary, the thesaurus and himself, not
to mention his readers, but he forged ahead with his autobi-
ographical ramblings. Unscientific though they were, all
that's really known of this particular expedition comes from
Jaxson's log, an erratic dissertation to which history must
occasionally defer. Here, then, another entry, from page 17:

*I was born the experimental, New Era way, in a rancid pod
beneath a field of icicles in a sea of slime, and I always felt
that attributed to my creamy complexion. I never met my
parents and they never met each other, so it shouldn't come
as such a great shock that my communication skills were
somewhat lacking. It was all new territory, this interaction
thing, but I craved it like a butterfly bursting from its cocoon.
I was moving into full adulthood, after all, and I was ready to
experience all the ups and downs that come along with full
integration into society. A guy, a chick, maybe a few rancid
pods following along behind, that's what it was all about, as
far as I could tell.*

There were lots of questions that Jaxson couldn't answer.
Like what he was doing on that spaceship in the first place?
Ship Observer, indeed. He'd been thwarted at every turn
from simply trying to do his job. The fact is, the who-what-
when-where-why of the mission seemed more elusive than
ever. Jaxson's thoughts of mutiny, never far from his mind,
took on new urgency after Wambold threatened to have him
suspended by heliotropes in the afterchamber and have his
memory modules zapped by freiburg pulsars. And why? For
asking too many questions? What was a reporter supposed to
do if not report? Jaxson was convinced that the captain, for
all of his remarkable discoveries and his sterling track record
and his beloved reputation, was ill-suited for leading such a
mission. Wasn't the simple fact that he had kept the Ship
Observer in the dark for so long evidence enough that he was

incapable of communication with his crew? If Wambold couldn't talk to *Jaxson*—the least jaundiced newsman ever to have strapped on a zeigfried belt—then who could he talk to?

Jaxson tried to engage his crewmates in a bit of friendly banter, but they had all tuned out long ago. His traveling companions, after all, were an odd lot who had been hand-picked from some humorless universe that valued a good joke about as much as a poke in the eye. Raleigh couldn't be reached by hook, crook, or a joy buzzer in his pants. Teller was as funny as diphtheria, Oblivia never knew whether to laugh or to cry, and Marta-2 was a joke in search of a punch line. Which left Marta-1.

Jaxson found her in the ship library, a cramped space overflowing with technical manuals, plotting tools, and a bank of video screens which displayed an incomprehensible collection of polar charts, cosmographs, and frequency polygons. Jaxson felt queasy the moment he walked in, the visible practice of science not agreeing with his constitution. He far preferred alchemy to chemistry, metaphysics to physics, and astrology to astronomy, whereas Marta-1 favored the concrete to the abstract, the real to the imaginary, and pretty much anyone to Jaxson. She was so deep in concentration she barely heard him come in. "What are you studying?" said Jaxson, peering over her shoulder.

"Earth, if you must know," said Marta-1, shooting him a sidelong glance and barely disguising her distaste for the interruption. "You've heard of it, I presume?"

"Sure. Earth, one of my favorite mystery destinations. Nice beaches, breathtaking views, easy parking. Open 24 hours a day. Can't wait to get there."

Jaxson's attempt at humor fell predictably flat. Marta-1, whose stretched canvas look was all the rage those days, showed no sign of molecular activity in the pleasure centers of her face, commonly expressed by a slight upturn of the lips or a glistening of the eyes. "You know nothing about it, do you?"

"Actually, that's why I'm here," he lied. "I was hoping to get some insights from the Chief Behavioral Scientist on what to expect in the extremely unlikely event that we ever get to wherever it is we're going. You know, get some background information so that readers back home will understand the challenges we faced on the journey."

"You mean, you want me to do your job for you."

"I just thought we might share some ideas."

"Humph," said Marta-1, an odd expression of approval/disapproval characteristic of the two minds fighting it out inside her. The social Marta-1 wanted nothing to do with Jaxson while the scientific Marta-1 was tempted by the opportunity to engage in some didactic discourse. Like any good scientist, her inner pedagogue won. "I shall attempt to elucidate for you the scientific basis of the present undertaking, by which I mean the theory, implementation, and expected outcome of our mission. Captain Wambold warned me that this day might be coming and suggested that I keep my tutorial at a very basic level—I believe the term he used was 'childish'—so I shall avoid as many technical terms as possible and use common devices such as graphs and charts, and, if necessary, puppets and dolls to make clear what anyone with even minimal academic qualifications should have learned in his *Introduction to Basic Energy Theory*."

"Has anyone ever told you that you have the most beautiful eyes this side of the Quantic Divide?" said Jaxson.

Marta-1 pretended not to hear. She walked over to an empty data board and picked up a pointer, even though there was nothing for her to point at. It reminded Jaxson of his dusty old professors at the Institute of Applied Learning who were always pointing out one thing or another, while never really getting to any point at all. This brought on another bout of queasiness, but he suppressed his fight or flight instinct and settled in for what was sure to be an elucidating experience. "Now then," she began, "as you may know, our discovery of Earth initially wasn't much more than a curiosity. Astral imaging devices decoded a light and sound source from among the countless hums and dins bouncing around the universe, and a team of mapping engineers managed to isolate the precise coordinates of the broadcasts. Once our tracking systems zeroed in, we were able to capture radio, television, and other planetary transmissions which allowed us to construct a history, topography, and social analysis of the faraway sphere." Marta-1 pointed to a thick volume sitting next to one of her screens. "I refer you to the work of Professor Hannibal Jacoby for a full accounting of the techniques used in the building of the hypothetical model."

Jaxson pretended to jot down the name on his pod pad. "Pro... fessor... Hanni... bal—"

"Earth turned out to be quite remarkable, given the chemical composition of its atmosphere, its climatic variables, and the general physiognomy of the place. It appeared to be a veritable spitting image of Obsidia, a fraternal twin in the crazy quilt of life forms sprinkled throughout the skies. As for the Earthlings themselves, they appear to be just like Obsidians in almost every way—"

"Except for that 200 year gap in evolution—"

"Yes, yes, but their height, weight, pulse rate, brain function, and nervous system are all identical. The research indicated a planet of quaint innocents, an unsophisticated lot forging slowly ahead in a universe running on overdrive. Unfortunately, Earth was much too far away to be of any real interest. After an initial burst of interest, the data got stashed away in some laboratory, along with all the other flotsam and jetsam of university research. It almost certainly would have stayed there forever were it not for—"

"Helgi Quince?"

"Yes, Helgi Quince, an undergraduate design student who, on a drunken dare, broke into the Records Room and

stole the first file she laid her hands on before being arrested
by the campus police. She was summarily expelled but when
the data from her file came to light, she, and it, became a
cause célèbre. Something about this faraway planet resonated in the soul of Obsidian youth—"

"The innocence of an earlier time... the fascination with
the unknown... the curiosity about a foreign culture..."

"And so, with a kind of twisted humor that only craven
youth could grasp, all things Earth became an obsession with
Obsidians.

"Hey, I *was* one of those craven youth!" said Jaxson wistfully. "That was one of the best times ever."

"Why am I not surprised?" said Marta-1. "So you remember then that it was all a big joke at first, a crazy fad em-
braced by bored college students, but before you knew it,
people were naming their children after ancient Earthlings,
dressing in old-fashioned rayon shirts and pleated pants, and
dancing to jazz music."

"*It ain't the blues 'til you paid the dues,*" said Jaxson, holding up his harmonica.

"My point exactly," said Marta-1, turning away to arrange
some books on an already perfectly neat desk. "In such ways
crazy fads are born all over the universe."

Jaxson leaned on the desk, trying to look casual. "There's
something I wanted to talk to you about," he said, grabbing
his chance to change the subject.

"Oh?"

"You've probably been wondering why I've been so, well,
kind of remote since lift-off."

"I've wondered no such thing," said Marta-1, scratching a
small red welt that appeared on her arm.

"I just wanted you to know that it's nothing personal. I've
been so busy maintaining the logs, I haven't really had time
to engage in interpersonal relationships."

"Okay, that's it," said Marta-1. "This tutorial is over."

"The truth is, it can be very alienating out here in the vast unknown without someone to share the more, shall we say, intimate moments with. Of course, you, as a behavioral scientist, are all too aware of the pitfalls of extended space travel upon one's emotional well-being when crossing the deepest, darkest zones of a throbbing universe."

"Are you hitting on me, Ship Observer Epsilon?" said Marta-1, with due alarm. "Because if you're hitting on me, I'll have you before the Investigative Tribunal so fast your maelstrom tank will spin."

"No need, no need," said Jaxson, shifting direction so quickly Marta-1 could almost hear the gears grinding. "It's Captain Wambold I'm talking about. Don't you think his behavior is totally bizarre?"

"He's under a great deal of pressure," said Marta-1 caustically.

"My point exactly. Not everyone can deal with such enormous responsibilities. It's not unnatural that somebody would crack under all that weight."

"I've seen no such cracks. What exactly are you referring to?"

"The way he flits around, jumping from the computer to the observation post to the command bridge, barking out orders like some kind of tyrant."

"I wouldn't question the Captain too much, if I were you. Take that as a fair warning."

"Okay, I just want you to know that if the crew ever thought about replacing the Captain with someone a little more flexible, well, I'm available. We could be home in no time, if you catch my drift."

"Are you suggesting a mutiny, Jaxson? Am I hearing you correctly?"

"Mutiny is a bit strong. A peaceful transference of power is more what I had in mind."

Marta-1 burst out laughing. "A transference of power?" she

howled. "From Captain Wambold to you? That's the funniest thing I ever heard!"

"Yes, well, I'm glad to boost your spirits," said Jaxson, slowly backing away.

Marta-1 grabbed the first book she could find—Huspence Killjoy's *Statistical Probabilities & Probable Statistics*—and tossed it at Jaxson's head. "You're nothing but a snake in the grass! An agitator! A traitor!"

"You've got me all wrong," said Jaxson as the book flew past him and bounced off a wall. When a bank of emergency lights began flashing red and orange, he decided to postpone his courting ritual until a more propitious time. Jaxson always felt that his personality worked better in the lower, subconscious realms and was a taste best slowly acquired and savored before spitting out. Leaving the evisceration for later, he fled from the library and managed to run straight into Marta-2, who was doing exercises in the corridor outside. "Hey! Be careful!" he yelled as he pulled back from a meta-carpal knuckle thrust that landed within an inch of his life.

"Oh, sorry," said Marta-2 after nearly decapitating him with a wild chop from her other-mind reservoir of kwan consciousness. "I didn't realize anyone was here."

"A guy can't even stretch his legs on this spaceship without taking his life into his own hands," said Jaxson, having almost been done in by two Martas in one fell swoop.

"I know, it's hard to find a place to unwind. I'm just trying to stay alert, do my job, and not get too blue. It's hard, sometimes, don't you think? Here we are, rushing wildly through space, never knowing what lies ahead, everyone so busy with their endless tasks, not even taking a moment to reflect upon the larger issues, the issues of life and death and meaningfulness. I mean, why plunge headlong to the other side of the universe when we don't really know what lies at the bottom of our own oceans? Why expand our horizons into the vastness of space when we haven't even mastered the basic elements of existence on our own planet? It's all so disturbing, don't you think?"

"Yeah... yeah... disturbing," said Jaxson, barely listening. From a far corner of the spaceship, he could hear a rumbling noise and the shuffling of feet.

"Sorry to bother you with all this talk," said Marta-2. "I'm just feeling a bit emotional tonight." A dull alarm sounded in the distance and more footsteps clanked along the metal grating above the relaxation chamber. "Do you think you might show me a few tunes on the harmonica sometime?" she said with disarming innocence.

"I'm pretty busy these days," said Jaxson, resisting the urge to tell her that what he was most busy with was staying away from her. The fact is, Marta-2 made him nervous. Who knew what a lonely molecular biologist might do in a moment of weakness? She could split his nuclides or screw with his enzymes or get ziggy with his zygotes or whatever it is that they do. Better safe than sorry when dealing with a lab rat, that much he knew.

"Oh, yes, of course. I don't mean to be a bother. I just thought that if you taught me one of those beautiful songs, I could entertain myself without disturbing anyone."

"Yeah, sure, we'll see."

Teller appeared in the corridor armed with night vision goggles and radiation meters. Before Jaxson knew what hit him, a blast from Teller's sonar tube exploded just inches from his head and nearly burst his eardrums with the reverberation of pulsating sound waves. "Intruder in Section 7!" Teller yelled out.

The shock waves flattened Jaxson against the corrugated steel walls of the hallway. He felt like every bone in his body had been rearranged as he struggled to pull himself upright. "Damn it, Teller, it's me!"

Teller wiped some steam off his goggles and took a closer look. "What are you doing down here?"

"Stretching my legs, if you must know. I didn't realize I needed your permission to breathe."

"If you needed my permission to breathe, you would've been dead long ago."

Jaxson forced a little laugh. "Good one, Teller."

"I don't think he's joking, to be honest," said Marta-2 in a low whisper.

Jaxson saw that Teller had his finger on the firing pin of the sonar tube and was looking for any excuse to shoot. "Listen, Teller, you really, seriously need to calm down," he said.

"A good soldier shoots first and asks questions later," said Teller. "I repeat, what are you doing down here?"

"I'm leading a mutiny," said Jaxson with matter-of-fact sarcasm.

Teller's finger twitched a little and he had to force himself to pull it off the trigger. "There will be a full report on this," he said. "You know that, don't you?"

"I wouldn't expect otherwise."

"I'll be writing you up in triplicate, Jaxson. One for the Captain, one for High Command, and one for my personal records."

"How about one for me?" said Jaxson. "And one for posterity? And one just for the hell of it?"

"With pleasure."

"Knock yourself out," said Jaxson.

Teller marched off down the corridor, ramrod straight. Marta-2 couldn't help but smile as she watched him make a sharp 90 degree turn at the end of the hall. "So," she said to Jaxson, "I'll be waiting for that harmonica lesson."

"Don't hold your breath," he said.

"Oh, I see," she said, her smile quickly fading. She stared at the floor, careful not to make eye contact.

"No, that's your first lesson. Don't hold your breath. Just let it flow in and out."

"Okay," she said, looking up. "I'll remember that."

Jaxson tipped his cap, just like he'd seen them do in those old Earth movies that had gotten transmitted all the way to Obsidia, and escaped through a hatch to the other side of the spaceship. They were cool, those guys in the black and white flicks, cool as cucumbers. He stared through an observation portal into the cold blackness of space and wondered if he'd ever get a chance to see the real deal for himself, on Earth. It was out there somewhere, that long gone planet, and he could almost see it now, a bunch of cool cats and hot chicks, everybody dancing to the beat, just waiting for him to pick up on the groove.

A thick cloud of pungent smoke hung over the stage as the band kicked in to a slow blues. That's the way I liked it, down and dirty, every beat sharp and clean and right on the money. I could feel the bass reverberating through the plywood floor, the guitar plucka-plunking up my spine, and the drums snapping off downbeats like gunshots in the night. A bunch of cool cats and hot chicks danced to the beat, just waiting for me to pick up on the groove. I did a little run in A-minor to shake off the cobwebs, then bent a reed so low it nearly snapped. I held it right down on the floor for a couple of extra beats, let it growl good and heavy, then brought it back up into the ozone. A woman fainted dead away on the dance floor, then another, but I wasn't in the mood for mercy, not tonight, baby, Jaxson Epsilon's on stage and I ain't takin' no prisoners, it's just you, me, some slow shuffling blues, and a six-pack of Schlitz. Sit tight and hang right, boys and girls, we're groovin' 'til sunrise.

Chapter 5

*"I guess all songs is folk songs. I
never heard no horse sing 'em."*
—Big Bill Broonzy

The Hudson Commodore rumbled down the road, its oversized tires flopping against the asphalt, its engine growling like an old blues singer on a late night tear. Esmeralda was behind the wheel, the top was down, the radio was up, and the great American midsection lay straight ahead. Nick hadn't felt this free since his release from the army and Esmeralda hadn't felt this free since, well, forever. They were like two crows on the loose, stretching their wings, flying instinctively, heading for a magnificent new nest. "We're moving from the outhouse to the cathouse," said Esmeralda, the wind brushing through her hair. Nick just smiled, not having the heart to correct her. Anyway, one man's cathouse was another man's penthouse, and wherever they were going, it was bound to be better than where they'd just been.

Frankie Laine, Peggy Lee, and the McGuire Sisters blasted out of the car speakers and if that wasn't a miracle, nothing was. The idea of a song being sent across the airwaves *and* being picked up in a moving vehicle was almost too much for Esmeralda to grasp. What's next, Django Reinhardt dancing on the dashboard? She cruised through the Illinois countryside, carefree as a Gypsy in a flea market, while Nick nodded off to the rhythms of the road. The highway can do that to you, keep you so awake you can barely close your eyes or send you straight into an undulating slumber. When he awoke a couple of hours later, he wasn't on the highway at all. He found himself all alone in the car just outside St. Patrick's Cemetery in Joliet, a town with little to recommend it other than the Illinois State Penitentiary, and that was no recommendation at all. Esmeralda was nowhere to be found, which was particularly disturbing since Nick had no intention of roaming through the cemetery to find her. He chose instead to sit tight in the car and bide his time, if one can call it that. Time passes slowly outside a cemetery—if at all—and Nick imagined a horde of hungry zombies coming to exact revenge for his impersonating a ghost, or whatever it is he did to so upset Mister Montgomery and his minions. What would they do? Feast on his face? Bathe in his blood? *Oh, God, where was she?*

Esmeralda appeared in the stairway of a shabby apartment building across the street from the cemetery. Half a step behind her was an older woman whose thick black hair was tied with a red scarf that hung down over one shoulder. She wore long, dangling earrings that brushed against her neck and a heavy silver necklace that bounced off her generous bosom as she crossed the street and approached the Hudson. "Now, *this* is a car!" she said with true admiration. "Is that real chrome on the fender?"

"Of course it's real," said Esmeralda. "Are they gonna put tin on a car like this?"

The woman ran her fingers over the trim and up along the hood. "You have done well. The back seat is bigger than my room."

"Don't get any ideas."

Nick saw the unmistakable resemblance between mother and daughter. The beady eyes, intense stare, and suspicious glint in the eye could only have been passed through the same steamy gene pool. "It's nice to meet you, Mrs. Kurlansky," he said. "Esmeralda told me all about you."

"There is no Mrs. Kurlansky, unless Esmeralda's father had a mother, and that I doubt. My family is Wasso, from a long line of Wassos, but you can call me Persephone since that's my name. Whatever she told you, there are two sides to every story."

"I assure you, it's only good things. Have you recovered from your operation?"

"Operation?"

"Your *back* operation," said Esmeralda, fixing her with a stare.

"Oh, yes, my *back* operation," said Persephone. "I never felt so good. It's a miracle what these doctors can do with a knife and a saw."

"Yes, yes," said Esmeralda. "So, this is Nick, a very famous musician from a very famous family of industrialists."

"Pharmacists," said Nick. "Rexall Drugstore, open until eight on Friday and all-day Saturday."

Persephone took a deeper look at Nick, like she was studying his aura, or the shape of his head, or the thickness of his wallet. She took his palm in her hands and felt the flexibility of his fingers and the shape of the knuckles. She then studied the way his life line deviated from his fate line and got a worried look. "I see trouble in your future," she said.

"Oh?" said Nick.

"Don't listen to a word she says," said Esmeralda. "Persephone saw trouble in my future since the day I was born."

"And was I wrong?"

"It's always the same thing with you, isn't it? You make predictions that don't come true, give suggestions that don't work, and see things that aren't there."

Persephone ignored her daughter and told Nick that he should avoid swordfish and chickpeas, walk on the north

side of the street, and sleep with one eye open. Then came
the required stories of the family's origins, as if the Wassos
were descended from a Neolithic tribe—which, in fact, they
well might have been—and the subsequent tales of the
crossing of a mythic desert, the parting of a river, and the
wandering through foreign lands. It was a stream of conscious narrative that went off in a dozen directions at once
and was rife with inconsistencies, improbabilities, and
outright lies. Still, Nick was able to piece something or other
together about a family of nomadic roof repairmen who
descended upon Joliet several decades earlier and very
nearly—but not quite—robbed the town blind. They were
sent up the river, that river being right outside the courtroom
and winding less than a mile to the outskirts of town.
Persephone waited for a release that never came while
reading palms, telling fortunes, and keeping the Earth's axis
properly off-balance. Then came a traveling vacuum cleaner
salesman who got his foot in the door and a whole lot more.
He had a brand new Electrolux V, the one with the chrome
trim and the sleigh bars, and that was enough to drive any
girl crazy. It was a wildly romantic affair, what with the
vacuum bags and the suction tubes and the ingenious
attachments, but when it was all over, Persephone was left
with a baby girl and Jacob Kurlansky was long gone, Panama
hat and all. The gonif.

"Yes, yes, well, that's ancient history, isn't it?" said Esmeralda, finally getting her two cents in. "This is now, and
now is now and then was then and maybe we'll meet somewhere in the middle. Meanwhile, it's time to boogie, Mama,
so be good, take care, and we'll catch you on the flip side."

"You'll be careful?"

"Of course we will. We'll be in California before you know
it. I'll send you some wine."

"You have to watch out with those Kurlanskys. They give
you their name and leave you with all the bills. You'll be

lucky they don't make you pay rent."

"Don't worry about Esmeralda," said Nick. "She's plenty sharp."

"Sure, she's sharp. She's her mother's daughter."

"Yeah, okay," said Esmeralda. "Let's go before the sky falls on our heads."

There were hugs and tears, promises to write, plans to meet, tickets to be sent, and bank accounts to be filled, and with that Esmeralda and Nick were back on the road, the cemetery and the old apartment and the penitentiary mere specks behind them in the rear view mirror.

"Any more surprises?" said Nick.

"You never know," said Esmeralda.

Afternoon hit Chicago like a jab to the chops. It was too hot, too humid, and altogether suffocating as the sun languorously crept across a sky bisected by towers, cranes, and unfinished skyscrapers. Mister Montgomery sat behind a big mahogany desk staring at a bottle of Remy Martin, trying to decide if it was too early to take the edge off the day. The intercom on his desk buzzed. "Ray and Dirk to see you," crackled his secretary's voice over the air.

Perfect. It was just the excuse he was looking for. He reached for the bottle and the intercom with one fluid motion. "Send them in."

Ray and Dirk appeared in the doorway, looking unsure of themselves. Should they go right in or wait for an invite? Should they take off their hats now or when they go in? Should they wipe their feet on the mat or take a chance on the carpet? Montgomery motioned them in with an impatient wave of his hand. "Well?"

Ray led the way to a couple of seats in front of the desk. He and Dirk stood there, unsure whether to sit or not. Montgomery gave no indication either way, so stood they did. "We just wanted to bring you up to date on the situation," said Ray.

"Let me take a wild guess," said Montgomery with a thick dose of sarcasm. "You looked everywhere. You spent the whole night checking every street in the neighborhood. You called your boys and told them to keep a look out. You covered the bus station and the train station and Midway Field. Then you doubled back and looked again, but the guy clear got away, just like that. That sound about right?"

"Pretty much so," said Ray, looking downcast but not completely defeated. "Except for one thing. Dirk pointed out something real interesting, how the guy was limping when he ran out of the house and since nobody laid a hand on him, we got to thinking how that limp must've been there all along—"

"So we got to thinking, who do we know with a limp?" said Dirk. "Well, there's Father Murphy over at the rectory, there's old lady McGinty over at the cleaners, and, oh, yeah, there's Nick the harmonica player over at you-know-where. The very same guy we delivered your message to just the other day."

"That's right. We delivered the message—"

"—loud and clear—" interjected Dirk.

"—yeah, we told him what's what and who's who, just like you said—"

"And?"

"Well, I don't know, boss, he said he wanted to talk to you—"

"Which we discouraged—"

"And then he got smart-alecky—"

"Which didn't sit right—"

"And then he walked right out the door—"

"Poof, into the night."

Montgomery sat back and ran it down. He hadn't figured Nick for a fool, but then again, what do you make of a guy who hangs his hat every night on the bedpost of a crazy-ass bar girl and keeps coming back for more? Guy like that could get invisible on you at the first sign of trouble. "Go on—"

"So, Dirk and I started adding things up and we decided to pay Esmeralda a little visit, well, just because."

"And?"

Ray nervously ran his hand over the top of the chair. "Well, the thing of it is, boss, she's gone."

Montgomery leaned forward almost imperceptibly and stared at Ray without blinking. "What do you mean, she's gone?"

"Cleared out. Lock, stock, and barrel."

"And how, exactly, did you come to this conclusion?"

"Well, Dirk here, he put his shoulder into the door, and it just kind of gave."

"There was nothing but a pile of junk inside. Table and chairs kind of stuff. But all her clothes, her valuables, her shoes—"

For the first time, Montgomery looked truly worried. "Her shoes?"

"We looked high and low for any sign of anything, boss," said Dirk. *"Nada."*

Ray pulled a business card out of his pocket and handed it to Montgomery. "Just this card from some Jew lawyers we found on the floor." Ray stood there a moment, not quite sure what to do. "Sorry about this, boss," he said. "She's a real crazy bitch."

"Is that your professional opinion, Ray?"

"Just my gut."

Montgomery knocked back the rest of his drink and studied the card. "Check out this guy Whitley," he said. "See what he knows. Give him a little push if you have to. Think you guys can handle that?"

"Consider it done," said Ray.

The Hudson glided through the Illinois countryside, the pistons purring, the engine humming, the cylinders clickety-clacking to the steady push forward. Nick was itching to drive, but Esmeralda kept saying, "Later, later," until he finally began to suspect that later would never come. At Moline, she somehow made a wrong turn, which was no easy task since all she had to do was continue driving straight, but straight was not Esmeralda's natural inclination, not ever, and they found themselves going south instead of west. They passed altogether unnecessarily through Kewanee and Galesburg before righting themselves and getting back on the road at Rock Island. Nick, careful not to upset the delicate balance of Esmeralda's inner navigator, offered some sage advice: "All you've got to do is keep driving straight, sweetheart. Highway 6 takes us all the way to California."

"I don't like straight."

"I know that, but if we want to get to California, there are certain concessions we've got to make. California is in a particular direction and we need to follow a particular road to get there. It doesn't just move around on a whim."

"Too damn many rules, Nick. Let's just keep it simple, okay?"

"Whatever you say, baby," he said.

Esmeralda came up and over a gradual incline, then sped along a straightaway that reached to the horizon. It was a good opportunity to put the Hudson through its paces and she gave it full throttle. The car zoomed along the highway, faster and faster, the wind cascading through her hair, the thrill of unencumbered speed coursing through her veins. She was a Gypsy stallion galloping free and wild through the Balkan steppes—no responsibilities, no bills to pay, no rent due, no shadows on the walls, nowhere to be and all the time in the world to get there. A primal freedom enveloped her, an openhearted acceptance of life's great adventure that had been nearly buried in Chicago. She was where she'd always been meant to be, on the open road under a sunny sky, without a care in the world. She was a flamenco dancer, she was a violin, she was a dancing bear, she was leading a caravan through the Anatolian plains.

Esmeralda's caravan suddenly hit a bump in the road, as caravans tend to do. There's something about the creaky wheels or the crooked axles or, in this case, the geyser of steam spewing from under the hood, that slows every Gypsy down. The engine sputtered, then coughed, then belched as the car coasted to a stop along the side of the road. Esmeralda's Jewish side was immediately reawakened as her carefree life became so unexpectedly precarious. She was reminded of a painful diaspora, of confinement in penned-up little villages, of bad luck and trouble. It was as if her inner crow got blasted out of the sky and fell in a heap on the side of an Iowa cornfield.

Nick got out of the car and stared helplessly at the eight cylinder engine. The thing had completely conked out and he didn't have a clue what to do. There was no point in telling Esmeralda that she'd been driving too fast, just as there was no point in her telling Nick that Gypsies don't have speed limits, so instead they said nothing at all. They sat at the side of the road, waiting for God-knows-what. A guy came by in a tractor, waved, and kept going. Then another guy came by in another tractor, waved, and kept going. Then a third guy came by in another tractor and didn't even wave. "Are we gonna die out here, Nick?" said Esmeralda. "Are we actually gonna die in the middle of an Iowa cornfield?"

Nick stared at his palm, noting how the life line and fate line diverged into what looked exactly like the border between Iowa and Illinois. "I'm not sure, Es, but I just want you to know it's been a real pleasure knowing you."

"Me, too, Nickie, me too."

Ray and Dirk were in no mood to mess around. They staked out a corner of the lobby of Greenberg, Greenberg and O'Shaughnessy and watched as John Whitley ambled slowly down a brightly lit corridor, stopped to talk with his boss, waved to the telephone operator at her desk, said good night to the janitor, got a shoeshine in the lobby, put a flower in his lapel, bought a newspaper from the man in the kiosk, paged through the sports section, readjusted his tie, and stepped out onto the street. That was as good a place as any to ask a few questions, but it was an even better place to simply clobber him over the head, toss him into their car, squeal off down the road, screech to a halt, hustle him into a building, slam him to the floor, kick him in the ribs, and slap him across the choppers. It took no time at all before Whitley spilled the beans, yammering out every name, date, and address he ever encountered while in the employ of Greenberg, Greenberg and O'Shaughnessy.

When Montgomery's door swung open moments later, Ray and Dirk stood there with full confidence. "We got the straight poop," said Ray. "The guy was blabbing so much, we could hardly get him to shut up." Ray got a big grin on his kisser like he was a Lake Geneva comedian. "God, these lawyers can talk! No wonder they charge by the hour. It takes them that long to tell you what school their kids go to."

"Get to the point," said Montgomery.

"Turns out our girl Esmeralda's been holding out on you, boss. Hell, she's loaded. She's got herself a real nice spread out in California. Whitley cashed a check for her and before you knew it, she was running off to a Hudson dealership downtown. That's the last he saw of her, but five'll get you ten she's on her way to the coast with that boyfriend of hers."

Montgomery sat back and took stock of things. All in all, he was doing pretty well for himself. His various operations were all showing a profit, he instilled fear in his enemies, and he was surrounded by sycophants, yes-men, and women of questionable virtue who would jump at his slightest request. Life, however, had thrown him one curveball, a curveball named Esmeralda Kurlansky who seemed to think she could live outside the rules and regulations of his little criminal empire. This time she'd gone too far. Montgomery flung his shot glass at the door, smashing it into a hundred pieces. "That's it! No more! It's time to pick up the pieces!"

Ray and Dirk stared at the fragments of glass, wondering if they should pick up the pieces. "Right, right," said Dirk.

"I don't care what it takes. I want you to find those two and get them back here, one way or another. Do I make myself clear?"

"Perfectly clear," said Ray. He and Dirk tipped their hats and disappeared into the hot, humid Chicago night.

Nick and Esmeralda leaned against the Hudson as the last rays of sunlight disappeared behind some lonely grain silos that dotted the horizon. The Iowa night was dead quiet except for the chirping of crickets, which sounded like a thick electric current buzzing through the atmosphere. When even the chirping stopped, Esmeralda nervously grabbed Nick's arm. "You think somebody's out there?" she said.

"Out where?"

"Out *there*," she said, pointing everywhere and nowhere at once. "I saw a movie where the crickets stopped chirping and two minutes later the place got lit up with machine gun fire. Like they knew or something."

"It's just late. Even the crickets gotta sleep."

"Yeah, I suppose."

Two minutes later the place got lit up with the shaky headlight of an old truck that came wobbling down the road, creaking and groaning and listing to one side like a tugboat about to capsize. Nick leapt into the middle of the road, determined to stop the vehicle at all costs, but the driver was already slowing to a stop by the time he saw them. He was an old coot, his bones as creaky as his truck. He climbed down from the cab, scratched his head, rested his thumbs in his overalls, and chewed on the stem of a corncob pipe. "Got you a little trouble, looks like," he said.

"Looks like," said Esmeralda as she flicked a dead bug off the windshield.

"Just boiled over, did she?"

"Brand new car and all."

"Brand new, you say?"

"Brand new."

"And how many miles you say you got on this vehicle?"

"How should I know? A hundred or two I suppose."

"Well, Miss, you could just take a look see on the odometer."

"And where would I find this odometer thing?"

"I expect you could find it right under the speedometer. You got one of those, don't you?"

"Yeah, yeah," she said, leaning over the dashboard. "It says—*hey, wait a minute!*—it says 12,214 plus another number that's stuck between the 6 and the 7."

"Goodly number of miles for a brand new car."

Esmeralda leaned against the driver's door, her face burning redder than an Iowa tomato at sunset. "That can't be. I just bought this car right from the dealer."

"Well, Miss, were me, I'd take this Hudson right back to that dealer and give him what's for."

Nick stepped in before Esmeralda completely blew her top. "We can't really do that."

"Well, you sure as heck can't just stay out here. Night's coming up real soon. Tell you what. I'll tow you into the next town and you can figure it all out over there. It's just a couple of miles up the road."

"That would be much appreciated, Mister. Much appreciated, indeed."

The auto repair shop in Brooklyn, Iowa, was closed for the night, as was the movie house, the gas station, the pharmacy, the grocery store, and the newsstand. Nick and Esmeralda left the car in the driveway of the repair shop and walked a couple of blocks to a Howard Johnson's that just happened to have a room available. "You're lucky," said the desk clerk with a perfectly straight face. "It's high season."

"You hear that, Nickie?" said Esmeralda. "Man says we're lucky."

"Where you headed, if I might ask?" said the desk clerk.

"California," said Esmeralda. "We've got a farm out there."

"That so? What kind of farm?"

"Money farm. We've got money growing on trees. There's so much cash on those trees, we hardly have time to pick it all."

"Whoo-ee. You don't need any farmhands, do you? I could leave tonight."

"Keep your bags packed. You never know."

Nick and Esmeralda checked into a room that was exactly like every other motel room in mid-America. There was a mirror, a lamp, a closet, a desk, a fan, a waste basket, an ashtray, a nightstand, a Gideon's Bible, a wash basin, a Kleenex dispenser, a calendar, a room rate sheet, a flower pot, a bed frame, a mattress, and sheets that smelled of Tide. Esmeralda flopped onto the bed, stared at the cottage cheese ceiling, and pondered the silence. There was something about Iowa silence that was different from Illinois silence. Illinois silence was more subtle. It had little hiccups in it like car horns, ambulance sirens, and screaming babies that kept things from getting too quiet. Iowa silence, on the other hand, was the real thing. It was end of the world silence that put funny thoughts into her head. "Nick," said Esmeralda, "there's something I've been wanting to tell you."

"What's that?"

"Well, that first night we met at the bar? When you bought me all those drinks? I had you figured for a real chump."

"I figured."

"Every nickel of change from your tab went straight into my pocket."

"I figured."

"A couple of those drinks never even got poured."

"I figured."

"And when I took you home that night, I went through your wallet."

"I figured."

"I just wanted you to know, Nick."

"That's okay, hon. I got it all out of your purse the next morning before I left. I even grabbed an extra ten for the trouble."

The light above the bed snapped on. Esmeralda looked at Nick with anger. "What do you mean?"

"What's fair is fair, is all."

"Good night, Nick."

"Good night, Esmeralda."

Nick dreamt of the foxholes in Italy, the same dream he had dreamt every night since leaving Europe. It was raining and there was mud everywhere—mud dripping from the sky, mud dripping from the trees, mud dripping from his helmet. He dug himself deeper into the hillside as airplanes roared overhead, cannons boomed, and flares lit up the sky. There was a sudden barrage of machine gun fire, a splattering of bullets biting into the ground, a groan, a splash of blood, boots pounding the dirt, and footsteps squeezing into the mud. Nick twisted his body in the foxhole. There was no up, no down, no friend, no enemy. It was nothing but a swirl of death and madness. The guy next to him, a kid, really, a kid just like him, stood up and raised his hands to the heavens like some kind of crazed John the Baptist. Nick grabbed him, but it was too late. A burst of gunfire cut through his chest and severed his spine. The mud, the blood, the flesh and the bones mixed into a throbbing ball of putrescence. Nick thought how it was time to leave—north, south, east, west, it made no difference—it was time to get the hell out of there, and then he felt something burningly, scorchingly hot ripping through his leg. It left a metallic taste in his mouth and burned as if he were on a stake in medieval Italy. That's what was in his mind—he was burning at the stake in the town center—the hordes watched in horror, some cheering, some crying, his leg sizzled like meat on a spit, so hot, so hot, so very, very hot—

"Nick... Nick... are you all right?" said Esmeralda, waking up with a jolt in the middle of the night.

"Yeah, I'm okay," he said, groggily coming out of the dream.

She held him tenderly in her arms and wiped the sweat off his forehead. "Try to just forget about it, okay, honey?" she whispered into his ear.

"Sure thing," he said, hoping he could somehow stay awake. He stared out the window at the cornfields in the distance. If only he could stay awake, he wouldn't have to dream, not tonight, not tomorrow, not ever. That's how he fell asleep, thinking about the cornfields, hoping he wouldn't have to dream.

Chapter 6

"There was one Sonny Boy and that's it, just
one, and I don't mean that second one!"
—Little Walter

Esmeralda awoke with an angry stomach. She had a full eight hours to digest the mishap with the car and she didn't like it one little bit. All she could think of was how she would invoke a Gypsy curse upon the Hudson dealership the likes of which had never been seen on the shores of Lake Michigan. There would be fires. There would be brimstones. There would be frogs falling from the sky. By the time she was done with them, the car lot would be turned into an auto graveyard that would whistle in the wind, smell of formaldehyde, and make the blood run cold. Then maybe they'd remember that nobody screws with Esmeralda Kurlansky. Not now. Not ever. No way. No how.

Esmeralda rustled Nick out of bed and marched over to the automotive repair shop on Main Street, where a young mechanic was already admiring the sleek lines of the 1947 Hudson parked outside his garage. "This baby yours?" he asked as they approached.

"Who wants to know?" asked Esmeralda, eyeing him suspiciously.

"Name's Marvin. My Dad's the proprietor of this shop."

"And what does that make you, the good son hustling up

business on the street? I know that game backwards and
forwards. The cute little kid charms the pants off the gadjos
while Dad robs their house blind. Well, it ain't gonna work,
buddy, not with me."

"I'm, uh, I'm not sure what you mean—"

"You know exactly what I mean. It's the oldest con in the
books. You wouldn't be a couple of shyster mechanics looking to take advantage of a couple of city folks, would you?"

"Well, now, ma'am—"

Nick read the situation for what it was—a potential disaster in the making—and jumped in. "We'd just like you to
take a look at the car," he said, before the kid called in the
National Guard.

The kid looked them up, down and sideways, then finally
yelled through the garage doors. "Hey, Pops! Couple of people
to see you."

A weathered old geezer in greasy overalls ambled out and
got an eyeful of the strangers and their car. "Um-hmm," he
said, walking around the vehicle and taking note of some of
its stellar features: "Hudson Commodore 8... maroon paint job
with black convertible top... arm rests on the doors... twin air
horns... locking glove box... thick carpeting front and back."

"You looking to fix this thing or sell it to us again?" said
Esmeralda.

Pops stopped in front of the driver's door and rubbed his
grizzled face. "Don't rightly figure I could sell something that's
not mine," he said, not fully grasping her sarcasm.

"Look here, Pops," said Marvin. "It's got a radio built right
into the dashboard."

Pops leaned over and took a gander. "A Philco, no less.
That thing work?"

"Better than the engine," said Esmeralda. "Goddamn thing
steamed right up on us."

"No need for that kind of talk, ma'am," said Pops as he
opened the hood and checked the water level in the radiator.

"Did I say something wrong?" whispered Esmeralda to Nick.

Nick shrugged, Marvin smirked, and Pops gave the car the once over. "What you have here is an overheated engine," he finally proclaimed. "Could be any number of things gone wrong. Bad hose, bad belt, maybe cylinder trouble. If you're real unlucky, could be a crack in the engine block."

"I've got no idea what that means," said Esmeralda, "so let's just keep it simple. Can you fix it or not?"

"Well, let's just take a look see." He poked around the engine for a minute, then nodded to himself. "Um-hmm, just like I figured. Looks like a loose fan belt. Marvin, hand me that spanner wrench."

Marvin dug around in a tool box and came up with a mechanic's best friend. "Here you go, Pops."

The old man loosened the bolts holding the fan belt in place, spread them an inch or so farther apart, and retightened them. "Okay, ma'am, say your prayers and give that ignition a turn."

Esmeralda did as he asked—minus the prayer business— and the Hudson started right up. "Well, that's more like it," she said.

"You see, it doesn't always have to be a problem."

"Yeah, good, so what do I owe you?"

"Let's just call it 50 cents."

Esmeralda looked up from the driver's seat, wondering if she was hearing right. "For what? You didn't do anything."

"Now, ma'am—"

"I'm tired of getting screwed by you galoots. You didn't even replace any parts."

"A quarter will be fine."

"Hmmph," snorted Esmeralda.

Nick dug into his pocket and handed over a dollar's worth of change. "This should cover it," he said. "Thanks for your trouble."

The mechanic counted up the coins and shook Nick's hand. "Got yourself a temperamental travel companion there."

"Maybe you could just point us toward Route 6?"

"Son, you're *on* Route 6. Ain't no other road and ain't but two ways to go. Back. And forth."

"In that case, we'll be heading forth."

"Straight ahead, then," said Pops, dropping down the hood and squeezing it closed. "Good luck to you, son. I suspect you'll need it."

Ray and Dirk headed down their own stretch of Route 6 in a gray Chevrolet Special, an old clunker that had maybe one good car chase left in it, if that. Lousy car, lousy trip, lousy job—it was a punishment of sorts, an exile from the center of the action to the margins of nowhere. And for what? Taking the initiative? Putting two and two together? Tracking down a deadbeat dame? The more Ray thought about it, the more his ulcer acted up, especially as he viewed the distended belly of America stretched out before him. Joliet, Moline, Rock Island, and God knows what other two-bit burgs lay ahead, each of them deader than the next. Which was exactly how Ray imagined Nick and Esmeralda after he and Dirk got through with them. They figured a new Hudson with Illinois plates shouldn't be that hard to find, not when it was being driven by a curly-haired floozy and a guy with a limp. They stopped at gas stations, hamburger joints, and roadside bars, always asking the same question: "You haven't seen a curly-haired floozy and a guy with a limp in these parts, have you?"

"Not rightly so," would come the answer.

"Okay, well, if you do see them, tell them not to get too comfortable."

"Not too comfortable, you say? Okay, we'll be sure to let them know."

That's when Ray would light up a Viceroy, Dirk would

break off a toothpick between his teeth, and they'd stare those hayseeds right in the eyes. Just because.

Ray slowed down in some town or other while Dirk looked up and down every side street for any sign of a convertible Hudson. They passed a bar, a barbershop, a hardware store, a five and dime, and a general store that looked pretty much exactly the same as every other no-count town in Illinois. *"Nada,"* said Dirk as he scanned the half-empty streets.

"Big surprise, hey, Dirk? Like somebody's gonna spend more than five minutes in a dump like this. These little towns give me the heebie-jeebies."

"What do you figure people do out here? What makes them get up in the morning?"

"Who knows?" said Ray. "Me, I'd go crazy in two days just from staring at the squirrels."

"They got squirrels?"

"I don't know. It's just an expression. Squirrels, trees, sidewalks, it's all the same." Ray stepped on the gas and got back on the highway. "They're out there somewhere," he said. "We might have to go clear across Nebraska, but we're gonna get them, you can bet on that."

"I can? Okay, ten bucks says Omaha."

"Twenty says before."

King Biscuit Time was on the air, which meant that it was noon in the heartland. Every black-owned radio within 500 miles of Helena, Arkansas, was tuned in to KFFA, and a few white ones, too. The 15 minute broadcast was timed to coincide with lunch hour on the surrounding plantations, where farmhands dropped everything to listen to the jumping, jiving Delta blues the way they were meant to be played. The King Biscuit Entertainers were live in the studio and Nick was thrilled to find them right there at 1360 on the AM dial. Pinetop Perkins was on piano, Robert Lockwood, Jr., was on guitar, James Curtis was on drums, and the star of the show, Sonny Boy Williamson, was on harmonica. Williamson played a searing harmonica solo that almost blew right through the dashboard and sent a shiver up and down Nick's spine.

"*That's Sonny Boy Williamson and the King Biscuit Enter-tainers,*" said the announcer, "*and this is King Biscuit Time live from the KFFA studio in beautiful downtown Helena, Arkansas. Have you tried the latest from King Biscuit Flour? To turn out the best cornbread you need the best cornmeal. All good cooks know this. It's a very simple job to turn out piping hot cornbread dishes using the famous Sonny Boy Meal. So why not pick up a bag of Sonny Boy Meal today and see for yourself all the delicious cornbread dishes you can cook up. Just read the recipes on the back of the 5-lb. or the 10-lb. bag. Muffins, cakes, or just plain skillet cornbread. Get it today. Either plain or the new Sonny Boy Mix.*"

What Nick didn't know was that Sonny Boy Williamson was *not* Sonny Boy Williamson. The station couldn't afford a big name like that, so instead they hired a guy named Rice Miller and *said* he was Sonny Boy Williamson. Not long afterwards, Miller claimed to be the "original" Sonny Boy Williamson and even got fake ID to prove it. Nobody seemed to know a lawyer, so from that day on the world had two Sonny Boy Williamsons and so much the better. You couldn't really go wrong with either one.

The band played *Stop Breaking Down* as Esmeralda drove through Iowa. The land was flat, the sky was blue, the air was heavy, and the bugs were thick as molasses. That was some-thing she hadn't figured on—the bug attack—and there was already a whole delicatessen of animal by-products covering the windshield, the grill, and the hood. It was July, after all, and the bugs were celebrating their exquisite existence by dive-bombing the car at every imaginable angle. They swooped in with glee and plopped their red-yellow guts right down the center divider of the window. If there was some nobility in this multi-winged kamikaze attack, Esmeralda couldn't see it. All she saw was a raw stew of spindly legs, spiky bodies, and skeletal frames, and it made her question for the first time her decision to flee Chicago.

> *Stop breakin' down*
> *Baby, please stop breakin' down*
> *Stop breakin' down, now*
> *Baby, please stop breakin' down*
> *I don't believe you really, really love me*
> *I think you just like the way my music sound*

Esmeralda figured that Sonny Boy Williamson had it just about right, but what was he doing in Helena, Arkansas? No siree, the blues were Chicago and Chicago was the blues. The windy, crooked city combined hope and despair in just the right amounts—10% hope, 75% despair, and 15% for the waitress—and that's what you needed to drag yourself out the door night after night. She glanced into the rear view mirror, as if hoping she could spot Old Town in the distance. It was a momentary thing, this nostalgia for the Flame Club and the crummy coldwater flat, and it would pass soon enough. But for now, she wondered if she'd made yet another mistake in a life fully packed with error and miscalculation.

Illinois turned into Iowa, a geographical event that went unnoticed by all but the state police, and they barely noticed either. One flat piece of dirt looks pretty much like any other, especially when the sky hangs low and threatens to collapse of boredom at any moment. Ray was getting itchy and his ulcer needed feeding before it got good and irritated. After passing 50 miles of corn and alfalfa, an orange and black A&W Root Beer stand appeared out of nowhere at the side of the road. What would induce someone to open a restaurant in an alfalfa field was anyone's guess, but Ray wasn't in the mood for guessing games. He pulled off the highway onto a gravel driveway and before the cloud of dust even settled, a teenaged car hop appeared with a heavy metal tray. "Howdy," he said, as he undid the mechanical contraption and inserted it in the window panel of the driver's door.

"Careful there," said Ray, "this is an auto-mo-bile, not one of your farm implements."

The kid fully caught the sarcasm. "What can I do you for?" he said, folding down the tray with exaggerated caution.

"What's the specialty of the house?"

"Root Beer. The hot dogs won't kill you. The fries might. The potato chips been sitting there since winter. Steer clear of anything brown."

"Those hot dogs. Are they grilled or boiled?"

"They're going around on one of those rotisserie things."

"Pork or beef?"

"You're kidding, right? How should I know?"

"Tell you what," said Ray. "Bring us two beers and two dogs. Think you can handle that?"

The kid tipped his cap, a ridiculous-looking thing made of flimsy orange and black paper, and headed for the kitchen window.

Ray glanced out at some railroad tracks that ran alongside the road, a couple of scruffy trees, and a half dozen farms in the distance. The place was a real action central. Dirk paged through the local newspaper, killing time. "Listen to this," he said. *"Secretary of State George Marshall announces a plan to rebuild Europe with American money and ingenuity.* Can you believe it? They're gonna take our hard earned dollars and send them over to those wops and krauts? I thought *we* won the war."

"It's all fixed, Dirk, the whole system. It's fixed up at the top, and guys like you and me gotta scramble just to make an honest buck. The whole thing stinks."

The car hop came out with their order. "Two beers and two dogs. Lemme know if you need anything else."

"Actually, there is something," said Ray. "You haven't seen a curly-haired floozy and a guy with a limp in these parts, have you?"

"I might've seen a floozy," said the kid, "but I don't know about any limp."

Dirk narrowed his eyes. "How about a convertible Hudson with Illinois plates?"

"No, no, I don't think so."

Ray lit up a Viceroy, Dirk broke off a toothpick between his teeth, and the two of them stared the kid in the eyes. The kid just stood there a moment, then shrugged and moseyed on back to the stand. Dirk reached over for the root beer. The mug was so cold that ice dripped off the sides. "How do you figure they keep these glasses so cold?"

"I don't know, Dirk, these locals got a way with things."

"What, way out here? They got a fancy Frigidaire or something?"

Ray raised an impatient eyebrow. "It's just ice, Dirk. It's not a goddamned miracle."

"I dare to disagree. A cold glass of root beer on a day like today is a miracle right up there with brats and sauerkraut."

Ray took a deep drag of his Viceroy, exhaled slowly, and watched the smoke drift lazily up along the windshield and into the visors. "You're a real simple man, aren't you?"

"I try to appreciate the little things," said Dirk, rising to the challenge. He loved these little word games with Ray and saw a rare chance to put one over on him. "It's what separates us from the apes."

Ray thought about it for a moment, then snubbed out his cigarette on the window tray. "What are you telling me, that apes don't like root beer?"

Dirk balanced the ice-cold mug against his hairy arms, then lifted it with his short stubby fingers to his gaping mouth. "When was the last time you saw an ape chugging an A&W?" he said with a self-satisfied grin.

"You don't want to know," said Ray as he watched the last few drops of root beer dribble over Dirk's lips and down his chin, "you really don't want to know."

The Hudson cruised down Highway 6, headed ever west. Morning became afternoon and the cornfields transformed from yellow to golden orange. Rich farmland stretched as far as the eye could see, dotted here and there with tractors, threshers, and harvesting machines. As afternoon became evening, the sun set, the moon rose, and a whole new world of nocturnal bug life splayed itself against the windshield. Iowa was eerily quiet at night. The farmers were long asleep, the townsfolk were tucked away in their homes, and the air was still as the Flame Club after closing. As one shapeless patch of earth migrated into the next, Nick and Esmeralda experienced the strange dislocation of travel as their bodies were transported over the plains of the American heartland.

The moment they crossed the Missouri River into Nebraska, Esmeralda's imagination came alive with visions of nightclubs, dancehalls and saloons. Omaha was the biggest city for miles and held out hope for some action at last, but when they rolled down Dodge Street, they found nothing but sleepy hotels, closed lunch counters, and locked-up stockyards. Nothing was open, not even the Texaco and Conoco gas stations that dotted every other street corner. Nick wanted to bed down in the first available room, but Esmeralda refused to stay in a city whose sidewalks rolled up at 8:00 P.M., so they just kept on going.

Back on the highway, they drove past cattle ranches and slaughterhouses that spread their putrid smells straight into the atmosphere. Everything smelled of manure—the road, the trees, the grass, the car itself. Finally the wind changed direction, their olfactory systems recovered, and Esmeralda pulled off the road to a secluded spot alongside a country lake. They snuggled together in the back seat, Nick's head in Esmeralda's lap, staring into a vast, starry sky that was unblemished by factory smoke, burning coal, or chemical residue. Nick's mind slowly emptied, his muscles relaxed, and he began drifting off into sleep when a crackling in the bushes sent him bolting upright with a start. For an instant, he was back in the foxholes of Italy, his eyes darting from one creeping shadow to the next.

"Nickie, Nickie, it's nothing," said Esmeralda as she pulled him back onto her lap and tried to soothe him.

"How do you know it's nothing? Who knows what the hell is out there?"

"I'll tell you what's out there. There's a bunch of flying insects just itching to climb in here and do a number on my nice vinyl trim."

Nick leaned back into her lap and tried to block out the memories. "I'm sorry, baby, it's just—"

"I know... I know," said Esmeralda, holding him tenderly in her arms. "I wish I could've been there with you."

"What, in the foxholes?"

"I could've ironed your shirt or something while you were killing Nazis."

Nick half-smiled and leaned up on his elbows. "Es, you never ironed a shirt for me even once in Chicago."

"Weren't any Nazis."

"Anyway, I never killed any Nazis."

"Who'd you kill, then?"

"I didn't kill anybody. What the hell'd I want to kill anybody for? They never did anything to me."

"That's what I like about you, Nickie. You need at least half a reason before you go messing with someone. Not like those gonifs in Chicago."

Esmeralda snuggled into his shoulder and closed her eyes.

Nick pulled out his harmonica and played a couple of notes that seeped into the reeds and muffled down to the bottom of the lake. Crazy, he figured, thinking about the war out here. "What do you think Muddy's doing right now?" he said.

"Right this minute? He's probably sweet-talking some innocent girl into buying him a drink. If I was her, I'd hit the road, but Muddy knows how to hypnotize the ladies with that maple syrup voice of his. One minute you're sitting on a barstool minding your own business, the next thing you know, Muddy's leaving a rose petal on your pillow."

Nick played a quiet blues and pictured himself onstage with Muddy and Willie and the boys. He could almost see them now, standing on the plywood with slightly stooped shoulders, feeling the shared weight of the world. Muddy would growl out some lyrics, Willie would fwap his bass, Nick would take a long, crazy solo and for a few minutes, at least, they'd all be connected. They celebrated life's misfortunes, reveled in its disappointments, and drank to its gross inequities. Who knew what it all meant? Life in the foxholes; life in the club; life in the backseat of a Hudson convertible; it was hard, sometimes, to tell them apart.

Chapter 7

"The energy of the mind
is the essence of life."
—Aristotle

S tasis is death," as was famously noted by H. Lavender
Laroche in his *Introduction to Basic Energy Theory*, "and
thus our need to keep ahead of the energy curve lest
the energy curve get ahead of us." It was a mantra known by
every schoolchild on Obsidia. *Stasis is death. Stasis is death.*
Obsidia had been operating for decades on antiquated
hydrogen power and the primitive machinery of freeze-dried
fusion. Once the energy grids began faltering, new resources
were urgently needed to fuel expansion, since without growth,
society was in danger of stagnation.

Laroche argued that the elemental energy of the brain
itself could be tapped. Given that even the simplest thought
caused countless millions of neurons and synapses to fire
every instant, couldn't those electronic discharges be captured, distilled, and converted into a source of endlessly
renewable energy? Thoughts, after all, weren't just disembodied mental constructs floating through the air, they were
actual, physical phenomena that left their mark in the brain.
Thoughts were imprinted in binary code in the nooks and
crannies of the centromedial nucleus of the amygdala, and
Laroche believed that if one were able to unlock that code,

the energy of the thought itself could regenerated for other uses. "If the power of thoughts could be harnessed, the potential energy is virtually as unlimited as the imagination itself!" he proclaimed.

The idea was simple enough. If someone could imagine a tornado, the vast power of that tornado must be imprinted somewhere in the brain. Once its binary code was located and decoded, the energy of the tornado itself was ready to be harvested. The more profound the thought, the more complex the code. The more complex the code, the greater the amount of released energy. Laroche's theory stood untested for years until post-doctoral fellow Pygmalion Shaw established in his laboratory an actual transference of what he referred to as "primal mental energy" by decoding a single thought into its binary components, running it through a radium wash, and bombarding its electrons with magnetic strips of ilium, kurtium, and vonnegutium.

That single famous thought, retrieved from the brain of laboratory subject Anna Olshansky, was the simple image of a stalk of steaming asparagus. While the energy captured from Olshanky's imaginary asparagus was barely able to run a dishwasher through one full cycle, it proved beyond a doubt that even the most insignificant thought pattern, when properly decoded, could provide an absolute, measurable, and quantifiable amount of transferable energy. Shaw's experiment opened an entire new field of energy research, most notably the furthering of Laroche's theory by the iconoclastic scholar Opium Elegans, who posed the now-famous conundrum: *If an asparagus can run a dishwasher, imagine what a dream could do.* It was the logical next step. Dreams, being thoughts that were uninhibited by the normal parameters of time and space, were much richer in the amount of code imprinted in the brain and were consequently a potential source of much greater energy retrieval. Since dreams were unlimited in dimension, scope and variety, they could provide a nearly *infinite* source of energy. They merely needed to be harvested.

"Think about it," said Elegans, "our conscious thoughts center around the everyday issues of sustenance and survival, whereas our dreams are the mind unleashed. In our dreams, we can fly, perform unimaginable feats of strength, experience unfathomable terror, die, resurrect, and enter the eye of a hurricane. That's energy worth talking about. That's energy worth exploiting."

That's where Reverie Energy entered the picture. They developed a method to decode dreams, run them through their energy retrieval system, and come out with pure, measurable energy. The only problem was that the system was still in the theoretical stage and was deemed to be far too dangerous to test on laboratory subjects. The function of dreaming was still not completely understood, but it was widely assumed that dreaming was necessary to relieve the fears and anxieties of everyday life. Behavioral scientists, in particular, were concerned that if the dream code of a significant number of people was tampered with, it could magnify those emotional problems and lead society into a kind of mass psychosis. What they needed was a neutral setting, somewhere unregulated and far from the inquisitive eyes of their competition. A place like Earth, for example, a sister planet that shared Obsidia's characteristics but wasn't advanced enough to worry about the consequences of experimenting upon its backward population.

With the stakes so high, the great distance to this faraway planet suddenly wasn't quite so daunting and plans were laid for an expedition. If a crew of experienced scientists could somehow get there, all they needed to do was retrieve the code from Earthling dreams, process it through Reverie Energy's patented Rev-It-Up® retrieval system, and send it back home to their power hungry planet.

"Easy," said Jaxson, as he thumbed through Reverie Energy's

prospectus, peer reviews, and financial filing papers, hoping to make sense of what exactly they were up to, "if you happen to be a genius." That was the one thing no one had accused him of. Jaxson's mind was becoming a big pile of steaming hablum in which time, space, speed and sewage were all mixing into an indistinguishable mess that had no beginning and no end, just an interminable middle that kept repeating over and over. He tried everything to keep from going crazy but he, like everybody else on board, was showing signs of "space fatigue," an altogether ridiculous euphemism for the complete mental collapse of a crew deprived of light, love, and laughter. Jaxson would've jumped at his own shadow if he even had a shadow anymore, but that, like everything else in this endless darkness, had been stripped away from him. All that was left was his log, to which he—and we—reluctantly return in an effort to shine some light on these darkest of hours.

I'd given up on practical jokes, impersonations, and stand-up routines—some of my most endearing qualities—long ago. I had the toughest audience this side of the city morgue, a bunch of stiffs who wouldn't know comedy if it was a feather that came up under their latrine stalls and tickled their ass (and yes, I tried that on more than one occasion before giving up). I even began worrying that I was becoming one of those gray-faced automatons myself, a man devoid of hope, humor, and hilarity. If I don't have that, then who, exactly, am I? Maybe deep space isn't the best place to have an existential crisis, but then again, maybe it's precisely the best place. Ah, life, what's it all about? You're born in an antediluvian ice palace, you live, you die, your ashes get fried by zapruder rays, and you start all over again. The whole damn thing is a mystery to me. What's the point of rushing around the universe when you don't even know where you're going or why you're going there?

That aspect of the journey was still unchanged. Jaxson's

reportorial skills were being challenged at every turn and he was left with a journal made up solely of innuendo, lies, and half-truths. Captain Wambold was stonewalling him and apparently relishing every moment of his grand deception. "Later, later," he would say every time Jaxson asked him anything about the expedition but later never seemed to come. No one else could be bothered to even grunt a response anymore to Jaxson's inquiries. Did it really matter to them that he hadn't trained as an intern at this gazette or that aftenbladet or some other daily zeitung? What is a reporter anyway except for a pretty face, a pair of eyes, and the ability to tell it like it really is? More to the point, what was Jaxson, of all people, even doing on this expedition? What was he, a sci-phobe if there ever was one, doing among six of the most brilliant mechanical engineers, molecular biochemists, and behavioral scientists ever to be assembled in one place at one time? What particular skill set did he bring to the table that made him an indispensable asset to this hand-picked team of Reverie Energy's best and brightest?

The truth is, dear reader (and please don't be made to feel uncomfortable by my taking the liberty of such a familiar form of address), I am, for all of my warts and imperfections, essentially an old-fashioned storyteller. My being the official note taker on this journey fell into my lap like most everything else in my life—completely by accident and totally unwanted. The fact is, I flunked out of more than a few science classes and it wasn't because I was so far beyond my classmates that I failed out of boredom. No, I was bored all right, but I was bored because I couldn't keep more than two formulas in my head at the same time and that, as they say, left me at least one formula short of a full equation. Hence, all those embarrassing F's and too-generous D's intermingled among just enough C's to get me out of the Institute of Applied Learning before I died of old age.

Jaxson's entering the Institute had been a giant mistake of

mythic proportions and was based solely on a clerical error for the ages. Through some sloppy shuffling of papers, a mighty gust of wind, and a window left carelessly ajar, a confluence of events had conspired to jumble his test scores, rearrange his academic profile, and determine that his intellectual potential was off the charts. His teachers had been saying the same thing for years, although it was the other end of the charts they were referring to, an opinion he found impossible to dispute.

Imagine my surprise—and theirs—when I was suddenly hustled across town and thrust dead center among the most intellectually gifted of the academic elite. Now, there are fish out of water and petunias out of potting soil, but I was a red snapper stranded on a sand dune, a goldfish flopping in a canary cage, a sockeye salmon snaggled in a bear's den. Having been cast adrift among a school of übersharks, I decided to clam up and make no waves, but when thrown in among a group of pathological overachievers, my silence was taken not as stupidity but rather as a kind of profound self-assurance. It was one of the few things I learned at the Institute for Applied Learning, that stupidity and arrogance are nearly indistinguishable, a lesson that was to serve me well in later years.

Jaxson managed to sneak and cheat his way through two years of higher yearning before being summoned by the headmaster, who informed him that a review of his admission papers had revealed an error of the most serious nature. It seemed that his actual intellectual quotient was—how should we say it?—subpar, and should the circumstances of his acceptance to the Institute be found out, it would prove to be embarrassing in the extreme since he had—unwittingly, of course—neglected to inform the Institute of his obvious academic deficiencies, and had—unwittingly, needless to say—taken up valuable space that could have been used by someone far more deserving, and had—unwittingly, to be sure—made such a mockery of the selection process that were anyone to find out, the very funding of the Institute could be in jeopardy. The headmaster kept reiterating the unwittingness of his actions as if looking for an avenue of escape, like maybe Jaxson would just shuffle off out the front door and never be heard from again.

Now, Jaxson might've been a halfwit, and an unwitting halfwit at that, but he wasn't such a complete idiot as not to recognize an opportunity when it knocked him right over the head. After some complicated negotiations, he suggested that it was better to let sleeping dogs lie than for him to expose this sordid tale of academic flimflammery. He proposed his surefire technique of slipping between the cracks, making himself invisible, and acting the dummy even though, as the headmaster insisted on pointing out, it wasn't an act. The headmaster, no dummy himself, saw the benefits of their little subterfuge and granted him graduation with full honors in exchange for keeping his mouth shut. It proved to Jaxson yet again that silence is the best answer when one doesn't even understand the question.

Upon entering the real world, Jaxson was due for a rude awakening. After all, no amount of fakery and chicanery can get you through life—at least that's what they tell you—but he saw no reason not to at least give it a try. With employers lining up to hire the bona fide young geniuses from the Institute of Applied Learning, he parlayed his checkered academic career into a corner office at the illustrious Reverie Energy, where everyone awaited what was sure to be his meteoric rise to the top. Imagine his surprise—and theirs— when he discovered that unlike the four year vacation known as upper school, he was actually expected to produce something tangible, marketable, and profitable. With reality slapping him in the face, he knew it was only a matter of time—and not much time, at that—before his intellectual deficiencies sandbagged him and exposed him for what he really was, a second floor talent perched on the twentieth floor of a fantasy that was about to collapse.

It was time to make my first presentation to the Board of Big Cheeses (my name) and there was no way I could fake it past a half-dozen heavyweights who actually knew what they were talking about. The only question was whether I could escape before one of those cheeseheads put 2 and 2 together and came up with the square root of 16. I packed everything I could carry into one oversized briefcase (and okay, I admit it, a few of those electronic devices weren't technically mine) and slipped into the Express Elevator to the ground floor where, with unbelievably bad luck, three of the Directors were waiting to enter the very same elevator on their way up to the very meeting I was escaping from. And so, amidst no little fumbling and stumbling, we were whisked straight back up the building to the Penthouse office where the rest of the fontinas and camemberts were awaiting my sure-to-be-stunning presentation.

It was stunning all right, as Jaxson relied yet again on his old heroic device of clamming up like a 160-pound cephalo-pod. He announced to a rapt and entirely hushed audience that the project he was overseeing was far too sensitive to be discussed even in that forum, that they couldn't be certain they weren't being monitored by their competition and, in fact, it was so important to the future of the company that he staked his entire reputation—hah!—on expanding its funding, putting it on the fast track, and moving the launch to the earliest possible date with, ahem, him, the boy genius himself, on board to make sure everything was on the uppity-up.

It was thus—and here would be an appropriate moment to reiterate that old chestnut about arrogance and stupidi-ty—that Jaxson killed two birds with one stone and managed not only to exit himself from a situation in which he was sure to be found out at any moment, but also managed to put himself into extremely close proximity with Marta-1, who just might've been the love of his life, even if it meant taking Marta-2, who was critical to the mission, along for the ride. The next thing anyone knew, six of Reverie Energy's brightest stars, plus Jaxson, were being strapped into an aging spaceship, the gyro clock was counting down, the retro rockets were engaging, and off they went. It was either a great adventure into the future or a great escape, depending on who was talking. A few minutes later, the black curtain of empty space dropped and that was it. Endless, eternal, unchanging nothingness. The darkness. The void. The big sleep. Good-night, Obsidia. Sweet dreams. Wake us when it's over.

And then it all changed. On an undetermined day of a forgotten month in an unknown year, Captain Hieronymus Wambold came rushing through the observation chamber, a crazed look in his eyes, his arms swinging like windmills. Jaxson figured he was done for, that the old man had finally lost it and was going on a wild rampage. He ducked as Wambold went rushing by, but it wasn't Jaxson he was swinging at, it was the broad expanse of space to which he reached out in excitement. "It lies straight ahead!" he proclaimed. "There, at the conjunction of the 17th coordinates!"

It took a moment for the crew to climb out of its catatonic stupor, but slowly his words began to sink in. They strained their eyes and saw what appeared to be a small pomegranate floating in soup far in the distance. A gasp was heard, then some clearing of throats, then some peculiar sounds that had been long buried in the collective larynx of the crew, and then a cheer, but not just any cheer, it was a cheer of unbridled relief and joy, a cheer of discovery and invention, a cheer of pure exaltation and rapture.

"*E-a-a-r-r-t-t-h-h!*"

Jaxson did a little jig around the control room, kicking up his heels and thrusting out his knees like a sub-Subian ankle dancer. "Yes, yes, yes!" he kept chanting, and indeed the answer to everything was yes—yes to life, yes to the future, yes to camaraderie, yes to the mission, and yes to Captain Wambold, the greatest pilot of them all, the greatest visionary, the greatest leader—oh, how could we have ever questioned him? "Three cheers for Captain Wambold!" Jaxson cried out. "Three cheers!"

Marta-1, Marta-2, and Oblivia formed a spontaneous circle and twirled about with carefree abandon. Raleigh came out of his trance long enough to stare in wonder at the filling of his conscious mind-void, and even Teller had a little spring in his step. There were a million things to do—dials to be checked, gauges to be observed, data to be entered—but for one brief moment, at least, the crew joined together to share their success. They were making history and this was one of those snapshot moments that would be imbedded in their minds forever.

Having been deprived of any kind of external stimulus for so long, they gazed in wonder at a distant planet that seemed to grow right before their eyes. Everything became expanded, as if they were wide-eyed children whose visual field was being filled to overflowing. That bowl of soup way out in the distance steadily grew larger and transformed from a thin broth of consommé into a thick chowder of meaty stew. Suddenly they were in it, whipping around planets and moons and asteroid belts that appeared to be so enormous as to defy description. As official observer on the flight, it fell to Jaxson to provide literary allusions so that the folks back home would one day understand the dimensions of this strange new world. But words, like most everything else in his life, failed him. How does one describe a planet so big that its mountains stretch to eternity and its oceans float on a bottomless abyss? A sky that cascades into a panoply of colors as if exploding from a prism of infinite dimensions? A landscape so vast and varied as to defy measurement and categorization? How does one describe such a sight, indeed, when in truth Earth was exactly the same size as Obsidia? Such is the trick the mind's eye plays when escaping the eternal blackness of space.

Captain Wambold consulted his charts and appeared, for the first time since lift-off, to be completely at a loss. Where does one land one's ship when overwhelmed by the very real possibility of being consumed by a hostile terrain? As they approached the planet, it became impossible to even distinguish the plateaus from the mountains, the rivulets from the seas. All was a profound vastness that threatened to imprison them in terminal oblivion. The crew grew quiet as each of them contemplated their place in this greatly expanded universe. What exactly were they getting themselves into?

Teller's terse voice suddenly crackled over the intercom, breaking the silence. "Spaceship at 3 o'clock!" he implored.

Wambold's head jerked back dismissively. "Impossible!" he said. "This planet is too primitive to have orbiting spacecraft!"

Impossible or not—and the crew was reluctant to disagree with Captain Wambold about anything anymore—they couldn't help but notice a vehicle right outside the observation portal. "Um, Captain..." said Raleigh.

"It can't be," continued Wambold. "The Earthlings have only recently figured out how to split an atom. There's no way they could launch a rocket."

"There's one other possibility," said Raleigh.

"And what would that be?"

"It's not theirs."

"It's not theirs? Then whose is it? Who would dare approach these godforsaken territories? It's *our* sister planet, damn it, no one else's!"

Raleigh stared out the observation portal at a vehicle with

strange markings—seven circles of increasing radius inside a collapsing parallelogram. He checked his identification logs and found no such insignia from any known galaxy. "It's an unlisted number," he said.

Wambold watched as the ship made no attempt to take elusive maneuvers and passed by with nary a hello. "The arrogance," he said.

"Fleet of ships at 7 o'clock!" came Teller's next warning. Wambold hurried across the bridge to find three more star craft flying in formation just outside the portal.

"Captain," said Marta-1 with a worried voice as she came running up from her post. "The skies are full of traffic. Six, possibly eight vehicles. They're everywhere."

Wambold had heard enough. "Teller! Engage communication! Find out what's going on out there!"

Teller took a quick scan of the skies. There were a half-dozen ships, all of unknown registry. "It looks like we've got competition, Captain. Cargo ships, freighters, supply convoys, you name it. They're milking this place dry!"

"Not on *our* planet, they're not!"

Marta-2 appeared on the bridge with a distressed look. "Technically, Captain, it's not our planet. It exists in a nebulous legal cloud."

"That's impossible. What right do any of these interlopers have to come here and make off with our resources? It's *our* sister planet, not theirs!"

"It's a tricky legal morass. There are cases on appeal—"

"I say we don't let them get away with it," said Teller.

"Just relax, Teller," said the Captain. "We'll go by the book on this one. Send out the cease and desist requests and ask them to stand down."

"Is that an order, sir?"

"Of course it's an order."

"Because if we show any sign of weakness—"

"Teller!"

"I'm on it, sir."

Teller turned on a dime and marched to his post. Wambold went back to his computers and entered some calculations. Jaxson just sat there, watching and waiting. It was quiet on the ship. Too quiet, if you asked him. He liked to hear the fans and the coolant and the little creaks and groans of metal rushing through space a million miles an hour. He loved the little ping of asteroids bouncing off the reflector shields and the incandescent pop of comet showers on the windscreen. It reminded him he was alive.

Teller sent off every official document he could find to dissuade the passing spaceships from trespassing on what was clearly Pulsar-7's realm of influence. He tried a dozen different protocols before finally connecting on a common communication frequency, but it was all a waste of time. He got a few polite no-thank-yous, a bunch of no-replies, and one or two squiggly little drawings that looked a lot like someone giving him the finger. Teller, having little patience and even less sense of humor, didn't take kindly to the slights. "Captain, permission to address command."

"Granted."

"Permission to speak freely?"

"Out with it, Teller."

"Sir, I really think we need to be a bit more aggressive with our posture vis-à-vis the intruding spacecraft."

"Oh? What do you suggest?"

"A quick blast across the bow of one of those ships would send the correct message, sir."

"Are you crazy, Teller? You'll do no such thing!"

"They're laughing at us, sir."

"Are you even remotely aware of the Pact of Nations? We foreswore the use of arms years ago."

"I've always considered the Pact to be a very good theoretical model for the rules of engagement."

"There's nothing theoretical about it. It's the law."

"Some think of it as more of a suggestion."

"Tell you what, Teller. Get back to your post and send out the rest of those requests."

"Is that an order, sir?"

"Yes! It's an order! Go!"

Teller returned to his station. The rest of the crew watched and waited. There was a whiz and a buzz from the communications center and then a long silence. Suddenly, a burst of crackling came over the intercom, then some screeching feedback, and finally Teller's voice: "Code B! Code B! Attack craft at 5 o'clock!"

Everyone looked at each other. "What?"

"Urgent! Urgent! Unidentified warship approaching unannounced! Assume battle stations!"

"*What?*"

Red warning lights strobed across the bridge, metal protective barriers swooped down from the ceiling, and exterior deflective shields automatically deployed. The noise was nearly unbearable as metal screeched against metal in the rush to secure the ship. In the background, Captain Wambold's voice could be heard rising over the cacophony. "Teller! What are you doing! Stand down! Stand down!"

It was too late. Teller was off in his own little world, a world in which friends became enemies and enemies became combatants. Without warning, he launched a preemptive strike in which a bright yellow trail of light burst out from a laser tube embedded in the nose of the Pulsar-7. The crew, none of whom had ever seen a weapon outside the Museum of War, stared in stunned silence. The laser screamed across the sky and directly hit the underbelly of the oncoming spaceship. There was a burst of light and then another as the ship broke apart into a dozen pieces. The wings and engines scattered haphazardly into space, while the crew chamber circled wildly just outside their observation portal. It spun, wobbled and rotated as it orbited in ever greater circles. For

Jaxson, it was, quite simply, the most terrifying thing he'd ever seen. He caught a glimpse of three crewmen who were desperately trying to salvage what was left of their craft and saw fear itself magnified a thousand times. The red capillaries of their eyes were like rivers of blood that ebbed and surged as the spaceship was buffeted by the gravitational pull of the planet below. Finally, Earth's outer atmosphere reached out and grabbed the ship and slowly sucked it in like the tentacles of an octopus. There was another burst of light and then a wild array of pulsating colors that reflected off its translucent skin. The chamber hung in space for a moment, silent and hulking, then broke apart and fell toward Earth's surface below. It twisted and turned and tumbled as the atmosphere ate away at its outer edges. Flames burst forth. A contrail streamed behind. A pulse of light etched into the sky. Finally, the chamber crashed with a terrible thump into a barren piece of terrain, leaving behind a massive cloud of dust, soot, and sand.

The other spaceships from the alien fleet hovered in the outer atmosphere for a few shocked seconds, then shot out of their orbits into deep space. They were gone in the blink of an eye. Jaxson looked at Marta-1. She looked at Raleigh. He looked at Oblivia. She looked at Marta-2.

"Teller!" screamed Captain Wambold over the hushed silence. "You are relieved of your post!"

Chapter 8

*"Crows everywhere
are equally black."*
—Chinese Proverb

The Nebraska sky was like a pin cushion of light shining through an ocean of blackness. Nick sat in the back seat of the Hudson staring into the firmament. He could see Ursa Major and the Big Dipper and what appeared to be either Venus or Mars, although he could never remember which was which. Funny how the sky was pretty much the same wherever he happened to be. The constellations might be different and everything was moved around a bit, but the sky made him feel both bigger and smaller no matter where he was. Bigger because his problems diminished when set against that endless backdrop, smaller because he was barely a pinpoint in his own field of vision. Whether on a lake in Nebraska or a hill in Italy, Nick could look up and get lost in some story. Tonight the sky told him about a guy who walked along a rain-splattered city street. The lights from a restaurant cast a lonely glow as two lovers touched hands over a bottle of wine. The guy buttoned up his coat against the wind and wandered the back alleys, his footsteps click-clacking off the cobblestones and echoing along the narrow passageways. As night became day and day collapsed into a dull haze, the rain beat down without end.

He walked in an ever-widening circle, reaching out for something that was always just beyond his grasp—a thought, a feeling, a plan, a reason to keep on going after seeing what he saw in the war—

Two dots of light moving across the southwestern sky interrupted his reverie. At first Nick thought a meteor was burning itself out in the earth's outer atmosphere, but then the lights flared rather than flamed and he figured it must be a comet sweeping across the sky. When the object suddenly turned on a dime and made an impossible loop, he wondered if he was seeing things. He turned away, figuring his eyes were getting jiggy or his mind was playing tricks on him or his bum knee was shooting magnetic sparks into the air, but when he looked again and still saw those crazy lights out there, he rustled Esmeralda from her uneasy sleep. "Esmeralda? You awake?"

"I am now."

"You see those lights in the sky?"

Esmeralda squinted her eyes. "It's probably a reflection from the lake."

"You think? Why would there be lights in the lake?"

Esmeralda turned impatiently. "How should I know? I'm not an expert in what goes on out here. I'm a city girl."

Nick kept looking at the sky, unable to take his eyes off the erratic lights. "No, they're up there all right, up in the sky."

Esmeralda kept her eyes on the sky, following the little points of light. "They're just lights, Nick. It's no big deal. Why shouldn't there be lights in these backwater burgs? For all we know, there might be an all-night casino just down the road."

"Sure, Es, that makes sense."

They both watched the sky, transfixed, until one of the lights came to a dead stop, moved backwards, dipped a bit, and suddenly blew into a thousand pieces. "Whatchawhocha!" gasped Esmeralda. "What was that?"

"I've been trying to tell you—"

They watched for a few seconds and then, before either of them knew what happened, it was all over, as if someone had turned off a big switch in the sky. The lights were gone and so was the afterglow and so were any signs of meteors, comets, or asteroids. Nick and Esmeralda stared into the blackness of space in total silence. They snuck a glance at each other but kept their own council, neither of them wanting to be the first to say anything. Sometimes the brain is like that: it presents incomprehensible information, then just switches off. Nick put his arm around Esmeralda, leaned back, and got lost in the kaleidoscope of stars. Esmeralda wrapped a blanket around their legs, snuggled into his arms, and immediately dozed off. All that could be heard was the gentle lapping of the lake against the shore and the creaking of a rowboat against a dock. Nebraska was quiet. Crazy quiet. And buggy. Bedbug buggy. Buggy as a June bug in July.

Ray and Dirk also saw the lights in the sky. They were driving down Route 6 somewhere outside Des Moines when there was a burst of light high above the horizon that looked like a Fourth of July fireworks display. That made sense since American independence was important enough to be celebrated far and wide, but it didn't *really* make sense given that it was, in fact, already July 7th. Either somebody had their dates screwed up or light really did take a long time to travel across the skies or something else altogether was going on that was unexplainable, inexplicable, and downright incomprehensible. When the lights disappeared as quickly as they materialized, Ray fidgeted in his seat and cleared his throat. "You see that?" he finally said.

"Nope," said Dirk.

"Me, either," said Ray.

And that was that.

Morning hit Iowa like cornbread on a skillet. The sun was sizzling, the fields were baking, and the new day smelled of butter and molasses. Ray and Dirk polished off a breakfast of pancakes, griddle cakes and corncakes in a Newton diner, replenished their ammo at a bait, tackle and firearms exchange in Des Moines, and headed for Omaha. Omaha was famous for its Omaha steaks and would be a good place to stop for dinner and drinks, before hunting down Nick and Esmeralda. Even though Ray's ulcer was acting up and Dirk was getting fidgety, all in all, things could've been worse. Their late night misadventure in Chicago was already a distant memory relegated to the trash heap of good intentions gone bad. It had been a failure by any measure, but just being in on some action had left them in a good mood. There is, after all, something about chasing after somebody in the middle of the night that is cathartic, invigorating, and good for the digestion. It balances the acids and keeps the gastrointestinal system healthy and harmonious. And harmony, let it be said, is not unimportant, especially in these most unsettled of times.

Daybreak found Esmeralda behind the wheel, her high-heeled shoes finding a comfort zone when pushed all the way down on the accelerator. Nick was still asleep in the back seat and she took the opportunity to get off the highway and do a little Gypsy wandering through the empty back roads. Amongst the endless hills and dales, it was a half-dozen red and white shaving cream signs that both stoked her curiosity and forced her to slow down. She stole a couple of nervous glances at the placards, careful not to drive off the road.

DON'T STICK
YOUR ELBOW
OUT SO FAR
IT MIGHT GO HOME
IN ANOTHER CAR
BURMA-SHAVE

Esmeralda pulled away before she got too close, then gazed upon a countryside that was veritably ripe for development. She figured a fortune telling parlor could go in a field just off the road, a palmist over here, a dozen dancers over there, and up ahead a hundred tents running carnival attractions, freak shows, and shell games. Lost in an entrepreneurial paradise, she zoomed past a radar trap hidden in the cornfields, the wind blowing through her hair, a Gypsy guitar ringing in her ears. Seconds later a black and white Highway Patrol vehicle was on her tail, its siren squealing.

Nick rustled in the back seat. He dreamt that he was a human cannonball being shot through a circus big top, soaring past trampolines, girls on the flying trapeze, and blasting right out through the tent flaps. He kept climbing higher and higher until gravity finally reached out and grabbed him by the throat. When he awoke, he found himself a central character in a high speed chase being conducted down a two lane bumpy road. "Esmeralda!" he shouted as the Hudson kicked up a cloud of dust, a mound of leaves, and quarry full of gravel. "Pull the hell over!"

Esmeralda wouldn't hear of it. "Hang on!" she yelled back, as she bore down on the center divider.

"Haven't we got enough trouble already? Stop the damn car!"

Esmeralda's Gypsy genes were in heated battle with her Jewish genes as to whether to run or to hide. Two thousand years of wandering on one side came up against two thousand years of wandering on the other side and it was a match made in wanderer's heaven. "No... no... no... no..."

Nick climbed over the front seat and grabbed the wheel. As the car wove back and forth between the lanes, the siren got louder and louder until the cop car seemed to be right on top of them. When Esmeralda realized she couldn't outrun the fuzz, she finally took her foot off the gas and let the car roll to a stop, even then refusing to cooperate with the law by not applying the brakes. "Man, you are really something," said Nick, the blood drained from his face.

"I was born bad," said Esmeralda with a shrug.

"Just try and act nice if you can," said Nick, knowing better than to get into it with her right then and there.

"Oh, I'll act nice all right. I'll be sweet as molasses."

"Don't overdo it."

A jowly patrolman pushed himself out of his cruiser, then slowly walked over to the Hudson. "Morning, ma'am."

"Something wrong, officer?" said Esmeralda in a timid, innocent voice.

"Going a little fast there, don't you think?" said the cop.

"Why, no, I don't believe I was."

"I had you clocked at 78 in a 55 mile an hour zone. Out here in Nebraska, we'd call that a little fast."

"There must be some mistake. I never trusted those radar machines. Is that what you're using? They're wrong more often than they're right, if you ask me."

"Ninety-nine percent accurate, ma'am, that's the latest studies."

"See what I mean? Nothing is perfect."

"Would you mind showing me your license and registration?"

"Not at all," said Esmeralda. She reached across the dashboard, opened the glove compartment, and began digging around. "Keep quiet," she whispered to Nick as she gathered together the documents, plus a crisp five dollar bill to hold them all together. She handed over the little bundle to the cop with a wink.

"What's this, ma'am?" said the officer, fingering the money.

"Oh, my," said Esmeralda with exaggerated innocence. "I don't know. Must've slipped out of the glove compartment. Oh, well, why don't you just keep that for the next Policeman's Ball?"

"That's mighty kind of you, but we're not real big on dancing out here." The cop studied her papers as if they were written in some foreign tongue. "Says here you're from Chicago, is that right, Miss, uh, Miss Kurlansky?"

"That's right, Chicago, Illinois, the city that takes care of its own."

"You see, ma'am, maybe this is the way you take care of things in Chicago, but out here in the sticks we do things a little different. We go more by the book."

"What book is that?"

"Would you like to step out of the car, ma'am?" said, the cop, losing his patience. Esmeralda debated the issue for a moment, then pulled her skirt above her knees, opened her blouse another two buttons, and swung open the door. The cop couldn't take his eyes off her butt as she yo-yoed it out of the front seat and did a slow and easy around the world. "You haven't been drinking, have you, Miss Kurlansky?"

"I had some V-8 Juice for breakfast. That okay?"

"Would you like to walk along that line on the road for me?"

"Not really."

"Ma'am, why don't you just go ahead and do as I say."

Esmeralda sashayed down the road like a haughty burlesque queen. Nick watched through the side mirror and sank a little lower in his seat. "Look, officer, she's had a rough couple of days. First time out of the city and all."

"What exactly are you two up to out here?" said the cop, looking at Nick out of the corner of his eye.

"We're headed to California. Got us a farm. Looking to

raise a family. Maybe a couple of goats."

The cop watched Esmeralda wobble down the road in her high heels and turned to Nick with some fatherly guidance. "If I were you, I'd stick to the goats."

"That's probably good advice. The truth is, I'm just back from the war and Miss Kurlansky, well, she's had a rough time of it."

"The war, you say? Which theater?"

"Italy."

"Um-hmm. Pretty tough out there, was it?" Nick nodded without saying a word. The cop glanced again at the registration, then at Esmeralda, then at Nick. "Now, if I run this car through the teletype machine," he said, "I'm not going to find out it was stolen, am I?"

"You've got my word."

"All right, then, soldier. I'm letting you off with a warning. Our jail probably couldn't hold Miss Kurlansky, anyway. That woman would eat right through the bars."

"You won't be sorry."

"I'm already sorry. Tell you what, how about you drive from here out?"

"Love to," said Nick, sliding behind the wheel.

"We'll just pretend this never happened. No speeding, no car chase, no attempted bribery." The patrolman shook his head and muttered to himself—"I must be crazy"—then motioned for Esmeralda to return to the car. "You take it easy now, hear?" he said, handing back her license, registration and the five dollar bill. "You've got a long road ahead of you."

Esmeralda harrumphed herself into the passenger seat and stared straight ahead. "Can we go now?"

"God speed," said the cop as he tucked his ticket book into his pocket. "Which, by the way, is 55. Got that, ma'am?"

"Got it," mumbled Esmeralda. Nick turned on the ignition, the cop squeezed into his black and white, and Esmeralda buttoned up her blouse.

"You drive careful now, son. You wouldn't want to rile any-one up."

"I'll remember that," said Nick as he pushed back the seat, adjusted the mirror, and pulled out onto the road.

A black crow soared overhead, watching the Hudson, the cop car, and the cornfields which dotted the horizon. There was a good wind that day and the crow could catch an updraft just by dipping one of his wings with the slightest flicker. Whoosh, whoosh, a stream of air would tickle his under-feathers and send him 20 feet higher without so much as a flap. This was his domain, the upper layers of the lower atmosphere, and woe be it to any sparrow, robin, or yellow-headed chickadee that got any wise ideas and tried to horn in on his airspace. Hawks and falcons, needless to say, were always welcome to fly by and hang for a while so long as they kept a respectful distance. It was the law of the jet stream and the hierarchy of the skies. Know your place, honor your elders, and keep your beak clean.

The crow was headed west for no good reason other than he wasn't going east, and that was that. Things didn't always have to be so goddamned complicated. Also, there was that Hudson which he had spotted way back in the Chicago Loop, or, as the crow liked to think of it, the Big Smorgasbord. There was something whimsical about that car, maybe the color of the hood or the shininess of the chrome or the reflections of the hubcaps. Whatever it was, the crow decided to follow along and see if the Hudson might provide some entertainment on the lonely flight to the Pacific mating grounds.

A hundred feet below, where the rubber meets the road, Nick drove west past rows of pale yellow cornstalks, each tall as a man, separated every couple of miles by an alfalfa field, and then more corn. Nick didn't know any jokes about corn, and Esmeralda wouldn't have listened anyway, so they sat quietly watching the steam rise up off the tarmac, trying not to become hypnotized by the wavy lines of heat radiation. KFFA wasn't coming in anymore, and the local stations broadcast nothing but farm reports, so they listened instead to the wind flapping off the visors and the rubber tires sloshing on the hot asphalt. The sounds of nature were disturbing to Esmeralda and it was only a matter of time before she was fiddling around with the radio again, looking for a diversion. She flipped through the static until the somber voice of the national news reared its ugly head:

"Did you see lights in the sky last night? If so, you're not alone. Reports have been flooding in from all over middle America. Here's a dispatch from network headquarters in New York."

"Nick, you hear this?"

"Turn it up."

"The American Broadcasting Company and affiliated stations presents Headline Edition with Taylor Grant. To stay in step with history in the making, stay tuned to Headline Edition." The broadcast paused for ABC's signature beeping sounds of a Morse code keypad. *"July 8th, 1947. The Army Air Forces has announced that a flying disk has been found and is now in the possession of the Army. Army officers say the missile has been inspected at Roswell, New Mexico, and sent to Wright Field, Ohio, for further inspection. Our correspondents in Los Angeles and Chicago have been in contact with army officials endeavoring to obtain all possible late information. Joe Wilson reports to us now from Chicago."*

"Oh, my God—"

"Shhhh."

"The Army may be getting to the bottom of all this talk about the so-called flying saucer. As a matter of fact, the 509th Atomic Bomb Group Headquarters at Roswell, New Mexico, reports that it has received one of the disks, which

*landed on a ranch outside Roswell. The disk landed at a ranch
at Corona, New Mexico, and the rancher turned it over to the
Air Force. Rancher W. W. Brazel was the man who discovered
the saucer."*

"You don't think it's aliens, do you?"

"Who said anything about aliens?"

*"In Fort Worth, Texas, where the object was first sent,
Brigadier General Roger Ramey says that it is being shipped
by air to the AAF research center at Wright Field, Ohio.
General Ramey described the object as being of flimsy construction, almost like a box kite. He says it was so battered
that he was unable to determine whether it had a disk form,
and he does not indicate its size. Ramey says that so far as
can be determined, no one saw the object in the air, and he
describes it as being made of some sort of tinfoil."*

"I'm telling you right now, Nick, if we're going to be attacked by little green men, I'm bailing out. I had enough of
little green men at the Flame Club in Chicago."

*"Other army officials say that further information indi-
cates that the object had a diameter of about 20 to 25 feet,
and nothing in the apparent construction indicated any
capacity for speed, and there was no evidence of a power
plant. The disk also appeared too flimsy to carry a man. Now
back to Taylor Grant in New York..."*

Esmeralda snapped off the radio. "You don't think—"

"What, last night? I'm sure there's an explanation—"

"There's *always* an explanation. That doesn't mean it's
true."

Nick drove west, looking to the future while keeping one
eye peeled on the rear view mirror to make sure the past
wasn't catching up with them. The open prairie lie straight
ahead, endless and mysterious. There were a few buttes and
mesas in the distance silhouetted against a clear blue sky. To
the north was the odd rock formation, to the south a long
expanse of dusty plains that fell off to the horizon. Other-

wise, there was nothing out there but a crow, a glow, and a half-dozen signs along the roadside:

DON'T LOSE
YOUR HEAD
TO GAIN A MINUTE
YOU NEED YOUR HEAD
YOUR BRAINS ARE IN IT
BURMA-SHAVE

Chapter 9

There are no Burma Shave signs in space, not because space travelers don't shave, but because they're crazy about their cold fusion razors. There are plenty of other signs, though—signs of fatigue, signs of boredom, and signs of trouble. And trouble, like a pot of steaming hablum, was brewing. The crew waited for the other shoe to drop, expecting allies of the downed spacecraft to reappear and squash them like bugs against a windshield. After all, the aggrieved parties had every right to retaliate after Teller's insane attack put the entire mission, if not Obsidia itself, at risk. There would be trouble, that was for sure, and the crew's best hope was that the victimized fleet would take them to the Court of Last Resort, where Reverie Energy's own fleet of lawyers could challenge, delay, finagle, and try to obfuscate the compilation of facts which, when you got right down to it, was completely indisputable. All of this sister planet stuff— the supposed "special relationship" between Earth and Obsidia—was pure baloney in the legal system, since no one had ever established any protocols for dealing with extra-planetary visitation rights, proprietary considerations, eminent domain, or lack thereof. *Arma in armatos sumere jura sinunt.*

The pressure on the crew was nearly unbearable as they viewed every reflection outside their portals as a potential copernicus wave of radiation that would render them transitory puffs of flesh and blood. They were sitting ducks constrained by a cryptic message from the Court of Last Resort that was anything but reassuring:

REMAIN IN EARTH ORBIT UNTIL FURTHER NOTICE.
SUSPEND ALL EXPERIMENTS UNTIL FURTHER NOTICE.
ACCEPT NO OTHER NOTICES UNTIL FURTHER NOTICE.

And so, they waited, a state of being with which they were all too familiar. At least now there was a sense of time, given the obvious distinction between night and day, but rather than relieve their anxieties, the sunrises and sunsets only exacerbated their sense of dislocation. Earth was right there, hanging in the sky like a piece of forbidden fruit, and they hovered above it, afraid to take a bite. Around and around they went, through the dark and the light—five revolutions, ten—and still no sign of their friends whose mother ship they had so ingloriously blasted out of the sky. Communication with the home planet, slow in the best of times, was now further delayed by bureaucratic encumbrances of the hitherto, forthwith and henceforth nature, and they began to wonder if maybe it *was* all in the hands of the lawyers. In the absence of clear orders from mission control on Obsidia, Captain Wambold had to consider the nearly unimaginable—taking a risk and making an actual decision.

As usual, it all fell on his shoulders. Teller was persona non grata until further notice, Raleigh was in his "be there then" state of quasi-consciousness, and Oblivia couldn't put two sentences together without causing a communication train wreck. Still, the crew was united in its desire to land on Earth. It was far too dangerous to stay in orbit, regardless of what the Court had dictated. More to the point, they were visibly frustrated by the idea of having traveled halfway across the universe only to be thwarted from completing their mission at the last moment. They had given up everything for this journey and it was unthinkable to quit now. If that weren't enough, Raleigh's latest celestial calculations determined a whole other problem: they had exactly seven days to land, conduct their experiment, and depart. "After that, the aphelion of the Earth's orbit makes our return home impossible. The solar power isn't sufficient to boost us out of the elliptical orbit and the perihelion isn't for another six months."

Even Jaxson, who didn't understand much of anything when it came to direction or navigation, knew that when a planet was farthest from the sun, its solar resources were barely enough to spark the ship's plugs, much less blast it into deep space. "Captain, I think I speak for everyone when I say we should proceed with our plan and deal with the consequences later," he said.

"Oh, you do, do you?" said Wambold. "You think we should simply contravene the orders of the Court and go our merry way?"

"Well, yes, sir, that sounds like a good plan to me."

"That's why I'm the Captain and you're the Observer."

"Captain, if I might say—" said Marta-2.

"I'll be in my quarters," said Wambold, waving her off. He took several steps, then turned back. "I assume you're all in agreement about landing?" The crew nodded as one. "Yes, of course you are," he said. "You don't have to deal with the consequences."

"You have our full support," said Marta-1.

"Thank you, Chief Behavioral Scientist. Your loyalty is noted."

The Captain's quarters were unremarkable. There were the usual extra accoutrements provided to the senior executive—

the private wash basin, the matching set of hablum snifters, the embossed personalized stationary with its unfortunate misspelling of "Hieronymouse" Wambold—but notably missing were any photographs of friends, family, or any other personal effects. The Captain was a real lifer to the service, meaning he had no life whatsoever outside the organization. He took pleasure in completing his missions with a minimum of fuss and bother and had an exemplary log book to prove it. Where others might reminisce about youthful escapades and romantic interludes, the Captain could look back upon a lifetime of service with nary a blemish or infraction.

It was, therefore, with an uneasy feeling that he paced his chambers contemplating the proper course of action. Or, as he much preferred, inaction. That was something he'd learned along the way. *When confronted by a situation whose outcome is uncertain, do nothing.* It would have been the perfect motto to hang above his command post would it have not been so blatantly uninspiring. The problem with doing nothing was that every once in a while the doing of nothing was actually the doing of something, as if by default. If a tri-wheeler is coming right at you and you choose to do nothing, aren't you, in fact, making a very particular decision? It was a form of mental gymnastics Wambold avoided at every turn. One thing, though, couldn't be denied. There was a very big tri-wheeler headed his way and he had to decide whether to jump on or get run over. The Court of Last Resort, after all, took no prisoners.

The Captain paced, turned, stopped, pondered, and paced some more. To land or not to land, that was the question. To take a daring step or to blindly follow orders. To be safe or to be sorry. Because one thing was for sure: he was facing the end of the line on what was probably his last mission. What would be his legacy? To be the man who lost control of his ship to a rogue engineer? To be the faithful captain known only for the temperature scale that bore his name? Or to tweak those suckers and go for the glory?

With nothing else to keep him occupied, Jaxson secluded himself in the library and pored though the ship's intergalactic database of fun facts and fractious figures. He discovered that not much in the way of personal accounts was known about the faraway way station they were orbiting. Earth had never been a particularly popular stop on anyone's itinerary as it was known to be unwelcoming to travelers, unhealthy for the spirit, and unsavory in its habits. He made due with some generic data about Earth's topography, demographics, rainfall totals, crop distributions, and gross national products. You could learn a lot about a planet from its statistics, Jaxson figured, and what he lacked in actual knowledge he could more than make up for in unconfirmed assumptions. Just like a *real* scientist.

Marta-2, ever eager to make her presence felt, showed up in the library as well. She pretended to double-check some formula or another, but it was painfully obvious that what she was checking out was Jaxson himself. "Researching Earth, are you?" she said, sneaking a peek at his data scan. "It's a strange name, isn't it? A bit harsh to the ear."

"As best as I can tell, they named it after a famous singer named Eartha Kitt. She looks like a cat."

"Really? How interesting. You know, I have a great curiosity about other people and other cultures. I think it's what drove me to science in the first place, even though my work with energy transference might seem far afield."

"Uh-huh," said Jaxson, trying to figure out a way of getting her out of there. He had bigger fish to fry, mackerels, mostly, which on Earth reputedly could grow to 42 inches and weigh upwards of 30 pounds. It was one of the thousand obscure facts he was entering into his log, just in case anybody asked what he was doing there.

Marta-2, poor girl, was completely incapable of taking a hint. She lingered nearby, glancing through his log. "Maybe I can add a little something," she said. Under the guise of trying to help Jaxson write his report, she insisted on providing him with a full and complete explanation of the fine points of energy transference, a subject with which he had no familiarity and even less interest. It was, however, the central point of their mission and would fill some sorely needed space in his Observer's Log. Reluctantly, he jotted down a few notes.

Now, this is the part of the story, dear reader, where most observers would try to impress you with how much they know and bore you to tears with all sorts of formulas, theories and highfalutin speculations. Well, not me. You should know me well enough by now to realize that I have neither the time nor the inclination to wallow in obtuse scientific foofaraw that does neither you nor me any good whatsoever except to impress some young pod at a cocktail party with our supposed sophistication. So let's just say this whole business of transforming the energy of dreams into a pure dynamic energy that can be crushed, crunched, and compacted is done through a series of intricate maneuvers in which the particles are zipped around from one reflective surface to another, expanded, contracted, frozen, cracked, chomped and refracted a half dozen times again through vacuum tubes, resisters, capacitors and a bunch of other shiny metal gadgets that are guaranteed to give you a headache. It is, in other words, all done with mirrors.

By the time Marta-2 finished her dissertation, Jaxson was sweating with trace memories of all those forgotten formulas from the Institute of Applied Learning. It still amazed him that no one ever realized he wasn't cut out for science. Couldn't they see that he was a poet at heart—a man of letters, a masticator of vowels and eviscerator of consonants?

"I owe you one," he said, giving Marta-2 her due for helping him fill in his notebook while urging her toward the door.

"Maybe you can teach me one of those beautiful songs," she said, completely misinterpreting his offer. Did she really not understand that when somebody says he owes you one, he's telling you he owes you nothing at all?

"Yeah, sure," he lied, "anything you want."

There was an awkward moment of silence, interrupted thankfully by Captain Wambold's scratchy voice coming over the intercom. "This is your captain speaking. Prepare for landing. Please be sure your seatbacks and tables are in an upright position."

"*What?*" said both Jaxson and Marta-2, wondering if they were hearing right. Could it be? Were they actually going to put down on Earth at last? Jaxson, rarely at a loss of words, was rendered nearly speechless. A single syllable, hardly material to be entered into the annals of space exploration history, escaped his lips: "Wow."

"Have a good touchdown," said Marta-2, squeezing his hand.

"Yeah, you too," he said as he hurried out of the library, down the corridor, and up to his pod chamber above the Observation Deck. He strapped himself into his bunk space and tried to breathe. It was hard to believe that after all this time in the vast nothingness of space they were actually headed for terra firma. He only hoped the terra wasn't so firma that they'd disintegrate upon landing, but he put that idea straight out of his head. This was no time for negative thoughts, not when a vast new world lay before them. What an adventure it would be! With his thermies in one hand and swimsuit in the other, Jaxson was ready for whatever this crazy outpost had to throw at them.

Earth! I still couldn't help smiling at the strange name and the little tickling sensation it created at the base of my larynx. The place actually sounded primitive, as if the populace had barely evolved phonetically. Earth. Birth. Dearth. Mirth. What were they, a bunch of savages? Anyway, who cared? We were getting out of the frying pan of space and if Earth was the fire, we'd just have to find a way to put it out. Better a date with Earth than a fly-by with incoming copernicus waves.

Captain Wambold piloted the ship into progressively lower orbits in order to give the crew time to adjust to Earth's outer atmosphere, but the pull of gravity proved to be more disruptive than Jaxson had imagined. They'd been zooming through space with zero resistance for so long that he'd forgotten what it felt like to be attracted to a planetary body. Flexing his hands, lifting his arms, and stretching his legs required more effort than he was used to, and it was as if his muscles were moving independently of his wishes. He felt a tingling along his neck, a not altogether unpleasant experience, but when he discovered that the tingling was caused by a patch of skin that had been pulled and distended by g-force gravity, he was less amused. That, it turned out, was only the beginning. Earth, a bombastic rock out in the middle of nowhere, was so dense (or, as Jaxson would later come to believe, so full of itself) that steering the rocket ship was very nearly impossible. Captain Wambold, a master pilot, had to pull out every imaginable maneuver from his bag of tricks just to keep them from imploding. They were buffeted by solar winds, atmospheric speed bumps, gravitational voids, intrepid wave forms, precipitate dew drops, and a whole host of other meteorological events that were completely foreign to them. They were pushed, jabbed, rocked, wobbled, lashed, flailed, flogged, and fustigated, and that was only in the outermost layers of the exosphere. Their descent through the thermosphere and mesosphere was such torture as to defy description, even by such a silver-tongued wordsmith as Jaxson. How does one even begin to explain the sensation of having the enamel pulled off your teeth, the color out of your hair, and the taste out of your tongue?

I found my mind spinning in reverse, spiraling back in time like a corkscrew gone amok, digging deeper and deeper into the nether regions of my subconscious where every negative aspect of my life played out before me. There I was, falling out of my crib, kicking and screaming and flailing against an unlistening world, let me grow up, that's all I ask, I'm born to be free, don't you understand, free like the wind, let my spirit soar like a pterodactyl shot from a cannon, yes, let me glide over the mountaintops and swoop into the sea, I'm a dreamer, a lover, a poet, not an orphan, there must be some mistake, what am I doing in a sterile room with a silver light shining from a phosphorescent bulb, no, let me just slip outside and take a look around, you go right and I'll go left and we'll meet somewhere over the moon, hey, people, don't you understand, I'm built for speed not stability, Jaxson be nimble, Jaxson be quick, Jaxson jump over a candlestick, and that's exactly what I did, I kept running and running, nimbly and quickly, and then the spaceship hit the troposphere and my mind went totally black and then it went totally blue until finally there was nothing at all but the screeching of metal on metal, the scraping of rubber on sand, and the sound of thunder on the distant shore—

Chapter 10

*"The mind is not a vessel to be
filled but a fire to be kindled."*
—Plutarch

It was raining over the central plains of North America, a
not unusual phenomenon in early July. A fast-moving
cloud cracked open violently as if the hand of God had
slapped it silly. There was a terrible clap of thunder, an angry
discharge of lightning, and an Earth-shattering sonic boom
as the Pulsar-7 came blasting through the inner atmosphere
5000 miles an hour too fast. This was too speedy even for the
long arm of God Himself, who pulled back and let the
spaceship go kerplunk in an agnostic-inducing hard landing.
When the clouds cleared on a high mesa 20 miles north of
Arapahoe, Nebraska, the tailpipe and exhaust chamber of
the Pulsar-7 poked out of a desolate patch of prairie brush,
looking for all the world like the leaning tower of Pisa. From
a distance, the ship blended in seamlessly with the plateaus
and buttes that jutted up from the plains. Only upon closer
inspection would one notice that this was no prehistoric rock
formation but was, in fact, the latest in 22nd century poly-
plasmatic technology. Luckily, closer inspection in these
parts was more likely to come from a wild goose, a prairie
dog, or the odd peripatetic gopher than any human beings.

The escape hatch of the Pulsar-7 creaked open and Cap-

tain Wambold poked his head out. His forehead was bruised
and his chin bloodied but all in all he didn't look the worse
for wear. He took a deep breath, let the air linger on his
palate, and slowly exhaled as if he were a judge at a wine
tasting. He took a second, more confident breath, relieved
that the atmosphere of Earth didn't burn a searing hole
through his lungs and larynx. Even though all the studies
pointed to Earth being respiration friendly, studies are only
as good as the scientists behind them and scientists are, as
Jaxson liked to say, prone to the occasional misdiagnosis,
miscalculation, and miss by a mile. Speaking of which, it
appeared that Captain Hieronymus Wambold, aka the
Embodiment of Most High Perfection Itself, seemed to have
missed his destination by a mile and then some. He had
aimed for the deserts of New Mexico, hoping to catch a
glimpse of what, if anything, was left of the unfortunate
recipient of Teller's attack, but the rough welcome to Earth's
atmosphere had deposited them well away from their
destination. "We seem to have been blown off course," said
Wambold, rubbing his chin with consternation.

"That's the least of our problems," said Teller, after taking
a preliminary scan of the spaceship's systems. "We have
major damage in the steering chamber, engine failure, heat
shield malfunctions, and a whole host of lesser issues."

Wambold looked at him gravely. "Give it to me straight,
Teller. What's the prognosis?"

"Well, sir, to put it in Earth terms, our goose is damn near
cooked."

"I have no idea what that means. Is that good or bad?"

The rest of the crew slowly gathered around their Captain
as he stepped back from the escape hatch. Each of them had
been shaken by the rough landing and were still gathering
their senses. Raleigh was dead quiet as he shook off his aches
and pains and entered suborbital othermindedness, Marta-1
was in a state of molecular dissociation that left her unable

to feel her fingertips, elbows and kneecaps, Marta-2 was so dizzy she had to hold onto Jaxson to keep from falling, and Jaxson was so discombobulated he didn't even mind. Only Oblivia seemed to be unaffected, not a great surprise since she had long ago spun into an orbit of her own making.

Teller ran his data—food supplies, astral mapping calendar, climate prognosis, galactic disturbance graph, fuel reserve variables—through the tripometer. "It's like Raleigh said," he said. "We have seven rotations of the planet before we have to depart. Getting the ship into operating condition in such a short time is one hellacious task."

Wambold's face darkened with a rare look of worry. "Do we even have the human resources to rebuild the ship in seven days?"

"We'll need Raleigh for the structural issues, me for the engine work, you to oversee the project—"

"What about the experiment?" said Marta-1, listening in with growing concern. "Have you forgotten the reason we're here?"

"Yes, the experiment," said Wambold. "What are the minimum requirements?"

Marta-1 pulled Wambold aside and lowered her voice to a conspiratorial whisper. "Me, Oblivia, and Marta-2 is all we need. We've been running through the procedure ever since liftoff and it's in our bones. Put me in charge, Captain, and we'll make you proud."

"I like your confidence, young lady. Let me think it over."

Jaxson, the seventh wheel on a ship that needed only six, lingered nearby and caught just enough of the conversation to set off his inner smoke detector. He'd looked forward to a change of scenery in order to rekindle his romance with Marta-1 and the wide open spaces of Earth was for him a whole new enchilada. Which, incidentally, he discovered during his research, was a popular dish in the southwest United States, just like in sub-Subian Obsidia. Marta-1... an enchilada... a candlelight dinner... what could be better? "We can't just send them out there alone, Captain," he said. "It's not safe."

"Why not?" said Marta-1. "The engineers get the ship ready for lift-off while the scientists proceed with the mission. That's what we've trained for all along."

"True," said Wambold, "the training was approved by the top brass back home—"

"No, really, Captain," said Jaxson. "It's far too dangerous. I volunteer to accompany Marta-1 and the others on their expedition."

"What do you think, Teller?"

"We certainly don't need him here, Captain."

"We don't need him out there, either," said Marta-1, pleading her case. "He'd just be in the way."

Wambold weighed his options. The crew seemed edgy and he needed to make a decision. "Jaxson will remain behind with the engineers," he said. "Marta-1, Marta-2, and Oblivia will conduct the experiment."

"But, Captain—"

"That's enough, Jaxson. Try to make yourself useful." Wambold released the escape hatch valve and an extension ladder of polyprotopulsium unfurled to the rocky surface below. He stepped out onto a platform, then backed his way down some 30 steps, stopping every rung or two to look out at the vast landscape that surrounded them. They were perched on the flat tablelands of a mesa, a thousand feet above a lonely plain that appeared to be even flatter still. There were little clumps of trees dotting the terrain, with the occasional bush and some rolling sagebrush adding a bit of variety to a mostly monotonous panorama. It reminded Wambold of the outer quadrants back home that were used mostly to grow yeast and malt for hablum but were otherwise a wasteland. Taking a deeper breath, he trod down the final few rungs of the ladder and officially became the first

Obsidian to set foot on Earth. Jaxson caught the historic moment and recorded Hieronymus Wambold's first words in his Observer's Log: "Don't everyone all pee here at once."

We followed the Captain down the ladder, nearly breaking our necks in the rush to touch ground at last. Chief Navigator Raleigh ran some dirt through his fingers, Data Transfer Officer Oblivia brushed her hand through the air, and Molecular Biochemist Marta-2 dug her toes into the warm soil, but it was Behavioral Scientist Marta-1, as always, who shined in the light of day. She was cool as a cucumber as she took climatic measurements, evaluated chemical compositions, and did some preliminary soil analysis. Chief Engineer Teller, meanwhile, had served out his period of banishment from the rest of the crew and was now back among the living, albeit on probation. One or two more screw-ups like the last one and he'd be relegated to outcast status, a position I had earned with no little effort and was not anxious to share. One outcast is one thing, but two outcasts is the beginning of a trend, and before you know it the outcasts are in the majority and everybody's *goose is cooked.*

When Jaxson touched ground, he cautiously jumped a few inches just to make sure he wouldn't keep on going right into the stratosphere. "It's got good gravity," he said with the innocence of a teenager kicking the tires of his first car.

"It's got good gravity?" said Wambold, staring at him and wondering—not for the first time—how Jaxson ever got assigned to the flight. Was this the future of science? He shuddered to think. "Raleigh, establish coordinates."

Raleigh consulted his hand-held gyro, put his finger into the air to measure wind currents, and established magnetic north. "We are precisely 290 Earth miles north-northeast of Denver, Colorado, the 25th largest city in the United States of America and considered to be perfectly representative of the national average for intelligence, emotional stability, and psychological aptitude. If we're looking for the typical

American, we couldn't do better, sir."

"It will have to do," said Wambold. "One good subject is all we need."

"I really think I should go along, Captain," said Jaxson, "just to be safe."

"That decision has already been made."

"But, sir—"

Marta-1 headed back to the ship, satisfied that Jaxson's pleas had fallen on deaf ears. She headed up the extension ladder, her fingertips, elbows and kneecaps still numb from the landing. As she flexed her extremities to get the blood flowing, she managed to miss a rung and tumbled to the ground. Marta-1 blinked open her eyes, flexed the muscles in her arm, and groaned in pain. "No... no... no..."

The rest of the crew watched in stunned silence, then hurried to her side. Jaxson, the first one there, saw the sickening sight of Marta-1's twisted and dislocated shoulder. "Easy now," he said to her, "don't move." Jaxson gently felt around her shoulder blade, trying not to upset anything further. "I don't think anything's broken."

"Of course nothing's broken!" said Marta-1, pushing him away with her one good arm. "Can someone help me who actually knows something?"

The crew gathered closer, unsure what to do. "Where's my medical kit?" muttered Wambold after an untoward delay, knowing full well there was nothing he could do but pre-scribe a couple of carbasides and tell her to call him in the morning. Medical training was the captain's one area of total ineptitude, owing to a secret fear of anything that oozes, blisters, festers, drips, trickles, dribbles, seeps, slobbers, or secretes from the body. All such issues were to be handled by the Medical Officer, which would have been fine if only such a person were onboard. Unfortunately, there was only room for seven crew members and it was determined that due to the historic nature of the flight, that seat would be better occupied by a first rate Ship Observer, especially one who came so highly recommended from the planet's top scientific institute. Wambold stared at Jaxson with a look that would kill if only it wouldn't leave such a mess of pus, excretion, and other revolting bodily discharges.

While the rest of the crew stood by helplessly, Oblivia stared off into space and went into one of her patented trances. Her eyelids flickered, her eyebrows rose as if to give her optical orbits more space to maneuver, and her corneas expanded into a murky brown sea. Then, without a word, she bent over, took a deep breath, and yanked Marta-1's arm almost clear out of its socket. Marta-1 cried out in pain, but within seconds she was able to flex her fingers. "It's better," she said. "Much better."

Wambold was thankful for the medical miracle and even more relieved to be off the hook. "Three days rest," he proclaimed. "No lifting, no pulling, no walking."

"Impossible!" protested Marta-1. "What about the mission?"

"It will have to wait."

"It can't wait!" said Marta-1. "We've just barely got enough time as it is!"

"The Captain is right," said Marta-2 as she calmly took Marta-1's hand and tried to comfort her. "It's much too dangerous for you to leave the ship. I know the entire procedure, your part as well as mine. I can handle both roles without a problem."

Jaxson's imagination stirred with the realization that all was not lost after all. Marta-1 would be at his side and he at hers. He leaned back and reveled in his first terrestrial daydream. He'd lift her into his arms, then firmly but oh-so-gently carry her up the ladder to his very own quarters where he would look after her day and night, nursing her back to health, attending to her needs, dressing her wounds, massaging her shoulders, rubbing his fingers slowly, lovingly, up along her clavicle, down her neck, brushing gently across her breasts—

"No!" said Marta-1, gritting her teeth and pulling away. "It takes three people for this mission!"

"Well, somebody else then," said Marta-2. "I can show someone the ropes along the way."

Wambold stepped in with rare decisiveness. "It's decided then," he said. "Jaxson, you get your wish. You're going after all."

Jaxson's nursing fantasy exploded like a broken heart valve. Him? With Marta-2? And Oblivia? It was a recipe for disaster if there ever was one. "No, Captain, I think you were right. I'm better off here looking after Marta-1 and filling in for emergencies."

"We've already had an emergency. Now get yourself ready to depart."

"Please reconsider, sir," said Jaxson as panic began to set in. "Your initial impulse was surely correct... we all know how good your gut feelings are... we wouldn't want you to second guess yourself..."

"Jaxson!"

Marta-2, looking pleased with the turn of events, came to his assistance. "Don't worry," she said, "I'll watch your back."

"I'm sure you will," said Jaxson, hoping she wouldn't.

"All right then, it's settled," said Wambold. "Gather the equipment, establish the coordinates, set the contact points, confirm the readings, and proceed to wardrobe."

The Pulsar-7 did, indeed, have a wardrobe. The Mylar boots, skin-tight leotards, and polystabilized nanofibers of Obsidia weren't going to blend in on Earth, so researchers at mission control had provided the crew with a change of clothes for their date with destiny. There was a burst of activity as final preparations were made. Bags were packed, machinery unwrapped, and equipment tested. Jaxson studied some maps, Marta-2 went over a list of procedures one last time, and Oblivia did some eye exercises, an interesting choice that raised a few eyebrows itself. Wambold watched her a moment, wishing he could go along to make sure that the mission went as planned. He spoke to them gravely, reiterating the seriousness of the mission. "Make your way to Denver," he said. "Find some poor soul and conduct your experiment."

"We'll manage, sir," said Marta-2. "No need for concern."

"Get in, get out, and get back here as soon as possible," said Wambold.

"Not to worry, Captain," said Jaxson. "I'm shooting for midnight."

"You have seven days," said Wambold, ignoring Jaxson's usual irreverence. "Not one hour more."

As the trio listened to their last minute instructions, Raleigh added one of his patented nuggets of transcendental wisdom: "It has been said that at a train station one can catch a train."

"Be it so," said Wambold, pointing down the mesa to a dusty country road in the distance. And with that, the three intrepid explorers left their safe cocoon in search of a train, a brain, and a place called Denver.

Chapter 11

*"The outer space beings are my brothers. They
sent me here. They already know my music."*
—Sun Ra

Ray and Dirk crossed the Missouri River on the Ak-sar-
ben Bridge, a toll bridge that only weeks before had
been liberated by the Knights of Ak-sar-ben. The
Knights were neither a fraternal order of Masons, nor an
exotic tribe of native Americans, nor a cult of crazed Ku Klux
Klansmen, but rather a group of businessmen from Nebraska—Aksarben spelled backwards—who were tired of paying
a nickel every time they crossed the river. It was un-
American, they figured, so they formed a beneficent society,
bought the damn bridge, and said to hell with the tolls. This
was the America that Ray loved, a land of stubborn individu-
alists willing to stand up and take things into their own
hands. He was ready to take a few things into *his* own hands
as well, namely Nick's neck and Esmeralda's ass. First,
though, was an appointment with an Omaha steak, an 18
ounce T-Bone that had Ray's name on it ever since the
middle of Iowa.

The steak was good, so good that Ray and Dirk wobbled
up to their room at the old Blackstone Hotel and passed out
like a couple slabs of beef. Morning brought the smell of
more steak broiling in the restaurant below. How anybody

could eat a 12 ounce steak for breakfast was anyone's guess, but Ray and Dirk were up to the task. As they rustled themselves out of bed, the smell of the stockyards and slaughterhouses wafted through the room and put a couple of sharp creases into their pants. Dirk stretched and took a deep lungful of air. "It's good to be alive, eh, Ray?"

"It'll do," said Ray.

"This country air is good for you. Probably good for your ulcer. It's invigorating."

"I'll feel more invigorated when we wrap up this job."

Ray and Dirk packed their bags—bulging with towels, soap, shampoo, and anything else that wasn't nailed down—and headed for the lobby. The desk clerk looked the other way when they glanced through the registry—two bits went a long way in this town—to see if Nick and Esmeralda were stupid enough to stay somewhere so obvious. "You haven't seen a curly-haired floozy and a guy with a limp in these parts, have you?" said Ray to the desk clerk.

"Not that I recall," said the clerk.

"Okay, well, if you do see them, tell them not to get too comfortable."

"You bet."

Ray lit up a Viceroy, Dirk broke off a toothpick between his teeth, and they froze the guy with a stare. They took a last look around the lobby, glanced inside the dining room, then headed for the nearest steakhouse. They had their choice: the place next door, the place across the street, and the place next door to the place across the street. That's the one they chose, just because. Thirty minutes later, they dug into their top sirloins with rare gusto. For them, everything was rare—the idea of steak for breakfast, the idea of steak with eggs, the steak itself. The bloody red meat was so rare it boosted their levels of aggression to wild dog status. They licked their chops, threw down a bloody good tip, and set off in search of their quarry. They checked the registries at the Paxton Hotel, then the Magnolia, the Cornhusker, the Fontenelle, the St. Nicholas, the Grand Central, and the Sanford, all to no avail. By the time they looked in on a couple of saloons, pool halls, and record stores, it was time for lunch. "How about an Omaha steak?" said Dirk.

"Sure, I could go for a snack," said Ray. After a couple of prime ribs, Ray lit up a Viceroy, Dirk broke off a toothpick between his teeth, and they stared out the window of some joint on Dodge Street watching the cows go by. "They're not here," said Ray.

"How do you figure?"

"Whenever that crazy bitch is nearby my ulcer starts acting up, and my ulcer hasn't been this copacetic since Chicago."

"Maybe it's the air," said Dirk.

"It's not the air. They're somewhere west of here, I can feel it. Lincoln or Fairmont or Hastings, one of those places. We'll go straight to Colorado if we have to."

Dirk glanced at the menu one last time, took a deep breath of invigoration, then pushed away from the table. "I'm gonna miss it here," he said.

"Yeah, me too," said Ray. "Oh, by the way," he said as they headed for the door, "you owe me ten bucks."

"No problem," said Dirk. "You owe me twenty."

High above the plains of Nebraska, the crow climbed into a steady funnel of wind, then glided aimlessly over the barren terrain in search of a berry bush or a stray gopher or even a baby sparrow if things got really desperate. Nebraska was for amateurs, not for big black flappers who could plan, connive, and soar with the best of them. This was a crow out of his element, a city crow stuck among country bumpkins, a bird whose multitude of talents was being wasted by an unappreciative audience of dull farmers who'd actually planted stick figures all over their fields with bugged out eyes and flailing arms. As if it wouldn't take a hell of a lot more to scare a crow than one of those idiot mannequins.

The crow sensed a kindred spirit in the car below. Esmeralda's hair was like a big black nest that blew every which way in the wind. There was, after all, a bit of the Gypsy in the crow, and a bit of the Jew, too. They were two pious peoples who didn't take their Gods too seriously, and that was pretty much the way the crow saw the world, too. A little respect for the higher forces was due, but no need to go overboard, not when there were bigger fish to fry, mackerels, for example, which were a religious experience in themselves when braised with a dash of tarragon.

Nick and Esmeralda cruised down the desolate country road doing 55 and not one mile an hour more. Everything was aces, for about two minutes, that is, because Esmeralda's clock was always running and two minutes was about all she was good for until something or other needed winding up. "Are you sure we're going the speed limit?" she said. "It feels like we're standing still." Nick didn't even bother to respond. He pulled out his harmonica and played to the rhythms of the tires clacking on the asphalt. There was something about the movement of the car that pushed the music itself. He cupped his free hand around the metal casing and formed a vacuum that acted like an echo chamber. He bent the reeds with a thin stream of air that started deep in his larynx, rose up through his throat, and crested at his lips, then hit a high note that called to the heavens, sang to the clouds, and warbled to the birds above.

The crow was not immune to soulful warbling, even if it came from a ten-holed metal instrument that glistened in the sunlight. When he dipped down a little closer to get a listen, however, he sensed trouble ahead. Way up the road, three figures were walking right down the center divider and if the crow had his trigonometry straight, it was pretty obvious that a triangle of humanity was about to get its hypotenuse bisected by a slab of speeding metal. It didn't take a Pythagoras to figure out that however you squared it up, the sum of those parts was about to become a lot less than its whole. This was a time for action, something bigger than a caw or a pee or a poop. The crow swooped down like one of those kamikaze pilots who had been so popular with his cousins across the ocean a couple of years back and threw all caution to the wind.

There was a flurry of activity—a wild mixture of hands and feet and wings and beaks—as the Hudson's windshield suddenly became a canvas of flailing arms and flapping wings. There were faces both human and avian, a jumble of plume, quill, corduroy and denim, a shriek, a yell, a caw and a squawk. Then came the screeching of brakes, the burning of rubber, and the skidding of tires. There were feathers everywhere, the ruffled feathers of man and bird, and when it was over, the Hudson ground to a halt on a dusty country road just inches away from three hitchhikers who had appeared from out of nowhere with their hands upraised in the universal signal to stop. It was an old-fashioned group dressed in early-century attire, Reverie Energy's wardrobe department having miscalculated their date of arrival by at least five decades. They appeared to be Mormons, if not Amish or Mennonite—Jaxson in a dour, brown, ill-fitting corduroy suit, Marta-2 and Oblivia in black, full-length denim dresses and high-necked lace. In the middle of it all, almost forgotten, the crow landed ever so briefly in a nest of black, curly hair before Esmeralda swiped him away with a scream that woke the night owls of Hidden Valley. "Jesus Christ!" she yelled at the crow, at the hitchhikers, and at life itself.

"Oh, sorry," said Jaxson, dusting himself off. "We were just hoping for a ride."

"Whatever happened to standing on the side of the road

with your thumbs out?" said Nick, still shaking from the near miss.

"I wasn't quite sure of the signal."

"Yeah, well, that's the signal," said Nick. "A thumb, got it?"

"Got it."

"Where are you going that's so important?"

"The train to Denver."

Nick took a deep breath and gradually regained his bearings, relieved that no one was hurt. "Yeah, well, good luck. There's probably a station in the next town."

"Oh, good. Well, thank you for the advice."

Esmeralda took a quick read of the situation. These were clearly people of the Book and that could only mean trouble. Persephone had always warned against getting too close to people who took the written word that seriously—couldn't be trusted, she said—and in this part of the country, they probably threw that book at you just for looking at them the wrong way. Still, a person could die in an arid landscape like this—probably of boredom as far as Esmeralda was concerned. "We can't just leave them out here," she whispered to Nick.

"Do you really want to get preached to for the next 20 miles?"

"Just do it."

"All right," said Nick, turning back to the hitchhikers. "Arapahoe's not too far up the road. I guess we can take you to the depot. Hop in."

Jaxson, Marta-2 and Oblivia climbed into the back seat, careful not to catch their long coats and billowing dresses on anything. They settled in, Marta-2 on one side, Oblivia on the other, Jaxson in the middle. The seat was surprisingly plush and gave them plenty of room to stretch their legs. "Thank you for your kindness," said Marta-2.

"Don't mention it," said Nick.

"Why not?" said Jaxson.

"I don't know. Just don't mention it."

"It seems to me that if someone does someone else a good turn, the other party should mention it."

"You see? I knew it," Nick muttered to Esmeralda. He stared at Jaxson in the rear view mirror. "Look, I'm not going to argue with you about it. If you want to mention it, then mention it."

"Thank you."

As Nick pulled back onto the road, Jaxson, Marta-2, and Oblivia leaned back to enjoy the scenery, sparse as it was. Even the most barren rock formation was a feast for their hungry eyes. "Pretty lonely out here, isn't it?" said Esmeralda.

"Yes," said Jaxson, "you are the first life forms we've seen in miles, not counting the round-tailed ground squirrels and the long-tongued bats."

"Where you from?"

"Oh, way back there," said Marta-2. "A little place you wouldn't have heard of."

"Try me."

"It's a little town called Hflafenjørg," said Jaxson, "about two sequesters this side of the Outer Realms."

"Sure, sure," said Esmeralda, "I think I met a guy from there once. Melvin, or Alvin, or something. Pretty good tipper. So, what's up in Denver?"

"We have a short mission, then we return."

"A Mormon mission? You dunk people in water or something, don't you?"

"Um, yes," he said. "We dunk each other all the time, like donuts."

"Donuts, you say?" said Esmeralda. "I gotta warn you, this religion stuff isn't for me. No offense, but I think it's a bunch of hooey."

"Hooey and kablooey," said Jaxson, trying to be agreeable. "It's complete nonsense."

"What's that?" said Esmeralda, wondering if she was

hearing right.

"Religion is a crutch for the philosophically disabled," said Marta-2, quoting an old Obsidian proverb. "All you need is purpose."

"You don't say," said Esmeralda, slowly warming to the strangers. "That seems just about right, doesn't it, Nick?"

"Just about," said Nick.

Esmeralda put her arm out the window and felt the wind rushing through her fingers. "Let me tell you a little story. My mother's people were from Bulgaria way back when and they had this legend about how the Bulgarians built a church and the Gypsies built a church. The Bulgarians, who had a couple of extra bucks, built their church of gold. The Gypsies, who had nothing, built their church of cheese. Time passed and the Gypsies roamed the countryside the way we like to do and after a while we got hungry and started to eat the church. A little slice here, a little slice there, and before you knew it, the church was a goner. Now, you go over to Bulgaria today and what do you see? You see that the Bulgarians have themselves a country and they have themselves a church. And what do the Gypsies have? Nothing. No country. No church. Nothing at all. There's a lesson in there."

"Yes, yes, of course," said Jaxson. "Break out the bread and wine and hope the cheese isn't too sharp."

"Exactly," said Esmeralda. "You see, that's what we're doing. Going out to our vineyard in Petaluma, California, to wait for the grapes to ferment. Sell them or drink them, that's what I say. We win either way."

"Win-win-win if you decide to bathe in them," said Jaxson.

"Hey," said Esmeralda, patting Jaxson's arm. "You're okay."

"You are, too," said Jaxson. He settled back to experience the sensory pleasures of the 78% nitrogen, 21% oxygen, and 1% trace elements that were blowing through his hair. It wasn't bad, this planet's atmosphere, not bad at all. A little sour, perhaps, but not so disagreeable as to leave a bad aftertaste. As he filled his lungs almost to bursting, it occurred to him that he was actually there—on Earth!—and he was riding in the back seat of an internal combustion engine automobile with two hipster guides. He could tell they were hipsters by the way Nick slouched in his seat and hung his arm out the window and the way Esmeralda wore her hair wild like Rita Hayworth in *Gilda*, one of the films he'd loved back at the Institute on Friday Night Noir. He had to pinch himself.

Nick pulled out his harmonica and played along to the rhythm of the wheels on the highway. He played a boogie that kept repeating itself, chugging along the open road, hitting the same notes over and over, bending them a little farther each time until they growled like the muffler of the Hudson. Chugga-chugga-chugga, the rhythm kept pushing on as the car kicked up pebbles and gravel and zoomed down the road. It climbed over a brief incline and the harmonica went right with it, reaching to the middle octave as the wind blew in over the visors, down along the dashboard and out along the back seat.

Jaxson and Marta-2 tapped their feet and listened with particular interest. "I guess everybody plays harmonica on Earth," whispered Marta-2.

"Yeah," said Jaxson, "what a cool planet."

"Why don't you play along?"

"You don't think he'd mind?"

"Why would he?"

The wind, the road, the car, and Nick's harmonica combined into a kind of blues band that played all the parts, and then came a solo that rode right over the top of it—*rat-a-tat-tat*—a cluster of sharp notes ran up and down the scale in perfect counterpoint to the rhythm as Jaxson pulled out his own harmonica and slipped in a blistering riff that punched and kicked to Nick's driving melody. The two harmonicas ran inside and outside each other, finishing each other's phrases, hitting together in unison, higher and higher—

Nick looked in the rear view mirror and caught Jaxson's eyes and something passed between them—a connection, a sense of recognition—and yet, at the same time, there was a certain uneasiness. The harmonicas disappeared as quickly as they had surfaced.

"No more?" said Esmeralda. "That sounded great."

"Maybe later," said Nick.

"Yeah, later," said Jaxson.

"Okay," said Esmeralda as she shrugged, reached over to the dashboard, and turned on the radio. She skipped through the usual farm reports and country music stations before coming upon the national news. A deep, stentorian voice crackled through the static:

"An examination by the army revealed last night that mysterious objects found on a lonely New Mexico ranch was a harmless high-altitude weather balloon, not a grounded flying disk. Excitement was high until Brigadier General Roger M. Ramey, commander of the Eighth Air Forces with headquarters here in Fort Worth, Texas, cleared up the mystery."

"You hear this?" said Esmeralda to Nick, turning up the radio.

"The bundle of tinfoil, broken wood beams and rubber remnants of a balloon were sent here yesterday by army air transport in the wake of reports that it was a flying disk. But the general said the objects were the crushed remains of a ray wind target used to determine the direction and velocity of winds at high altitudes."

Jaxson, Marta-2, and Oblivia shot each other nervous glances. They sat there quietly, not moving a muscle.

"Warrant Officer Irving Newton, forecaster at the army air forces weather station here said they use them because they go much higher than the eye can see. The weather balloon

was found several days ago near the center of New Mexico by
Rancher W. W. Brazel. He said he didn't think much about it
until he went into Corona, New Mexico, last Saturday and
heard the flying disk reports. He returned to his ranch, 85
miles northwest of Roswell, and recovered the wreckage of the
balloon, which he had placed under some brush. Then Brazel
hurried back to Roswell, where he reported his find to the
sheriff's office. The sheriff called the Roswell Airfield and
Major Jesse A. Marcel, 509th bomb group intelligence officer
was assigned to the case. Colonel William H. Blanchard,
commanding officer of the bomb group, reported the find to
General Ramey and the object was flown immediately to the
army air field here. Ramey went on the air here last night to
announce the New Mexico discovery was not a flying disk."

"I knew it," said Nick. "These things are never what you
think they are."

"Thank goodness for small favors," said Esmeralda, turning off the radio.

The Hudson cruised through the countryside. A few
farmhouses appeared on the horizon, followed by a cluster of
feed stores, fertilizer suppliers, and tractor dealerships. As
they approached Arapahoe, more houses dotted the landscape, then came the usual gas stations, five and dimes,
hardware stores, and food shops of small town America. The
passengers took in the sights as if they were tourists on a
lark. "Do you know how you can tell when you're in a small
town?" said Jaxson.

"How?" said Nick.

"When the closest Dairy Queen is 50 miles away."

"Uh-huh, good one," said Nick.

Jaxson was on a roll now, a bottled-up comedian with an
appreciative audience at last. "Hey, did you hear the one
about the chief engineer who fell off the wagon?"

"Why, no, I don't think so," said Esmeralda.

Marta-2 grabbed Jaxson's arm and reigned him in before

he went too far. "Maybe some other time," she said.

Nick drove down Main Street, turned at the edge of town, and pulled into the train station. There were the usual wood shacks, water towers, and coal hoppers that stretched from one end of America to the other. "Well, this is it," he said as he parked the Hudson at the curb.

Esmeralda glanced up at the departure board and saw that the train to Denver was just about to arrive. "You're in luck," she said. "I was afraid you'd have to sit here all day in this dump of a town."

The travelers climbed out of the Hudson and gathered their things. "I guess this is goodbye," said Jaxson, reaching out to shake hands with Nick. "It's been a gas."

"You're going to be all right?" said Nick, a hint of worry in his voice.

"Sure," said Jaxson. "We're old hands at this travel game."

"Good luck on your mission," said Esmeralda as she helped Marta-2 and Oblivia with their suitcases.

"And good luck on yours," said Marta-2 as she headed for the depot.

And with that, the Earthlings and the Obsidians parted ways on the high plains of Nebraska. They each had a long journey ahead of them, whether by rail or by road. It was still a couple hundred miles to Denver and that was a formidable jaunt, even as the crow flies.

Chapter 12

Jaxson Epsilon's
Earth Log
—July 8, 1947

Okay. The gloves are off. This is it, dear reader, the real deal, the straight scoop, the unvarnished truth, straight from the horse's yapper. I'm here on Earth and it's time to let loose. Captain Wambold's no longer looking over my shoulder, Teller isn't checking my grammar, and Raleigh's no longer leading me on cryptic verbal end runs. In honor of my ink-stained brethren the galaxy over, those poor unsung heroes of press rooms far and wide, I'm dropping all pretense and telling it like it is, like it was, and like it always will be. I write this for you, future generations, so that you'll understand what this mission was really about. This is Jaxson Epsilon unplugged and uncensored.

We parted ways on the high plains of Nebraska. They were pretty cool, my first two Earthlings, especially the one called Esmeralda, who was total aces. Nick was a little on the chilly side, but he warmed to my personality after one of my bravura comedic performances. As gases go, our meeting was definitely high octane. Which sounds like a good expression to try out in my next encounter with human beings. These Earthlings seem like a good audience for my brand of sophisticated humor, an acquired taste that too often goes undigested back home. I will certainly inquire about the possibility of an engagement at a Denver comedy club.

The Arapahoe train station wasn't much to look at. There were just two tracks, one going this way and the other going that way. There was a ticket office, a magazine rack, a snack bar, a tourist center, a telegraph office, a tobacco counter, and a postcard stand all jammed together in a tiny booth run by a ten-armed man in a visor. Or so it appeared, so fast was he moving. He stamped this, tore off that, reached over here, pulled over there, and sent an old lady toddling off into the waiting room with a ticket, a newspaper, and a pack of Wrigley's Chewing Gum, the use of which was unclear to me. We got so dizzy watching him juggle 50 tasks—have they *really* never heard of robots on this planet?—that we decided to bypass his bustling department store and went straight to the platform, where a half dozen people waited for the 3:10 to Denver.

We stood there waiting for I knew not what. My encyclopedic library research indicated that methods of transportation had evolved slowly on Earth, and I wasn't quite sure if we were in the era of diesel, electric, or hypermagneto hovertrack. Soon enough we heard a muffled, whooshing sound coming from the tracks, then a faint rumbling, a tremor, a chugging, and finally a clacking that grew louder and louder. When a locomotive appeared at the mouth of the station, we jumped back in disbelief, stunned to see a big black mountain of steel screeching along the tracks, its wheels churning and engine belching. I actually saw human beings shoveling great piles of a dark and sooty rock into a furnace, where it was fired and the steam captured as a source of power. Was I dreaming or had we entered into some prehistoric world of environmental madmen? Were they trying to choke us to death?

The station dissolved into a center of insanity surrounded by an air of lunacy wrapped in a sheet of chaos. People got on

and off the train amid frantic shouting and yelling. Conduc-
tors, stevedores, and porters appeared with carts, suitcases,
and steamer trunks. Bags were loaded, carts pushed, parcels
delivered, snacks gobbled, and tickets punched. Meanwhile,
sweat from the locomotive evaporated into the air and great
clouds of steam rose into the sky as the engine shook and
shuddered. I stared at the iron monster, trying to understand
how the mechanism actually worked. It appeared as if all
those parts were somehow connected and that pushing here
caused that to turn which made this thing spin and that
other thing compress. Or something like that.

"What do we do?" said Marta-2 as we stood motionless
along the tracks.

"I don't know," I said. "There must be some way that we
get lifted inside." The other passengers on the platform had
disappeared and I had no idea if they'd been uploaded,
rerouted, or possibly tossed into the furnaces with the coal.

A burst of pure white steam and three high piercing whistles shattered the air. "All aboard!" a cry echoed down the
tracks.

The wheels creaked as the engine churned impatiently to
be let loose from the confining walls of the station. Another
burst of steam and another whistle was followed by a snort of
air as if the train were a wild animal about to burst from its
pen. "C'mon, let's go!" I yelled as I grabbed our bags and leapt
up the stairs of the nearest car.

Marta-2 grabbed Oblivia and followed me up the steps as
the train began moving down the tracks. It was an odd
sensation as the mechanism started, stopped, and jerked
from side to side. Despite my gravest doubts, we actually
began picking up speed and headed for the open air. Just as I
was about to kick back and enjoy the ride, Marta-2 cried out
in distress: *"Oy-oy-oy!"* I turned to see that Oblivia was
hanging halfway out of the car and was headed straight into
the arms of a giant cactus that was growing along the tracks!

I sprung into action, leaping like a sub-Subian jumping bean, grabbing her around the midsection, and pulling her in before the cactus decapitated her. As we slammed against the doorway, several passengers watched us with what might have been concern, amusement, loathing, or some combination of the three, since it was anyone's guess what they were thinking.

We stood next to the open doorway as the train slowly picked up speed. The car creaked and shuddered as vibrations from the wheels shook us from side to side. When I realized that we were in danger of being bounced right out through the open portal, I decided to lead the way deeper into the inner chambers of the train. We held on for dear life as we stumbled down the aisle, careening from side to side as the train wobbled unsteadily along the tracks. The car was made up of smaller compartments, each of which was teeming with humanity. Despite all of my research into the habits and practices of Earth's mid-century transportation systems, I had never anticipated a form of travel in which the *passengers* were the cargo. These Earthlings had either developed survival skills that allowed them to adapt to such torturous conditions, or they were even more thick-skulled than studies had indicated and had been rendered insensate. The optimist in me hoped for the first, but the realist in me settled sadly on the latter.

We held our stomachs and tried to regain our equilibrium as we inched our way down the aisle. We glanced into compartments that were full to overflowing with humans of all sizes and ages. I noticed that the women tended to wear flowery, billowing dresses with no discernible shape or form while the men favored loose-fitting burlap overalls with multi-pocketed straps and bibs. These hardly seemed to be the hipsters I was hoping for but appeared more like some kind of long-lost country cousins. As the train herky-jerked down the tracks, we edged forward, holding onto windows, doors, light fixtures, air vents, and anything else we could grab hold of. Then, just when I thought we were home free, the train made a sharp turn around a bend and tossed us unceremoniously into an open compartment. When I recovered my bearings, I found myself face down in a woman's lap, a breech of just about every imaginable form of Earthly etiquette.

"*Eeeeeeek!*" the woman squawked.

"*Aaaaaaah!*" I shot back.

"*Oy-oy-oy!*" Marta-2 added.

I pulled myself up and busied myself with cramming our suitcases into the overhead luggage rack. "Sorry... oops... excuse me... beg your pardon..."

"Young man!" harrumphed the woman. "Do you mind?"

I finally got everything situated and plunked myself down between Marta-2 and Oblivia, just like in the back seat of the Hudson. Seated across from us were the aggrieved woman and a man who was so old it looked like his skin had been spread over his bones with a putty knife. He had a hollow look in his eyes, a deathly pallor, and no discernible awareness of his surroundings. Luckily, he was seated directly across from Oblivia and they could stare into each other's blankness until the cows came home. Which, in this part of Nebraska, I suspected could be pretty much at any time at all.

I settled into the cushioned seat and gazed out at the passing landscape. There wasn't much to see, just a barren terrain broken up by the occasional mesa or butte. "Nice, isn't it?" said Marta-2, trying to muster up her enthusiasm.

"Not bad," I said, staring out at the empty prairie. "Not exactly what the brochures said, but you know how they always exaggerate those things."

"They might've gotten a little carried away with all that business about fruited plains, purple mountain majesties, and amber fields of grain."

"From sea to shining sea, no less."

Marta-2 laughed at my bon mot—I can't help it if I'm funny—then gazed back out the window. "Do you ever think about what you'll do when we get back to Obsidia?" she said.

I wasn't crazy about her prying into my affairs, but I figured it would help pass the time. "I don't know. Start a band, maybe."

"Really? The girls will all go crazy."

"That's not the reason you start a band," I said with self-righteous indignation. "It's for the music, not the girls."

"Um-hmm," said Marta-2, blushing slightly. "I just know you'll be a great success. Why, the way you play..." Her voice faded away and I could only imagine what she was thinking.

Nebraska passed by in a blur. The land wasn't barren enough to be considered a desert but it was too parched to sustain much in the way of life. It was just land for the sake of being land, a kind of midzone between something and something else, a place holder, a respite, a stretch of space to keep areas of real life from getting too close to each other. Even here a farmer had staked his claim, a misanthrope, no doubt, a loner in a lonely land seeking nothing more than solitude. He wore overalls and a straw hat and worked a field at the edge of the tracks. Dangling from his lips was a small tube of paper with some kind of filtering device at one end. He inhaled it every few moments, creating a cloud of smoke and an ember of ash, both of which magically dissipated into the air. In front of him was a long-horned cow being held prisoner through an intricate system of straps, belts, and wooden yokes. The beast was dull of eyes and ponderous of movement, swaying this way and that as it plodded along the ground. A long stream of saliva dripped from its mouth and it looked to me like it was ready to fall over at any moment as it hung its head and snorted the dust from its nose. I expected the farmer to share his smoking tube, but instead he whipped the hairy beast across its buttocks, encouraging it to move forward. The cow twitched slightly, took a few steps, and pulled an iron plow along the ground. This in turn caused the crude mechanism to shred big chunks of dirt and leave rows of turned soil up and down the field. I wondered if I was actually seeing right or if I was experiencing some kind of post-terrestrial hallucination. *"Are they mad?"* I muttered to no one in particular. I wondered if this was some kind of absurdist performance put on just for our benefit. No one, after all, would even imagine trying to harness energy from a harnessed animal. *Would they?*

"This is abominable!" said Marta-2, overcome by the shocking site of abuse. "It breaks a hundred universal laws and goes straight to the heart of the covenant between mankind, animalkind, and kindness itself!"

For a brief moment I was tempted to take her hand and soothe her, but luckily I came to my senses before any crazy ideas were planted in her imagination. These molecular biologists can't distinguish compassion from chemical attraction and the next thing you know they're all over you sucking the spinal fluids from your brain pan.

Our little troupe of vagabonds from the future clickety-clacked to our date with destiny. Denver was certain to be loaded with a nice variety of brains and all we had to do was locate a top notch specimen, conduct our little experiment, and then cut loose in some clubs. I could hardly wait to see who was playing. Was Sonny Boy Williamson in town? Tampa Red? Memphis Slim? I was ready to move with the groove and get down with the go-around. To actually hear the blues the way they were meant to be played was way up there on my things-to-do-on-Earth list, right after visits to Hoover Dam and Madame Tussaud's Wax Museum. I could almost hear the bands tuning up right now.

The clacking of the wheels on the tracks created a natural rhythm, a kind of open-ended boogie that dug right into my soul. I couldn't resist the swaying of the train, the motion of the carriage, and the pounding of the wheels on the track. I pulled out my harmonica, slunk down in my seat, and played a few quiet chords that blended in with the whooshing sound of the locomotive. The notes rode over the rhythm as the train rose and dipped over the rolling plains, *ch-ch-chugga, ch-ch-chugga,* the melody built in little waves, lapping up against an ocean of sand that stretched to the horizon, *ka-chugga-chugga, ka-chugga-chugga,* the rods and pistons laid down an incessant beat that shook through the furnace and right down the spine of the train, the valves pounded like a drummer gone mad, the wheels clanked like high hats, the boiler groaned out the bass, and I leaned back and blasted out a staccato run that echoed off the walls of the carriage and straight into the heart of the engine, *ka-chunka-chugga, ka-chunka-chugga,* I bent the notes through the cylinders and condensers, the pumps and injectors, the springs and regulators, I twisted them and pushed them and squeezed them and caressed them, and then the engineer chimed in with a piercing whistle and the wheels clacked against the tracks with a steady 4/4 beat, the rims clanked against the rails with a twang and a clang, the couplings shook with an echoing tremolo, the notes pushed and stretched against the roof, and then the door swung open, a shadow crept across the floor, and a voice boomed out—

"Tickets, please."

"Huh?" I said, like a true blues cat.

"Tickets," repeated the conductor, eyeing us suspiciously. "I need to see your tickets."

I scanned my memory bank for anything pertaining to the requirement to produce a "ticket" for the privilege of being bounced around like a bag of broken drum sticks. My inner encyclopedia sent back some legalistic garbage that was as confusing as it was dry. "By tickets I assume you mean symbolic representations of the intention to compensate for services rendered, in this case the providing of a means of transportation in trade for a promissory note to be redeemed at the financial institution of the bearer?" I said in rote recitation.

"What are you, some kind of wise-guy country lawyer?"

"No, no, I didn't realize that one needed to pay for the privilege of being processed from one location to another."

"Yeah, the *processing* fee to Denver is two and a half bucks each," said the conductor impatiently. "That's seven-fifty for the three of you."

"By which I assume you mean dollars, is that right?"

"U. S. greenbacks. The ones with the presidents."

"No problem," I said, realizing there was a problem indeed. This was a situation that called for intelligence, intuition, and imagination. It was one of those moments that separate the men from the boys, the hablum from the chaff, the pods from the saline solution. It was... oh, God, where was Captain Wambold when we needed him! "Listen," I said in my most convincing impersonation of a feckless fool, "the moment we arrive in Denver, I would like to invite you to accompany us to the nearest Western Union station. There I'll place an urgent monetary request to our banking institution back home and we'll have the funds quick as a wink. How does that sound?"

"I'll tell you how it sounds. It sounds like either I throw you off the train at the next stop or I throw you off right now."

"If quick as a wink is too slow," I said with increasing panic, "I'm sure we could arrange something on the order of a quantum speed transfer. It just requires a few extra forms."

The old man seated across from us leaned forward a few inches, his bones creaking like a skeleton in a pathologist's lab. "Hit the road, jazz boy," he croaked, putting a punctuation mark on a conversation that didn't need one.

The reasons for so little touristic travel to this planet were beginning to become clear to me. The Earthlings were not the most welcoming of people, even to their own kind. I half wanted to tell the conductor that on Obsidia he'd be placed on a bed of marshmallows and slowly roasted to a sweet, gooey crisp, but it occurred to me that if they found out we were from a galaxy far, far away, there might be hell to pay. Especially after hearing that radio report in the car. What was that all about? Did they actually think we were weather balloons? Call me paranoid, but I had to wonder if there was some kind of cover-up going on at the very highest levels. And if so, why? And if not, why not? The reporter in me was bursting with questions. I roiled with frustration. There I was, on the cusp of the best story of my life, and I had to bite my tongue.

"Sorry for the inconvenience," I said.

"We didn't understand," said Marta-2.

"I need to pee," said Oblivia.

And with that we were unceremoniously booted from our seats, our cabin, and the train itself. Was this any way to treat visitors? I think not, dear reader, I think not.

Chapter 13

*"A crow will never
be a dove."*
—Bulgarian Proverb

There was less to Arapahoe than met the eye, which wasn't much to begin with. Nick and Esmeralda stopped at an A&W, had a couple of root beers—*how do they keep those mugs so cold?*—and got back on the road. What did people do here, Nick wondered. What dramas filled their lives? Was the widow on Elm Street plotting to run off with the pharmacist on Oak Lane? Was the old man on Cedar Avenue thinking of his son lost in the war? As the Hudson picked up speed and left Arapahoe, Nick realized he'd never know.

As they cruised through a section of land that nature had forgotten to finish topping off, Esmeralda found herself actually missing Iowa. At least in Iowa there were cornfields and crickets to drive you nuts, but here there was nothing but flat plains that led to flatter horizons. Brooklyn, Iowa, seemed like a cultural oasis compared to these creaky little outposts that people called towns but were really just a couple of shacks that fell off a truck and got a name stuck on them.

Esmeralda's mind wandered—never a good sign—and she found herself missing a lot of things. She missed the wind blowing in off Lake Michigan, she missed the sound of ambulances shrieking through the night, she missed the green-faced drunks at the Flame Club, she missed dusting it up with Muddy on a Sunday afternoon, she missed the skating rink at Lincoln Park, she missed circling the Loop on the elevated train, she missed the ladies room at Marshall Fields, she missed the deep dish pizza at Tony's on Indiana Avenue, she missed the guy at the bank who always gave her a wink, she missed running up the down escalator at the Furniture Mart, she missed the afterhours dives in Old Town, she missed the shadows on the walls of her dumpy tenement building, she missed the West Side suburbs and the smell of ground beef, she missed the duck-filled ponds on the highway out of town, she missed the comic pages in the Chicago Tribune and the obituaries in the Joliet Herald-News, she missed Sonny Boy Williamson and the King Biscuit radio show, she missed the rolling hills of Illinois and the rich black earth of Iowa, she missed the people who looked you in the eye and told you what they thought, she missed the people who lied to your face and rummaged through your pockets, hell, she missed the people who weren't even people, at least not the kind she'd come to know. "You think they'll be all right?" she said, gazing into the vast nothingness of south-central Nebraska.

"Who?"

"You know who. Those three. There was something strange about them."

"You think? I can't imagine what. A hipster comedian, a 19th century school marm, and a glassy-eyed girl who never says a word? What's strange about that?"

"Maybe that's just the way people are around here."

Up ahead was McCook, Nebraska, famous the world over for being located exactly halfway between Omaha and Denver. The town had been built by the old Burlington & Quincy Railroad Company as a place to fill the locomotive boilers with water and wipe the coal dust off the engineer's face.

Esmeralda could hardly wait. She'd been good for too long and was ready to let her hair down. Unfortunately, like all things Nebraska, the town was a grave disappointment for a former bar girl seeking anything approaching a good time. McCook looked like it was modeled after a collection of black and white Depression Era photographs. There were a couple of one-story buildings, a couple of two-story buildings, a couple of streets, a couple of parks, and a couple of taciturn townsfolk who had little to say and even less reason to say it.

The only real color was provided by Esmeralda herself, who got out of the car and paraded up and down Main Street just to let the locals know that the circus was in town and she was it. Her hair was tied up in a pink bandanna, her waist was wrapped in a purple shawl, and her shoulders were draped in an outlandish paisley cape. The plainer the town, the deeper Esmeralda dug into her suitcase to counteract the dreariness, and Nick feared she was reaching the bottom of the barrel. God knows, she might light something on fire or dance on hot coals or start a craps game just to keep from dying of boredom. He hobbled over on his bum leg, grabbed her around the waist, and escorted her back into the Hudson.

"C'mon," she implored him. "I'm itching for some action."

"Save it for Denver," he said. "We'll have a night on the town."

"Promise?"

"Promise."

Nick's knee was bothering him. Sitting in the car hour after hour was the worst thing he could do to keep the joint from tightening, but it was his driving knee and the only other option was to let Esmeralda drive. That, of course, meant the possibility of winding up virtually anywhere on the North American continent, if not central Asia.

"We're a real pair, aren't we, Nicky?" said Esmeralda. "You with your bum knee and me with my, well, you know."

Actually, Nick *didn't* know. He was afraid to ask. He ran

down the possibilities. Esmeralda's criminal record? Her life on the lam as a parole violator? Her legendary array of behavioral disorders? Her escape from a lunatic asylum? Her secret Nazi past? Her double life as a Russian spy? It helped pass the time, this tabulation of troubles real and imagined. It was kind of like spotting out-of-state license plates or counting the number of mileage markers on the highway or keeping a running count of dead bugs on the windshield. It all helped him keep his mind off things, things like what were they even doing on that highway, where were they headed, and why were they headed there.

Chicago seemed like thousands of miles away and another lifetime ago. Nick tried to remember what exactly led him and Esmeralda into this crazy adventure, but the whole thing was already becoming a haze. Was it only a few days ago that he was playing in a South Side blues band? Was he really now running for his life after attempting armed robbery disguised as a ghost? It suddenly occurred to Nick that perhaps *he* was the crazy one in the relationship, a sobering thought when considering his competition. Even Esmeralda had never stooped to "attempting robbery while invisible," a crime so ludicrous it didn't even register in the criminal code.

As Nick drove farther into the barren landscape, he couldn't escape the fact that all of this was merely window dressing for what was really bothering him. And what was really bothering him was that he had no idea what was really bothering him. All he knew was that he'd come back from the war a different person than the one who left. Now, nearly two years had passed and he was still trying to find the missing parts. He vaguely remembered that he once wanted to be somebody—oh, yeah, he was a guy with a dream, a man with a plan—but after Europe he just wanted to get through the day without leaving too big a mess. Today's today, tonight's tonight, and tomorrow's somebody else's problem. So much the better.

The sun began to set over the western mesas. The light shimmered in the clean, clear air and cascaded a warm blanket of yellow, red, and orange over the prairie. Nick pulled the sky around him like a loose sweater and warmed himself to the last moments of daylight. Maybe this was all that life meant. A wisp of a pink cloud hovering against a baby-rattle-blue sky. A flat-topped mesa sinking into the rust-colored sand—

"Uh, Nick?" said Esmeralda, interrupting his reverie.

"Yeah?"

"Do you see what I see?"

Nick glanced down the road and shaded his eyes against the sun. As he adjusted his vision to the harsh light, he saw the silhouettes of a man in a loose-fitting suit, two women in long, shapeless dresses, and a couple of suitcases stacked along the road. "It can't be," he said.

"It is."

"I'm not stopping," he said, jamming on the gas.

"Why not?"

"The guy's a pain."

"I thought he was kinda cute."

"Damn it, Es—"

"Pull over, Nick. Pronto!"

Nick reluctantly pulled over to the side of the road. Jaxson, Marta-2, and Oblivia stood there calmly with their thumbs out, as if nothing were amiss. "Oh, hello," said Jaxson.

"*Hello?*" said Nick, nonplussed. "Is that all you have to say? Isn't it a bit strange that we left you back in Arapahoe and now we run into you 50 miles later on the same road?"

"Yes," said Jaxson, slowly thinking it over. "It's as if you were the only car on the highway. How do you explain that?"

Nick just shook his head and stared over at Esmeralda. "What happened to the train?" she said.

"Well, therein lies quite a tale. There was a minor disagreement—"

"I'll bet—" said Nick.

"A tiny bit of confusion about certain procedures—"

"Sure, it's complicated—" said Esmeralda.

"Some questions about compensation—"

"It's called paying the fare—" said Nick.

"Something about inappropriate behavior—"

"You? No way—" said Esmeralda.

"Charges of improper touching—"

"Look, just get in already!" yelled Nick. "We'll take you to Denver!"

"Really?"

"Yes, really."

"Denver, Colorado?"

"Yes, Denver, Colorado."

"We'll be there by midnight," said Esmeralda, happy to have a little company. She reached over to open the door. "Rocky Mountains, here we come."

The relieved travelers slid into the back seat, taking up their old positions—Marta-2 on one side, Oblivia on the other, and Jaxson in the middle. "Once again, thank you for your kindness," said Marta-2.

"Don't mention it," said Nick as he pulled back on the road.

Jaxson started to say something, then thought better of it and kept it to himself. He leaned back in the air-foam cushioned seat, gazed out at the mountains in the distance, and settled in for the journey. He took comfort in the knowledge that after their brief misadventure, everything was back on track. Train, car, it was all the same. They'd be in Denver before they knew it, and from there it was sure to be a snap. A day or two getting down to business, then time to shake a tail feather. He could almost hear the blues clubs in Denver right now. Jaxson, they beckoned him, won't you come in and play?

Chapter 14

"Energy is an eternal delight, and he who desires, but acts not, breeds pestilence."
—William Blake

C hief Engineer Teller stared at the 654 engine parts and heat shield components he'd disassembled and lined up along the corridor. It was a giant jigsaw puzzle he had laid out before him, except this puzzle was three dimensional and allowed for a geometric increase in the number of possibilities in which Side A of Piece B might fit into Side C of Piece D, right on down the alphabet. Adding to the difficulties, it was completely unclear which piece was which since Teller, in his haste, had neglected to label any of the parts he'd impulsively pulled apart in order to get the show, as he called it, on the road. None of this came as any great surprise to Captain Wambold, who had concluded long ago that Teller couldn't be trusted to do anything but make a mess of things. Petty Officer Raleigh wasn't much better, his Rubik's cube of a brain proving to be useless with spatial relationships unless they were color coded and shiny. Which left Behavioral Psychologist Marta-1 and her bad shoulder to try to mix and match a bunch of gears and valves into some semblance of machinery that would get them the hell off this planet.

"All right," said Wambold, consulting the Pulsar-7 Owner's

Manual, "connect the octahedral combustion joint to the cryptophallic sparking mechanism using the included fallopian wrench."

Marta-1 dug through a half-empty toolbox and came up with some bottle caps, a couple of broken saw blades, and some rusty steel files. "There is no wrench," she said with a measured calmness that indicated she was fast approaching the end of her rope. Behaviorists, after all, were famous for concealing their true temperaments inside a Skinner Box of fake fronts, false bottoms, and phony sides.

"No wrench, you say? Of *course*, there's no wrench," said Wambold. "Why would Reverie Energy think to put a two dollar wrench into a mission designed to save them millions?"

"Lack of discipline is leading us down the path of anarchy," said Teller, quoting an outlawed slogan from the centuries-old Obsidian Reclamationist Party, a collection of nuts, crackpots and screwballs who briefly held power during the Forlorn Years.

"Careful there, Teller," said Raleigh, "people have been court-martialed for less."

"That's why Obsidia is where it is," said Teller, "a mere shadow of its former glory."

"And not a single war in 200 years," said Wambold. "I'd say that's pretty good, wouldn't you?"

"We've lost our edge, Captain. Complacency breeds contempt. Work makes you free."

"Then why don't you see if you can put together a few of those valves?" said Marta-1. "You're just wasting precious time."

Teller haphazardly dug through some sigmoid transponders and walrus bolts. It was anyone's guess where to begin. If only he could get a bunch of Earthlings to slave away day and night—

There was a sudden loud knock that reverberated down the corridor from out of nowhere. "What's that?" said Wambold.

Everyone looked up and listened. There was a second knock, a short delay, then another knock. "I think it's coming from somewhere outside the portal," said Marta-1.

"Outside the portal? What do you mean, outside the portal? Who could be outside the portal?"

"I don't know, Captain. The crew is all present and accounted for, and the expedition is well on its way, so who does that leave?"

"Earthlings?" said Teller, wondering if his prayers had been answered so soon.

"Don't anybody breathe," whispered Wambold, trying his best to hide his anxiety. "Maybe they'll go away."

There was another knock on the door of the spaceship, then three louder, more insistent taps. "Hieronymus Wambold?" a voice echoed out. "Are you in there?"

"Who could possibly know my name?" said Wambold, recoiling in fear.

"Perhaps your legend has preceded you, Captain, even to this faraway outpost," said Marta-1.

"Not bloody likely," said Wambold, ever the realist.

"Captain Hieronymus Wambold!" came the voice, more urgently. "Open the door immediately!"

Wambold jumped to attention and quickly headed down the corridor. The rest of the crew followed close behind, like lemmings to a cliff. When they arrived at the main control area, they stared silently at the door, wondering if they were victims of some kind of mass hallucination.

"We're waiting!" said the voice, breaking the silence. If this was an hallucination, it was an impatient hallucination at that.

Wambold turned the escape valve and cautiously opened the door a crack. There were two people standing on the ledge of the polyprotopulsium ladder. A man and a woman. The guy in a black fedora pulled down over his forehead, almost to his eyes. The woman with red, almost black, lipstick and a cigarette dangling out of her mouth. "Loquacious Landry," said the guy, flipping open a leather case to reveal a badge, an ID number, and an optic scan code.

"Me, I'm Kalamata Quayle," sneered the broad between puffs on her ciggie. "If you haven't guessed who we are by now, you're dumber than we thought."

"You must be from some relief agency—"

"You really *are* dumber than we thought," said Kalamata, looking at him askance. "We're from the Court of Last Resort, bozo. Congratulations. You won the lottery."

Wambold's shoulders noticeably slumped. "We were expecting you," he said.

"No, you weren't," said Landry, eyeing Wambold through the narrow opening. "Now, you gonna invite us in or do we have to kick the door down? We're tired, we're dirty, and we're pissed off. You decide."

Wambold immediately opened the door wide. "No, no, come in, come in. You're most welcome."

"I figured you'd see it our way," said Kalamata as she flicked ashes on the inside doormat. "Nice to know your noggins aren't completely fried."

"Yes... well... can we offer you some refreshments?"

"Sure, Cap, I'll have a scotch on the rocks. Don't skimp on the knockout drops."

"Make mine a double," said Kalamata, pushing her way past Teller and plopping herself down on the closest pod. In the bright light, Wambold could see she was a real looker. He mixed their drinks, then brought them over on a ceremonial platter he'd received years ago from some commission or another. For service above and beyond the call of duty, it said, blah, blah, blah—

"Okay," said Landry, "let's get down to brass tacks. We're the brass and you're the tacks. As in nailed. Which you are. By us. Real smooth move blowing that ship out of the sky. Took some real imagination. No, wait, not imagination. How about brainless stupidity? Which you've got. In spades. Had to dust off the court records to even find a case so outrageous. What did you think? That nobody'd care? That nobody'd notice? Takes my breath away. How dumb you are."

"Don't you even want to hear our side of the story?" said Wambold, shrinking in the face of the facts.

"You've *got* a side?" said Landry. "I don't think so. I think you've got nothing but a rabbit in your hat. Go ahead. Pull it out. Amaze us."

Wambold shuffled his feet and stared at his empty hands.

"Just like I thought," continued Landry. "No rabbit. How about a dove? You got a dove? Nope, no doves. No doves, no unicorns, no three-headed snakes. So, that's it, boys and girls. Case closed. Guilty as charged."

"I take full responsibility," said Wambold, manning up.

"No!" said Marta-1, rushing over to his defense. "It was all Teller's fault!"

Kalamata put up her hand like a giant stop sign. "Take a breather, sister," she said. "We'll take over from here. Don't get your panties all twisted out of shape."

"I refuse to see Captain Wambold charged with actions for which he was not responsible!"

Kalamata knocked back her drink and held out the glass. "Tell you what, sweetheart," she said, squeezing Marta-1 on her tush, "why don't you be a dear and top this off. Leave the legalities to the pros."

Marta-1 took the glass, filled it to the brim, handed it back to Kalamata, and shrunk into the shadows.

Landry paged through a sheaf of court orders. "Says here your unprovoked, deadly assault on a peaceful interplanetary aircraft requires a full investigation which, I think we all agree, has now been completed."

"That was quick," said Wambold.

"There is still a matter of even greater concern, that being your wanton disregard for orders requiring you to remain in

Earth orbit until further notice." Landry looked up from his rote reading of the orders and added some genuine, full-bodied sarcasm. "Imagine our surprise to find no one there at all, no welcoming committee, no forwarding address, no nothing."

"I can explain," said Wambold.

"No you can't," said Kalamata. "There *is* no explanation for disobeying direct orders from the Court of Last Resort. You might as well have painted a big mural in the sky with a stiff middle finger that said fuck you and your mother."

Teller had been listening quietly at the edge of the conversation but all this talk of order and duty set off a mother lode of repressed anger that would've shaken the rafters, if only the Pulsar-7 *had* any rafters. "What about the aphelion and perihelion of Earth's orbit?" he screamed out. "Those geniuses at mission command never accounted for that, did they? Seven days to complete our mission? Are they kidding? I say, shove it!"

"Shove it?" said Landry to Kalamata. "Did he say, shove it?"

"I think he said, shove it," said Kalamata.

Landry calmly pulled out a magnetic schiller, pointed it at Teller's chest, and squeezed the trigger. Teller shook twice, then exploded into 16 separate body parts that bounced off the rear wall and crumpled into a pile of discombobulated flesh and bones.

"Teller?" said Raleigh, staring into an eyeball that was lodged between a finger and big toe. "Is that you?"

"He'll be all right," said Landry.

"Okay, everybody needs to just calm down," said Kalamata. "I see here that seven crew members were assigned to this mission. Now, arithmetic was never my favorite subject, but my fingers tell me there's only four of you here which—wait, I've almost got it—tells me that we're missing three of you. Is that right, angel face?" she said, turning back to Marta-1 and giving her a big wink.

"Yes, well, three is probably the correct number."

"And I'm just going to guess that since the three aren't here, they must be somewhere close-by, like maybe hiding in the laundry room?"

"Something like that."

Kalamata ran her tongue around the outer edge of her glass, then walked slowly over to Marta-1. She studied her from head to toe, then came a little closer, leaned over, and kissed her full on the lips. "Where are they, honey?"

Marta-1 felt her knees go limp as her spine tingled from the base of her neck right down to the tip of her ass. She finally came out of the kiss with a dreamy swoon. "Denver," she said, without giving it another thought.

"You could have resisted," muttered Raleigh under his breath.

Landry's face reddened with the realization that their job wasn't complete after all. He grabbed Raleigh by the nape of his neck and pulled him right off the floor. "What's happening in Denver?" he said, leaving no room for any resistance whatsoever.

"It has been said that in Denver one can see to the end of time," said Raleigh, wisely choosing discretion over valor.

"I see," said Landry, dropping Raleigh to the ground. "So, not only did you disobey orders to remain in Earth orbit, you disobeyed orders to suspend all experiments until further notice."

"Now, look here, man," said Wambold, trying to reassert his authority, "the aphelion and the perihelion demanded that—"

"Enough!" said Landry. "I want their names! I want their locations! I want their asses back on this ship before night-fall!"

"That's pretty unlikely," said Wambold, pointing out the portal to the setting sun.

Landry closed his eyes for a moment, then turned to

Kalamata. "All I wanted was to get a good buzz-on," he said, finishing off the scotch. "Halfway across the universe and we're still not finished. You ready?"

"Ready as I'll ever be," said Kalamata. She straightened her nylons, pulled her double-breasted jacket closed, and touched up her lipstick. "Don't go anywhere," she said to Marta-1.

"I won't," said Marta-1 with the hint of a smile.

Kalamata gave her a knowing look, then followed Landry out the door, down the polyprotopulsium ladder, and into the night.

Chapter 15

*"Our truest life is when we
are in dreams awake."*
—Henry David Thoreau

The foothills of the Rocky Mountains rose up, up, and
up, leaving Jaxson, Marta-2, and Oblivia light-headed
and a little loopy in the back seat of the Hudson.
Obsidians were more susceptible to oxygen deprivation than
Earthlings, and they responded by laughing uncontrollably
at virtually anything Nick or Esmeralda said. At first it was
kind of amusing—this addictive giggling that passed from
seat to seat—but Nick soon tired of it, especially when they
passed an army convoy that elicited completely unprovoked
howls of laughter. There were a half dozen trucks painted
standard khaki green, with military insignias, unit numbers,
motor pool designations, and the words "Roswell Air Base"
stenciled across the doors. In the middle of the cavalcade
was a larger flat truck with flashing warning lights, red caution flags, and an "Oversized Load" sign. An unusual-shaped
object was tied down to the trailer and covered with tarps
that snapped sharply in the wind. One of the tarps blew back
slightly to expose what could have been the wing of an air-
plane were it not so large.

"Will you look at that," said Esmeralda, turning to look as
they passed it on the road.

"I never saw anything like that back on my base," said Nick. "I don't know how they'd even get something that big into the air."

Another section of tarp was breeched by a funnel-shaped device that glowed slightly in the mountain air. When Jaxson caught sight of the dull, translucent observation port, he nearly fell over laughing. Whether this was because of oxygen deprivation or just plain nervousness was hard to say. Jaxson had absolutely no idea why he was laughing—there was nothing funny at all about seeing the crumbled spaceship—but laugh he did, uncontrollably and hysterically, and the infectious giggle soon passed to Marta-2 and then to Oblivia until tears poured from their eyes. *Oh God, it's the funniest thing I've ever seen, wait a minute, hold on, I can't take it anymore, I'm gonna split a gut—*

The Hudson traversed a High Plains mountain pass, then slowly descended into the South Platte River Valley, where the lights of Denver shone in the distance. The terrain transformed from the barren surroundings of the outlying townships to the neatly planned developments of the suburbs to the burgeoning bustle of the urban center. They arrived not a moment too soon as far as Nick was concerned, even if it was too late to do anything but find a place to bed down for the night. All he cared about was getting away from the incessant jokes, witless wisecracks, and nonstop merriment emanating from the back seat. He stopped at the Cameron Motel on Colfax Avenue, the first place that flashed a neon vacancy sign, and checked in so fast he barely got the car doors closed.

"Well, sleep tight," said Jaxson, calling from the back seat.

"Yeah, yeah," said Nick, disappearing with Esmeralda into their room.

Jaxson was excited to spend his first night in an Earthy motel—Earthian? Earthly? Eartherial?—but the Cameron was nothing to write home about. Despite being located on the lively tourist strip of downtown Denver, the rooms defied any sense of fun with their drab walls, cottage cheese ceilings, and musty carpets. He was surprised to find that his quarters offered nary a hyperbolic heat chamber, facial demoleculizer, or foot pod stabilizer to rekindle his precious fluids after a long day traversing the highways and byways of America. As for late night entertainment, the Cameron simply wasn't on the circuit, be it blues, comedy, or ballroom dancing. There was no nightclub, no lounge, no bar—nothing at all but an ice machine and candy dispenser.

Jaxson had a room to himself since the manager refused to place him with two women—the Cameron being a family motel and all—so Marta-2 and Oblivia took the double room at the corner, Nick and Esmeralda took the double at the end of the hall, and Jaxson lounged in his own double right between them. He felt like the lettuce leaf in a sub-Subian club sandwich.

Jaxson had hoped to catch at least a few numbers at some local dive before turning in, but his exploration of American night life would have to wait another day. Instead, he slipped into his jammies, nestled into the oversized pillows of the big double bed, flicked on the night light, and glanced around at his new temporary quarters. If there had ever been a question, he could now definitely confirm that he was on Earth. Huzzah and hurray! He didn't miss for a moment his cramped bunk space on the Pulsar-7, nor Teller's incessant snoring, nor the Captain's pacing throughout the night. Speaking of which, he reminded himself to turn off his wrist-top communication module, since the last thing he needed was to be awakened in the middle of the night by an urgent message from the ship regarding some missed protocol or another.

Jaxson was too excited to sleep, so he amused himself with a Gideon Bible that was sitting on his nightstand. It was all very humorous reading, especially since God, as everyone on Obsidia knew, did not exist, at least not in the way they imagined him on Earth. God wasn't a person, or an essence, or a force—God was a dimension somewhere beyond length, width, depth, and purpose where all worldly assumptions were gloriously refuted and stacked end to end in a giant slinky that boinged around the universe. Jaxson loved the Earthling's attempts to personify God, be it a man on a cross, a 12-armed dancing girl, a boy with the head of an elephant, or an old guy with beady eyes and a white beard. The closest they'd come to getting it right was one of those 8-foot scarecrows he'd seen propped up in the middle of a cornfield in Nebraska. The thing looked downright insane, with bulging eyes, a crooked smile, and arms that flailed wildly in the wind. Nobody paid him any attention—how Godly can you get?—not even a large black crow that had been circling overhead and landed right on his head as if daring him to do something really, really wrathful. Scarecrow, indeed. But that's God for you, he just stood there and took it, reveling in the indignity of it all as the bird took off for a convertible cruising down the highway. The scarecrow never blinked. He just watched and waited and worked his charms in ever mysterious ways.

Jaxson fell asleep with the open Bible on his lap, nodding off to a wildly entertaining passage about a plague of frogs, lice, flies, and locusts. Hadn't he just been through all of that on the train to McCook? He dreamt he was back on that train as it clickety-clacked through the plains. His compartment had been converted into a sleeper unit and his eyelids were getting heavy with the rolling of the wheels and the swaying of the car when he felt the train came to a sudden stop. He looked outside to see that Marta-1 had flagged it down with an urgent romantic request: "Stop this train in the name of love! My man's inside and I won't be denied!" Jaxson dreamt that Marta-1 climbed inside his sleeper and cuddled up next to him in the cool Colorado night. The train rose into the foothills of the Rockies, chugged through dark mountain tunnels, rose and fell through undulating passes, up, down, up, down, they rolled through precipitous rocky crags, steel wheels churning, coal furnace crackling, engine chugging, Jaxson breathing heavily, Marta-1 holding him tight, whistles blowing, headlights flashing, the train shaking to the passions of an explosive burst of steam lighting up the sky.

In the room next door, Marta-2 trailed off into her own dream world. She was backstage at a sold-out concert, looking out over a cheering audience that simply couldn't get enough of Jaxson Epsilon and His Obsidian Blues All-Stars. She was holding his harmonicas, an avid fan who couldn't get enough of Jaxson, either. She could simply drink him up and savor the aftertaste forever. He was a shot of fine hablum that warmed her throat, a soft incandescent light that illuminated the corners of her heart, a burst of warm air on a cold winter's night, a romantic hero aching to take center stage in her unwritten love story. Jaxson played a soaring melody, accented it with a burst of heavenly notes, then left the stage and came right over to her. They were in a haze—just the two of them among a crowd of thousands, the two of them holding each other, looking deeply into each other's eyes, heading off into the warm, sparkling night.

Esmeralda dreamt of a vineyard. She was walking through a row of vines, picking ripe, luscious grapes, when a flock of chickens appeared, took her by the hand, and transported her to another world. These weren't everyday, garden variety, henhouse chickens, no, these were dancing chickens and they were dancing across the stage of Radio City Music Hall. There were 20 of them, maybe more, with bright red lipstick painted on their beaks and thick eyeliner etched around their eyes. They wore low-cut tops revealing top grade breast meat and skimpy skirts showing off their juicy thighs. They kicked their legs high in a precision dance routine, then flapped their wings into a giant sequined fan that undulated across the stage. More chickens joined the line as they broke into a six-pointed star, a daisy, and a diamond, and then they formed two dance lines which slowly separated to reveal the star of the show—Esmeralda Kurlansky, herself—dressed in feathers from head to toe. The spotlights were on her alone, the sexiest chicken ever to spank these hallowed planks. The orchestra blasted a punchy riff, the dancers spread their wings, and Esmeralda rose to the balcony on a hydraulic lift shaking a tail feather and wiggling her tush. It was Esmeralda Kurlansky on stage at last, right where she was always meant to be.

Oblivia, too, was lost in her own dream. She was a swatch of color orbiting a field of bubbles and she felt little effervescent pops as she zinged from one magnetic field to another. She was a champagne glass on New Year's Eve sparkling in the neon light, she was a babbling brook rippling down the side of a mountain, she was a hot lava stew gurgling in the pit of a volcano, she was an underwater vent fizzing beneath the tide, she was a thin film of soap wafting into the sky, she was a piece of Wrigley's Chewing Gum splattering on a child's cheek.

Nick dreamt the same dream he dreamt every night. Foxholes, rain, and mud. Airplanes, cannons, and machine guns. Groans, blood, and boots on the ground. And then, as always, something burningly hot ripping through his leg, shaking him from his slumber, jolting him wide awake—

The Denver Western Union office was conveniently located just a couple of blocks down Colfax Avenue from the Cameron Motel. Jaxson was waiting at the door when it opened and when he went in, it was like entering a museum of archaic equipment. On display was an unwieldy collection of telephone wires, telegraph machines, and Morse code pads that would've brought a pretty penny in an Obsidian antique store. Another guy in another visor—just like the ticket agent at the train station—was running the place and it intrigued him, this visor, as Jaxson could find no practical use whatsoever for the short brim and adjustable strap. It looked cool, though, and Jaxson made a mental note to get himself one before heading back to Obsidia. If he was going to form a blues band, he needed to look authentic.

Jaxson pulled out a wallet full of fake identification that had been prepared back home for moments just like these. He'd found a guy named Blacky in the Outer Realms who whipped up a driver's license, a birth certificate, and a social security card to make him look more American than most Americans. Blacky's associate, Shorty, had tapped into New York Bankers Trust and created a bogus account for Jaxson with unlimited funds. It was laughably easy to hack into a system that was only now discovering computers, and Shorty could have just as easily brought down the whole financial system with a couple of taps on his keyboard if he were so inclined. Actually, he *was* so inclined, but Blacky got him to back off before there was an intergalactic incident. That, after all, was what got them sent to the Outer Realms in the first place.

Jaxson studied a few forms and tried to figure out what information went where. Forms weren't his thing—forms being loaded with numbers—and numbers were nothing but a sad reminder of the Institute for Applied Learning and all of its arcane formulas. No matter, he had to figure out how much money to withdraw, and having paid no attention to the cost of things on Earth, he had no idea what to request. All he needed was enough to pay for a couple of nights at the motel, a few dinners, and a bit for incidentals. He jotted down the first number that came into his mind.

"Two thousand dollars?" said the clerk with a surprised look when he glanced at Jaxson's withdrawal request.

"Is that enough?" said Jaxson.

"That's more than enough, friend, unless you're planning on buying a house. I'm not even sure we've got that much on hand."

"A little more or a little less doesn't matter. Whatever you've got will be fine."

"Uh-huh," said the clerk, looking at Jaxson out of the corner of his eye as he tapped in the telegraph order. "Have a seat. This'll take a while."

Jaxson sat down and glanced around the office. There was a portrait of a chap named Harry S. Truman, a photograph of the Denver skyline, and not much else. The occasional clicks of the keypad kept him occupied for a few minutes, but he soon tired of the tedium of Morse code. Luckily, there was a magazine rack in the corner with the very latest issue of *Life Magazine*. Perfect. He could do some first hand research into the zeitgeist of the times and make it seem to the folks back home that he was actually doing something. Jaxson paged through the glossy magazine and made some important discoveries: rayon blouses were big this season, as were stacked heels and long-playing records... vodka martinis were popular, along with Ipana toothpaste and *Miracle on 34th Street*... Pablo Picasso, weekends at Cape Cod, and Kool cigarettes went well together... Waterford Crystal, Seagram's Seven Crown Whiskey, and Ajax Cleanser left a good impression... Marilyn Monroe, Albert Camus, and Jackie Robinson made good dinner guests... Instant Sanka, Minute Maid Frozen Orange Juice, and Reddi-wip couldn't be beat... Bugsy Siegel, the Hollywood Black List, and *A Streetcar Named Desire* were good topics of conversation... Harley-Davidson motorcycle jackets, plastic lenses, and Eames side chairs were absolute winners—

"Mr. Epsilon?" called the clerk from the counter. "Your transfer is here."

"That was fast."

"You're in luck. The wires must be good and greased up today. How do you want it, tens or twenties?"

"Whatever you've got will be fine."

"You keep saying that."

"I don't like making waves," said Jaxson, coolly running his hand over an imaginary ocean.

The clerk, ignoring the hipster jive, walked over to the safe and counted out some stacks of currency. "You're cleaning out my till, friend, hope you know that."

"I can leave you some, if that would help."

The clerk took another long look at Jaxson, taking note of the old-fashioned suit, the high-collared shirt, and the pocket watch on a chain. "Tell you what, Mr. Epsilon, why don't you just take this money and go straight to wherever it is you're going. Don't stop and talk to anyone, know what I mean? No drinks at the bar. No games of dice. No betting on the horses."

"Smooth," said Jaxson, as he stuffed the money into his pockets and exited the office posthaste.

"Real smooth," replied the clerk, watching as Jaxson turned right, stopped, looked around, scratched his head, turned left, and headed back along Colfax Avenue.

Oblivia stared into a plate of hash browns, toast, and runny eggs, not knowing whether to eat them, drink them, or rub them on her face. Marta-2 watched her nervously, hoping she wouldn't make a spectacle of herself. "Try the toast," she said. "You just put it in your mouth and chew it."

Esmeralda sat across from them in a booth at McVittie's Restaurant, a diner down the street from their motel, watching the weird scene unfold. She knew Oblivia was an oddball, but did she really not know how to eat? "So," she said, searching for something to say, "did you sleep okay?"

"Oh, yes, very well," said Marta-2. "I had some lovely dreams."

"It's the mountain air. Cleans out the cobwebs in the old braineroo."

"I do feel just the slightest bit lightheaded."

"Cuppa joe will take care of that. Only thing that works after a night of knocking 'em back... oh, right," said Esmeralda, catching herself. "I forgot. I guess you don't do that."

"Well, I don't make it a habit."

Esmeralda motioned to the waitress for a refill of coffee. "I gotta tell you, it's good to get away from the fellas for a few minutes. I couldn't move Nick out of bed this morning with a pitchfork."

"I'm sure he could use the rest. Driving a car seems like quite a source of endomorphic fatigue."

"No, no, my Nicky's not into morphine. Hell, no."

Marta-2 glanced up at the clock on the wall. "Jaxson should be back any time now."

"So, let me ask you something," said Esmeralda. "You and Jaxson, are you an item?"

"Oh, no," said Marta-2, "we're just colleagues."

"I see. Colleagues. What is it you do exactly?"

"We're in a new field of study exploring the possibility of energy transference at megaphysical levels."

"Uh-huh," said Esmeralda, not understanding a word. "Sounds complicated."

"Oh, yes, it is," said Marta-2. "Very complicated, indeed."

"But you and Jaxson," said Esmeralda, returning to more familiar territory. "I see the way you look at him."

"It's nothing," said Marta-2, blushing profusely. "He doesn't even notice me."

"Men are a funny breed. They either can't get what they want or they don't want what they can get. It's up to us to get them so confused they can't tell the difference."

"You sure know a lot about men. I've never really been very lucky with the male of the species."

"You see, that's the problem. They're not "the male of the species." They're suckers, mugs, goons, punks, eggs, geese, greasers, hombres, jaspers, and palookas. You gotta see them for what they are."

Marta-2 nodded in appreciation of Esmeralda's insights. "I sure wish I had some of your pizzazz."

"Look, honey, if pizzazz came in bottles, they'd be selling me by the ounce. But that doesn't mean I've got an exclusive on the stuff. You hang out with me long enough, some of it just might rub off."

"That would be swell."

Esmeralda sat back and looked at Marta-2 and Oblivia in the morning light. The morning light, much like the afternoon light and evening light, did them no favors. They looked like 19th century missionaries working the outer banks of the Amazon. "Let me ask you something," she said, mustering up all the subtlety she was capable of. "This, uh, this dress you're wearing, how attached to it are you?"

"This thing? Oh, not really at all. It was just kind of there."

"I see," said Esmeralda. "And your friend here?"

"I'm afraid that Oblivia doesn't have much of an opinion about fashion. Or food. Or footwear. Or—"

"Tell you what. What do you say we gals go shopping downtown? We'll just kind of look around a bit. I know you're not too flush, but maybe we could find something that wouldn't break the bank."

"Sounds like fun. Doesn't it, Oblivia?"

Oblivia craned her neck like a bird listening for worms. It was hard to say if she was nodding yes, no, or maybe. Maybe she was simply eyeing Jaxson, who entered the restaurant from one door and Nick, who entered from another. They nearly bumped into each other as they searched the crowded room for Marta-2 and Esmeralda. They wove their way between Formica tables and Naughahyde seats before finally spotting their booth... and each other. "Man, what a town!" said Jaxson, plopping himself down.

"Did you find Western Union all right?" said Esmeralda.

"More than all right. The place is totally aces. You tell them what you want and just like that, there it is."

"It's a real miracle," said Nick, sliding across from him into the booth. It was hard to say if he was referring to the miracle of Jaxson finding the place or to the miracle of Jaxson actually having some money in a bank.

"Tell you what," said Esmeralda. "How about you two fellas entertain yourselves for a couple of hours." she said. "We're going to explore a little."

"Me and him?" said Nick, shifting uncomfortably in the booth. "What are we going to do?"

"I don't know, sweetheart. You'll figure it out."

"But, Es—"

The women got up and gathered their things. "You might need this," said Jaxson, reaching into his pocket and handing Marta-2 a couple stacks of twenties.

"Oh, yes, this would be necessary in case of barter opportunities."

Esmeralda looked at the wad of money with wide eyes. "We'll meet you boys back at the motel."

"Have fun," said Jaxson.

"Yeah, have fun," said Nick.

The women left the two of them sitting in the booth, looking forlorn. Nick studied his fingernails. Jaxson contemplated the ceiling tiles. Nick finally broke the silence. "You play pool?" he said.

"Sure," said Jaxson, glad that he'd brought his swimming suit after all.

Nick left a couple of bucks on the table and got up. "Let's blow this joint."

Jaxson tossed down a couple bucks of his own and followed his lead. "Yeah, let's hit it."

Chapter 16

*"A bad rendition of you is better than
a good rendition of somebody else."*
—Willie Dixon

Daniels and Fisher Department Store had just about everything Esmeralda could imagine. Denver wasn't a hick town like Des Moines or Omaha or all those other two-bit truck stops they'd been in since Chicago, no, this was the real deal, a real store with a half dozen floors, and a tower that climbed to the sky, and elevators operated by guys in gloves, and escalators with rubber railings, and big broad aisles that let you breathe, and chandeliers made from real crystal, and plush carpets that stretched from wall to wall, and whole departments with nothing but shoes, oh, yes, shoes of every imaginable variety, high heels, low heels, medium heels, no heels at all, shoes and boots and dresses made of silk and cotton and linen, not to mention nylons—*see these, girls?*—shoes and boots and nylons and gloves and jackets and coats and hats—big playful hats that angled this way and that—and cute little things you wore to the side, and casual robes to lounge around in when you didn't feel like doing anything at all, and frilly little dresses just for the hell of it, and fancy dresses for entertaining, and a whole section of silk nighties and teddies with red bows and blue buttons, and—*oh, my!*—Christian Dior's new collection of billowing skirts and nipped-in waists with the laciest lace and the silkiest silk—bodices, corsets, and petticoats with high-heeled shoes and chiffon gloves—and the colors, why, these were colors that made a Gypsy heart sing! They were the colors of an expanding universe and it was expanding right before their eyes. "I think I've died and gone to heaven," said Esmeralda.

"So, you think this apparel is more in keeping with the fashions of the times than what we have on?" said Marta-2.

"No offense, honey, but a burlap bag is more fashionable than what you have on."

"Yes, I see," said Marta-2, running her fingers through a chiffon petticoat. "The absorbency quotient of the fabric and the sequential shape analysis of the thread would allow the material to adhere to the body with more of a draping effect."

"Yeah, that's right, your boobs will bounce and your hips will swing, instead of the other way around."

"And that is preferable?"

"That all depends on whether you're trying to attract a man or a swarm of flies."

"Well, if you put it that way," said Marta-2, blushing. She peeked at the price tag with a look of concern. "Is it expensive?"

"Sure, it's expensive. It's crazy expensive. How are you feeling? Adventurous?"

"I believe so," said Marta-2, doing a quick analysis of her enthusiasm to risk quotient. "You only live once, isn't that what they say?"

"That's *exactly* what they say."

"Then let's do it!"

Pederson's Poolhall, a joint on 15th Street and Glenarm, was just a stone's throw from the Cameron Motel, especially if the stone was thin and light and skimmed over the surface of the street without scratching too many car doors. Pederson's had four tables, each crummier than the next, with ripped felt, uneven surfaces, and irregular rail cushions. That didn't stop Nick, who was desperate for any distraction whatsoever, and Jaxson, who didn't know the difference between eight ball, nine ball, straight pool, and dirty pool. Nick racked the balls and hit a break shot that scattered cleanly over the table. The three ball fell in on the break and he followed with the two and seven before missing the six. Jaxson, more intrigued by the various customs surrounding the game than the game itself, applied some chalk to the tip of his cue—just as Nick had done—then bent over, formed a nice bridge with his fingers, and blasted the ball right across the poolhall. "Are you trying to kill somebody?" said Nick, leaping out of the way.

"Sorry," said Jaxson, "I gave it a bit too much ketchup."

"The expression is *mustard,* and any more mustard than that gets us thrown right the hell out of here."

"So, the object of the game is to hit the ball into the hole?"

"That's the object. It's all angles, spin, and English."

"I see," said Jaxson, summoning up trace memories from his days of arm wrestling with lower mathematics. "So, for example, that yellow ball with the stripe, it is obviously lying at a 37 degree angle to the plain from the white ball."

"Obviously."

"And if I were to tap the ball to the lower left with a bit of pulling action, the cue ball would return about eight inches and set up an easy shot on the green ball?"

"Uh, yeah," said Nick.

Two guys in T-shirts and tight jeans watched with interest. "Hey, you guys up for a game of doubles?" said one of them as they ambled over.

Nick knew a hustle when he saw one, but before he could beg off, Jaxson burst in. "Sure, love to!" he said, eager to expand his network of American hipsters and these guys looked positively cooler than cool. One of them was well-muscled, slouched a little to one side, and had a crooked nose that looked like it had been broken in more than one fight. The other was a bit shorter, with dark brown hair that fell over his forehead, and a handsome face that radiated a kind of otherworldliness.

"What do you say a friendly little game for, oh, I don't know, two bucks and a pitcher of beer?" said the taller of the two.

"Sounds good," said Jaxson, reaching out his hand to shake. "I'm Jaxson. That's Nick."

"I'm Neal. That's Jack."

"That's funny," said Jaxson. "Nick and Neal, Jaxson and Jack."

"How about that beer?" said Neal. "Pabst suit you boys?"

"Sure," said Jaxson, "I drink nothing but Pabst in the morning."

"Hey, Pete," called Neal to the bartender. "Send over a pitcher."

Neal racked the balls with a wooden triangle, wedging his fingers inside to get a tight rack. Nick could tell right away that he knew what he was doing. Big surprise. The only question was how much they would lose and how fast they would lose it. "Eight ball?" said Neal. "Lag for the break?" He set up the cue ball, tapped it against the rail, and watched as it rolled to a stop just a few inches from his hand. Nick conceded the break and stood back as Neal lined up his shot. "You guys from around here?" said Neal.

"Just passing through," said Nick. "I'm heading for California. Wild man here is going back to wherever."

"Road warriors, you say? I like that. Me, Denver's my home but it doesn't take much to get me going this way or that. New York, Mexico, California, just put me behind the wheel. Never know who you'll meet out there, that's what I like, not knowing, just keep on going, see what lies around the next bend." Neal looked over at Jaxson, who was studying the table, trying to figure out what was going on. "What about you, Slick?"

"I'm from out there," said Jaxson, pointing out the window to somewhere beyond the great American beyond.

"Sure, sure, *out there*," said Neal. "There's where Jack's from. *Way* out there. Isn't that right, Jack?"

"That's right."

"Four in the corner," said Neal, lining up a shot. "Now, you see, California has it all. The ocean, the mountains, the deserts, what more do you want? And chicks. Man, those blonds won't leave you alone for ten minutes."

"You don't say," said Jaxson.

"I *do* say," said Neal, knocking in the ball. "Jack's headed for California, ain't that right?"

"That's what my bus ticket says. East coast to west coast with ten days in Denver with my pal Neal."

The bartender came by and dropped off a pitcher of Pabst and four glasses. He barely got back to the bar before Neal called to him, "Pete, pour another." Neal downed a glass in one long gulp, then bent over a little glassy eyed and missed his next shot by a good three inches. "Damn it. You guys see that cushion move?"

Nick put in a shot, missed the next, and left Jack with the cue ball kissing the rail. Jack hit a carom shot that circled the table and just missed dropping the seven in the corner. With Jaxson up next, everyone stood back and guarded their heads and testicles. He pretended not to notice, especially when his dreaded days at the Institute of Applied Learning unexpect-edly rumbled to the front of his mind, the long hours of geometry and trigonometry making a most unusual payoff as he studied the arrangement of balls. "Six in the side," he said, as he smoothly stroked the ball in. "Two in the corner... five off the rail... nine in the side." The others watched in wonder as Jaxson cleared the table. After knocking in the eight ball on a near impossible double rail shot, he rubbed some chalk on his cue and calmly looked up. "Another game?"

Neal and Jack decided they'd had enough pool for the day and retreated to their table in the corner. Nick and Jaxson joined them, pushing aside ashtrays, newspapers, and a pile of manuscript paper. Jaxson caught the title on the cover page: *The Town and the City, by Jack Kerouac.* "Is it yours?" he said to Jack. "Some kind of personal log?"

"Something like that."

"How do you like that?" said Jaxson. "I write a log, too!"

"You don't say."

"I *do* say. Man, I'll tell you, it never ends."

"Tell me about it."

"Well, it's about my experiences—"

"No, no, I don't want you to *tell* me about it."

"Can I have a look?" said Jaxson, running his thumb along the stack of pages.

"If you must."

As Jaxson began reading the manuscript, Nick leaned back and savored the few moments of relative calm. It didn't last long. The bartender brought over another pitcher and everybody raised their glasses. Neal and Jack were old hands at the game and looked like they were just getting started. Jaxson, drinking as if it was hablum happy hour, felt the room beginning to spin but assumed it was some kind of Earthly orbital aberration and just kept on going. Nick, feeling dizzier than he could remember, wasn't that big of a drinker to begin with, especially not at this hour, and the Denver altitude only made him more lightheaded. What was he doing drunk before noon in a poolhall with two hipsters and a 19th century pool shark who was full of endless surprises? "Life is crazy," he mumbled into his beer.

"Crazy and sweet and wild," said Neal, knocking back his drink. "Who knows what's coming next, nobody, it's all a big, glorious mystery, right, Jack?"

"That's right," said Jack, draining his glass and matching Neal drink for drink. "It's a big mystery and we're just along for the ride." He poured another round and leaned across the table with a twinkle in his eye. "Look out that window, look at those mountains, it's the mountains of America stretching from the lakes to the deserts, it's a jazzy bebop riff of undulating crests and valleys, an endless horizon that rises and falls to the beat of the universe, I tell you, man, I can hear it, I can hear saxophones in those mountains, bop-de-bop-de-bop, they're off on a wild solo, tossing boulders off the peaks, big volcanic explosions burning red hot and sizzling, it's the rhythm of nature itself, it's the flow of rivers bursting from their banks, it's the mist of clouds hanging low in the sky, it's the breath of air so fresh it will burst your lungs, it's a long vibrating pulsating trembling solo that shakes the rafters and eats right into the soul and pulls us along, every one of us, it pulls us down a jaggy jazzy road and drops us off on a precipice that looks out past life and death and into the womb of eternity itself."

Jaxson looked up from the manuscript, nodding his head to the rhythms of Jack's extemporaneous riff. "Oh, yeah, daddy longlegs," he said. "Our man Jack Kerouac telling it like it is. I dig your jive."

"Oh, you do, do you?"

"It's fresh and clean like the brisk mountain air," said Jaxson, digging deep into his memory bank for all the hipster slang he could remember from *Hartnell & Slipshod's Dictionary of Idiomatic American English.* "I'll tell you, it spins me right out there into the ozone."

"You hear that, Neal? Our writer friend is hip to the word. An aficionado of fine nouns and finer verbs."

"Oh, yeah, I dig the whole package," said Jaxson, still tapping his fingers to the beat and knocking back another drink. "The rhythm and the rhyme, it's like a slow cool blues on a long hot night. That's how you should write."

Jack grew deadly quiet. He put down his glass, unsure whether to feel flattered or offended. "What's that supposed to mean?" he said, looking Jaxson straight in the eye.

The alcohol had loosened Jaxson's tongue and there was no going back. "Look," he said, paging through the manuscript, "this book of yours is good, but it's a *book*, know what I mean, it's a book like everybody else writes. I put it down as soon as you started talking. *That's* where the magic is."

"You don't say," said Jack, half-irritated and half-intrigued.

"I *do* say—"

"Don't mind him," said Nick, interceding. "He likes to get under your skin."

"No, I want to hear it. Tell me, Mr. Critic, how should I write?"

"Like before. Spontaneous. Off the cuff. Impassioned."

"You hear that, Neal?" said Jack, laughing. "Jaxson here is giving me permission to get jiggy and jazzy and break the rules."

"You listen to him, Jack," said Neal. "This guy speaks the truth."

"I've been writing like that for years," said Jaxson, polishing off another beer. "Real loosey-goosey. Feel free to run with it, Jack, I won't sue you. You just need to let go and tap into what the universe is telling you. Just say whatever's on your mind."

Jack swilled another drink. He was drunk now, tottering at the edge of the table. "If I said what I *really* thought, if I was *really* spontaneous, the whole damn world would stop spinning."

"Do it, then!" said Jaxson. "Shake it up, baby! Take it to the edge!"

"Better quit while you're ahead," whispered Nick as he leaned over and shot Jaxson a look that could've frozen the obtanium deposits on Anterom.

Jaxson didn't want to miss a word, but he felt the call of nature. "Sorry, fellas. Gotta take a whizz." He pushed back from the table and stumbled uncertainly toward the men's room. His face was flushed and his fingers tingled. He tried to remember the sensation. Oh, right, that's what it was like to feel *good*. He laughed at the simplicity of his discovery, then he laughed at the "Gents" sign on the bathroom door, he laughed at his reflection in the mirror, he laughed at the porcelain urinal, he laughed at the zipper on his baggy pants, he laughed at the river of pee filling the tank, he laughed at the hot water faucet that didn't work, he laughed at the cold water faucet that did, he laughed at the liquid soap container, he laughed at the paper towel dispenser, and he laughed at the wrist-top module he'd forgotten to turn on that morning. And then he stopped laughing. There were 94 messages from Captain Wambold and the title of each was:

URGENT. CONTACT IMMEDIATELY.

Something was up, that was for sure. Ninety-four messages? All the same? Wasn't that a bit excessive? Jaxson pined for the good old days of Western Union when a telegram took long enough for you to gather your thoughts, but the text pulse he sent to Wambold came back so fast it almost made his head spin.

ABORT MISSION. RETURN IMMEDIATELY.
COURT OF LAST RESORT EN ROUTE
TO DENVER. GET OUT NOW.

This was bad, worse than he thought. This was so bad it knocked the buzz right out of his head and sobered him up so quickly his neurons nearly snapped. Jaxson returned to the table, feeling deflated. The buzz was gone, the tingle was gone, and the warm glow of feeling good was dead and gone. All that was left was a feeling of terrible disappointment. "Nick," he said under his breath, "think we can go back to the motel?"

Nick looked up at him with heavy eyes. "Yeah, I'm not feeling so hot myself."

As Nick got up, Neal looked up from his glass and Jack rustled himself from his own thoughts. "Leaving so soon?" said Jack.

"Never stay in one place too long," said Jaxson.

They watched as Jaxson walked to the door. "That cat's got it down," said Neal. "What did he say? Write like you speak?"

"Something like that."

"That's the best damn advice anybody ever gave you, if you ask me."

"Maybe so," said Jack, pouring another drink. "Maybe so."

Jaxson opened his suitcase and tossed in his cold fusion razor, protopulsic toothbrush, and restabilizing soap powder. He didn't have much to pack but what he had was enough to weigh him down with the deep regret of a mission gone awry. To have come all the way to Earth and not even seen a single blues concert was disappointing in the extreme. What would he tell his friends back home? That he couldn't find a club? That he couldn't get a ticket? That they wouldn't let him in? There was also the little matter of the reason the rest of the crew was there—the dream experiment—and that bothered him as well. Not as much as the blues fiasco, maybe, but enough to give him a good case of professional remorse. Maybe he'd write about it one day. Sure, why not? It could make for a good blues song.

Jaxson zipped up his bag and was about to snap off the lights when he heard a knock on the door and what sounded like a muffled giggle. He opened it to find Marta-2 and Oblivia standing there like anxious dates on prom night. Marta-2 had on an ensemble that made her look like a voluptuous figure eight, the dress showing off her substantial breasts, thin waist, and womanly hips. Oblivia was equally elegant in a full flowing skirt and a strapless top that exposed more than anyone needed to see. "Well, what do you think?" said Marta-2.

Jaxson wasn't at all sure *what* he thought. At first he thought she was messing with his mind. Then he thought she was playing him like a banjo. Then he thought everybody was in on some joke except for him. "I like it," said Jaxson.

"It's called *The New Look*. The girls would go crazy for this back on Obsidia. Nobody's ever seen anything made from real fabric."

"It suits you. It kind of brings out your figure."

"I didn't think you'd noticed."

"Yeah, well—"

Marta surprised even herself with a confidence born either of her new wardrobe or of her afternoon spent with Esmeralda. "What do you say we go out on the town tonight?" she said. "Maybe check out some of that music you're always talking about?"

Jaxson couldn't take his eyes off of her. Maybe it was the afternoon light, or the red silk dress, or the eyeliner and lipstick, but she actually looked pretty good to him at that moment. Pretty, almost. Yeah, definitely pretty. Funny how he hadn't really noticed before. Too bad about that. Too bad about a lot of things. "Look, I'd love to go, I really would, but we have a situation—"

"Oh, I almost forgot!" said Marta-2, grabbing a bag from outside the door. "We have something for you, too."

"For me?" said Jaxson, as he picked up a Daniels and Fisher shopping bag. He reached inside and pulled out a pair of triple pleated rayon pants and a Hawaiian shirt with palm trees and hula dancers. "Man, these shirts are a gas and a half! Do you have any idea what these would sell for back home?"

"An arm and a leg?" said Marta-2. "Isn't that the expression?"

A conflict arose inside Jaxson's mind the likes of which he'd rarely known. Should he follow orders or follow his dreams? Would a couple of hours really matter in the overall scheme of things? What would be the difference if they left now or first thing in the morning? He looked at the shirt. The hula dancer wiggled her hips in the breeze. "Come," she seemed to say, "dance with me under the starlight."

"Sure," said Jaxson. "Why not?"

The Woody Herman Band played, the Rainbow Ballroom rocked, and the walls shook to the beat. It wasn't the blues, but it was the next best thing and the Obsidians danced like there was no tomorrow. Which there wasn't going to be, of course, at least not for the three of them in Denver. It was a night to cut loose, and cut loose they did. They'd been cooped up in cars, trains, and spaceships for so long they could barely remember what their extremities felt like, but tonight was a chance to unleash some energy. This was what it was all about, to bust out of the straightjacket of endless black space and have some real fun.

Jaxson and Marta-2 fit right into the crowd with their new duds and moved smooth to the groove and alive to the jive, and then there was Oblivia, oh, yes, indeed, Oblivia danced with every guy in the place, jitterbugging to the music as if she was born to be swung over some guy's hip, twirled over his shoulder, and pulled between his legs. The band launched into *Caledonia* and the dance floor bounced like a trampoline. Oscar Pettiford and Shelly Mann laid down the rhythm on bass and drums, Zoot Sims and Stan Getz traded sax solos, Lou Levy cradled the keyboard, Terry Gibbs played the vibes, and Woody Herman himself let loose on his signature clarinet riff that soared right through the ballroom. A slick cat in a zoot suit danced Oblivia to the center of the floor, where they did a shoulder twist, a hip twirl, and a quick stop drop. "Hit that jive!" somebody yelled as they spread out and did a hesitation Shorty George, then danced toward each other swinging their wings and whipping their hips. "Solid!" someone called out to Oblivia as she shimmied, collapsed in a heap, arose to the beat, and shook it once again.

Jaxson and Marta-2 danced closer as the night wore on, their cheeks accidentally brushing a few times, then not so accidentally, then with what could only be described as real purpose. Maybe it was only the mountain air, or the pounding of the music, or the throbbing of the crowd, but Jaxson felt a tingling in his spine as Marta-2 leaned into his chest and rested her cheek against his neck. The band played *Down Under* and the horn section sizzled. Denver sparkled that night as the music pushed the nomadic wayfarers into some higher altitude where they looked down on the world as if they were floating on clouds. That's how they felt, like crows gliding in the thin night air, peering down on a world that didn't know how to fly.

When they returned to the Cameron Motel, Marta-2 lingered outside Jaxson's room for a moment, hoping to be invited in. The alcohol and altitude left her a bit lightheaded and slightly loopy as Jaxson fumbled with his key. "How about a nightcap," she finally said, "to cap off such a lovely night."

"Uh, yeah... that'd be nice," said Jaxson, hemming and hawing, "but we've got a big day tomorrow."

Marta-2 wondered how Esmeralda would handle the situation. After all, Esmeralda wasn't one to take no for answer. No, Esmeralda would grab that key, swing open the door, and flop onto the bed with her shoes still on. "Is it really so late?" said Marta-2, surprised at her own forwardness.

Jaxson, for his part, wondered how Nick would handle the situation. Nick was always in charge, doing whatever he wanted to do without having to explain too much. Cool as a cucumber and steady as a rock, that was Nick all right. "You don't understand," said Jaxson. "It's about the experiment."

"I know, I know. First thing in the morning, we need to find a suitable subject, then there's the prep work, the run-through, the equipment check, and the test itself."

"There *is* no test," said Jaxson after a long moment.

"What do you mean?"

"I heard from the Captain. We've been ordered back to the ship."

"But... that's impossible," said Marta-2 in a halting voice.

"We have to leave first thing in the morning. The Court of Last Resort has suspended the mission."

Marta-2 leaned against the wall for support. The effects from the alcohol were gone. The warmth of the evening was gone. All that was left was a feeling of numbness. "All my life I've wanted to do something meaningful," she said. "I've given up everything to be part of this mission and now they want to take it all away?"

"I know how you must feel."

"No, you *don't* know how I feel!" said Marta-2. "Every-thing was all set! There's got to be something we can do."

"What can we possibly do? Orders are orders."

"You're just like the rest of them," said Marta-2, looking at Jaxson with bitter disappointment. "I thought you were dif-ferent, that you had something inside, real substance, real soul. I was wrong. Blues musician, indeed!"

Jaxson felt like he'd been kicked in the groin. "Hey, wait a minute..."

There was a moment of strained silence, followed by a distant, discombobulated voice which emanated from the shadows: "What if we already had a subject?" said Oblivia, stepping into the hallway.

"Yeah, well, we don't," said Jaxson.

"But what if we did?" Oblivia repeated, as she glanced down the hall to Nick and Esmeralda's room.

"No... not Nick..."

"Why not?"

"Because... it's dangerous!"

Oblivia fixed Jaxson with a stare, then took Marta-2's arm and hurried down the hall. Jaxson stood there a moment, feeling bluer than he could ever remember. How could they even think of experimenting on Nick? The guy gave them a ride! Twice! He stared into the cold, endless sky as a slow, sad, 12-bar blues trickled into the night.

Blues and trouble
came knockin' on my door
Blues and trouble
came knockin' on my door
I ain't gonna answer
my door no more

Chapter 17

*Jaxson Epsilon's
Earth Log
—July 9, 1947*

It should be pointed out, dear reader, that on Earth there are all sorts of doors. There are doors to enter and doors to avoid. There are doors of hope and doors of despair. There are doors of opportunity and doors of no return. Knowing which door to open and which to close can make all the difference in the world. You walk through the wrong door, you might never come out the other side. Me, I always preferred revolving doors since they give you a chance to change your mind at the last minute and just keep on going. That's me all right, a revolving door never quite sure where to stop or what to do when I get there. Now, though, I was about to enter a door to a whole other dimension whether I liked it or not. Ladies and gentlemen, may I present for your enjoyment and entertainment, Jaxson Epsilon, Cranial Energy Explorer.

It had kind of a nice ring, don't you think? If nothing else, it would look good on my resume, should I ever want to apply for another job that required boundless stupidity, unflinching bravery, and zero regard for life and limb. My "volunteering" to go along on this little excursion outside the spaceship was about to reward me with the opportunity to be the first Obsidian to extract dream energy from the brain of an actual living person. What that meant was anyone's guess, but it was too late to bail out now. Since I had no training whatsoever in the science of energy extraction, I was to be nothing but a puppet in Marta-2's hands, following her instructions explicitly and without question. So said Captain Wambold in his final orders when he forced me out the door and down the ladder of the Pulsar-7. Good luck on that one, to her, to him, and to me.

So there I was, both a reporter and a participant in my own story. To maintain objectivity under such circumstances is no small task, but I pulled out my notebook and un-quivered my ceremonial plume pen for the historic occasion. I felt like a reporter from the old days, when they dipped feathers in ink, scratched out hieroglyphs on papyrus, and kept a spare cigarette behind their ear. I was, after all, a story-teller from way back. What others called pathological lying I saw as the continuation of an age-old oral tradition. To say I was conflicted is an understatement to which I am rarely prone. I'm more of the new wave of brash and bold Obsidian journalists who refuse to hide behind truth, honor, and objectivity. I'll not only tell it like it is, I'll throw in the bonus of telling it the way I'd like it to be at no extra charge. Which is my way of saying I wasn't all that crazy about involving Nick in this experiment in energy retrieval. Not that Nick was such a good buddy, but the idea of something going wrong and leaving him with a pile of cooked cauliflowers for brains wasn't my cup of hablum. Which reminds me.

RECIPE FOR STEAMED HABLUM:
Take six micres of fresh hablum
Add a pinch of flatula
Boil in three lucres of pani
Stir until spent
Let sit
Inject

Still, I was left with no choice but to go along with the ad hoc plan, since our options were somewhere between one and none. I'm not particularly proud of not having taken a stronger stand and at least arguing on Nick's behalf, but for that we have the Hawaiian shirt to thank. The fact is, the moment you put a palm tree and a hula dancer on your chest is the moment you become sapped of all revolutionary spirit. No one wearing a Hawaiian shirt has ever stormed a Bastille, led a sit-in, or battled the police, of that am I certain.

Now, then, where was I? Something about doors, right? I was always good with doors, going all the way back to the orphanage where I was adept at hiding behind one door or another whenever there was work to be done. Given my history of lurking in the shadows, Marta-2 left it to me to devise a plan for breaking into Nick's room. I worked up a scenario in which we would insert molten wax into the keyhole of his door, wait for it to harden to +16° Wambold, create a negative space flexible mold, fill it with ionized liquid metal, let it dry, sand off any rough edges, and let ourselves in with our newly fabricated fake key. Then it would simply be a matter of zapping Nick and Esmeralda with six-hour doses of sustained release Somatime, "for those occasions when you *really* want to sleep like a log."

Marta-2 was duly impressed with my blueprint for action but suggested we could save about three hours by simply trying the handle, since Earthlings of the mid-twentieth century were known to rarely lock their doors. When the tumbler opened without a hitch I reluctantly tossed my plans into the dustbin of history, which was located right next to the door of opportunity and just across from the sands of time. Here, dear reader, I find it necessary to reiterate that all of my following activities were done under protest and that, as was clearly defined in the protocols established after the Forlorn Years, I was, in fact, only following orders.

Nick and Esmeralda were sound asleep when we entered the room, Nick breathing quietly and Esmeralda snoring arhythmically with a little huff, a little puff, and a long exhalation that made the sheet rise and fall like a pink parachute. Marta-2 approached them on tiptoes, then sprayed Somatime Mist into their nostrils, *psst-psst, psst-psst,* and that was that, they were out like sub-Subian trance dancers overdosed on mushrooms. Marta-2 immediately began setting up the equipment we'd carted along in our suitcases. There were at least 20 modular pieces which, when connected together, formed a portable laboratory with enough gauges, meters, and dials to run an interstellar communications station. Marta-2 was pretty good with pipes, joints, and nozzles, that much I had to give her. Oblivia, whose function on the mission was completely beyond me—what did Data Transfer Officer even mean?— guarded the door against unwanted visitors. I suppose she was capable of warbling out some kind of warning, but I imagined her tripping over the first syllable and uttering sub-audible cries that might be recognizable to small dogs and geese but certainly not to either of us. Still, I saw the wisdom in keeping her occupied as Chief of Security since it kept her a safe distance away from Nick's brain, which, after all, needed to be kept in some kind of pristine condition lest he catch a bad case of Obliviation.

Marta-2 wasted no time. She attached electrodes to Nick's temples, sensory modules to his fingertips, and pulsation anipodes to his toes, then set the wireless terminals on the Rev-it-Up® unit to full receive. With a couple flicks of a switch, a 60800 GHz Insonia Thetamax Monitor flashed a remarkably clear, detailed view of Nick's brain. The magnetic resonance utility provided a multidimensional look inside and as far as I could tell, all the pieces were there, meaning the brain roots, the gray stuff, the juicy fluids, plus all the plugs, sockets and wires you'd expect to find in a living, breathing Earthling. I was actually quite proud of Nick at that moment. He was just like us—a thinking, feeling, caring biped—even if he was 200 years in arrears on the evolutionary scale.

"I'm afraid there's no time for training or a run-through or anything like that," said Marta-2, "so you'll just have to learn as you go."

"Learning isn't really my thing," I said with my usual self-deprecating humor, minus the self-deprecation part. "I'm more a monkey-see, monkey-do kind of a guy."

"There's nothing to worry about, Jaxson. Just remember, I've got your back."

"It's not my back I'm worried about. It's the top, bottom, and sides I'm not so sure about."

Marta-2 picked up a vacuum-sealed pouch that crackled and popped when she opened it, kind of like the breakfast cereal back at the orphanage. Inside was a pair of matching Eisenberg gloves and socks made of a transmutational material that was both thin and strong, flexible and malleable, and ultra-sensitive to the touch. "Put these on," she said. "Don't worry about the fit. They'll adapt to your hands and feet."

She was right. Once I pulled them over my knuckles and toes, they stretched here, contracted there, and expanded anywhere else that was necessary. "Not bad," I said. "Do you have anything with stripes?"

"Think of them as just another layer of skin. You might even forget you have them on, but if you look closely, you'll see that the insides are lined with microscopic sensors that read your fingerprints, the lines in your palms, and the reflexology zones of your feet. They give us a map of your entire physiognomy and emotional state. Anything that can be measured and quantified gets analyzed and thrown into the hatch."

"The hatch?"

"That's what we call the central nervous system of the machinery, the area where all the readings and statistics get juggled together, then replicated and reanimated into the 9% of Jaxson Epsilon who will lead us into the bright future of energy independence."

To say that I was lost would do injustice to the memory of every intergalactic explorer who turned left instead of right and was never heard from again. I was lost all right and not just 9% lost, I was 99% lost and counting. "Sure, I get it," I said, relying on my old technique from the Institute of Applied Learning of copping to what I knew, faking what I didn't, and hoping the bell would ring before anyone found out.

"No, you don't," said Marta-2, patiently. "Let me explain. We're going to isolate your essence, the 9% of Jaxson Epsilon that is necessary to recreate a three-dimensional alter ego of who you are, and then we're going to send you, well, not *you*, but the new *embodiment* of you, into Nick's brain to retrieve the dream code that will fire up our lights back home. It's all based on the Eisenberg Paradox which states, of course, that *"the material and immaterial nature of a body's mass are identical yet opposite aspects of the same phenomenon."*

"You realize that I have no idea what you're talking about, right?"

"It's just basic energy theory, the stuff they drummed into our heads all through school."

"Yeah, well, I might've missed a couple of days."

"Jaxson, we really don't have time for this," she said, wondering how she was going to teach me enough in two minutes to keep me from blowing out my brain, Nick's brain, and the entire circuitry of the machine. Did the poor girl actually think she could give me a crash course in dream theory at this late date? "Look," she said, trying to stay calm, "in the old days, the accepted scientific theory was that you couldn't get something from nothing, that energy was a constant that always had to be accounted for. It wasn't until

H. Lavender Laroche and Pygmalion Shaw discovered that *nothing* and *zero* are quite different concepts that dream energy became a reality."

"There's a difference between zero and nothing?"

"Nothing is nothing, but zero is the flip side of one, and that opens the doors to a whole other way of perceiving energy. The day you understand the difference between zero and nothing is the day you'll understand dream energy."

"Yeah, okay," I said, lost, as always, in the ozone.

"Look, it doesn't really matter. We'll just wing it as we go. Now, listen. I'm going to flick a switch and the sensors will be activated. You'll notice a slight glow around your hands and feet, which might look a bit odd, but don't worry about it. It's a totally normal change of hue reflecting your various emotional states and thought patterns. It means everything is working. After a minute or two, you'll feel yourself getting tired, then moving into a quasisomnescent state in which you'll be here but not here, aware but not aware, awake but not awake. It's what we call Conscious Hibernation™."

"That's the state I was in all through school."

"That's when it all begins. Once you're under, your alter ego awakens and integrates with the image on the monitor. It's you but not you, an embodied entity which enters into the very real world of Nick's brain. Think of yourself as a ghost who is able to walk through walls, knock over lamps and slam doors, but is hovering somewhere outside reality." She paused for a moment and looked at me with concern. "Does any of this make sense?"

"I'm a harmonica player. All I have to do is keep track of 12 bars that repeat over and over. Ba-bop, ba-bop, ba-bop, the turnaround... ba-bop, ba-bop, ba-bop, the turnaround... know what I mean?"

"Don't worry," she said. "You'll be all right." And with that, Marta-2 flicked a switch. Sure enough, I noticed a slight glow around my hands and feet. A moment later I began to feel tired, like I wanted to just stretch out and lie down in a cave somewhere. And then I saw myself staring back from the far edge of the monitor. I was in there, all right, a kind of shimmering ghost in the machine. It was just like Marta-2 said. It was me but not me. I was there but not there.

"Do you hear me?" she said. "Are you all right?"

I wanted to answer but when I tried to formulate the words, I discovered that my voice had disappeared, apparently part of that 9% that had been siphoned off for more important matters. But then I answered anyway. "Yes, I'm fine," I said, only it wasn't me, it was the me on the monitor and I wasn't quite sure who was who anymore. Not that I disagreed with the answer—no, no, I agreed wholeheartedly—I just wasn't sure whose answer it was. The "I" I had come to know pretty well after all these years had become a "we."

"Before you become completely discombobulated, I want you to understand something. The Earthlings got pushed off track hundreds of years ago when a philosopher named Descartes convinced everybody that the mind and the body were two separate entities. Descartes' dualism messed them up terribly and they're still stuck in the quicksand. You have to understand that you're an essence interacting with Nick's essence. He's not separate from his thoughts and you're not separate from him."

I gave her a ghostly nod as I both understood and didn't understand at the same time. Deep down inside, however, I did feel a kind of unity of purpose with Marta-2, with Nick, and with this whole idea of a kind of common energy roiling through us all.

"Are you ready?" asked Marta-2.

"I'm as ready as ready can be," I said, feeling just about as unready as unready can get.

"Get in quickly and get out quickly," said Marta-2. "Follow the established guidelines, take no unnecessary risks, and exit at the first sign of trouble."

I nodded three times—once to acknowledge her instructions, once to affirm my well-known self-destructive nature, and once just because—then took a deep breath and dove in. My shimmery self shimmied across the monitor like I was still dancing to Woody Herman's band which, in fact, maybe I was. There was a kind of rhythm in my ears, or Nick's ears, or wherever I was, a rhythm that glided I and me and we and they across his external auditory canal.

Marta-2 turned to the monitor, flicked another switch, and watched a secondary image that was being transmitted through the me inside Nick's head. My optic nerves were doubling as video cameras—lights and all—and were broadcasting everything I saw directly to the screen. I moved transparently along the tissue and cartilage of the bony pathway, wiggle-waggling my way along the slippery inclines and steep drops. It wasn't long before I reached the eardrum, a big movable gateway that pulsated with Nick's each and every breath. I paused for a moment, examined the porous membrane, and realized something: I was seeing in stereo! Part of my vision was coming from my embodied self inside Nick's head and part was coming from the video image on the monitor. The two me's were seeing more than three dimensions!

"Is something wrong?" said Marta-2 into her headset.

"I don't think I can explain it."

"Don't even try. Everything looks fine from here. Just go right through."

"Okay... I'll just... go right through," I said as I approached the tympanic membrane and stood before a kind of dematerialized doorway. Sure enough, a channel opened and I slipped through into a wide-open cavity. Inside the inner ear, it was pitch black everywhere except where my artificial light shone. I proceeded farther, moving along the hammer-shaped malleus, then to the incus and stapes. I stood there a moment, searching the inner walls of the cave. There were fissures everywhere and hairy little growths that gave the place a spooky appearance. As if on cue, a church bell clanged outside the motel, a dozen birds flapped in the branches of a tree, and Nick's head moved imperceptibly. My arms darted across the video screen and I held my ears as if my head might explode. "What was that?" I said in a startled voice.

"It's nothing," said Marta-2. "Just some little noise outside."

I turned my head and caught sight of Nick's eardrum pulsating. The malleus, incus and stapes moved sequentially one after another, like three bones doing a skeleton dance. The whole inner cavity seemed to be vibrating. "Your little noise outside is like a tornado down here," I said as I braced myself and headed along the outside of the Eustachian tube into a system of canals. I think it was at that moment that it dawned on me that I, Jaxson Epsilon, was actually inside a human cranium, that I, Jaxson Epsilon, was the first Obsidian to have made such a journey, and that I, Jaxson Epsilon, would forever be a part of history. I felt oddly patriotic, humble, and nonplussed all at the same time. "Dampness noted," I said, using the dry, technical tones of how I imagined a real explorer might speak. "Surface slightly slippery. Walls waxy and reflective."

"You're in the cochlea. Stay to the sides if you can, then head for the eighth cranial nerve."

I rose up over some prickly hair cells that dotted the vestibule, then slid down the auditory nerve canal. It was quite a ride, as good as any videocoaster at Breughel Park back home. Next thing I knew, I was staring at the outer surface of Nick's cerebral cortex. "Bingo," I said.

Marta-2 did a quick spectroscopic analysis of the image on the monitor and charted the location. "I have you at 52°, 7 minutes left of median, 29°, 3 minutes right of lateral," she said as she zeroed in on a closer view of the quadrant. "You're directly above the Sylvian fissure of the temporal lobe. You'll want to cross the Sagittal plane to the medial temporal lobe which, by my calculations, is 3° east of the median." As I edged along the surface of the cortex, a lunar-like landscape of neural tissue appeared on the monitor. Marta-2 followed my movements from one fold to another until I reached the trans-occipital sulcus, an area that looked like a big, curved wave formation. "That's it, Jaxson," she said. "You're at the doorway to the limbic system. Can you see anywhere to enter?"

"There are fissures all over the place. I could try any one of them."

"The choice is yours."

I inspected several of the crevices, then found a tunnel which appeared to snake its way right down to the hippocampus. I entered, quiet as a ghost, then shimmied down along the outer wall of the channel.

The video image on the monitor became blurry in the lower light and all Marta-2 could see was a dull gray mass illuminated by an occasional sliver of light. "The hippocampus is the center of memory and dreams," she said. "That's the region we're looking for, the place where thoughts are encoded in the brain."

"What does that mean exactly?"

"Think of the brain as a giant computer running in four lobes. Every thought, every memory we've ever had is encoded in billions of files that are fragmented across its hard drive. When we sleep, the brain reassembles certain of those files by firing billions of neurons and synapses in order to connect them together for a few minutes. The accumulation of those files is a movie we call a dream."

I continued on lower down the channel, through the cracks and crevices of the limbic system.

"There are two kinds of dreams," said Marta-2, "ones that come from an area higher in the cerebral cortex, and ones

that come from a darker, more primitive zone. Those are the
ones we're after, where the real energy is. The upper cortex
dreams are nice and easy, but the lower cortex dreams are full
of anxiety and despair. They're called REM state dreams and
we can see them in the rapid eye movements of the dreamer."

I groped around in the dark of Nick's brain, hoping not to
run into anything too disturbing. This was no time for ghost
stories, especially since *I* was the ghost.

"Now, listen, you should start picking up signals from the
hippocampus. Think of yourself as a kind of digital medium.
The same principle that allows you to dematerialize in Nick's
brain allows you to rematerialize the coded information from
his dreams."

"Yeah, yeah, the Eisenberg Paradox. How about we leave
the science to you and the driving to me?" I said, having had
enough for one day. As I descended, I felt my forehead beginning to perspire. "By the way, it's pretty damn hot down here."

"Just a bit farther—"

A burst of electrical interference made my legs tingle and
caused the video monitor to flicker. Marta-2 waited in
anticipation of something that only a scientist could appreciate. What was it? A multi-colored cloud formation? A
spiraling hexahedron? A throbbing, pulsating brain wave?
No, it was even more spectacular. The screen lit up with the
most beautiful image of them all:

101011100000001101000000001101011
110000000000010000010000100010
0011111110110101010111000110100101
111000000010101010101000000000

Marta-2 ran the code through a visualization adapter,
then looped the information back into the monitor so there
was a kind of digital collision, the result of which was the
unfolding of a whole new image on the screen that was

neither numbers nor clouds nor patterns nor brainwaves, no, it was, in fact, the broad panorama of a towering waterfall in a beautiful forest beneath a rainbow sky. Nick stood beneath the cascade with Esmeralda, letting the mist wash over their bodies. They strolled arm in arm, kissed in a field of rhododendrons, and disappeared into a golden sunset.

Marta-2 watched Nick's dream in silence. She felt a kind of peacefulness that brought a warmth to her body and a cool breeze to her head. "It's a beautiful dream," she said.

My voice broke through her reverie. "Were you able to read it?"

"Yes, Jaxson," said Marta-2. "I read it fine."

From my perch in the hippocampus, I watched the ones and zeroes from Nick's dream come flying out like little doves that flapped into the air, never to be seen again. From my *other* seat in the motel room, I watched the code zipping by at light's speed as it was gathered and deposited into an unseen receptacle at the heart of the machine. There was a low hum. A light flickered. A meter oscillated.

Marta-2 turned her attention to the compacting, destabilizing, stripping, sterilizing, varnishing, and reanimating of Nick's dream. We had a million lines of code stashed away in our machinery but until it was transmitted back home, it was just a bunch of useless ones and zeroes. It was time for Oblivia to take center stage. "Oblivia," said Marta-2. "It's time."

Marta-2 slid a chair in front of the control panel of her portable laboratory, dabbed some alcohol on Oblivia's temples, and attached two wires which wound around from the back panel of her machinery. It was time to animate Oblivia's brain with Nick's dream and that required a lot of knob turning and dial watching. Marta-2 turned on the unit and punched in some instructions. A light flickered, a meter activated, and a concave lens at the top of the faceplate began glowing like a watery bulb. Little waves of light crossed over the surface, then broke into pixilated geometric forms. Pulsating hexagons tiptoed along the edge of the lens, rhomboids bounced back and forth, and tetrahedrons ping-ponged off each other. The patterns slowly began to merge and the lens took on a glimmering luminosity. I found myself drawn into it as if it were a warm bath that was washing away my thoughts. Strangely enough, I felt myself letting go of something intangible and indefinable and I wasn't even the one attached to the machine! Oblivia, with her tenuous grasp of reality, must've been flying with the fishes and swimming with the sparrows. She sat there absolutely comatose and looked for all the world like a toaster oven with those two wires poking out of her skull. I half expected her tongue to brown.

The Dream Machine began blinking and buzzing and reminded me of one of those laboratory experiments back at the Institute that I never quite managed to get right. My experiments blinked where they were supposed to buzz and buzzed when they were supposed to hum, and that, ladies and gentlemen, is pretty much the story of my life. This, though, was science writ large, the culmination of thousands of years of theories and hypotheses, and I was lost in the dust. As Marta-2 had laboriously explained, this was the part of the process with the zipping particles and the reflective surfaces and the resisters and capacitors and I barely comprehended a bit of it. Me, I like a good melody and a glass of babinka to get the juices flowing, but these were juices of a whole other order and as for flowing, well, the whole room seemed to be flowing, like right out the window. The lights were blinking ever faster when two mirrored, rectangular plates rose up out of opposite sides of the contraption. An amorphous mass of electron particles began flowing between the plates, creating a kind of shimmering effect, like wavy lines of heat radiation. Marta-2 twisted a few dials and the electron images sharpened as they danced from one plate to the other. There were thousands of images—of water, mist and vapor, of rivers, lakes and streams, of electrons, protons and neutrons—and each was like a miniature photograph that bent crisply, then vibrated and disappeared. The plates accumulated the images like pages in a book and bounced them back and forth, faster and faster, from mirror to mirror, until a thousand different movies were all being shown at the same time, and finally the streams joined as one and a big cinemascopic funnel burst through the air. Oblivia, perfect blank medium that she was, twitched once and fell over as the pure dynamic energy of Nick's dream was shot through space.

I watched with amazement. It worked! It actually worked! For the first time in history, we had located, commandeered, and transmitted the full, unbridled energy of a dream across the stars! And most incredibly, it really *was* all done with mirrors! "Oh, man..." I uttered. For one of the first times ever, I was very nearly out of words.

"Man, indeed!" hooted Marta-2. "Hooray! Huzzah! We've proven that the system works! Now we just need one more dream, this one from the lower cortex."

"I was afraid you'd say that," I said. In truth, this little trip down Nick's memory lane wasn't so bad, but I was ready to leave. It was hot and humid in his cerebral cortex, which was probably a healthy sign for doctors and dreamers, but a bit too jungle-y for me. Me, I'm a blues cat, I dig back alleys, attics, and basements, not the neurological muck inside some human head laboratory. I yearned to get back to my old self sitting in the motel room, where an ice cold Pabst Blue Ribbon was just waiting to get popped.

A lone candle danced in the wind. Nick rustled slightly in his bed and Marta-2 glanced over to make sure everything was all right. She watched as his body relaxed and entered a deeper sleep in which nothing stirred. The candle dipped and twinkled and glistened, then grew still. Marta-2 was about to turn back to the monitor when something caught her eye. A kind of subliminal impulse drew her to Nick's eye sockets which she realized were suddenly twitching almost uncontrollably. "Um, Jaxson?" she said. "Are you almost there?"

"Almost."

"Okay, well, Nick has already entered the REM state. You need to proceed with due urgency."

I poked around in the dark entryways to the lower cortex. It was a real mess of ganglia and nerve cells. "Okay, I'm just looking for a spot for a nice soft landing—"

"You need to gather the code and return to the cerebral cortex. There's really no time to lose."

And that's exactly what would have happened had everything gone smoothly. But *nothing* goes smoothly in the life of Jaxson Epsilon, not ever—not in the womb, not in the saline wash, not in the orphanage, not at the Institute, not on the expedition, and certainly not now, because the instant I entered the lower cortex, a huge crack of thunder and blast of lightning erupted from the centromedial nucleus of Nick's amygdala and his whole cranium shook like a hula dancer in a hurricane. I was bounced around like a pinball in the neural tissue until I finally came to a rest in a web of synaptic thread. Above me, on the inner walls of the cranium, a dark, disturbing lightshow flashed in the windows and pathways of the brain. Dull bursts of aubergine mist intermixed with heavy clouds of rust and bursts of black lightning. Powerful tympanic waves shuddered through the Sagittal plane, sounding like explosive discharges echoing through a mine shaft. I felt like I was half buried in mud—unable to see, unable to hear, unable to find a way out.

On the monitor, the ones and zeroes of Nick's dream reunited into the familiar landscape of a foxhole in the hills of Italy. It was Nick's recurring nightmare unleashing all of its terrible power in a series of digital bursts that filled the screen. It was raining and there was mud everywhere—mud dripping from the sky, mud dripping from the trees, and mud dripping from his helmet as he dug himself deeper into the hillside. A squadron of airplanes roared across the sky, dropping bombs and strafing the ground with machine gun fire. Flares hung bright in the night sky, shining like pink neon on New Year's Eve, while bazooka shells exploded into a thousand shards of shrapnel. Bullets pinged off the sides of trucks, off pots and pans, and off the helmets of dead soldiers. Blood soaked into the foxhole—the blood of Nick's comrades—and the guy next to him began screaming into the barrel of his gun, then stood up and raised his hands to the heavens. It was too late—too late for him, too late for everyone. Nick grabbed him but a burst of gunfire cut through the guy's chest and severed his spine. The footsteps of enemy soldiers approached, then the groan of crankshafts, and Nick saw the darkness surround him. He saw the end— he saw his *own* end—and he climbed blindly out of the foxhole into a maze of horror. He crawled a few feet, then felt something burningly hot rip through his leg. He looked down to see that a bullet had shattered his knee. He tasted metal in his mouth and imagined he was burning on a stake in medieval Italy. He crawled some more, but it was no use: his leg was a dead weight behind him. The ground began to shake—it shook like the earth was regurgitating itself—and he looked up to see a heavy German tank headed right for him, its steel tracks slashing through the dirt, cutting up and eating the bush and vegetation and anything else in its way, and now *he* was in its way—he couldn't crawl, he couldn't move another inch, there was nothing left in the world but him, the mud, and a thousand tons of churning steel, and that's when—

Chapter 18

*"All that we see or seem is but
a dream within a dream."*
—Edgar Allan Poe

The door to Room 212 of the Cameron Motel burst open. Before anyone knew what hit them—*phwack-phwack, phwack-phwack, phwack-phwack*—Oblivia was tied to the bed, Marta-2 was handcuffed to the chair, and Jaxson was face down on the desk. Loquacious Landry yanked the electrodes off Nick's forehead, pulled the sensory modules off his fingertips, and detached the pulsation anipodes from his feet. Kalamata Quayle took Esmeralda's pulse, checked under her eyelids, and gave her another hit of Somatime Mist, just in case.

Loquacious flashed his Court of Last Resort terrafoil badge at his captives so that they could see just who they were dealing with. The multidimensional Hall of Justice hologram quivered with self-importance, as did Landry himself, so overwrought was he at the site of the modular pipes and joints of the Rev-It-Up® retrieval system. "What is this?" he said, running his fingers over the archaic mechanism. "Some kind of joke?"

"It's no joke," said Marta-2. "It's an important experiment. The future of Obsidian energy independence depends on us."

"Better break out the candles in that case. Reverie Energy

is closed until further notice. Your research is unauthorized and unlawful. Which is why your business is our business. And our business is making right. What's wrong."

"Please. We're almost finished. I'll do anything—"

"Impressive," said Kalamata, looking at Esmeralda's generous bosom, "but you're finished all right, sister, and finished good. Now, what do you say we get a move on? We don't want to be around when these two wake up from their naps."

"But you don't understand!" said Marta-2, taking hold of Jaxson's limp hand. "My colleague is still deep inside the subject's cranium!"

"And what does that mean?"

"I don't *know* what it means. That's the whole problem. That's why we're conducting the experiment."

"You should've thought of that before we came," said Loquacious.

"But, *look* at him!" said Marta-2, staring into Jaxson's blank eyes.

"Rather not, sweetheart, not on an empty stomach."

Marta-2 could see that she was getting nowhere. "What are you going to do with us?" she said, trying a different approach.

"Take you back to that rattrap of a rocket ship," said Loquacious. "Then the whole lot of you get to face the music. Which will not be pretty. At all."

Oblivia slumped against her bedpost, Jaxson remained dead quiet, and Marta-2 faced her captors with steely resolve. "Then so be it," she said. "We have nothing to be ashamed of."

"That so? You think you can just contravene court orders like they didn't exist?" Loquacious kept looking at Jaxson out of the corner of his eye, as if waiting for him to say something. "What about you, Sluggo?" he said, nudging Jaxson with the business end of his magnetic schiller. "What have you got to say for yourself?"

Jaxson lifted his head from the desk and stared at Loquacious blankly. "The mind-body conundrum lies at the heart of the energy problem."

"See what I *mean?*" said Marta-2, wondering what had become of the old Jaxson.

"He seems fine to me. What are you gonna tell us next? That he was only following orders?"

"He *was* only following orders," said Marta-2. "My orders."

"I see. So you must be the brains behind this bunch of bananas. Which, by the look of things, is not saying much."

"Think what you want. I take full responsibility."

"Sure, sure, we get you, sister," said Kalamata, glancing from Oblivia to Jaxson. "You take the fall so these two go free. I don't think so. Not for a minute."

Loquacious gathered up the modular tubes and hoses from the machine and dumped them into the empty suitcases. "Makes me wonder sometimes," he said with sudden weariness. "If I'm in the right line of work. I could've had a business. Pharmaceuticals maybe. Or surgical supplies. Tubes and hoses. Who knows what they're worth? You name your price and that's that. Nobody argues over the price of a surgical hose. Or a catheter tube. You gonna take a chance on a cut-rate catheter tube? Of course not. You almost *want* a catheter tube to cost a lot just for the peace of mind. But no. I had to get into the private dick game. Chasing cheats, geeks, mopes and dopes halfway across the universe. Because they pose a threat to the natural order. Or some such thing. What do I get out of it? Satisfaction? Hardly. Recognition? Don't make me laugh. Camaraderie? Please."

"So why do you do it?" said Kalamata, growing weary of her partner's constant belly-aching.

"Because one of these days I want to be able to look in the mirror and say, there's a guy who stood for something. Even if he wasn't quite sure. What it was."

Kalamata smoothed out the bed sheets, fluffed the pillows,

and straightened the blankets. "Okay, time to go," she said, motioning Jaxson, Marta-2 and Oblivia to the door. As they filed out of the room, she glanced back at Nick and Esmeralda, who slept the sound sleep of humans unconcerned with intergalactic tribunals and outernational protocol. Nothing moved but for the pink bed sheet, which expanded and collapsed to Esmeralda's irregular breathing. Kalamata watched her for a moment, made sure that everything was in order, and flicked off the lights.

The visitors from across the skies headed across the parking lot to where a taxi was waiting. "Nebraska," said Loquacious to the cabbie, "and make it snappy."

"You got it, buddy," said the driver. "You want the scenic route or the flat-top highway?"

Loquacious stared at the outlandish four-door contraption that was painted yellow as a canary and probably moved about as fast. "Just get us there," he said. "Think you can do that?"

"Well, let's see," said the driver, heavy on the sarcasm. "That's Nebraska, U.S.A. you're talking about, isn't it? Why don't you just sit yourself down and leave the driving to me?"

By the time Loquacious squeezed himself into the front seat, the meter was already at 40¢ and running. "Christ!" he said. "Let's get moving!"

The Checker Cab descended through the foothills of the Rocky Mountains and headed back along Highway 6 to the Great American In-Between. Whatever giggles the high altitude had once induced in the Obsidians were now fully evaporated, leaving them with the heavy feeling of too much oxygen, not enough nitrogen, and nary a molecule of helium at all. Jaxson, Marta-2, and Oblivia were in their usual positions in the back seat, Oblivia staring straight ahead into the back of the driver's seat, Marta-2 staring out the side window into the darkness, and Jaxson seated between them, staring at nothing at all.

"No," said the cab driver, a heavy-set guy with a round face and a cropped crew cut, "this House Un-American Activities Committee is a good thing. Gotta root out the commies before they take over the whole country. They've already got Hollywood by the short hairs. I say send the whole lot of them to Russia, they can make movies about cabbage and potatoes. Now, this senator from Wisconsin, this is a guy who's going places. Joe McCarthy for president, that's what I say, show them who's boss. Why don't they make a movie about *him*, that's what I want to know. I'll tell you why, because Hollywood is crawling with lefties who aren't man enough to carry Joe McCarthy's gavel. I'll tell you something, when he calls those meetings to order, you can hear a pin drop. Don't mess with Joe, that's what I say. He asks one of those are-you-now or have-you-ever-been questions and you can just see them starting to squirm. Half of them can't wait to start naming names just to save their own asses and the other half start hiding behind the constitution. Hell, I don't know which is worse. I say send them all to Siberia and let them show their movies to the elks and Eskimos."

"Are you now or have you ever been what?" said Loquacious.

"A communist! Isn't that what we're talking about? A pinko! A red! A writer!"

Kalamata, seated between Loquacious and the driver, stared out into the darkness. She lit up an unfiltered Lucky Strike, took a deep drag, and let it hang low off her lip, too bored to even bother holding it. Earth just wasn't her kind of place. At least not the mesas of Nebraska or the mountains of Colorado. She was more of a cave dweller, comfortable with bats, night owls, and other late-night revelers. Kalamata would've been right at home in a 1920s speakeasy, a place where you whisper a secret word through a slot in the door, slip a fiver into the bouncer's mitt, and plop a Mickey Finn into the glass of some broad who caught your eye. A bottle of hard booze, a dexy or two, and she could go all night. But she was 20 years too late for that, and she was too late for World War II as well, and now, of course, she was too early for the delicious possibilities of a Cold War that appeared to be right around the corner. Wartime was her specialty—making deals for black market nylons and illicit cigarettes, trading favors for information, breaking codes and knuckles when needed. Couldn't she just once get an assignment worthy of her talents? A secret agent in the house of love—that was her calling—a shadowy, slinky vamp who knew all the answers and most of the questions. "How much longer?" she said.

"Hard to say," said the driver. "It all depends."

"On what?"

"You've got the traffic, the road conditions, the tempera-ture, the wind, the humidity, and the barometric pressure, and then, who knows, there's the possibility of cows on the road, highway construction, bugs, visibility issues, detours, backups, gas station delays, and the ever-present unknown variables. I figure six hours, give or take."

Kalamata leaned forward, straightened her nylons, and casually pulled her skirt an inch or two above her knee. "Is that the best you can do?"

The driver got an eyeful and managed to give the gas pe-dal more toe and less heel. "Well, maybe five hours if we're lucky," he said, sitting a little taller in his seat. Outside, on the darkened road, the headlights of the cab illuminated some roadside signs:

WE KNOW

HOW MUCH

YOU LOVE THAT GAL

BUT USE BOTH HANDS

FOR DRIVING, PAL

BURMA-SHAVE

Loquacious felt a vibration in his pocket and pulled out an ultra-thin telemodule which glowed in the dark, shone in the light, was your pal in the day, and let you sleep at night. "Unbelievable," he muttered under his breath as he read a message.

"What is it?" said Kalamata.

"Those newspaper reports about Wright Field were bull. Looks like a cover-up at the highest levels. The damn thing is right here in our own backyard."

Kalamata crushed out her cigarette in the ashtray and lit another one. "Let me guess," she said coldly. "We've got new instructions?"

"What do you think?" said Loquacious as he shoved the module back into his pocket and leaned toward the driver. "We need to make a little detour. Town called Julesburg. It's supposed to be not too far off the road."

"You're the customer," said the driver. "We can go to Argentina as far as I'm concerned."

"Julesburg will be fine."

The driver continued on for a few more miles, then turned off on Highway 138 and headed northeast. The taxi meter held steady for one-fifth of a mile, then clicked from $86.20 to $86.40. Loquacious pulled his hat lower over his forehead and tried to get a little shut-eye. Kalamata flicked ashes on the floor of the car and exhaled smoke from her nose. The passengers in the backseat glanced at each other and wondered what, exactly, was up.

The taxi drove through the dead of night and into the rumor of morning. The driver continued his nonstop commentary on the state of the world, lacing politics, geography, and economics into his all-encompassing view of a nation on the brink of, well, something or other. As they neared their destination, he delivered a history lesson designed either to keep himself awake or to keep the others from sleeping. "Well, now, Julesburg was known as the 'Wickedest City in the West' back there in the 1860s, oh, yes, those were the days. Young fella named Jules Beni started up a trading post in this little corner of Colorado. Wasn't much of anything there except for the fact that the Pony Express rode through on its way to California. Eventually, one thing led to another—as things tend to do—and a couple of beet farmers moved in, a saloon opened, and a town was born named Julesburg, mostly because I guess nobody wanted to call it Beniburg."

There was a collective groan, but the driver got a good laugh out of his little joke which, truth be told, was pretty good. "Go on," said Kalamata, not understanding for an instant what was so funny.

"Then came some so-called massacre of the local Indians, which is neither here nor there, but the government figured they'd better come in and build a fort to protect the settlers from whatever Indians were left."

"Since they were angry," said Marta-2.

"Sure they were angry. The settlers had enough to worry about already."

"I meant the Indians."

"The Indians?" said the driver, looking confused. "Who cares about the Indians? The point is, the building of Fort Sedgwick was just another good idea gone bad. You see, those crazy tribals rode on over one night and burned the whole thing right down to the ground. Nice guys, huh?"

"Real nice," said Kalamata.

"Well, that was the last straw for old Jules. He figured it was time for a career change and he decided to become a horse thief instead of a shopkeeper. I mean, could you really blame him? The money was better, the hours were shorter, and the horses were just there for the taking, what with the Pony Express almost begging to be robbed."

Loquacious stirred slightly under his hat and twisted in

the front seat. "What? What robbery? Where?" he muttered, then fell back into his tenuous sleep.

"After a short while, Jules had himself a real thriving business selling stolen horses, the Indians went back to being Indians, and the town went back to being a town. Until this other fella named Jack Slade showed up, that is. Slade worked for the Pikes Peak Express Company and he tracked Jules down somewhere outside town and tried to put him under arrest. Now, Jules, you see, didn't take kindly to strangers, so he just up and shot Slade five times and left him for dead. But this fella Slade was one tough hombre. Bullet wounds and all, he caught up with Jules a little while later down the road. Slade pulled his gun, tied Jules to a fence, then shot off his fingers, blew out his brains, and cut off his ears as souvenirs."

"Souvenirs?" said Kalamata. She stared at the driver as if he were some rare exhibit in the human zoo.

The driver glanced over at Kalamata, glad to see he was making an impression. "Guess he put them in a box or something. Now, there was probably a lesson in this for the residents of Julesburg, but damned if anybody ever quite figured out what it was. Julesburg became known far and wide for its gamblers, prostitutes, scofflaws, outlaws, thieves, crooks, con men, and dance hall girls. Oh, yes, it was a town that put starch in your spine and vinegar in your veins. It put the wild into Wild West, let me tell you."

"But that was then," said Kalamata.

"And this is now," said the driver. "You see, then came *real* trouble. The townsfolk found religion. Which ruined everything."

"As always," mumbled Loquacious.

"Hell, these days Julesburg is slow as molasses. The saloons have been rebuilt into churches, the whore houses have been knocked down and turned into hardware stores, and the dancehalls have degenerated into schools. Fort

Sedgwick is nothing more than a couple of broken-down buildings outside of town that nobody bothers with anymore, not even the Indians. The Army comes by every once in a while to rearrange the dust, but that's about it."

"And so ends our little tale?" said Kalamata, hoping she could finally get a moment's rest.

"I'm afraid so," said the driver.

Or so he thought. A few moments later, the Checker Cab pulled up on a dirt road that was three miles from a fork in another dirt road and halfway to a curve in the South Platte River. At exactly that spot, the passengers came face to face with a large, khaki green truck that was mired in the mud. Three words were stenciled across its door:

ROSWELL AIR BASE

The flat bed was empty except for several large tarps which flapped in the breeze. The windshield was splotched with bugs, dirt, and the various detritus of what appeared to be a long journey. Not far away, a couple of jeeps and civilian vehicles were parked near an aluminum shed which might have doubled for a small airport hangar or barracks hall. There were no windows and only one door, which was unmarked and unremarkable but for the fact that it appeared to be slightly ajar. Security was apparently nonexistent, not that there was much need for protection in these most barren of outposts. "We'll be a few minutes," Loquacious said to the driver, as he and Kalamata quietly slipped out of the car. "You can stretch your legs if you want, but those three," he said, pointing to the occupants in the back seat, "are not to move an inch."

"Locked and loaded," said the driver as he delivered an exaggerated salute, a thumbs-up and a V for Victory all in the same motion.

The first rays of the morning sun bounced off the alumi-

num roof of the shed and got bent back up into the sky, as if
to give the universe a chance to reconsider whether it really
wanted to start the day. Loquacious and Kalamata moved
through the shadows to the door and pushed it open. Inside,
a desk sat empty except for a cup of cold coffee, a Look
Magazine, a Reader's Digest, and a half-finished model of
the Pentagon made of toothpicks. Behind the desk was a
1947 RCA 721-TS, an early model television set with a tiny 10-
inch screen scrunched inside a large mahogany console. On
either side of the television were a couple of file cabinets, a
lamp, a chair, and a waste basket. A short hallway led to the
door of a room whose circular window allowed an unimped-
ed look inside. Loquacious pushed his hat against the glass
and gazed down at a scene that made him nearly retch in
disgust. He wondered if he was even seeing right or if he was
experiencing some kind of hallucination brought on by too
much Earth and not enough sleep. He looked again, hoping
his imagination was playing tricks on him, but what he saw
was real and it broke every rule of every planet of every
galaxy since the day that matter met antimatter and decided
to uncoil the universe.

Two Earthlings were dressed from head to toe in hazardous material suits which allowed them see through glass
shields, breathe through artificial air canisters, and feel
through pliable synthetic gloves that were sealed tight into
their arm guards. Laid out on cold, steel tables were the three
bodies from Teller's laser attack and subsequent crash into
the New Mexico desert. They were completely naked,
mouths open, eyes rolled back in their heads, lifeless and
inert. Their bodies showed signs of the violent collision with
the Earth, with burn marks, contusions, and general external
trauma. One of the deceased had a gaping wound that
extended from his right upper thigh down past his knee and
into his lower leg, exposing bone and cartilage that had been
mangled almost to the point of nonrecognition.

The room itself was a simple laboratory set-up, with the usual marble-topped tables and desks, plus a calendar, a wall clock, a telephone, a ventilation system, a sink, and several trays of surgical instruments. Loquacious watched as one of the humans picked up a forceps and made some preliminary markings on the chest of the most severely injured pilot. He drew a line down the center of his chest, then followed it out along the stomach to the thighs. Next, he made an incision below the clavicle and then, almost unbelievably, he took a kind of snub-nosed scissors and actually began cutting away the pilot's ear! It was as if the ghost of Jack Slade had returned and was reenacting the final scene in the life and death of Jules Beni. "I could work this job 20 more years and never again see anything like this," said Loquacious, watching numbly from the window.

"It's unbelievable," said Kalamata, watching with the kind of morbid curiosity one saves for a ten-ship pileup in an asteroid storm.

"You know what this is?" said Loquacious.

"An autopsy, I suppose, although for what purpose I can't imagine."

"No, it's evidence. It's evidence for the Court of Last Resort that's going to nail these Obsidians once and for all."

"Yes, if we get this on film, there can't be much question—"

"I'm not talking about film. I'm not taking any chances."

"You can't mean—"

"That's right," said Loquacious, pulling out his magnetic schiller. "Damned if we're going to leave these three here to wind up in formaldehyde bottles in some circus sideshow. Are you ready?"

"Ready as I'll ever be," said Kalamata.

"Okay, then," said Loquacious. "Let's do it."

Chapter 19

Jaxson might've been trapped in the back seat of a Checker Cab, but Jaxson's essence was trapped inside Nick's subcortex without a roadmap of any kind. The black lightning from Nick's centromedial nucleus filled his field of vision as he floated blindly in the nooks and crannies of the amygdala. As he pinballed among the nests of neurons and synapses, Jaxson's essence truly took on a ghostly presence in the machinery of Nick's brain. There was just thunder and lightning for its own sake, an unrelenting assault on whatever senses were left to him.

As for Nick, his dream took on a whole new dimension. With most of the ones and zeroes stolen away, he was left with a nightmare that was even more disjointed than before. It was as if the dream images had been tossed around and rearranged like the files from a hard drive that suddenly crashed during download. Now, the dream was not only terrifying, but it barely made sense. This disconnection of images is what the old-fashioned psychologists on Earth might've called cognitive dissonance or, in later years, delusional disorder, or, as the dream scientists at Reverie Energy had warned, paranoia. That was their greatest fear from the beginning—and the very reason for this journey to Earth. The truth is, even the Obsidians had no idea *why* we dream and what function it actually serves. There were all sorts of ideas—dreams served as a psychological release; they were the remnants of prehistoric fears; they allowed the brain to practice defense mechanisms—but no one really knew. The only thing sleep scientists were certain of was that if they prevented someone from dreaming, that person would exhibit psychotic behavior after only a night or two of dream deprivation. Extrapolating this to an entire society, they could predict the very real dangers of mass paranoia, economic disruption, and political upheaval—and the likely consequences of environmental breakdown, population explosion, and uncontrollable war. It was an endless argument that filled the chambers of Obsidian universities and the editorial rooms of its newspapers. Scientists, after all, were hardly immune to their own delusions of grandeur and attacks of unprovoked anxiety, but it seemed entirely possible that in serving the energy needs of their planet, they could inadvertently cause a complete collapse of society.

When Nick awoke at sunrise, he felt particularly lightheaded and disoriented. It took longer than usual to reconnect with his surroundings—where was he again? A motel in Denver?—and even longer to put together what he was doing there. Oh, yes, the incident in Chicago—the club, the apartment, Montgomery's poker game—and then the quick escape for California. He sat up on the bed, rubbed his forehead, and glanced slowly around the room. It seemed quieter than before, which was curious since it had been completely quiet from the moment he went to sleep. But this was a different kind of quiet, a quiet in which he could hear the air breathe and the atmosphere exhale. He watched Esmeralda, still in the netherworlds of her own slumber, and wondered where *she* was right now. Was she dancing with bears in the Bulgarian forest? Was she clicking castanets in the dance halls of Seville? Was she playing violin for pennies on the streets of Zagreb?

"Esmeralda," said Nick, stroking her arm.

"Huh? Huh?" said Esmeralda, as her eyes slowly flickered open from the haze of Somatime Mist.

"It's time for breakfast."

She leaned against the headboard and glanced around the room. "Man, what a crazy dream. My dad was in it, apologizing for being such a shit. And a whole lot of people kept flitting in and out, some real oddballs with wires and badges and stuff crammed into their suitcases."

"Yeah? Me, too. I feel like I've been bouncing around on one of those crazy teacup rides at a carnival."

"Must be the altitude," said Esmeralda, as she rolled out of bed and stepped into a dress that was waiting for her all balled up in a pile on the floor.

"Must be," said Nick, tossing her a pair of shoes.

Esmeralda followed Nick out of the room, still in a half-daze. In the hallway, she knocked on Marta-2 and Oblivia's door and tried to muster up some of her old enthusiasm. "Rise and shine, fashion plates!" she called out. When there was no answer, she knocked again, then tried the handle. It opened into a room that looked like it hadn't been slept in. "Strange," she said. "I don't see any bags."

"Yeah, well, who knows with those two?" said Nick. "C'mon, let's go."

"Let's try Jaxson's room. Maybe they're there."

"Do we have to?"

"It's only breakfast. It doesn't hurt to be a little friendly."

Nick reluctantly followed her down the hall. When she knocked on Jaxson's door, it swung open to reveal another empty room. Not only was there no sign of Jaxson, there was no sign he'd ever been there. "So much the better," said Nick.

"They didn't even bother to say goodbye?" said Esmeralda, nonplussed.

"That's gratitude for you. You give people a helping hand, they turn their backs on you."

"It doesn't make sense. They seemed so polite."

"I never much liked them from the beginning. And where did they get that pile of cash all of a sudden? One minute they're hitchhiking, the next minute they're buying out the department store?"

Esmeralda took a final look around the room, then closed the door. "My mother always said there's certain things you never question. Like money. She calls it divine justice. It's just divine."

"I say good riddance," said Nick, pulling Esmeralda down the hall. "Let's get out of here before divine justice nails them for robbing Western Union or cleaning out the bank or knocking off the train station. This Jaxson character is bad news."

McVittie's Restaurant was packed with working stiffs on their way to work, nightshift zombies on their way home, and an assorted group of transients, wanderers, and hoboes who found the Naughahyde booths more comfortable than the park benches and bus stations outside. There was a cook, a cashier, and a couple of snaggly waitresses in hairnets that made them look slightly yellow and waxy. A radio played a newscast in the background:

"Havoc in Hollister. Motorcyclists Take Over Town, Many Injured. That was the headline in the July 5 edition of the San Francisco Chronicle. State Highway patrolmen imposed informal martial law in downtown Hollister, California, to curb the riotous activities of an estimated 4000. The outburst of terrorism—wrecking of bars, bottle barrages into the streets from upper story windows and roofs and high speed racing of motorcycles though the streets—came as participants in the annual 'Gypsy Tour' sponsored by the American Motorcycle Association converged on Hollister for a three-day

*meeting. Riders, both men and women, steered their machines
into bars, crashing fixtures and bottles and mirrors. They
defied all traffic regulations racing full speed through the
streets and intersections. Hundreds loosed bottle barrages in
the worst 40 hours in Hollister history."*

"Whatever it takes to build up an appetite," said Nick as
he worked on a stack of pancakes.

Esmeralda sat across from him, half-listening to the news
while contemplating their fortune in the morning tea leaves.
She raised her teacup a few inches over the table and spun it
three times in a circle. Two clumps of leaves formed on the
inner sides of the cup, each spelling out the letter "M." The
letters were flattened and elongated and looked like serpents
hovering over a pond. "Nickie," she said, "who do we know
with the initials M-M?"

Nick looked at the tea leaves with his usual skepticism.
He was used to Esmeralda's reading of whatever was in front
of her, be it outstretched palms, tea leaves, napkin folds,
coffee stains, plate cracks, or breadcrumbs. "Beats me," he
said. "McKinley Morganfield?"

"Yeah, maybe."

The leaves formed a straight line that led toward the handle of the cup, where a little clump took on the appearance of
a bird in flight. Nick studied the formation for a moment,
then looked up and glanced across the room. His eyes,
already dark from the lack of sleep, blackened to the stony
ebony of a petrified forest when he saw two familiar figures
sitting at the counter. "Mister Montgomery," he said.

"Huh?"

"M-M."

"Oh, yeah. Good old Mister. He's probably wondering
where we are right about now."

"Es, it's time to go," said Nick in an urgent whisper.

Esmeralda put down her teacup and looked up at him,
surprised at the concern in his voice. "What is it?" she said.

"Just do as I say," he said as he dropped a couple of bucks on the table, grabbed Esmeralda's arm, and hustled her out the back door of the restaurant.

At the counter, old lady McVittie shoved a couple of plates along the Formica top to the customers in the last two stools. It was the usual breakfast fare, maybe a bit more robust than usual, with two sides of toast, two sides of potatoes, and a bowl of raw onions. The main course—McVittie's signature dish—was met with a shrug. The Denver Omelette, after all, was simply not in the same league as the Omaha Steak, which is maybe why it took so long for Ray and Dirk to show up in the Rocky Mountains in the first place. What was the motivation for their expedition halfway across the country? The green bell pepper? The cheese? The cubed ham? These were Chicagoans, after all, guys from the City of Big Shoulders, not Western namby-pambies who liked their eggs fluffy and beaten with a wisp, not with a hammer. There were even rumors that the Denver Omelette wasn't from Denver at all, that it came over with the Chinese railroad workers, and that it was actually egg foo yung buried between two pieces of bread. Wouldn't it be just like the Chinese to hide their real intentions inside a typically inscrutable dis-guise?

Ray poked at the potatoes with his fork and examined both sides of the toast. You couldn't be too careful these days, he figured, what with the Marshall Plan sending all their money to Europe and the Hollywood Ten plotting to overthrow the government. They were being attacked from within and without, and if that wasn't reason enough to give you an ulcer, the telegram from Mister Montgomery that was waiting for them at Western Union certainly was:

FIND THOSE TWO OR ELSE. STOP.
DON'T COME BACK EMPTY HANDED. STOP.
DON'T STOP. STOP.

Ray read it for the third time, in between bites of runny

eggs, as if looking for loopholes. The crisp capital letters didn't leave a lot of room for interpretation—no, Montgomery was still pissed off and their couple of days on the road hadn't soothed him one little bit. "You haven't seen a curly-haired floozy and a guy with a limp in these parts, have you?" he said to Mrs. McVittie.

"Does she have black hair?" said the old woman.

"Real black."

"And the guy's kinda cute?"

"Real cute."

"They're at that table over there," she said pointing to the middle of the room.

Ray and Dirk swung around on their stools to observe two red-haired floozies at one table, three blonde floozies at another, and one elderly floozy sitting alone whose hair had been dyed so many times it was hard to say what color it was. As for guys with limps, everybody in the place looked like they had a limp, like they were in some kind of orthopedic ward. "Okay, thanks, sister," said Dirk, accustomed to the ever disappointing news.

"Guess they blew," said Mrs. McVittie, glancing at the table that was now empty except for a plate of half-finished pancakes.

"Uh-huh," said Ray, turning back to his eggs, "gotcha."

Dirk couldn't take his eyes off one of the waitresses across the room. She was balancing three plates on one arm while clearing a table with the other. "Get a load of that one," he said.

"Never hit on a broad in a hairnet," said Ray.

"Why not?"

"Who knows what's she's concealing under that spider web? Could have a nest of scorpions crawling around in there, for all you know."

"Yeah, yeah, I guess that sounds about right."

"Trust me. I know about these things. It's one of the rules of the road."

Dirk nodded uncertainly. "So what are we gonna tell Montgomery?" he said as he bit into a fried green pepper.

"We're gonna tell Montgomery the truth—that there's no sign of either of them—that they got Shanghaied to China or abducted by aliens or kidnapped by that motorcycle gang."

"What the hell is this country coming to?" said Dirk, shaking his head in disgust.

"Damned if I know," said Ray. "The whole damn thing is coming apart at the seams."

Dirk mashed a potato between his teeth and thought things over. "Okay, good, so you gonna call him?"

"No, you are."

"Me? Why me?"

"You're good on the phone. I always admired your voice long distance."

Dirk broke off a toothpick and rolled it between his lips. "I'll flip you for it," he finally said.

"Fine," said Ray as he pulled out a quarter from his pocket and flipped it into the air. "Call it."

"Heads," said Dirk.

"Heads it is," said Ray, catching the coin and slapping it against the back of his hand. "You call."

"But, Ray, I won."

"That's right. Congratulations. You get to call. Tell Mister I said hello."

Dirk knew he was being played like a cheap violin but he also knew there was no point arguing about it since Ray always got the better of him in these little games of mental hopscotch. He shot him a quick look just to let him know that he knew what Ray knew and—who knows?—maybe even more. Dirk pushed his thick sausage of a body away from the counter, walked over to a phone booth at the back wall, and dropped in a fistful of coins. He listened for a dial tone, fumbled with the receiver, and began dialing a crazy-long series of numbers when the waitress with the hairnet appeared out of the kitchen with a tray of food. "Hey, there, big boy," she said, "where'd you get all those quarters?"

Dirk looked her up and down and then up and down again. "There's plenty more where those came from," he said.

"You don't say," she said, balancing the tray, rubbing up against his arm, and giving him a wink all at the same time.

Ray sponged up some egg with his toast and glanced over to make sure Dirk wasn't rubber fingering the rotor. A clown like Dirk, after all, would swear on his mother's grave that the line was dead just to be cute. As he turned back to the yellow blob on his plate, he noticed a reflection in the mirror that nearly made him choke on his egg foo yung: Nick was at the wheel of a Hudson Commodore and Esmeralda was right next to him, her mane of black hair frizzing in the wind like the Bride of Frankenstein shot out of a cannon. "Dirk!" he yelled out. "Hang up!"

Dirk didn't need to be told twice. Anything was better than talking to Mister Montgomery, even if the goddamn phone ate his coins. He smashed the receiver against the hook a couple of times, then yelled across the room. "What is it?"

"Get the damn car!"

"What, now?"

"Yes, now!"

Dirk dug around inside the coin return for loose change, then shrugged his apologies to the waitress. "Next time, sister," he said.

"Okay, big spender," she said. "I'll be waiting."

"Just one thing," said Dirk as he hurried for the door.

"What's that, honey?"

"Lose the hairnet, okay?"

"Sure thing, big boy, anything you say."

Chapter 20

"Something unknown is
doing we don't know what."
—Sir Arthur Eddington

T he trunk of the Checker Cab sprung open, its corrugated steel lid creaking and groaning in the breeze as the driver reached inside for some bags. He nearly disappeared inside the gaping cavern, a big mechanical mouth that looked like it could chew him up. It was amazing what a Checker Cab could carry in its oversized luggage space. There was Loquacious Landry's daypack, which was crammed full with documents from the Court of Last Resort, Rand-McNally roadmaps, a calorie counter, a currency converter, a magnetic chess set, a book of Chinese proverbs, homeopathic digestion aids, antidepressant medications, a bottle of mouthwash, and an assortment of police-issue restraining devices. Next to it was Kalamata Quayle's overnight bag, which was stuffed with dietary supplements, a carton of cigarettes, three tubes of crimson rose lipstick, an isometric forearm exerciser, a variety pack of Wrigley's Chewing Gum, a joy buzzer, a pair of spa slippers, a Serbo-Croatian dictionary, a Burmese cat's eye, a chart of Andean rainfall totals, and her own assortment of restraining devices, although certainly not of the police variety. The Obsidians' suitcases, containing a modest collection of early twentieth century fundamentalist attire, were now bulging with the addition of the Dior dresses and Hawaiian shirts and could barely contain all of the tubes and hoses of the Rev-It-Up® retrieval system. The equipment was haphazardly jammed together in a manner unbefitting a serious scientific inquiry, but such is the case when the police are left in charge of taking care of sensitive evidence. Jammed behind the suitcases was Fort Sedgwick's RCA television set, which Loquacious had confiscated just for the hell of it, and three body bags which had been tossed inside as if they were the afterthoughts of an archeological museum exhibit. These Loquacious insisted on removing himself, since he didn't want any squishy, three-foot, olive-green aliens popping out through the nylon zippers.

The cab was parked at the bottom of a mesa about 12 miles outside Arapahoe, dead center in the middle of no-where. "So, this is it, huh?" said the driver, eyeballing some sagebrush, cacti, and an irregular dotting of prairie dog holes.

"Home sweet home," said Loquacious, keeping himself between the driver and the mesa so that he wouldn't notice the two rocket ships parked in the distance. "What do we owe you?"

"$112.60, plus $6 for the extra bags."

"How do you figure?"

"Bags in excess of 40 pounds shall be surcharged at the rate of $2 per bag per excursion," said the driver, reading from a printed form pasted on the dashboard.

"You people never miss a chance to stick it to the tourists, do you?"

"What can I tell you, buddy?" said the driver, shrugging unconcernedly.

"Let me give you a tip," said Loquacious, counting out exactly $118.60.

"Sure," said the cabbie, sticking out his hand.

"Don't take any wooden nickels," said Loquacious as he

pulled his hat lower over his forehead and spun on his heels.

The driver got back into his cab without a word, started up the engine, and headed back toward Arapahoe. The travelers slung the television, suitcases, backpacks and body bags over their shoulders and embarked on the long climb to the top of the mesa. They were as quiet as the desert air—tired of the heat, tired of the bugs, and tired of Earth itself. Earth was becoming a giant albatross around all of their necks and was proving to be as inhospitable as had been rumored. What the Obsidians had seen as a great adventure—a foray into an old world theme park—was becoming a frightfully dangerous excursion.

Up, up, up they climbed, over craggy rocks and slippery boulders, stopping just long enough to catch their breath, then forging on to the barren plateau above them. The ground baked in the sun and little clumps of dirt and sand kicked up with each footstep as the travelers moved single file up the hill. Loquacious led the way, ever eager to put this distasteful mission behind him. Kalamata brought up the rear, making sure there was no funny business, although what exactly would constitute funny business in a group such as this was anyone's guess. It was a chain gang without a chain, a brain trust without a brain, a prayer group without a prayer.

Jaxson was feeling especially lightheaded, not surprising given that 9% of his essence was still trapped in Nick's brain. He'd been uncharacteristically quiet from the moment the detectives burst into the motel room and pulled the plugs on the machinery. Marta-2 had kept an eye on him ever since, making sure he didn't suddenly wander off a ledge somewhere. She felt responsible for Jaxson being on the excursion in the first place, having let her romantic inclinations intrude upon her scientific responsibilities. Ah, love. Who knows what chaos it might breed?

When they arrived outside the Pulsar-7, things didn't look

much different from when they'd left. The left ventricle wing
was crushed against the body of the ship, the forward observation portal was cracked in seven places, and there was still
a gaping hole through the ribbed skeleton of the underbody
that made stabilization impossible. What should have been a
beehive of activity was more like a hornet's nest of argument
and banter. Muffled voices could be heard from the forward
chambers, followed by sarcastic groans, curses, and slamming doors.

"Hieronymus Wambold!" shouted Loquacious from the
bottom of the polyprotopulsium ladder.

The door to the rocket opened a moment later and the
weary captain appeared in his rumpled uniform. "You're
back," he said.

"Of course we're back. Did you think we were going to
dilly-dally in Denver while the solar clock is ticking down?"

Marta-1 emerged from behind the door and stood behind
the captain. She peeked over Wambold's shoulder with a
look of anticipation until Kalamata caught her eye. "Hey,
toots," said Kalamata. Marta-1 blushed and retreated into the
shadows.

"Do you realize that we have less than four days to get off
this planet before the aphelion hits the fan?" said Loquacious.

"I'm well aware of the date," said Wambold, "although
keeping track of this slow moving sun is enough to induce
somnescence. Anyway, that's not the problem. The problem
is that you shot the one person who knows how to make the
necessary repairs."

"And why is that a problem? His body parts should've
recombined hours ago."

"Yes, they did, but—*how shall I put it?*—Chief Engineer
Teller awoke from his ordeal in a particularly foul temper."

"Oh, God," muttered Loquacious under his breath. "What
next?"

"He's being very difficult, to say the least."

Loquacious had had it up to there and was ready to blow a gasket. He spoke with measured words: "Get him down here—"

Before Loquacious could finish his sentence, the Chief Engineer burst through the door like a bear who'd been prematurely awakened from hibernation. He climbed down the rungs of the ladder two at a time, anxious to confront his executioner and reanimator. Teller was convinced that his various body parts had somehow been improperly realigned in the recombination process, which was ridiculous, of course, since reanimation simply doesn't work that way, but try telling that to someone whose eyeballs and wisdom teeth had only hours before been tucked inside his anal cavity. "You wanted to see me?" he growled at the detective. A spittle of saliva escaped from his mouth and dribbled down his chin, where it quivered a moment before evaporating into the hot morning air.

"You see these three bodies?" said Loquacious. "I thought you'd like to see up close. What you did." Loquacious unzipped one of the bags to reveal the shell of a body whose features were nearly indistinguishable. "This fellow, the one without a face, he probably has a wife and two kids. Daddy, daddy, they're crying out to him, tell us a bedtime story. But they're not going to hear any more bedtime stories. At least not from him. Not tonight. Not ever." Loquacious pulled open the top of another bag and separated the flaps. "This one, the little guy with the green gills. Maybe he's got an elderly mother who depends on his check every month. She's waiting for the doorbell to ring. She's waiting for the delivery man from the supermarket. But there is no delivery man. There's nobody. Nobody to look after her. Nobody to care." Loquacious zipped open the final bag and choked back a gasp as he turned away from the horrendous sight. "This victim of your foul play. Is only partially here. The rest of his organs are trapped in some laboratory. Where the Earthlings conducted experiments on him. What do we tell his parents? That they should just go ahead and bury him? Without his heart? And liver? Would you like to be the courier who has to deliver that message?"

Teller shrugged. "They're collateral damage. Couldn't be helped. Not like your shooting me. Which could've been. Helped, that is," he said, sarcastically mocking Loquacious Landry's tortured syntax.

"You're right," said Loquacious, seething at Teller's impertinence. "My decision was discretionary. I had a choice. Zap you with my schiller or turn you over to Miss Quayle. For final disposition. You know what they say about discretion, don't you? That it's the better part of valor?"

"I guess so."

"Don't believe it," said Loquacious. "Discretion is for dummies. Like me. But no more. I've learned an important lesson." He opened his bag and pulled out an assortment of butcher knives, parers and corers. "Kalamata, take this guy out back and feed him. To the crows."

"With pleasure," said Kalamata, reaching for the tools.

"Now wait just one minute!" said Captain Wambold, hurrying down the ladder. "That's my crew you're talking about. You'll have to go through me before you lay a hand on a member of my team."

"No problem," said Loquacious. "Miss Quayle, will you kindly take them *both* out back?"

Before Kalamata had a chance to perform her kitchen acrobatics, Marta-2 rushed between the detectives and the crew. "Haven't we had enough trouble already?" she pleaded. "Do we all want to go before the Court of Last Resort and explain how we broke every covenant between man and planet?"

"Well said," said Raleigh, appearing through an open portal in the aft shaft, "well said, indeed!" Raleigh was between trances and savored this rare moment of real life drama.

"From the mouths of molecular biologists come true nuggets of wisdom. Let us put this abject conflict behind us and work for the common good. What say you?"

"Oh, fuck off, you big bag of steam," said Oblivia, rustling herself out of her self-imposed silence with scathing vituperation. Everyone instinctively moved toward one another, like a rack of pool balls bouncing off the walls and headed for collision. It was as if Jack Slade and Jules Beni were going to engage in a fight to the finish when an entirely unexpected voice of reason commanded everyone's attention.

"The day we understand the difference between zero and nothing is the day we'll understand dream energy," said Jaxson, staring into the empty space between his hands.

"True... true..." muttered the gathered assemblage. Jaxson's wise council calmed everyone's tempers and put things into proper perspective. Well, almost everyone, that is.

"Are we really going to listen to *him?*" said Teller, still itching for a fight. He reached back to slug somebody—*anybody*—but before he could connect with Jaxson's jaw, Loquacious pulled out his schiller and blasted the Chief Engineer right between the testicles. Teller was propelled against the contextual wing of the Pulsar-7, where his body fragmented and disintegrated into a jumble of re-de-animated parts. His lips, which were lodged now between the folds of his stomach and the crevices of his kneecaps, flapped breathlessly in the wind. "Not again," they quivered, then fell silent, drawn and ashen, in the hot Nebraska sun, "not again..."

Marta-2 found Captain Wambold alone in his cabin, studying ship diagrams and engine maintenance schedules. She cleared her throat, then tapped on the door and stepped inside. "Did you notice anything strange about Jaxson, sir?" she said.

"How does one judge what is strange about Jaxson?" said Wambold, looking up from a blueprint of the Pulsar-7 exo-skeleton. "What is the metric one would use? A personality scale? A psychological profile? A social barometer? Where would one even begin?"

"I know what you mean, Captain. It's something I like to think of as the charm factor. He's really quite extraordinary, isn't he?"

"Quite," said Wambold, twisting his eyebrows into angry pretzels.

"But that's not what I'm referring to. There's something that happened in Denver you need to know about."

Wambold closed his eyes, as if he could block out any more bad news by simply ignoring it. "If you must provide the sordid details of your aborted mission, do it with due haste and a minimum of detail. My intestinal tract cannot take another eruption of gastric fluid activity."

Marta-2 looked at the captain with concern. He wasn't a bad guy, and he deserved better than this constant barrage of bad news. Still, a mission report was a mission report and she had her own responsibilities to fulfill. "Well, the good news is that we managed to find a suitable subject and were able to conduct the experiment after all, at least partially, that is, and I wish to report that we were able to extract nearly ten minutes of pure, undiluted dream energy without any problems whatsoever. The retrieval was an unequivocal success, to the degree that we were able to complete the process, that is, which, unfortunately, was only halfway, given the unexpected arrival of detectives Landry and Quayle who, in their haste, abrogated the experiment before Data Transfer Officer Oblivia had a chance to transfer the data from a second, more incendiary dream, said data being presently ensconced in the Rev-It-Up® retrieval system just waiting to be sent to Obsidia, if only the machinery were still in our hands. Which it is not."

"And the bad news?" said Wambold, waiting for the inevitable enumeration of deaths, accidents, and disfigurements.

"Jaxson's essence is trapped in the brain of a human."

Wambold sat there a moment digesting the news. Part of Jaxson, the *bête noir* of intergalactic space exploration, the *enfant terrible* of the outer spheres, was trapped in the brain of a human? Well, well, well. This was cause for—*hmm, let's see now*—well, what? Concern? Alarm? Panic? The captain ran through the possibilities and settled on a fourth option. Laughter. Pure, undiluted, unequivocal laughter that started deep in his belly and rose joyfully up his spine and exploded in a starburst of hilarity that would've shaken the rafters, if only the Pulsar-7 had any rafters. Which it did not.

"Uh, Captain?" said Marta-2.

"Terrible news... terrible news..." said Wambold, after finally pulling himself together.

"What should we do, Captain?"

"What *can* we do," he said with a faraway look in his eye, "except grin and bear it?"

"But don't you think—"

"That will be all, Chief Molecular Biologist," said Wambold, turning back to his diagrams. "Report accepted."

Jaxson was in a fog, and not just his usual fog, no, this was a real fog brought about by sitting in the steam bath of the Pulsar-7's spa for an hour and ten minutes, which was a full 50 minutes longer than recommended, but Jaxson missed that part of the instructions when, in an effort to blow out the cobwebs in his brain, he turned all the settings to full blast, but now there was pretty much nothing left *but* the cobwebs, cobwebs that mucked up his perceptions of the past, present and future, his whole brain had become a mess of spidery filaments that spread everywhere and nowhere, his thoughts jumped haphazardly from the orphanage to the

Institute to the twentieth floor of Reverie Energy, they were becoming jumbled together, the pranks and the jokes, the deceptions and the misbehavior, the lying and the cheating, who was he really, this Jaxson Epsilon of unknown parentage and questionable stock, was he a force of good in a world gone bad or merely a thorn in everyone's side, was he a soulful blues musician and man of the people or a complete and utter fraud, was he lover or a user, a heartbreaker or abuser, the memories sweated out through every pore in his body, it was raining thoughts until the cobwebs were nearly bare, there was more of Jaxson left in Nick's brain than in his own, he was an empty vacuum cleaner, a barren compost heap, a tarnished recycling bin, he'd lost his spark, his will and his edge, he was a mere shadow of his flamboyant former self, he was excess baggage, a guy just along for the ride, an observer with nothing more to observe, and then, for one brief second, Jaxson saw a glow around his hands, the glow from the skin-tight Rev-It-Up® gloves that shone briefly in the heavy mist, and at that instant the fog cleared and Jaxson saw a pair of fancy spa slippers with tassels and cheap jewels and then he saw a naked foot and a bare leg and then he saw another body and realized that Kalamata and Marta-1 were entwined in a deep, romantic embrace, and that's when his whole world exploded, Marta-1, the sole reason for his being on this excursion in the first place, was clearly and obviously romantically involved with... with... with... a *detective*, and this was beyond anything he'd ever imagined, this was beyond belief, this was beyond the beyond, and then the fog thickened and his vision blurred and Jaxson fell right through the door and out into the corridor where he twitched around like a frog on a hotplate, and when Marta-2 happened by and saw him staring blankly into his own reflection in a pool of sweat, she said, "That's it," and it was.

Chapter 21

*"I am accustomed to sleep and in my dreams to imagine
the same things that lunatics imagine when awake."*
—Descartes

The Hudson Commodore rumbled through Colorado
with a renewed sense of urgency. Nick headed west
through Idaho Springs, Kremmling and Steamboat
Springs, stopping only for gas, oil, and water, then getting
back on the road as quickly as possible. Not that Esmeralda
exactly shared his worries. When he told her about spotting
Ray and Dirk at the restaurant, she didn't believe a word of it.
After all, did it really make sense that Montgomery would
send those two gonifs halfway across the country to collect
on her lousy $800 debt? Hardly. It was more likely that Nick
was having a little delusional episode brought about by his
nightmares, his lack of sleep, his aching knee, his oxygen
deprivation, and his general disorientation at having spent
three days and nights cooped up in a car with Esmeralda
which, even she had to admit, could drive anyone a bit loopy.
"Don't worry about a thing, Nickie," said Esmeralda. "Just
focus on getting us to California before the grapes wither up
and die."

Nick might've been delusional, and maybe those slabs of
beef sitting at the counter merely *looked* liked familiar
palookas, but he didn't think so. No, he knew there was a

very good reason for Ray and Dirk to follow them—his ill-conceived attempt to rob Montgomery—and that was something he simply hadn't been able to bring himself to tell Esmeralda. It was a little secret that would have to wait for the right moment to be unveiled, preferably somewhere where she couldn't throw a lamp, a tire iron, or a kitchen knife at him. "Okay, baby," he said. "We'll just follow the plan."

"Good," said Esmeralda, reaching over and patting him on the knee.

"Es?" said Nick, after a moment. "We've *got* a plan, right?"

"Sure, sure, Nickie, what do you think?" she said with exaggerated patience. In truth, Esmeralda didn't have anything even approaching a plan. Plans were for suckers. You make a plan, you break a plan, and what are you left with but a pile of confusion and regret? No, dreams were more like it, since dreams were subject to whim, and whim was Esmeralda's specialty of the house. She lived her life with a dash of whim and a side order of whatchama-whocha thrown in just to keep them guessing. After all, the future was a big unknown and the past was just a sad old story trying to catch up with you and lay waste to your dreams. Better to live in the present, keep your purse wide open, and let the chips fall where they may.

There were all sorts of rumors floating around America in the summer of 1947. Rumors of flying saucers crashing into the New Mexican desert, rumors of dead aliens being shipped to secret army bases, rumors of communists plotting to overthrow the government, rumors of a powerful Russian A-bomb, rumors of a super-secret Central Intelligence Agency, rumors of a protracted Cold War, rumors of a nationwide television network, rumors of a black man playing in the Major Leagues, rumors of Al Capone dying of syphilis, rumors of tiny transistors powering giant computers, and rumors that *Gentleman's Agreement* would win the Oscar for Best Picture. Which it did. By a landslide.

Utah had its own crazy rumor, that the Mormons had taken to wearing magic underwear which gave them supernatural powers to ward off illness, deflect bullets, and protect them from evil forces. Nick laughed it off as a ridiculous superstition, but Esmeralda wasn't so sure. "Who knows what's what?" she said, looking at him with equal parts frustration and exasperation. Nick, unfortunately, was a small thinker and a hopeless realist. Realism held him down, just like every other Midwesterner she'd ever met. It was something about the weather, or the flat terrain, or the interminable open sky that pinched their imaginations and made them look at the world the way it really was, not the way it ought to be. A guy like Nick looks at a farm and sees a barn and a silo, he glances down the road and sees two lanes and a divider, he looks at a forest and sees bushes and trees. Hopeless, in other words. She'd been brought up on stories of magic rings, enchanted gardens and charmed shoes, and even if magic underwear did seem to be a bit of a stretch, she saw no reason to linger among the land of suspect undergarments. Not that they needed a reason to speed their way through Utah: this was no place for a bar girl and a harmonica player, especially since there were no bars and no bands within dancing distance of Salt Lake City.

Esmeralda wangled her way back behind the steering wheel and Nick pulled out his harmonica and played to the rhythms of the tires clacking on the cracks of the highway. As far as Esmeralda was concerned, Nick's harmonica was his saving grace. When he did a run up those scales, the real world faded away and gave way to an enchanted realm of diamond-studded shoes, sharkskin suits, and floppy hats that hung low over the forehead. That was the Nicky she loved, a guy who could swing to the beat and soar with the crows and thumb his nose at the universe.

Late in the afternoon, they came upon a barren landscape known as the Great Salt Desert, an endless salt flat that had neither hill nor valley nor speck of vegetation to break the monotony. It was as if nature had undergone an identity crisis and had simply thrown up its hands and given up when it got to this piece of parched earth. Trying to relieve the boredom, Nick unleashed a barrage of notes that reached for the sky but thudded mutely to the arid salt slicks. He soon discovered that the desert was no place to play the blues or anything else, for that matter. The desert took his notes and sucked them dry, evaporating them into the ether. There was no reverb in the desert, no vibrato, no echo, no bass, and no treble; there was just a thin sound wave that dissipated into the air the moment it escaped his lips. It was like whistling into a paper bag and equally unrewarding. What Nick needed was a wall of Fender amplifiers to bounce his sounds across the salt flats, whip the breeze into a raging sandstorm, and take a crack at the clouds.

There were only two times he felt like that—onstage and in Esmeralda's bed—and that was like being onstage in a whole other way. Nick thought about the first time they made love, how Esmeralda danced on his chest, wrapped him in her thighs, and buried him in her breasts, then finished with a girlish laugh of pure, unbridled joy. At first, he was offended, thinking she was laughing at *him*, but eventually he realized that was just the way she climaxed. It was unrestrained, unselfconscious Gypsy joy let loose on a nervous world. It was Esmeralda bringing down the house in a vaudeville road show, Esmeralda in her chicken suit, strutting and preening, Esmeralda giving a what-for and a why-not and a who-cares all at once, Esmeralda affirming a life force that couldn't be repressed, and after a while Nick waited for that laugh, he *lived* for that laugh, come, Esmeralda, come into my bed, deliver your punch line, bring down the house, they're calling for an encore, come, Esmeralda, come, enter stage left, take a bow and swing your hips and shake your shoulders until a burst of energy rushes through your spine and erupts into a big, broad, crazy chortle that shakes the bed and bounces off the walls.

The Hudson hit a bump in the road and momentarily pulled Nick out of his reverie. It was unusual—this free-wheeling turn of the mind—since Nick's dream world had taken up permanent residence in the foxholes of Italy. He stared out at the interminable nothingness and his mind began filling in the blanks. Consciousness hates a void, just as nature hates a vacuum, and Nick felt himself floating off again. Maybe it was the desert air, or the unwavering flat-lands, or the hypnotic thump of the tires on the straight shot of asphalt that shook loose his past, but images of family, home, and friends now danced through his mind. He saw himself playing on a swing, studying for a test, kissing a girl, and skating on a frozen lake. The dry, hot desert transported him to wet, cold Wisconsin—a place that wasn't often on his mind anymore—and he imagined himself in the body of a seven-year-old in the back seat of the family Oldsmobile, driving down a dirt road to a dead end where a couple of Indians manned a flimsy barrier upon which was scrawled:

PRIVATE TOLE RODE
ONEIDA INJUN NATION
PAY HEAR
THANX A HEEP

Nick's dad reluctantly agreed to fork over 75 cents for the patently illegal toll, but he decided not to argue with the young warriors lest they choose to scalp them in more serious ways. "Can't wait to see how much they'll soak us for the show," he said. He was right. They soaked them for the show, which was half-hearted at best, since to get a dozen Oneidas to dance for three tourists went against every show biz dictate, Indian or not. Nick and his parents sat in wooden bleachers as two guys hit tom-toms, an old lady clucked an atonal whoop, and a troupe of warriors did a desultory war dance. A young Oneida woman, dressed in full squaw regalia, dished out something brown and unsavory into clay bowls and passed it around. Nick's mom and dad begged off, which left Nick mortified since food was food, even if it came from the underbelly of a buffalo. As he nibbled at it, the squaw smiled and the old lady whooped a little louder, and Nick suddenly felt himself magically transported somewhere over the band of dancers. He looked down and saw himself in their circle, and then he looked at his parents on the bleachers and he knew at that moment that he would never become a pharmacist, that he would never take over his father's drugstore, that he would never live and die in Wisconsin, that he was destined for something different. "How is it, son?" asked his dad, and Nick stared into his buffalo stew and said, "Better than I thought."

While Nick thought about the past, Esmeralda stared down the middle of the road and imagined life in California. Let bygones be bygones—that was the Gypsy way—let the little crimes and misdemeanors of yesterday fade into history, let the memory be short and the tomorrows sweet. Sweet as grapes. In Esmeralda's future, she saw grapes everywhere—grapes on the vines, grapes on the ground, grapes in her hair, grapes between her toes. She'd dance in the grapes the minute they got to Petaluma—that much she knew—she'd dance a lovely jig to the grape gods and then she'd bathe in the wine and squirt it all over Nick and the two of them would revel in their newfound freedom. They'd run through the fields and feel the warmth on their feet, they'd roll down the hills and dip their toes in the streams and make love beneath the eucalyptus trees. Screw Montgomery and his 800 bucks. She'd send him a bottle of her special reserve Chardonnay and they could call it even.

"Want me to drive?" said Nick, staring across the Godfor-saken salt flats. There were a couple of Joshua trees in the distance, their crowns so top-heavy with spindly branches it looked like they could fall over at any minute. The Mormons had named them after that guy in the Bible who threw his hands to the sky in prayer in a fit of pique. The lonely trees looked equally distressed as they flailed their limbs at the desert sky.

"In a while," said Esmeralda, struggling not to drift off into a salt-induced coma. The sun beat down on the road and left squiggly little radiation waves that rose up off the as-phalt, then vanished into thin air. Esmeralda glanced at a passing car and tried to make sense of its license plate:

UTAH

THE BEEHIVE STATE

"Nick," she said, "have you seen any bees since we got to Utah?"

"Not a one."

"Well, wouldn't you call that false advertising or some-thing?"

"I would."

"I mean, nobody says, *Illinois, the Pineapple State,* do they?"

"Nobody that I know."

"You don't miss it, do you?"

"What, Chicago? Not at all."

"What's to miss, right?"

"Nothing," said Nick, as he leaned back and stared at the open sky. The truth is, he missed everything about Chicago. He missed the high humidity, he missed the noise of the el, and he missed the late-night ambulance sirens. "Remember those shadows on the wall outside our apartment?" he said. "I never quite understood that."

"Spooked you, didn't they? The place was haunted, I'm sure of it. Some old lady probably threw herself off the roof and her shadow got caught in the wind."

"That happens, huh?"

"All the time."

Nick was fascinated by Esmeralda's belief in the impossible. Laws of gravity and attraction simply didn't apply in Esmeralda's universe, where anything went so long as it could be explained in ten words or less. Esmeralda had no use for science and science had no use for her, allowing her to exist somewhere just outside the normal physical world. That's where Gypsies liked it, in that shady netherworld where the usual rules didn't apply. Gypsies were guilt-free, unencumbered by following laws they never recognized in the first place. Things like taxes, speed limits, and security deposits were for gadjos to worry about, something to keep them awake at night. Gypsies slept well, with nothing on their conscience to weigh them down.

Nick's mind wandered again. The desert does that to you—it twists your thoughts and pokes your consciousness and throws you somewhere else altogether. He imagined himself in New York, the war was over, and his transport ship had off-loaded 3000 weary soldiers. He limped out onto the streets, free at last, with no idea of where to go. He wasn't exactly lost—nobody who'd ever spent two years in the foxholes would ever again feel physically displaced—but he was lost in a larger sense, lost as to what to do from that day on, lost as to having a vision of any sort of future. When half your buddies have been blown to pieces you have to reconsider your career trajectory. Career? The very idea seemed absurd. How could anyone even imagine a tomorrow when yesterday was covered in layers of mud and dirt?

Nick stood on a corner and debated whether to go north to Harlem or east to the river or west to the transit hubs but something pushed him to Greenwich Village, where he could wander in peace. Everybody was wandering in the Village— ex-soldiers, ex-students, ex-husbands and ex-wives—the streets were full of a disconnected population whose vacant eyes darted from doorway to doorway, searching for somewhere new to enter, a bar or a restaurant or a club that would suck them into its cocoon and embrace them for an hour or two. Everyone was walking in circles—Nick, too—what else was he supposed to do, around and around he went, his battered body had been deposited on home ground while his friends had been buried in the mud. Why had he lived and not them, what made him so special, was he supposed to be thankful for the chance to stare into a meaningless future? He circled Sheridan Square and Waverly Place and Bank Street on the far west side, then looped back around to the center of the Village, to Bleecker Street and Fifth Avenue and Washington Square, then headed over to the Vanguard, a downtown jazz club where an atonal piano riff echoed out into the night. Inside some waygone cat named Monk kerplunked the keys while staring aimlessly into space, what was he looking at, it was anyone's guess, his notes were upside down and either too close together or too far apart, nothing made a bit of sense, yet it spoke to Nick as deeply as anything he'd ever heard, it was the music of a world teetering on the edge, a world that had lost its way and threw out a whole new melody, forget the old ways, it said, forget the house and the car and the job and the degree, none of that means anything anymore, a generation has died and a new one is digging through its remains for clues what to do next, come on, you wildman hepcats, celebrate your alienation, that's what Monk seemed to say, celebrate your detachment from a world that marched off a cliff, let's toss away our music sheets and our arrangements and our tired old melodies and live in that crazy dissonance between the notes.

As the thin desert air let in a flood of forgotten memories, Esmeralda stole a quick glance at Nick and felt a momentary pang of regret. She'd uprooted the poor guy in the middle of the night, pulled him out of his routine, and put his life in danger. It was strange, this descent into the rarified zones of bad conscience, and Esmeralda didn't like it. These were the moments when her father's untamed genes made an unwelcome appearance, bringing his thousand years of guilt to bear upon her head. *"Shame on you, Esmeralda,"* he intoned, *"for putting this nice boy into such a world of trouble."* Her Jewish guilt and Gypsy non-guilt struggled for supremacy. She tried to feel bad about not feeling bad, then felt worse when she couldn't remember exactly why she wasn't feeling better. "I'm sorry, Nickie," she said, the words colliding together as if surprised to find themselves in the same Esmeralda Kurlansky sentence.

"Me, too," said Nick, stuck in his own remorse.

"I never should've gotten you involved in this whole thing."

"Forget about it. It's water under the bridge."

"No, Nickie, you were right. I should've paid off my debt and been done with it."

"You did what you thought was right."

"I mean, all this over a lousy 800 bucks!"

Nick looked out at a solitary Joshua tree in the middle of the desert and wondered what ill wind had blown its seed to this most inhospitable land. He envied the tree at that moment, lost as it was in mindless prayer. That's what Nick wanted to do at that moment, pray, and if he had even the slightest belief in God he probably would have gotten down on his knees right there in the desert and tossed his arms to the sky and asked, why, oh God, why did I break into Montgomery's house and try to rob him of $800? What was I thinking, dear God, did I really think I could move invisibly through his parlor and grab the ante off the poker table and disappear into the night? Nick slumped back against the plump vinyl seat. "Es, I've got something to tell you."

"What's that, Nickie?"

"You remember that night you came looking for me at all the clubs in Chicago?"

"Sure."

"And how you asked everybody where I was?"

Esmeralda got a faraway look in her eyes. She tried to imagine where Nick was going with all of this. "Uh-huh..."

"And how I came home real late that night?"

Esmeralda replayed the evening in her mind and slowly began putting two and two together. Nickie: not at the club. Nickie: not at home. Nickie: in the arms of some two-bit hussy with bleach blonde hair and falsies. She jammed on the brakes with such violence that the Hudson fish-tailed across the road and spun in circles on the salt flat like a dreidel gone crazy on Dexedrine. When the car finally corkscrewed to a stop, Esmeralda grabbed Nick's shirt collar and pulled it so tight, a button popped off and pinged against the windshield. *"Who is she!"* she demanded. *"Who is she?"*

A cloud of dust twirled around the car and deposited a layer of salt on Nick's parched tongue. "Damn... it... Esmeralda," he sputtered through his compressed larynx, "there... is... no... she..."

Esmeralda punched him in the arm just for the hell of it, then slowly loosened her grip and composed herself. "Well, what then?"

"I did something stupid," said Nick. "Really, really stupid."

Esmeralda impatiently tapped her fingers on the dashboard. Her fingernails rat-a-tatted against the dial of the Philco radio like bursts of Morse code in an echo chamber. "I'm waiting."

"Well, I just couldn't stand the idea of you working the bar at the Flame Club again and I had to do something, I mean, a man has to be a man sometimes, and a lousy 800 bucks was standing between you and your freedom, hell, it was standing between you and *our* freedom, 800 lousy bucks, do you know how small that can make a guy feel, to have his girl working a place like that, so I thought about this and that and kept running into one wall after another, I could pawn my stuff but I had nothing of value, I could borrow some money but I had no friends, I could get a loan but I had no collateral, so what am I gonna do, who knows, I went a little crazy, I went over to Montgomery's place, don't ask me why, it was poker night, I figured I could slip in and slip out in no time, so I got in disguise, okay, a stupid disguise, but a disguise nonetheless, I got in disguise and slipped in and there it was, 800 bucks on the table, maybe more, one lousy ante stood between us and our freedom, so I grabbed it and it was easy as that, hell, I understand now why guys become thieves, it's not that hard, you just reach out and take something and what was theirs is suddenly yours, no muss, no fuss, except there *was* a fuss, an unexpected fuss, because Ray and Dirk showed up out of nowhere and all hell broke loose, guns, fists, money flying all over the place, and I swear, right on the spot, I realized I was the dumbest mug in Chicago, what did I know about grand larceny, nothing, and here I wish I could say that I stood up like a man and took the cash and fought my way out of there, but the truth is I ran like a scared rabbit, I jumped out the window and landed in some bushes and crawled on my stomach and limped away into the night, and that's probably what sunk me, that limp, because Montgomery obviously figured out who I was, it didn't take a genius, and that's why Ray and Dirk are after us, honey, it's not the 800 bucks you borrowed, it's the *other* 800 bucks that did us in, the 800 bucks I had in my hand for no more than ten seconds that we're going to be paying back from now until the end of time."

Esmeralda sat motionless in the car as a cloud of sand swirled around them. "You did that for me, Nickie?"

"Afraid so."

Esmeralda turned away so that Nick wouldn't see a tiny

tear forming at the corner of her eyes. "Well, okay, then."

"You're not mad?"

"How can I be mad?" she said, taking his hand. "That's just about the sweetest thing I've ever heard."

"Es, you realize that we might not even get out of this alive?"

Esmeralda wiped some dust off the windshield, pretending to be busy, then noticed a grove of Joshua trees that was growing just across the road. "Ghosts in the graveyard," she said.

"I guess that's us, all right."

"No, that's what they call those trees back home. There were a couple in the cemetery across the street. When they blossom they get shimmery all over and kind of float in the light."

Nick took a closer look at the trees. They were tall, maybe 25 feet, and at the end of each fibrous branch was a clump of leaves shaped like a bayonet. It looked for all the world as if the limbs of the tree were at war with their surroundings. "Es, let's go."

"Good idea," she said, turning on the ignition. The engine turned over a few times, then coughed and sputtered to a stop. Esmeralda tried again, giving the pedal more gas, less gas, and finally no gas at all. The result was the same each time. The engine was flooded. Or the battery was dead. Or the air filter was clogged. As night fell on the Great Salt Desert, they sat there staring into the vast emptiness of the desert and the stark blackness of the sky. They were two phantoms at the end of the world. Two shimmering figures in the sand. Two ghosts in the graveyard.

And the night had just begun.

Chapter 22

*"If it wasn't for bad luck, I
wouldn't have no luck at all."*
—Albert King

The 3:10 to Denver was right on schedule and this time Marta-2 was prepared when the conductor came by and asked for tickets. She had two first class seats stamped and paid for and even though the conductor thought something was up, he couldn't figure out what exactly it was. They looked familiar—these two hipsters in the Hawaiian shirt and the full skirt and strapless gown—but he couldn't quite place them and let it slide. "Have a nice journey," he said.

"Much obliged," said Marta-2, digging into her internal database of midcentury American idioms. It was up to her, after all, to lead the way, since Jaxson was in no condition to make conversation, much less any "earth-shaking decisions." That was another of those odd expressions that Marta-2 had difficulty with, since it seemed highly unlikely that a mere decision could exert the power to physically shake the earth. It was becoming evident to her that the people on this planet were given to grandiloquent overstatement and nothing they said could be taken too seriously.

As for Jaxson, he was in that obscure netherworld where his brain was trying to adapt to not being fully there, even if that was the condition everyone else claimed he'd been in all along. Ah, the brain—what a great invention! It really was right up there with rubber bands, paper clips, and twist-off caps. You throw something at the brain, it's only a matter of time before the brain turns it, twists it, and throws it back all wrapped up in a nice neat package. Even now, Jaxson's brain was working overtime to compensate for the fact that he was missing a very important chunk of gray matter. With his diminished motor skills, speech attenuation, and cognitive disabilities, his brain needed to rewire itself and find new neural pathways. Already there were little signs of recovery— the increasing glint in the eye, the occasional bon mot, the flash of humor. Jaxson might not have been his old, complicated self, but he was on his way to a passable version of himself—a Jaxson Lite, so to speak.

As any good brain scientist knows, the brain adapts. That's what it does. As far as Marta-2 was concerned, 91% of Jaxson was better than no Jaxson at all, and even in his diminished state she found him to be more charming than 83% of the guys she'd dated on Obsidia, a number she computed by using an old relationship algorithm from the *Molecular Biologist's Handbook of Social Interactivity*. No, this was the guy she'd fallen head-over-heels for, and given the four-inch Christian Dior pumps she had on, that was head-over-heels, indeed. Jaxson might've been a mess, but he was *her* mess, and he was sure to get better as soon as his neurons and synapses did the boogie-woogie and got back on track.

Marta-2 had decided to take the bull by horns, much like that lonely farmer out on the prairie, but with hopefully a bit more finesse. Since she was the one who'd gotten Jaxson into this predicament in the first place, it was up to her to get him out of it. With a daring that surprised even her, she'd slipped inside Detective Landry's space transport, made off with the central unit of the Rev-It-Up® retrieval system, and replaced it with a pillow under a blanket, just like she'd seen them do in the movies. Then she'd left a note for Captain Wambold, grabbed Jaxson by the nape of his neck, and fled down the mesa for the next train to Denver.

Marta-2's plan was simple: get back to the Cameron Motel, find Nick, put him back into a deep sleep, and send Jaxson back inside his brain to retrieve his essence. Then it would simply be a matter of catching the next train back to Arapahoe and returning before anyone was the wiser. The plan, of course, was not without risk. If anything went wrong, Jaxson and Marta-2 ran the risk of not getting back before the aphelion of the sun and that was trouble indeed. The Captain would be forced to make a difficult decision, but he'd have no choice but to leave without them. And that would be that. At least Jaxson would be whole again, and that was the choice on the table: return to Obsidia a shadow of his former self, or take the chance of regaining his essence, even if it meant possibly staying on Earth forever. It was a choice Jaxson was in no condition to make. So Marta-2 made it for him. No guts, no glory. Isn't that what the Earthlings said?

Jaxson and Marta-2 stood outside Room 207 of the Cameron Motel on a night as quiet as Quagmar Eve during a shale storm. The parking lot was deserted, the radios were silent, and the sky was clear but for the intermittent flash of a *Vacancy* sign that reflected against Jaxson's forehead in a brilliant pink-red neon. Marta-2 tried the door, which opened without a sound. It was unlocked, as usual, Earthlings being strangely trusting despite their propensity for violence, mayhem, and all-out war. Jaxson moved quietly to the bed while Marta-2 prepared her sleepy-time medication. He'd prop up Nick's head, she'd zap him with a couple of quick sprays to the nostrils, and they'd be in business. That was the plan, at least. It was a good plan, based on *P.D. Snowcastle's Probability Chart of Human Behavior,* which predicted a motel stay of four days and three nights, that being the national average, but failed to take into account the fact that this was Nick and Esmeralda they were talking about, which should have taken all bets off the table. Sure enough, Nick wasn't on the bed, nor was Esmeralda, nor was there any sign of them whatsoever. "They'll probably be right back," said Jaxson, already more talkative than before, but just as wrong as usual.

"I dare to disagree," said Marta-2 after an uneasy look around the room. "All indications are that they made a premature departure, considering the hour of the day, the ratio of open to closed dining establishments, and a handful of Hansgaard-Olafson variables that supports an unfavorable conclusion."

"Things don't always go right," said Jaxson with pointed understatement.

"Wait here," said Marta-2 as she headed back into the hallway. "Let me check with the front desk."

Jaxson flicked on a light and looked around more carefully. There was nothing to indicate either Nick's or Esmeralda's presence—not a suitcase or a toothbrush or a can of shaving cream or a change of underwear or a pair of spare socks. Nor was there any sign at all of the previous evening—no remnants of the experiment or the ensuing struggle. It was hard to believe that less than 24 hours ago he'd been inside Nick's brain and had sucked out a powerhouse dream that could power a dozen freeze-dried fusion plants back home. Now, the whole thing was a big jumble—his navigation through the nooks and crannies of Nick's brain, being trapped inside an Italian foxhole, the detectives bursting in, the ride in the taxi, the bodies at the army base, the shock of finding Marta 1 in the sauna—

"They checked out this morning," said Marta-2 upon returning to the room. "Last seen going west at a high rate of speed."

Jaxson stared at a painting of a rodeo cowboy on the wall. The cowboy was riding a bucking bronco and holding on for dear life. *"Gone, baby, gone,"* said Jaxson, mumbling a few verses of an impromptu blues song, *"and they won't be coming back."*

"I'm afraid not," said Marta-2. "Not anytime soon."

Pederson's Pool Hall was either half-full or half-empty, depending on which end of a bottle you were looking through. Marta-2 sipped at her Pabst Blue Ribbon, struggling to inject a little levity into their bleak situation. "Hey, Jaxson," she said. "Did you hear the one about the brain who walked into a bar?"

"I don't think I've heard that one," he said.

"A brain walks into a bar and says, *'I'll have a pint of beer, please.'* The barman looks at him and says, *'Sorry, I can't serve you.' 'Why not?'* asks the brain. *'You're already out of your head.'"*

"That's very funny," said Jaxson.

"Glad you liked it," said Marta-2 as she gave his hand a little squeeze. The crack of pool balls reverberated around the room. The tables were full, mostly with bored-looking guys killing time. Funny expression, that. Wouldn't it be enough to just *injure* time, maybe give it a punch or a smack or a kick in the groin? "Well, the good news is that we still have three days before lift-off," said Marta-2.

"All the time in the world," said Jaxson, slumping against the bar and aimlessly running his fingers around the rim of his beer glass.

"For what it's worth, I won't abandon you, Jaxson. If you choose to look for Nick, I'll be at your side every step along the way."

The idea of being forever trapped on Earth with Marta-2 suddenly didn't seem so bad, which made Jaxson wonder exactly which part of his essence was missing. Was it his good sense? His good taste? His good fortune? "Well, thanks," he said, returning her squeeze of his hand. "That's good to know."

"Don't mention it."

The door swung open and Neal Cassady trounced into the bar with a girl on each arm. It was hard to tell if he was holding them up or if they were holding him up or if gravity had simply caved in and placed a protective shield around the whole bunch of them. "Set 'em up, Pete," Neal called over to the bartender. His eyes danced and glistened after what appeared to be a full night of drinking and carousing. As he gallantly pulled out two chairs for the ladies, he noticed Jaxson at the bar and came right over, leaving the girls to fend for themselves. "Hey, Slick!" he said, pounding Jaxson on the back. "Back to hustle some unsuspecting locals?"

"Just a drink this time."

"Sure, sure, I can see why," giving Marta-2 the eye. "Who's the cheesecake?"

"Neal, Marta. Marta, Neal."

"Pleased to meet you," said Marta-2, shaking Neal's hand.

"Ever been to Mexico, angel face?" he said. "I think I remember you from a bar in Juarez."

"I've never been south of the border, but I'd love to visit," said Marta-2. "I understand they have some very peculiar rock formations."

"Sure thing, sister," he said, his eyes lighting up. "We can all hop in my Packard and be there by morning."

"We'll have to take a pass," said Jaxson, staring into his beer. "Something's come up."

"Why the mopey mug, Slick? You look like your best friend just died."

"Might as well have. He split this morning with his girl."

"I can dig it. You gotta move with the groove before the groove moves you. Hell, Jack hit the road today, too. Got on the Greyhound this afternoon for San Francisco."

"Seems like everybody's headed to California."

"You know, you got inside Jack's head. Not many people can do that." Neal turned and give Marta-2 a little wink. "Your boyfriend here has a real way with words, a nice turn of the phrase."

"Oh, yes, I know," said Marta-2, with no little pride. She savored the word "boyfriend" for a moment, just to give it a try. It fit awfully nicely, she thought.

"So when are the two of you joining the party out west? The west is the best, nothing left for the rest."

"We were just talking about that," said Marta-2. "You see, the thing is, Neal, we need to get to California quick as a wink. We need to catch up with our friends before the sun rises thrice and leaves an indelible print on the prairie."

"Thrice, you say?" said Neal with a smile. "Well, you came to the right guy, sister. You say you need to move—there's only one way. I know a guy who knows a guy and if we put a couple of crisp bills into the right hands, he can deck you out in speed and style, oh yes, the prairie will fly by, America will open its throbbing arteries and suck you down its endless road, the west is calling to you, can you hear it, come, it says, fly down the twisting highways and byways of our fair land, jump in and jump on and don't stop, no, not for even a minute, don't stop until the roiling surf tickles your toes."

"You hear that, Jaxson?" said Marta-2 with a hopeful look. "Neal says he knows a guy who knows a guy."

"I guess that's good enough for me," said Jaxson.

"Then it's been decided," said Neal, taking the two of them by the arm and leading them to the door. "Come with me, guys and gals, into the great big unpredictable tomorrow where the road shoots straight off into the far-gone horizon—"

Chapter 23

"There has never been a day like it before or since,
a day when the Lord listened to a human being."
—Joshua 10:14

The cold desert wind howled across the salt flats and momentarily stirred Nick from a deep sleep. He was cuddled up with Esmeralda in the back seat of the Hudson, the top was down, and the first hint of morning sun glimmered over a distant mesa. Nick pulled a blanket around them, readjusted his arms and legs in the deep foam cushion, and drifted back to sleep. In a matter of seconds, his eyelids began flickering and he entered into his usual dream state, only it was different this time, not the dream itself, but rather the moment where the dream began. The memories of the planes in the sky and the machine gun nests in the hills had been wiped clean by Jaxson's lifting of the code, and all that was left was the end of the dream—the part Jaxson had been unable to remove—and that's where Nick now found himself. As he drifted into unconsciousness, the steel tracks of the German tank cut across his field of vision, bearing down on him with unrelenting force. The throbbing sheets of metal churned the dirt and tossed it aside effortlessly, digging deeper into the mud and pushing ever forward. Nick grabbed his knee, the red-black blood caking on his ripped pant leg, and tried to pull himself away. That was the color of his dream, red-black, a kind of wrenching monotone that heightened his sense of dislocation. The sky was red-black, the dirt was red-black, the moon was red-black, the sun was red-black, and the rain was red-black. The metallic taste of the bullet spread from his tongue to his lips to the roof of his mouth. His muscles were numb and his tendons lifeless as he struggled again to move away from the oncoming machinery, but it was useless, his fingers dug into the mud and left him glued to the ground, the grinding roar of the engine was deafening, the steel tracks of the tanks rolled ever closer, tearing up dirt and twigs and trees, until he could feel the first brush of the tank's metal against his forehead, it was cold and dead and unforgiving—

"Well, look what we have here," said Ray, pressing the muzzle of his gun into the crease of Nick's forehead. He watched with utter fascination as Nick's eyes flickered open, then stared real beady-like, like a bird trapped in the corner of a room knowing there was no way out—a bird getting ready to be shot out of the sky. Ray wanted to savor the moment and it occurred to him that he should've brought his Kodak Brownie along with him for just such an occasion. He'd give anything to have a photo of the expression on Nick's face right now—the fear, the hopelessness, the desperation—it really was priceless. What did they say, that a picture is worth a thousand words? This was worth *ten* thousand words—gloom, despair, anguish, dejection, misery, grief, sorrow, discontent—hell, he could go on forever—agony, woe, suffering, torture, torment—Ray's mind was a veritable Thesaurus of inquietude, malcontentedness and discomposure.

"We were expecting you," said Nick, careful not to make too sudden a move lest Ray twitch or sneeze or have an impromptu gastric attack.

"Were you now?" said Dirk, standing on the other side of the car with his own gun pointed at Esmeralda. She was still in that deep Gypsy sleep where the rivers are paisley, the women dance on streets paved in gold, and the men play violins made of unicorn hair. "Wake up, fairy princess," said Dirk, nudging Esmeralda's nose with the butt of the gun. "Time to face the day."

Esmeralda brushed the gun aside as if it were the latest winged creature from America's nightmarish midsection and let out a little snore. She looked like her own nightmare after being scrunched up all night in the open desert. Her hair was tangled, her makeup was smudged, and her clothes looked like they'd been run through a dryer with her still in them. She stretched a few times, then cozied herself into Nick's arms, real comfortable-like, and that was enough to stretch Dirk's patience, of which he had none in the first place, to the breaking point. "Hey! Toots! Rise and shine!"

Esmeralda finally awoke to the barrel of a gun pointed right between her eyes and said, "I swear, your honor, I've never been to Chicago in my life!"

"Okay, boys and girls, what say you get out of the car real nice and easy?" said Ray.

"Sure, no problem," said Nick, "we could use a stretch."

"Oh, God, Nickie," whispered Esmeralda as she realized she had awoken to a true nightmare, "what have we done?"

"You hear that, Ray?" said Dirk, eavesdropping on his prisoner. "Miss Kurlansky wants to know what they've done."

"Gee, I don't know, Dirk, but it sure was nice of them to pull over and wait for us in the middle of the salt flats. Real thoughtful of them, wouldn't you say?"

"That's exactly what I'd say."

The two hoods pressed their guns into Nick's head and Esmeralda's back and pushed them out of the car. They stumbled onto a desert floor that was still cold from the raw night, feeling the icy pellets of sand between their toes. Esmeralda felt a shudder rush up her spine while Nick struggled with the tightness in his bum knee as they took a few uneasy steps. "What happens now?" said Nick.

"Well, let's see," said Ray. "We've got all sorts of possibilities. On one hand we could shoot both of you right here and let the buzzards pick your bones dry. On the other hand, we could have you dig your own graves and then let your bodies decompose in the salt, which might give a kind of nice pickled effect in case anybody digs you up in a few centuries—"

"Pickled Man," said Dirk, "last in a long line of cave dwellers and hunters and gatherers."

"Or we could shoot Esmeralda first and let you fill in the grave, or we could shoot *you* first and let *her* fill in the grave, or we could shoot the both of you at the same time and let some wild buffalo crap in the grave—"

"The possibilities are endless," said Dirk.

"Yeah, I can see you've got a real problem," said Nick. "Too many choices and not enough know-how to make the right decision."

"That's what you get when you put a couple of gonifs on the job," said Esmeralda.

"Gonif?" said Dirk, sneering at Esmeralda. "What's that, some kind of Gypsy jigaboo?"

"It's Yiddish, Dirk. You wouldn't understand."

"Yiddish, you say? Try me."

"Okay, then, a gonif's a thief, but not just a regular thief, he's a real unscrupulous thief, a crook, you understand, a crook too stupid to be a swindler and too shaky to be an embezzler, he's an opportunist, a scoundrel, a lowlife, a shady operator, a rascal, a conniver, a con man. Does any of that sound familiar to you?"

"Sure, it sounds like a certain broad who used to ply her trade on a stool at the Flame Club."

"Too much talk," said Ray, glancing at the fast-rising sun in the eastern sky. "I haven't even had breakfast yet. I hate taking care of business on an empty stomach, but I've got my eye on some Mormon Funeral Potatoes back in Salt Lake City." *[see Appendix C]*

"Good one, Ray," said Dirk with a smirk.

"So that's it, then?" said Nick. "You're just going to shoot us out here in the desert and let us rot in the sand? You think Montgomery is going to go for that? There's not much return on his investment, if you ask me. What does he get for all his troubles?"

"Satisfaction. That's worth more than its weight in gold."

"How will he even know we're dead? You think he's going to believe you after all this time?"

"We'll bring him your harmonica and her shoes and Montgomery can have them bronzed."

"Sure," said Dirk. "That's even better than a signed death certificate."

"I've had enough, Nickie," said Esmeralda with a huff. "Don't talk to them. Don't give them the satisfaction."

"You're right," said Nick, brushing his fingers against her hand. "It's you and me, Es, that's all that matters."

"That's real sweet, but it's time to move," said Ray, pushing them forward with the muzzle of his gun. "We've got a real special place picked out for you two lovebirds."

The four of them headed deeper into the desert. There was nothing around them but for the salt flats and four pairs of footprints leading away from the highway. Nick thought how soon enough there would be just two pair of footprints coming back, a couple of extra-large Thom McAns from a discount Chicago shoe depot. "Now, you see, I figure some smart detective is going to put two and two together and figure out what happened," he said. "There'll be a bunch of Utah State Troopers in station wagons, some police photographers, the county medical examiner, and a coroner or two. They'll find two decomposed bodies in shallow graves, the guy with a steel plate in his knee, the girl with black, curly hair, and there'll be two bullet holes in each of them, in the

back probably—isn't that right, Ray?—and it'll be a real
head-scratcher of a case, not a clue to go on, except for those
Thom McAns, that smart detective will have just enough of a
print to go and he'll trace it all the way back to the windy city,
and a guy in the shoe store will remember, sure, sure, it was a
couple of big dumb guys, and the next thing you know
there's a knock on the door in the middle of the night and
the detective is asking if you've ever been to the salt flats of
Utah, and my guess is that the two of you will trip over each
other making fools of yourselves—"

"Tell you what, Nick," said Ray. "Why don't you shut the
fuck up?"

"Yeah, smart ass," said Dirk. "Shows what you know. I
don't even *wear* Thom McAns."

Ray and Dirk pushed them farther along the barren terrain until they came to a lone Joshua tree that rose up out of
the flatlands. "Right over there," said Dirk, pointing to a spot
in the shadows of the tree.

Esmeralda felt it strangely appropriate that this scraggly
tree was to be the site of their final resting place. They could
truly become ghosts in their own graveyard, even if the
surroundings were a bit plain for her tastes. She'd have
preferred something with a touch of velvet or a couple of
polka dots to liven things up a bit. "It's been a real pleasure
knowing you, Nickie—"

"I wouldn't trade it for the world."

"Okay, you two, on your knees," said Dirk.

Nick and Esmeralda looked at each other, clasped hands,
and sank to the sand. They stared into each other's eyes,
trying to block out the world, grateful at least that their final
snapshots of life would be of each other. Esmeralda began to
feel a kind of quiet acceptance, relief almost, that it would all
be over soon. The hustling, the heartache, and the unfairness
of life would finally be evening out, and that's all she'd ever
really asked for, just to get an even break. She heard a gun

cock, and then Nick heard it, and while for her it was the sound of sweet release, for him it was like a crack in the fabric of the universe and he came totally, completely undone. "Oh, God, why have you abandoned us?" he cried out as he threw his hands to the sky.

Dirk flinched, then fired, wildly it turned out, since he was as startled by Nick's near perfect imitation of the Joshua tree as by the beseeching plea that accompanied it, not that it mattered, of course, a wild shot in the desert was but a shot into the eternity of endless space, except that the bullet traveled right over Nick's flailing arms and hit the flailing limb of the tree instead, dislodging a thick branch which knocked over a bayonet clump of leaves which split the bark in half which severed a conjoining limb which smashed through a nest of twigs which cracked open an oversized, tree-colored, oblong sac, a beehive, in fact, the very same beehive which gave its name to this woebegone prairie state, a beehive which shuddered and buzzed and whined and whirred like a Luftwaffe bomber being shot out of the sky, and when it landed on the branch below it disgorged 10,000 angry, insane, infuriated bees which descended like a cloud not on Nick and Esmeralda, who, after all, were the most innocent of bystanders, but on Dirk and Ray, bad guys of the worst kind, because bees, of all God's creatures, know who's who and what's what and thus keep the world spinning in its proper orbit.

"Run!" yelled Nick, not that Esmeralda needed to be reminded, no, she was already halfway to the car and by the time Nick caught up with her she had turned on the ignition, done her own quick prayer, and held her breath as the engine turned over and purred like a kitten on a brocade pillow. The radio came alive and the signal from KFFA magically homed in straight from Helena, Arkansas. It was *King Biscuit Time*, the band was playing *Up the Country Blues*, and Sonny Boy Williamson laid it down just the way it was supposed to be:

I'm going to take Highway 61
Man, I'm gonna ride it from coast to coast
I'm going to take Highway 61
Man I'm gonna ride it from coast to coast
Now, my baby's goin' up the country
Lord, n' she won't come back no more

Nick and Esmeralda blasted down the Bonneville Salt Flats, breaking land speed records and quite possibly some flight records as well. They kept going and going until the Utah prairie became the Nevada desert and there was nothing left behind but a cloud of swarming, stinging bees. Ray had a bee in his ear and Dirk had a bee in his pants and damn if the two of them didn't taste as sweet as Tupelo honey. That's the finest honey money can buy. You just slather some of that delta honey on a cornbread biscuit, kick back, and enjoy. *Jus' puttin' it down the way it's supposed to be.*

Chapter 24

W elcome back, dear reader, to what very well might be the last will and testament of Jaxson Epsilon, intergalactic wayfarer, cranial explorer, and recalcitrant dream thief. I might be but a shadow of my former self, but even a shadow can shed some light on the dark side of a mission gone horribly wrong. I write for you, future generations, diminished in mind and spirit though I might be. Bear with me, then, as I try to make sense of events that have conspired to strip me of my wit and wisdom and left me as insecure as a cub reporter on a weekly space standard.

Circumstances having left an important part of me trapped in the lower cortex of a moody, unpredictable Earthling, I found myself traveling on an archaic piece of machinery down the highways and byways of America, as Neal liked to call them. Oh, yes, I was piloting a 1947 Harley-Davidson "Knucklehead" motorcycle, a big black hog of a beast that frightened dogs, deer and great winged pterosaurs. Marta-2 was seated behind me with her arms wrapped tightly around my waist, wearing a matching black leather motorcycle jacket, Doc Martens boots and Ray-Ban sunglasses, and we were flying down the road like there was no tomorrow, which, I might add, was not entirely unlikely. Not that I had any idea how to operate a two-wheeled, ear-splitting, kidney-bruising piece of steel death, but Neal's buddy convinced us it was a snap and the next thing I knew my hands were high up on the handlebars, my knees were caressing the tear-dropped gas tank, and my hair was tossed back like a slick sheet in the wind.

It was fast all right—my God, was it fast—and we were nearly airborne when I gave it a squirt of gas. The engine growled its appreciation by blasting us through a dip in the road, hightailing it right over a bridge, and careening through a hairpin turn before depositing us in a miraculously upright position half a mile up the road. From there it was all downhill, there being a long descent through the Colorado Rockies, but then we hit the flatlands and I got used to the sensation of the sun on my head and the wind in my face and the rocketing sense of speed—*did I say rocket?*—well, dear reader, it was exactly the *opposite* of drifting on the Pulsar-7 through space—that was as much fun as walking on ping pong balls—no, this was a jarringly visceral sensation. I could feel every crick and crack in the road, every curve and bump and change of elevation and it was, as they say out there in the Utah hinterlands, really something, brother.

Utah, in fact, seemed like a nice place to kick back and chat with the locals, but there was no time for that. There was no time for anything other than getting where we were going as fast as the Harley could take us. I kept one eye on the road and the other on the lookout for a maroon Hudson Commodore, but no such luck. What do they say about blues musicians, that if we didn't have bad luck we wouldn't have no luck at all? That was me, all right, down and out and lower than low. Not that I wasn't still capable of knocking out a couple of soulful lyrics, even in this diminished state of mind:

Riding down the highway
Doin' ninety, ninety-five
Yes, lord, I'm riding down the highway
Doin' ninety, ninety-five
Got me a bee in my bonnet
Hope it don't eat me alive

"I like that one a lot," said Marta-2, hanging onto every word as usual. She was also hanging onto me, this being the perfect excuse to cozy up and press her breasts into the small of my back. They fit—the breasts, that is—which was odd since it didn't make any particular evolutionary sense that her breasts and my back would form a complementary unit unless, it turns out, man and woman were always meant to be blasting down the highway on 750 cc's of gyrating power. As the road wore on, I began to like it: the highway, the bike, the breasts, the wind, even the feeling in my kidneys, which were loose as a goose and cooking with kerosene.

"There's something about the road that brings out the poet in you," said Marta-2, an observation with which I couldn't disagree. There's a rhythm to the road—the clickety-clack of the cylinders and pistons, the whoosh of the tires on the asphalt, the pounding pulse of the wind in your ears. Marta-2 leaned her head against my back and dozed off into a dream about Bunsen burners and Petrie dishes, or whatever it was that molecular biologists fantasized about in their spare time. As for me, my head was still buzzing. The highway had put me on a roll and the reporter inside me saw the rare opportunity to interview the person who had now become the central character of this story, that is, me.

"Tell me, Mr. Epsilon, how does it feel to have 9% of your essence missing?"

"It's hard to describe," I said. "It's like chocolate cake without the frosting, beer without the foam, hablum without the zumzum powder."

"So it's kind of like going down to the beach for the most beautiful sunset and everything is there except for the sun?"

"No, it's like going to the beach for the most beautiful sunset and the *only* thing there is the sun."

"Hmm, I see," I said, having no idea what he was talking about. This Epsilon fellow was cagey, elusive, and hard to pin down. All I wanted to know was the who-what-when-where-why of the situation, but he was leading me through a maze of maybes, what-ifs, and you-never-knows.

"The best way I can describe it is that you're sort of there but not there, aware but not aware."

"So this motorcycle, this road, this journey, are you on it or not on it? Here or not here? Kicking it or not kicking it?"

"Yes."

The guy was getting under my craw, which was really saying something since I didn't even know what a craw was, much less how one got under it. There were lots of words like that on Earth, words like cockles, which apparently are located somewhere in the heart although no one knows where. "Help me understand," I said. "When somebody loses his essence, what exactly does he have left?"

"That's the question, isn't it? Maybe you'll understand the day you understand the difference between zero and nothing," he said.

My inner reporter receded into the shadows and the rest of me pushed ever onward, over hill and dale and plain and desert. I gave the Knucklehead some gas and screeched past a series of fading signs that might've given me pause, if only I knew where to find such a gear on the Harley's transmission:

GRAB YOUR PANTS
HOLD ONTO YOUR LOAD
YOU'RE ABOUT TO TAKE A RIDE
DOWN THUNDER ROAD
BURMA-SHAVE

Chapter 25

"God didn't create metal so that
man could make paper clips."
—Harley-Davidson

Jaxson pushed the bike to its limits, there being no time to
waste and no place to waste it, especially when he and
Marta-2 hit Nevada, an expanse of land that held nothing
of interest to anyone not inclined toward the study of rocks,
dirt, and sand. "Oh, look," said Marta-2, "those are some
pretty impressive alluvial fans, calcium carbonate deposits,
and non-foliated metamorphic rocks."

They tore down a straightaway, then zoomed up an incline of the Ruby Mountains, a desolate stretch of hills that
were best seen from the rear view mirror and at a great
distance. As they reached higher altitude, the engine suddenly sputtered, coughed, and conked out. Jaxson coolly
glided to a stop, did an impressive job of parallel parking,
and slid off the bike like John Wayne getting off a barstool.
He inspected the various joints and sockets, pretending to
know what he was doing. "Um-hmm," he said, rubbing his
fingers over his whiskered chin, "looks to me like the plugs
aren't sparking and the shafts aren't cranking."

"Do we have any tools?" said Marta-2.

"What do you need?"

She pointed to the drive chain, which was hanging limp

against the ground. "A flat-head screwdriver... long-nosed pliers... ¼" Allen wrench... calipers... mallet..."

"I think we've got everything except the screwdriver, pliers, wrench, calipers, and mallet."

"I was afraid you might say that."

They slumped against a boulder that was perched near the top of the summit. That boulder got Jaxson's full attention, since he would do anything to avoid thinking about the issue at hand, which was out of his hands altogether. Instead, he wondered how a giant rock could have wound up at the *top* of a hill, but then he remembered that everything on this planet was upside down. Only on Earth do rocks roll up and drive chains roll down.

"What do we do now?" said Marta-2, just the way those femme fatales from the Friday night movies would say while chomping a stick of gum and examining their fingernails.

Jaxson searched through his memory bank of probable outcomes and came up with death by starvation, death by heat, death by cold, and death by northwest. "Hard to say," he said, not because it was hard to say but because it was *hard to say*.

"Then I'll say it," said Marta-2. "We're in a dire situation with no clear way out. The only thing that can save us is divine intervention which, unfortunately, does not exist. Nor does Mormon underwear, although I admit that we should have purchased a pair when we had the chance. It would appear that we are in what the sub-Subian wart readers would call a real bucket of bangi."

At exactly that moment, they heard a distant roar and felt the earth rumble. Was it an earthquake to add to their woes? A tectonic shift that would toss them into the crevices of the mountain? A geologic cataclysm that would bury them beneath the rubble? As the ground continued to vibrate and the noise grew ever louder, they decided to climb to the summit of the mountain where, from their perch halfway up the sky, they saw a big, black mass moving toward them from out of the western plains. It was like a swarm of bees, only 10,000 times the size. "It's the wildebeest migration of the Serengeti plains," said Jaxson with a shudder.

"Serengeti is in another country on a different continent," said Marta-2 with kindly disregard. "These are wild beasts, all right, but they're of the motorcycle variety."

As a gang of 50 outlaw motorcyclists approached the incline of the mountain, Jaxson and Marta-2 saw a whole new form of body type than they'd been exposed to in the central states. These were a bigger variety of human, with broad backs, prodigious stomachs, and beefy arms. They were covered in tattoos, had thick, unruly beards, and wore their shirts open to the wind. Their jackets identified them as members of the Boozefighters Motorcycle Club, but if it was booze they were fighting, Marta-2 suspected the booze had won. Emblazoned across their backs was a green bottle with three x's on the label, and the words:

BFMC
A DRINKING CLUB
WITH A MOTORCYCLE PROBLEM

The Boozefighters rode their Harleys right up to the hill and gave Jaxson and Marta-2 the eye. It was red, that eye, red and bloodshot and half-drooping out of their heads. "Hey, Kokomo, you see what these two are riding?" said Wino Willie, the leader of the pack and apparently a connoisseur of fine alcoholic beverages.

"Sure, Willie, I see a shiny new Knucklehead," said Kokomo, as he slid off his bike and tucked his thumbs into his belt loops.

"A Knucklehead disabled on the side of the road," said Pappy, the old geezer of the group at a creaky 29.

"That's a crying shame," said Dink, jumping off his Indian Scout and bending back his fingers until the bones cracked like skeletons being dropped onto the highway.

"Yeah, a real tearjerker," said Red Dog, who was neither red nor a dog but rather more crimson-colored and hyena-like.

"Out here, in the middle of nowhere," said Fat Boy, eyeing Marta-2, then Jaxson, then Marta-2 again.

"Where nobody knows nothing about nobody no-how," said Vern, employing a rare triple negative that Marta-2 reminded herself to investigate the next time she got a chance to consult her *Essential Earthian Grammar Companion*.

Willie and Kokomo moseyed on over to their neck of the woods and took their measure. "Where you two headed?" said Kokomo.

"California," said Jaxson, "little place called Petaluma."

"Petaluma?" said Willie. "Never been to that particular burg. Now us, we're coming from California ourselves, town called Hollister. You heard of it? Sure, you did. All tore up, that's what the papers said. Bunch of bikers rolled in and showed them what a little fun looks like."

Dink apparently found that to be real funny and started laughing. It was a mighty laugh that started low in his sternum and worked its way up his chest into an explosive guffaw that shook his whole body. Then Vern started laughing, either because of the way Wino Willie had expressed things or because of Dink's reaction, and this caused a kind of contagion as Red Dog and Fat Boy chimed in, and then it was every man for himself and a few women, too, the whole lot of them were laughing like crazy, Jaxson included, and then Marta-2 joined in, and the whole bunch of them were laughing like loons, and the really funny thing was, not a single one of them knew why.

"Now, if you'd gone to Hollister coupla days back," said Kokomo, "you'd a found a nice sleepy little burg in the middle of nowhere. Hell, we took that place and gave 'em beach front property, that's right, put a river right through that town, a river of beer and piss."

"Used to have 21 saloons in Hollister, now they got one creaky old bar and a bunch of broken lumber," said Dink.

"Hollister," said Vern, "hell, that place'll never be the same!"

"And a good thing, too," said Jaxson, hoping to meld into the action. "What's life without a little fun?"

There was a murmur of approval, followed by a murmur of disapproval, which was followed a murmur of unknown origin. After a round of hacking, coughing, and a clearing of throats, the gang relaxed its guard and kicked back. "Now what's the problem with that bike of yours?" said Willie.

"Well, it seems the drive chain slipped and we don't have the tools—"

"Gus!" yelled Willie to a young guy with a scrawny mustache and the beginnings of a beard. "Get your ass over here with that toolbox of yours!"

Gus revved up his engine and drove over from the edge of the group to the Knucklehead. "Yep," he said, "looks like a drive chain problem." He jumped off his old V-Twin, opened up the side bags, and pulled out an array of tools that would have done any motorcycle mechanic proud.

"All right," Willie announced to his crew. "Might as well make camp here for the night." The Boozefighters revved up their engines, then rode their bikes into a big circle and dismounted. A couple of guys got a fire started in no time and hung a big pot of beans from a spit to cook. A cooler appeared as if by magic—*a cooler? Out here? Who carries a cooler on a motorcycle?*—and before the earth settled from all the shaking, Jaxson and Marta-2 were hoisting Pabst Blue Ribbons, which was quickly becoming their quaff of choice.

"To President Truman," said Willie, raising his bottle in a toast. "First in war, first in peace, first to break the landlord's lease."

Marta-2 observed the gathering like an anthropologist might view a rare species of outlaw malcontents engaging in

bilateral social rituals. She took note of posture, chin structure, forehead shape, and thumb flexibility while trying to
discern the degree of their enculturation, the internalization
of their moral codes, and the complexity of their ingroup-
outgroup dynamics. "So, what brings you fellas out to a place
like this," she said, using her best roadside vernacular.

"Where do you think we should be?" said Vern. "Behind a
desk somewhere?"

"No... no..."

"Not after jumping out of a B-52 over France, no-sir-ee,
not me."

"That's right," said Kokomo, "you engage somebody in hand
to hand combat, then try going to college on the GI bill!"

"Sure, I understand, it would be difficult—"

Willie leaned closer and nearly curdled Jaxson's skin with
his alcohol breath. "What do you think a guy's gonna do after
four years on some shithole Pacific island?" he said. "Sell life
insurance?"

"That really would be the height of irony," said Jaxson.

"I ain't got no idea what that means, but I'm with you,
bro," said Kokomo. "Live fast, die young, and leave a good-
looking widow, that's what I say."

A couple of biker chicks tramped over to the circle and
gave Marta-2 the once over. "Where'd you get the duds, Lolly
Pop?" said Betty Lou, whose breasts nearly burst through a
sweater so tight it looked like it was sewn directly to her skin.

"Oh, this little thing?" said Marta-2, twisting her butt ever
so lightly in her Christian Dior evening gown. "It's called the
New Look, just out of Paris."

"Is that so? Looks a tad uncomfortable to ride, don't you
think, Bonita?" she said, poking one of her gal pals in the ribs.

"Uh-huh," said Bonita, moseying on over. "Especially with
that black leather jacket and all." Bonita ran her fingers over
the fabric, then, quick as a wink, pulled a switch-blade from
her pocket, flicked it open, and—*zzziiippp*—cut a slit right

down the middle of Marta-2's dress. "Much better, don't you think, dearie?"

Marta-2 was instantly transplanted from her social laboratory to the harrowing back roads of the American jungle, where to agree was almost always the right answer. "Yes, thank you very much," she said. "I'll just tie the legs together at the ankles and we'll be off, isn't that right, Jaxson?"

"Right you are," said Jaxson, seeing that the drive chain was securely back on its moorings. "We wouldn't want to intrude any further."

"You sure about that?" said Kokomo. "You sure you wouldn't want to join up with us? We're headed somewhere the folks want us, up there in South Dakota, a town called Sturgis, a place where a man can be a man and a woman can be, well, whatever."

"Sounds tempting," said Jaxson, "tempting, indeed."

"The Sturgis Rally," said Willie. "Gonna be thousands of us on the road, that's where you should be headed, Sturgis, you hear?"

"Sure, Sturgis," said Jaxson as he and Marta-2 hurried to the bike. "We'll keep that in mind." He kick-started the Knucklehead, gave it full throttle, did a wheelie, and waved to the Boozefighters, just the way Roy Rogers did on the Friday night movies. A few minutes later, they were back on the road, the wildebeest migration was at their backs, and California lie straight ahead. It looked like clear sailing from here on out, with nothing out there but a couple of coyotes, a bird or two, and a guy and a girl laying rubber on the asphalt highway.

I sing to thee,
America,
To your hills,
Your valleys,
And your open roads.
Let us go loudly into the night.

Chapter 26

*"Dreaming permits each and every one of us to be
quietly and safely insane every night of our lives."*
—Charles William Dement

The deconstructed dream energy from Nick's waterfall reverie shot through space at several times the speed of lightsound, that being Oblivia's contribution to the experiment as a Class A energy medium. For all of her foibles and social embarrassments, Oblivia's perfectly blank mind offered access to the void of space without all of the unwieldy complications of human despair, regret, hope, and salvation. The little packet of 1's and o's careened around the universe at break-neck speed, zapping through black holes, supernovas, and anything else the stars could throw at it. Oh, it was fast all right, fast and wild and indestructable, everything, in fact, that Rutherford B. Halcyon had predicted when he proposed the Advanced Theory of Irresistible Force, an elegant hypothesis which, when broken down into its most basic elements, essentially said, get out of the way folks, this baby's coming through.

Nick's dream zoomed through space, leaving a shimmer and a warm afterglow as it traversed the Epicurean Conundrum, the Ecclesiastical Belt, and the Pneumonic Divide. Esmeralda's turquoise bandana left a glistening vapor trail and for one brief moment the universe was wrapped in her warm Gypsy bosom. The waterfall left particles of mist which refracted the solar rays into a magnificent rainbow that pulsated across the skies while the bundle of energy made its way for Reverie Energy's download station. It took somewhere between forever and no time at all before the digital stream made its way to the annotation transponders, where it was uploaded into its analog equivalent, that being a replication waterfall which could be reproduced into an infinity of images. It was, for those with a less scientific bent of mind, much like a mirror within a mirror within a mirror, each of which possessed the pent-up hydroelectric energy of several million gallons of water powering the biggest paddle wheel this side of the Pontifical Schism.

And so, the lights lit, first dimly, then with more conviction, then with full confidence. With a flick of a switch, there was an injection of enough pure dream energy to drive all the freeze-dried machinery that fusion had left in the lurch. Lights began to glow in every alcove and window and doorway as night became day and day became an endless kaleidoscope of bright lights and brighter tomorrows. Obsidia was alight with Nick's dream of waterfalls and Esmeralda's turquoise bandana blowing in the wind. People danced in the streets. The videocoaster at Breughel Park ran nonstop through the night. Convenience store clerks turned on both the heat *and* the air conditioning just for the hell of it. And above it all, on the twentieth floor of Reverie Energy, a team of project managers, financial officers, and board members watched the results of the experiment with profound interest: if one simple stolen dream could provide such pure, undiluted energy, imagine what the theft of *all* Earthly dreams could do...

Night fell too on the rocket ship—quickly, definitively, and without mercy. Night on the high desert has no time to waste, nocturnal high-fliers being an impatient lot, and once the last rays of the sun settled behind the mesas, the night-hawks descended upon the night crawlers, the night owls picnicked on the night mice, and the balance of nature was recalibrated all over again. For those other denizens of the desert—the beleaguered crew of the Pulsar-7—night held its own anxieties. Time was fleeting, the aphelion was almost upon them, and the ship was far from ready. While the portal cracks and undercarriage rips had been patched, the left ventricle wing was in total disrepair and the primary engine was still in a hundred pieces. It was little consolation that the Pulsar-7 at least looked better by night, its dings and dents less visible in the shadows of the moon than in the glare of the sun.

Despite the sense of urgency, the crew was limited by its own lack of manpower, material, and expertise. They were almost completely dependent on Chief Engineer Teller, who had re-reanimated one more time and decided to play along and be the good soldier, at least until given the opportunity to exact his revenge. And, oh, how sweet it would be! He imagined the punishments he would inflict on Loquacious Landry—the insults, the reprimands, the glorious retribu-tions. He would flay Landry, he would thrash him, he would hold him upside down and shake him until his insides clickety-clacked against his bones like coins dropping from a change machine. But for now, it would be yes sir, no sir, and anything else I can do for you, sir? Teller would follow orders so quickly, he'd make Landry's head spin, which, come to think of it, was yet another good method of settling the score.

Landry, for his part, was in his own little world, that being the confined quarters of his Space Transport Sprite 2000, a two-seater detectives' model that had been stripped down for fast chases, quick maneuverability, and a minimum of creature comforts, that being the trade-off in law enforce-ment vehicles the universe over. Other than the standard-issue hablum brewer, hallucination compartment, and helio-tropic imaginarium, there was nothing on the transport out of the ordinary except, of course, for the archaic television set that Loquacious had pilfered from Fort Sedgwick as not much more than a practical joke. The tiny 10-inch screen required 12 cubic feet of console space to squeeze in all of the vacuum tubes, condensers, and antenna coils needed to create what the Earthlings laughingly called a miracle of modern-day technology. The thing flashed and flickered as the National Broadcasting Company presented one of the first-ever live telecasts of a baseball game, the national pastime of a country with too much time on its hands. The things Earthlings did to occupy themselves was a source of endless amusement to Loquacious, who still couldn't grasp the difference between a pitch that was high and inside and one that was low and away. He was taking a well-deserved break, kicking back and watching the Christians being thrown to the lions, or the bulls being thrown to the matadors, or whatever it was that one side was throwing at the other. "Strike three called!" a chap named Red Barber screamed at the top of his lungs as a strapping fellow named Duke Snider of the Brooklyn Dodgers stood there watching the ball bisect the plate. Loquacious stared at the set in disbelief. Was the batter really that inept? Was he being paid by the opposition to perform so poorly? Was it possible that the umpire actually *was* blind? "Swing at the damn ball!" he yelled, already experiencing the existential angst of the mid-century American couch potato.

Across the mesa, on Pulsar-7, Wambold had his own problems. It had finally become apparent to him that he was in command of a crew of malcontents, misanthropes, and megalomaniacs. Was this how his career would end? Stranded on a backward planet with nary an individual to call his friend? He faced the very real possibility of being trapped on Earth for another six months—assuming the perihelion even appeared as scheduled on this unruly planet—and six months among these emotionally dispossessed people might prove to be his undoing. Wambold looked to the skies and uttered a rare confession: "Oh, Obsidia, how I miss you! Obsidia, with your barren plains and icy poles and infested swamps, embrace me once more in your slimy tentacles and hold me near!" The captain had good reason to worry, starting with a cryptic note he found under his door only hours after the crew returned from Denver:

CAPTAIN WAMBOLD. I REGRET TO INFORM YOU THAT JAXSON AND I HAVE LEFT THE SHIP IN AN EFFORT TO RECOVER HIS ESSENCE. I AM WELL AWARE OF THE POTENTIAL CONSEQUENCES OF OUR ACTION, BUT YOUR UNRESPONSIVENESS TO MY CONCERNS HAS LEFT US NO CHOICE BUT TO ACT IN THIS UNILATERAL FASHION. WE SHALL MAKE EVERY ATTEMPT TO RETURN TO THE SHIP WELL IN ADVANCE OF THE APHELION, BUT IF WE ARE UNABLE TO SUCCESSFULLY COMPLETE OUR MISSION IN A TIMELY MANNER, PLEASE KNOW IT HAS BEEN AN HONOR TO SERVE UNDER YOUR COMMAND, DESPITE OUR CURRENT DIFFERENCES. MAY YOUR RETURN TO OBSIDIA BE FAST, SAFE, AND WITHOUT FURTHER INCIDENT. MARTA-2.

Wambold crumpled the note into a wad and threw it straight out the door. As luck would have it, a southwesterly wind howled over the mesa and blew it right back into his cabin, where it lay untouched as a reminder of his loss of control. Ah, yes, control. Wasn't that what it was ultimately all about? Once the detectives discovered that Jaxson and Marta-2 were gone, they'd surely hold him responsible for not being in control of his crew, and who could argue with them? He could almost see his command slipping away from

him. The Court of Last Resort would be looking for a scape-
goat and who better than the captain of the ship to take the
fall? That simply couldn't be allowed to happen. If Captain
Hieronymus Wambold was going to go down, it wouldn't be
without a fight. Missing crew? *What* missing crew?

He slipped out of his cabin, looked both ways, and headed for the Rejuvenation Chamber. Not that *he* needed
rejuvenation—he was just fine, thank you very much—but
he had a few rabbits left to pull out of his hat in order to keep
the course straight and narrow. The chamber was in a dark,
out-of-the-way corner on the third larynx level that no one
ever visited. Wambold looked at the shiny terrafoil exterior
of the unit and brushed off a thin layer of cosmic dust. He
tried the latch door, cautiously at first, then with a firmer
hand, and forced it to creak open. It was musty inside, with a
blue-green glow emanating up from the brancusi slots. A
single control panel operated two adjoining compartments,
its brushed albino plate consisting of a singular knob with
only two possible settings: *On* and *Off*. It reminded Wambold that some of life's simplest problems are solved by the
most complicated equations, while the really tough stuff is
often resolved by the simple flick of a switch. This switch,
thankfully, was *Off*. The captain flipped a latch on the door,
slammed it closed, and locked it tight as a drum.

Occupied, it read.

Morning unfolded over the mesa with a stretch and a yawn.
The desert lulls the unwary with its gentle dunes, then
eviscerates them onto an unforgiving patch of parched earth.
That's where Raleigh found himself, a half mile from the
Pulsar-7 on a barren piece of wasteland where he could get a
lay of the land. With the ship's navigation system on the
blink, he had to rely on an improvised collection of knowledge ascertained from observation, calculation, and blind

luck. He drew a series of circles in the sand to annotate the position of the ship and whatever celestial markers were available in the high sky. He zeroed in on two stars in the Zoroaster Combine and calculated the celestial fix, then determined the prime vertical as the sun passed east-west through the zenith and intersected with the horizon. He adjusted his compass by calculating the azimuth of the sun, then projected the latitude line, took a meridian sight, and got a running fix. After assimilating all of the information, he concluded that if all went well—which, of course, it never would—the ship had a 50/50 chance of getting off the ground before the aphelion, a 60/40 chance of escaping Earth's atmosphere, a 70/30 chance of entering plus/minus orbit, an 80/20 chance of getting through the Helsingor/Helsingborg Straits, and a 100% chance of all-of-the-above or none-of-the-above ever happening, which covered all the bases and a few extra, just in case anybody asked, which, needless to say, they wouldn't.

When Raleigh headed back for the ship, he inadvertently stepped right into a gopher hole and sank straight up to his knees. He twisted and turned and tried to pull himself up, but it was useless—he was wedged in tight. He was just out of earshot of both the Pulsar-7 and Landry's space transport and he wondered if this is how it would all end: a conscientious navigator dying of thirst and starvation in a faraway, hostile land. Would they find his skeleton crumbled into the dust of the desert, his hands outstretched to the skies in plaintive prayer? Was this really all there was to a life lived probing the deeper questions of purpose and existence? He was trapped like a rat on a sinking ship in a terrible squall. Or, more accurately, like a chipmunk on a piece of flat ground in mild summer. What's the difference? All was lost. All hope was gone. All was finished. Raleigh's life passed before his eyes—the meditative trances, the otherminded states of presumptive consciousness, the emptying of the vessel and the filling of the void. Is this where it all had led him, to a gopher hole in a semi-arid, nameless desert? Raleigh's heart sank—a lucky piece of medical mischief—causing his torso to narrow, his leg to shift, and his foot to find firmer ground. He unconsciously pushed up on his toes, grabbed a little wrinkle of sand, and then, just like that, he stepped out of the hole. Huzzah! Raleigh brushed himself off and navigated to the ship, which shone with the warm glow of early morning. It was definitely time to retire to his chambers and contemplate the meaning of what had just happened. There were clues to be deciphered, after all, clues that maybe, just maybe, would lead him to the ultimate understanding of exactly what, when all was said and done, was what.

The left ventricle wing hung limp against the body of the Pulsar-7, clanging every few seconds in the wind. The weltenberg joints had completely sheered off during the rough entry into Earth's atmosphere, leaving nothing but the magellan coils and the congenital springs to hold things in place. That, as they used to say back in the real world, was simply not going to fly. It was up to Teller to find a solution— *of course* it was up to Teller to find a solution. Who else was going to do it? One of the behavioral scientists? The navigations officer? What a joke!—and what Teller lacked in imagination, he made up for in sheer will. He decided he'd simply yank that wing back into place, slap on some aloe oil, jam in some connective modules, and punch up the slots and grooves. Not everything had to be so damn complicated all the time, did it?

Teller gathered the crew around to hold the ladder and wing in place. He climbed up several rungs and gave the ventricle a good shake. "Piece of cake," he said, satisfied that the whole contraption wasn't going to collapse on his head.

It might have been a piece of cake, but Loquacious was aware of several missing layers. "Where's Jaxson?" he said, steadying the ladder with his shoulder.

"He and Marta-2 are in the Rejuvenation Chamber," said Wambold, quick to respond. If there was one thing he had learned from Jaxson, it was that if you're going to tell a lie, make it bold, outrageous, and loud.

"Oh?" said Loquacious, listening with more than his usual suspicion. He was surprised the captain would give approval to using an experimental recharging system that was meant only for the most extreme cases of physical and psychological depletion. "I was under the impression that the molecular revitalization process was nothing to mess around with."

"Well, no, it's not," said Wambold, his voice trailing off in swallowed syllables. "But desperate times—"

"Require desperadoes," mumbled Loquacious under his breath. He didn't trust these Obsidians any more than he trusted the Earthlings. There was a reason they looked so much alike, something a bit off in their makeup. And by makeup, he didn't mean lipstick, sweetheart. Loquacious smelled a rat, or at least a prairie dog, but which wool was being pulled over whose eyes was anyone's guess. He pulled his fedora down over his forehead and took a little look around the ship. Raleigh, as advertised, was in deep otherness and so much the better. Oblivia was spinning like a Sufi sewing machine, a mental image that predictably held no meaning whatsoever. Kalamata and Marta-1 were off checking out each other's etchings and that left only the Rejuvenation Chamber, or as Loquacious thought of it, the Hall of Lies. The chamber was located just down the hall from the spa and was only to be used in emergency circumstances, since its science was based solely on an unproven, theoretical model that was just as likely to strip the body down to a big nothing as it was to provide that little extra something.

Something didn't sit right. Would Captain Wambold, the

most risk averse commander Loquacious had ever encountered, really allow not one, but *two* crew members to have their bodies calcified, salted, spun, and depetrified only two days before departure? No, something was up, of that he was sure, and yet... and yet... there it was, two doors, a tight rubber gasket, and a sign that left little doubt: *Occupied,* it read.

Loquacious stared at it a moment, went to try the door, then thought better of it. Maybe something was up. Maybe it wasn't. It was hard. To say.

The wayward wing creaked and groaned as the Chief Engineer maneuvered it into place. "Higher and to the left," instructed Captain Wambold from his command post at the foot of the ladder.

"Yes, sir!" said Teller, as he elevated the wing toward its modular counterpart with his shoulder, his hand, and occasionally a nudge from his chin. It was the perfect job for someone possessing Teller's unique qualities since it required a certain birdlike instinct, plantlike intelligence, and rocklike determination.

"Do you need another hand there?" said Wambold, watching Teller's balancing act with growing concern.

"No, sir!" said Teller, wobbling on the ladder unsteadily. The truth is, he needed *ten* other hands, but damned if he was going to exhibit any weakness in the face of overwhelming odds. As bravery and stupidity know no bounds, it was entirely in character that Teller would bound for the wide chasm and take a mindless leap of faith. He felt his foot slipping as he pushed with all his might and two opposing forces took hold—gravity, which dictated that he tumble to the ground at 16 feet/second/second, and luck, which conspired to snap the tab of the ventricle wing precisely into the slot of the ship's prefabricated rudder system with a loud click. It was thus that Teller both fell on his ass and saved his ass in one fell swoop. "Anything else I can do for you, sir?" he said, pulling himself up from the ground and saluting smartly to the Captain.

"Why don't you take a few minutes," said Wambold, "then go see what you can do about reconstructing the engine?"

"I'd be happy to, sir."

"I didn't say anything about happy, Teller. Try not to over-do it."

"Of course not, sir."

Teller bounded up the stairs and headed for the breakfast lounge area. Marta-1 was already there, staring into her tea with a dreamy look. Raleigh soon sauntered in, followed by Oblivia and Wambold.

"Well, look here," said Teller, "Just like the old days. The crew of the Pulsar-7 coming together over a friendly break-fast."

"As it should be," said the Captain.

"Couldn't agree more," said Teller. "Seems like the perfect time to catch up on everybody's thoughts."

"What thoughts would those be, Teller?" said the Captain.

"Well, sir, I was just wondering what the big rush is to get off this planet when all we're doing is handing ourselves over as prisoners to the Court of Last Resort? Seems a bit, um, stupid, if you ask me."

"Hmm... yes... stupid..." said Wambold.

There was a brief moment of uncomfortable silence. Raleigh poured out a serving of experiential toasty puffs into a bowl while Oblivia stirred some instant cubic loops in a readi-carton with feigned concentration. "You're just worried because you're the one responsible for all of our troubles," said Marta-1.

"Uh-huh, well, screw you, too," said Teller. "You've already gone over to the enemy, anyway. You're not fooling anyone by slinking off after dark. We all know where you're headed."

Marta-1 turned a darker shade of pale and held her tongue.

"What do you suggest, Teller," said Wambold, "that we simply stay here forever? That's only delaying the inevitable. I'm afraid it's time we face the music, unpleasant though it might be."

"That's easy for you to say, Captain," said Teller. "What have you got to lose? You're too old to be flying, anyway. They'll simply put you out to pasture and erase your name from the records. The rest of us have our careers to consider."

"How *dare* you speak to the Captain like that?" said Marta-1. "Why, if it wasn't for him—"

"I don't see the point in turning ourselves over to some kangaroo court. What have they got us on but a bunch of trumped up charges? What, disobeying orders? Landing without permission? Conducting research? It's a sham trial if I ever saw one!"

"What they have is three disfigured pilots in body bags," said Raleigh. "Detective Landry will hold them over our heads as irrefutable evidence of criminal behavior."

"Yes, the bodies," said Wambold. "We'll have our hands full with that one, I'm afraid."

"Us? Why *us?*" said Teller in a mocking tone. "Aren't *you* the captain, sir?"

"You're right," said Wambold, catching Teller's drift. "The responsibility is ultimately mine."

"Now wait just a minute—" said Marta-1.

"That will be all," said Wambold. "Now, then, Chief Engineer, I believe the engine requires your attention."

"As you wish, Captain. I'm just following orders. As always."

"As always, Teller."

"Just to be clear."

"Perfectly."

Chapter 27

"I don't want you to be true;
I just want to make love to you."
—Willie Dixon

A black crow flew high over the Nevada desert, heading west into the jet stream, fighting the winds and the downdrafts and the boredom, oh, yes, even the sky above the desert is boring, the clouds are sparse and unconvincing, the refraction of light diffuse and unappealing, the prismatic effect almost nonexistent, the aura and halo and shimmer of the sun's rays depleted to the point of barrenness, no, the desert sky is no place for a crow with ideas, the thin air will sap the spine and the spirit, it will strip the imagination and weigh upon the soul. The crow flapped his wings with renewed vigor, not out of inspiration but desperation—get me out of here before I fall from the sky like a broken bombardier, take me on your whistling winds and transport me high over the baking sands, push me west, blessed guardians of the stratosphere, west to where the redwoods beckon, west to where the dew of morning fans the passions of the night, west to where a canopy of sequoias shades the brain from overheating, west to where the air is fresh and clean and unhinged from the old ideas of the past. The crow swept high over Battle Mountain, Winnemucca, Lovelock, and Reno, then climbed higher still over the steep escarpments of the Sierra Nevadas, battling the sudden gusts and urgent currents that swirled down from the mountain peaks and up from the valley floor, up, up, up he went, over the Truckee River and Lake Tahoe, over Fredonyer Pass and Freel Peak, over the Carson Range and the Tuolumne River, and then, like a welcoming draft of sanity, he flew over the central valley of California, its little villages clinging to the golden foothills—first Grass Valley, then Auburn and Roseville—and then the first hint of the ocean breeze, a taste of salt in the air, a breeze from the Pacific current, a breeze with the hint of islands and palm trees and exotic spices. The crow flapped with renewed vigor, his tired wings refreshed, his blurry eyes sharp and focused, his heart thumping to the beat of the western wall, while a thousand feet below a Hudson Commodore followed as if attached by a string—who, really, was leading whom?—the convertible pushed on over bridges and straightaways and mountain passes with its own one-mindedness, California or bust, no time to stop, no place to rest, get us to the Kurlansky spread before we're dead, and before the sun set twice, the passengers found themselves on a long, slowly descending highway through Sacramento and Woodland and Vallejo and into the center of a whole new world as San Francisco glistened in the distance like a pearl popped right out of the ocean.

The Swiss-American Hotel on Broadway was nothing fancy, but fancy doesn't count when you've been on the road for as long as Nick and Esmeralda had been, when you've traveled night and day and nearly been killed in the Utah salt flats. That was a topic never to be discussed by either of them. Upon mutual agreement, the names Ray and Dirk were to be permanently filed away since they were either in a morgue or an intensive care unit and wouldn't be bothering them again any time soon. Anyway, this was California and all thoughts of the past were off the table. Which was good, since their room didn't *have* a table. It had a bed, a dresser and a bathroom down the hall, though, and that was luxury enough.

It was early evening, too late to even think of continuing on up the coast, but too early to knock off, so the newcomers decided to take a look around, tired or not. This was San Francisco, after all, the legendary Barbary Coast, the edge of the continent, Babylon by the Bay. People were known to disappear in San Francisco—soldiers on leave, sailors waiting to ship out, musicians between gigs, guys looking for adventure, girls on the prowl. There was something in the air, a chill or a mist or a perfume, that called to the dispossessed— come, take a walk into the angular shadows of night, come, go left instead of right, come, turn north instead of south, come, enter this doorway or that corridor or those darkened alleyways. North Beach was the old Italian neighborhood, perched right up against Chinatown and the two districts rubbed against each other like first dates on the dance floor—slightly curious, slightly afraid, slightly ajar. There was the sense that anything could happen in North Beach, even though right now nothing much at all was happening. It was an area getting ready to ignite, just waiting for the match.

Nick and Esmeralda strolled the neighborhood, looking for some cheap wine and a bowl of spaghetti. There were plenty of bars—Gino and Carlo's, Tosca, 12 Adler Alley—and a string of hole-in-the-wall restaurants—Capp's Corner, the Gold Spike, Fior d'Italia—but they kept walking, past Broadway, past Pacific, down Jackson to Kearny, where they came upon a giant of a man standing on a stepladder. He was painting a sign above a doorway and looked spectacularly unsteady, either because the mechanism was wobbly or because his six-foot seven-inch frame dwarfed the ladder, or because his heavy-set body threatened to crack the rungs, or because he was marvelously drunk, evidenced by his off-key singing and glassy stare, but whatever it was, he was a sight and a half and Esmeralda had to stop and look. "Hey, mister," she said, "where's the action?"

"Right here," he said, "soon as I open up." He dipped his brush into a can of paint and eyeballed the lettering. It was a real mess, whatever he was painting, but he didn't seem to mind. The letters were all different sizes and shapes and had a kind of well-worn, homey look.

"The, uh, *hungry i*," said Esmeralda, trying to make sense of the sign.

"No, no, it's not done yet. The place is called the *hungry id*," he said, dipping his brush into the can.

"The hungry watcha-ma-calla?" said Esmeralda.

"The *hungry id*, you know? From Freud? Id, ego—"

"Uh-huh. Hope you don't mind my saying, but that's a terrible name. Anybody's hungry, they're gonna lose their appetite."

"It's not a restaurant."

Esmeralda glanced back at the sign, then at Nick, then at the guy. "You're losing me, mister."

"It's a nightclub. Music, poetry, jazz, comedy. I only book acts nobody else will touch."

"With a name like that, you're gonna get customers nobody else will touch, either," said Esmeralda.

"We're new to town," said Nick, jumping in before Esmeralda could stick both feet into her mouth. "Anywhere you'd suggest?"

"Depends what you want. You don't look like the type to go to Fisherman's Wharf or Playland at the Beach, am I right? Now, if it's music you want, there's jazz in the Fillmore, plus a couple of joints downtown that are okay. If you want to stay in the neighborhood, there's a spot on Broadway that won't leave you completely destitute. Then, if you're still around, I've got a blues jam downstairs on Sunday afternoon."

"Is that right? I play a bit of harmonica. What time did you say?"

"Whenever anybody shows up. Two, two-thirty, something like that. Just tell them Big Daddy sent you."

"Is that you?"

"Big Daddy Nord, at your service. This is my place."

"Okay, good, maybe we'll check it out."

Big Daddy leaned precariously over the doorway, trying to dip his brush into the paint can. As he dabbed at the bottom of the can, the ladder tipped and turned and nearly toppled over. "Shit!" he said, swinging from side to side.

"What is it?" said Nick, grabbing the rungs before the whole thing tumbled on top of them.

"I'm out of paint!" said Big Daddy, as he stabilized himself between the door, the sign, the ladder, and a window frame. "Wouldn't you know it? After all this chatter, the damned enamel dried up."

"Sorry, mister," said Esmeralda, "but if you ask me, you should just leave well enough alone. The *hungry i* is a whole lot better than the *hungry id*, anyway."

"You think?"

"I don't know what the hell it means, but it's kinda got a ring."

"Okay, then," said Big Daddy, "the *hungry i* it is. I was getting tired painting, anyway." He climbed down off the ladder, gathered his gear, and split. "Later, cats and kittens."

"Later," said Nick and Esmeralda, watching as he disappeared down a basement stairway. They crossed over to the produce market, which was closed for the night, down to the financial district, which was closed for the weekend, and over to the Chinatown opium dens, which were closed forever. There was a strange, sweet-smelling smoke wafting up from some windowless basement apartments, but if the welcome mat was out, it wasn't in English. They continued up Stockton Street, admired some roasted Peking ducks drying in the window of a meat market, tried on matching Confucian skullcaps in a tourist shop, and wandered through a herbalist emporium which had jar after jar filled with bizarre-looking roots, bones, and animal parts whose uses were left better to the imagination than to the prescription pad. Esmeralda made the mistake of sneezing, which brought a crooked little man running to the counter with a packet of powders.

"This good for cold!" he insisted, shoving the foul-smelling compound under her nostrils.

"That's okay, mister," she said, backing away. "It's just the dust."

"You sure? You look pretty sick to me."

"Believe me, I'm in the pink."

"How about you?" the herbalist said to Nick.

"Never felt better."

"You sure? Back okay? Stomach good? Pecker working?"

"Yeah, yeah, everything's tip-top."

Esmeralda grabbed Nick's arm and led him to the door as the herbalist followed them to the street continuing his pitch: "We've got rhinoceros horn, bear claw, gecko tongue—"

"We'll keep it in mind," said Esmeralda as she and Nick disappeared into a crowd around the corner. Before they knew it, they were back on Broadway where the neon lights bathed them in a cool purple-pink haze. Fluorescent martini glasses beckoned them from bar windows, music floated out from dance halls, and a cool saxophone wafted down from an upstairs studio. A saloon door swung open and they got swept inside to a bar where they knocked down a couple shot glasses of whiskey, nibbled on an olive, paid their tab, and were back on the street before the door swung closed. The neighborhood was coming alive with weekend revelers, out-of-town tourists, and locals out to unwind from the long week. A couple of curious onlookers stood around a television set in the window of an electronics shop, watching the Army-McCarthy Hearings. Uncle Joe McCarthy himself could be seen silently yapping at some poor government slob while the viewers watched with blank faces. A few drops of sweat hovered on McCarthy's forehead as he poked and prodded the witness. When the camera panned in for a close-up, the television screen flickered a few times, as if afraid of its own shadow.

Nick and Esmeralda continued their tour of North Beach and by the time they hit Columbus Avenue, they were ready to call it a night. They crossed over to the Swiss-American Hotel, climbed three flights of stairs, and headed for their room at the end of the hall. The hotel wasn't much quieter than the street. Music, voices, and car horns filtered in through the thin walls, and the floor boards pulsated to their own beat. The place could've used a coat of paint and a new carpet and a shot or two of disinfectant, but with a little imagination it was almost possible to think of it as being steeped in Old World charm. The newcomers stumbled down the hallway, a little tipsy from their first night in San Francisco, much like passengers crossing the Bay on an unsteady ferry. Nick fumbled for his key, Esmeralda fumbled for Nick, and they both fumbled for the door when a pair of heavy boots kicked past them along the carpet. The squeaky soles continued on down the hall, stopped, turned, stood there a moment, and came back to the two interlopers trying to get into their room. "Don't I know you?" intoned a sonorous voice over the cacophony of the street.

Nick turned to see his old buddy Jack Kerouac leaning against a wall, his hands stuffed into his pockets, his collar up around his neck. "Yeah, sure, Denver, wasn't it? Some crummy pool hall?"

"That's it, all right. Pederson's Death Parlor. I got out of there just in time."

"You and me, both. Denver nearly did me in. Not to mention my girl, here. This is Esmeralda."

"Nick didn't tell me he was traveling first class," said Jack, taking her hand.

"Pleased, I'm sure," said Esmeralda, outstretching a dainty hand and slipping into the slightly ditzy voice of a Chicago B-girl. The shots of whiskey had loosened her tongue and proved, once again, that you can take the girl out of Chicago but you can't take the bar out of the girl.

"Jack here's a writer," said Nick. "He's working on a book."

"Oh, sorry about that," said Esmeralda. "I hope you'll feel better in the morning."

"You got it, sister," said Jack, laughing to himself. "The words always look better by the light of day, least that's what I tell myself." He looked down the hallway for any sign of Jaxson. "So, where's your hustler friend? Out giving free advice to the unwary?"

"Hard to say," said Nick. "We kind of left Denver in a hurry."

"What, you left him in the lurch?"

"I guess you could say that."

"Good, a guy like that's better off in the lurch."

"Yeah, much better," laughed Nick.

"What exactly *is* the lurch?" said Esmeralda.

Jack thought for a moment, then shrugged his shoulders. "Haven't the foggiest," he said.

"Me, either," said Nick.

"Some writer," said Esmeralda.

Jack leaned back against the wall and studied their faces. "Weren't you supposed to be headed for a ranch somewhere up the coast?"

"Vineyard," corrected Esmeralda. "We're going to pick a couple bags of money off the trees."

"That's a nice gig if you can get it."

"Oh, we can get it, all right," said Esmeralda, twirling around in the hallway and clicking her heels together like a flamenco dancer gone batty.

"Don't mind her," said Nick. "She gets a little excitable sometimes."

"This town does that to you. It'll knock you on your ass if

you let it. Not that that's so bad. Me, I like the view from the sidewalk. Keeps a guy honest." Jack shifted his weight from one foot to the other and ran a hand through his hair. A couple of kids ran up the stairs, shaking the banister and sending a tremor through the floor. A car horn tooted from somewhere outside. An old lady came out of the communal bathroom, glanced around as if to remember where she was, and headed down the hall. "So, tell me, love birds, what do you think of San Francisco? Ready to claim your piece of the west?"

"I like it," said Nick. "It feels like home."

"It's a different kind of different," said Jack. "There's a craziness in the air, makes you want to loosen your collar and let down your hair. Listen to that hum outside, that's the hum of the Bay. This town has its own soundtrack, a saxophone over a piano over a drum. Man, I'll tell you, there's a beat to this city and it goes on all night long. You hear it? Listen. The foghorns echo off the bridges and a conga player beats his skins until the moon finally drops into the ocean, too exhausted to go on."

"You really *do* have a way with words," said Esmeralda.

"I'll be back here one day, that's for sure. I'm hitchhiking down the coast, then back east, but these streets are calling my name."

"Yeah, yeah, I can hear them now," said Esmeralda. *"Jack, Jack, grab a broom."*

"Sure, if that's what it takes. I'll sweep the streets. Hell, if I won't."

"I'm just pulling your chain. This neighborhood could use some sprucing up, but maybe it could be something. They could open a couple of jazz spots, a coffee shop or two, a strip joint, am I right, Nickie? Who knows, it could be almost as good as Chicago."

"Yeah, almost," said Nick, winking at Jack.

"Okay, I'm off for the streets," said Jack. "You two want to see if we can get into some trouble?"

"Not tonight," said Nick. "We've got a big day tomorrow. We'll catch you on the flip side."

"Okay, then, grab some of that wine for me and remember to drink the rest."

"We'll say a toast for you."

"Til next time," said Jack, raising an imaginary glass.

"Til next time," said Nick and Esmeralda, clinking the air.

Chapter 28

"Do not count your chickens
before they are hatched."
—Aesop

The Golden Gate Bridge swayed slightly in the morning
breeze. Actually, it swayed from side to side and up
and down and even a bit in and out, but that was all in
the design. Even though it had been perfectly safe for all ten
years of its existence, Esmeralda didn't trust it for a minute.
"What, exactly, is holding this contraption up?" she kept
muttering as Nick navigated beneath the impossibly long
suspension cables.

Esmeralda was suspicious of anything built after the collapse of the Ottoman Empire, which had nothing to do with
bridges and everything to do with fast exits, especially if you
were a Bulgarian Gypsy with itchy feet and sticky fingers.
Now, collapse was on her mind as they crossed the San Francisco Bay—collapse of the government, collapse of society,
collapse of civil protection against alien invasion, collapse of
her dreams. Oh, yes, especially the collapse of her dreams. As
the Hudson headed north through Marin County, she became painfully aware that what for her had been in the realm
of the imaginary was about to enter the world of the real, and
reality, as any Gypsy knew, was only as good as your latest
Tarot card reading.

Fear gripped her insides and turned her stomach to goulash. Her mouth went dry, her lips tightened, and the pores in her skin contracted. For the first time she faced the very real possibility that this whole journey had been a figment of her imagination. Was there really a lawyer in Chicago? Was there really a cousin in California? Was she even driving through Mill Valley and San Rafael in a Hudson convertible? Who knew what was what? Maybe life was just a shell game and she was the shell. Maybe life was just a stage and she was the usherette. Maybe life was just a dream and she was the part that went sh-boom, sh-boom.

Nick, off in his own world, veered toward some faded-out shaving cream signs at the side of the road and Esmeralda's miserable life passed before her eyes. Jail cells, detention centers, leatherette barstools, and shadows on the wall flashed by in a jumble of remorse. "Damn it, Nickie!" she yelled as she grabbed the steering wheel.

"Hey, okay, okay," he said, straightening the wheel. "Everything's cool."

"Oh, you think so? Did I ever tell you how my father died?"

"I think I missed that one."

Esmeralda leaned back into her seat, staring straight ahead. "I was seven years old. A cop came to the door one afternoon and said my Dad was last seen driving a lonely road up in northern Wisconsin when he wrapped his car around a Burma Shave sign. Seems he was trying to read the last line and got too close. They found him in a ditch, the victim of his own morbid curiosity."

Nick tried his best to keep a straight face. "It probably said don't drive too close to this sign or you'll go home in pine."

"The gonif," said Esmeralda with a shrug. "Got what he deserved."

As Nick drove on, Esmeralda reflected on her misspent youth. Even crossing into Sonoma County and seeing her first rows of grapes did little to assuage her anxiety. There they were, all those branches and leaves and twigs just waiting to sprout into bottles of Chardonnay and Chablis, but she couldn't shake the feeling that a lifetime of bad luck and trouble was catching up with her and trying to ruin her California dream.

The car rose over some gently rolling hills, then curled along Redwood Highway to the edge of the Petaluma River, where a couple of steamboats paddled upriver toward the mouth of the Bay. They followed Petaluma Boulevard into town and turned up Kentucky Street. Petaluma had the feel of old California, which is to say it had been around for maybe a hundred years or so, but in this part of the world you counted decades, not centuries. They passed City Hall, the Continental Hotel, Elite Bowling Parlor, and Star Bakery, then arrived at the cast iron facade of the McNear Building. An office on the ground floor indicated the presence of Mr. Morris Norris—Realty Agent, Notary Public, Tax Consultant, Legal Advisor, Court Clerk and Stenographer. All of these services could be found in the singular personage of Morris Norris himself, a hefty man who sat behind a $300 mahogany table on a 50¢ oak stool, which left a mixed message as to whether he was a man on the way up, on the way down, or on the way out. He glanced up upon seeing two living customers walk through the door and sneezed mightily. "Allergies," he said by way of introduction.

"Mr. Morris?" said Esmeralda.

"Norris," corrected Morris.

"I'm Esmeralda Kurlansky. A guy at Greenberg, Greenberg, and O'Shaughnessy said to look you up."

"Of course. Esmeralda Kurlansky. Abe Kurlansky's long-lost cousin. We've been waiting for you."

"You and me both. It's a long drive from Chicago."

"I trust the journey went well?"

"Oh, yeah, a real breeze."

Nick stood off to the side, the odd man out of an odd couple. This was family business, after all, and the only thing he knew about family businesses was that he wanted no part of it. "And you must be—" said Morris, extending his hand.

"The boyfriend," said Nick.

"AKA Nick Drake," said Esmeralda, introducing him as if he were the prime suspect in a lineup.

"Well, I'm very pleased to make your acquaintances. I think you'll find yourself quite comfortable in Petaluma. The climate's grand, the air is clean, and there's plenty of Jewish families."

"Jews? Here?" said Esmeralda.

"Well, sure. Didn't you know?"

"The only thing I know about Petaluma is that my cousin Abe put down roots here. What did he do, knock up half the women in town? The Kurlanskys are famous for that."

"No, Abe kept pretty much to himself. The Jewish folks have been around for quite some time. Must be over 200 families by now."

"You don't say. Well, that's nice, mister, but I'm about as Jewish as Nick the Mic here. The only thing my dad gave me was his name and a tendency to complain. I'm more what you call a half-breed, if you catch my drift. Half now, half on delivery."

"That's a good one," said Norris, slapping his knee and laughing too loud.

"Look, Mr. Morris—"

"Norris," said Morris.

"We're pretty anxious to see the spread. What say we sign whatever has to be signed and you give us directions to the ranch?"

"I'll do better than that. How about I just show you the way?"

"Why would you want to do that?"

"It's really no trouble. I close early on Saturday. In fact," he said, glancing at his watch, "it's almost noon."

"Oka-a-a-y, but no funny business," said Esmeralda, sus-picious as always of anyone with an office, a desk, and a light bulb.

"Funny business?"

"We're not hicks, Mr. Morris."

"Norris," said Morris.

"If you're thinking of squeezing out a piece of the action, or getting some percentage of this and that, well, you can forget about it right now."

"Believe me, Miss Kurlansky, I wouldn't dream of it," said Norris, raising his hands like some old varmint in a Western caught with too many horses in his barn.

Esmeralda took the opportunity to do a quick scan of his palm. His hand was as broad as a farmer's, with puffy fingers, a life line that was long and unbroken, a heart line that was straight and true, and a head line that showed a distinct lack of imagination. The guy was golden. She only wished she could sell him a new roof for his house. "Sure, we'd be glad to take you up on your offer, Mr. Norris."

"Call me Morris. I can see we're going to be friends."

"You're not messing with me, are you, Morris?"

"How do you mean?"

"Never mind. Meet you out front in five?"

"Five it is."

Nick followed Morris Norris's Packard out of town along Western Avenue, which eventually turned into Spring Hill Road and became a two-lane highway. They drove past a couple of horse stables, past a dairy farm, past some grazing cows, and then, after eight or nine miles of curves and bends, they turned on Guglielmetti Road, which wasn't much more than a dirt lane, and then they turned on Jewell Road, which wasn't even dirt, but more a jumble of gravel, stone, clay, and hay. Eventually, the tire tracks ended and a little shack appeared out of the weeds.

Esmeralda, ever hopeful, got out of the car and looked at the broken down cabin that lay at the end of an overgrown path. "You see, these vineyards are stashed out here in the sticks to keep prying eyes away. This must be the caretaker's shack."

Morris got out of his Packard and came over to them. "Welcome to the Kurlansky Ranch."

"Where is it exactly?"

"How's that?" said Morris.

"You know, the house, the cellars, the crushers—"

"The coops, you mean? I think they're just behind the back bedroom."

Morris's words flew right over Esmeralda's head like a chicken on laughing gas. "Oh, I almost forgot!" she said. "There's something we need to do." She hurried back to the Hudson and pulled three wine glasses out of the glove compartment. "How about you uncork one of our very best, Morris? I've got a thirst that just won't quit."

"Well, now, Esmeralda, I don't want to disappoint you, but if it's liquid refreshments you're referring to, I'm afraid Abe was pretty much of a teetotaler."

"What kind of Kurlansky was he?"

"One of the best, I assure you," said Morris, giving Esmeralda a reassuring nod. "Now, the house should be to your liking. We left everything just the way it was. Except for the sheets, of course. We had the sheets washed and ironed. Otherwise, it's got Abe's personality written all over it. Nice and simple and clean as a whistle."

Esmeralda tried putting two and two together, but things just didn't add up. She ran a few more numbers through her head, but they kept coming up all crooked and wobbly, like a broken slot machine. She turned to Nick with a confused look. "Nickie? Am I missing something? Did we go to the right town? Weren't we supposed to turn left somewhere back there in Nevada?"

Nick looked back at her with his own vacant gaze. He had a funny feeling that the churning in the pit of his stomach was trying to tell him something. "I don't think there's more than one Petaluma, baby."

"Oh, no, you won't find another Petaluma, you can be sure of that," said Morris. "It's a real one-of-a kind town. Folks around here are pretty proud of our little piece of paradise."

"Um, Morris?" said Nick. "Can I ask you something?"

"Shoot."

"Where's the grapes?"

"The... grapes?" Morris rubbed his chin with the back of his hand. "Well, there's plenty of grapes all over Sonoma County. Not so much in Petaluma, of course, but if you go up around Healdsburg and Glen Ellen and St. Helena, you'll find vineyards everywhere you look."

"And what is it that people grow in Petaluma?"

Morris looked at Nick like maybe he was pulling his leg. Morris decided that if he was, he sure could keep a straight face. "Well, eggs, of course. Didn't you know? We're known as the Egg Basket of the World."

Esmeralda found it suddenly impossible to look at Morris. She took Nick's arm and squeezed it so hard the veins nearly burst. "Did he say eggs, Nickie? Because I thought I heard him say something about eggs."

"That's what he said, honey. Eggs."

"Eggs?"

"Eggs."

Esmeralda leaned against the car and fell sound asleep on the spot. This bout of narcolepsy was something new for her, a rare but not unheard-of physical reaction to extreme stress of an almost unimaginable kind. She stood there entirely immobile, kind of like a cross between a mannequin and a pillar of salt. Esmeralda instantaneously entered into a deep dream state, the subcortical variety that is full of pent-up energy and exists in a parallel world where anything can happen and usually does.

A rooster crowed in the distance. There was a flapping of wings. Esmeralda danced across the stage of Radio City Music Hall in her chicken suit, weaving her way between two rows of feathery poultry who strutted their stuff in a zig-zaggy chorus line. The audience stood and cheered as she kicked her legs high in a precision dance routine. She dipped and swirled across the floorboards, then spread her wings to embrace a whole new world that was unfolding right before her eyes. It was a world of glamour, leisure, and infinite pleasures. She bowed deeply, reached down for a bouquet of flowers, plucked the petals, and tossed them high into the air. It was raining roses. The air was thick with the sweet smell of success. Life was a beautiful garden.

And then she woke up. Esmeralda's eyes snapped open and she glanced from the weeds to the shack to the chicken coops. She stood there for exactly 30 seconds, which was the time it took for the blood to rush from her fingers to her toes, then fainted dead away on the spot. She lay there in a heap, down and dirty as a chicken farmer on a Saturday afternoon. Esmeralda Kurlansky was right where she was always meant to be, home at last.

Chapter 29

*"Beyond a certain point there is no
return. This point has to be reached."*
—Franz Kafka

The Harley-Davidson Knucklehead drove through the
night, through the day, and into the night again,
stopping only for gas, water, and food. That's what the
signs said every 50 miles or so—Gas, Water, Food—and
Jaxson, who was especially open to suggestion now that his
essence was gone, took pretty much every suggestion offered.
Marta-2 didn't object, since her kidneys had long ago gone
into full revolt and even a five minute stop was a welcome
chance to let her organs settle into a temporary state of
corporeal balance. Their motorcycle jackets had already
developed a patina from the salt flats, the sand dunes, and
the mountain passes and formed to their bodies like fitted
suits. Their boots were scuffed, their pants tattered, and their
skin tough and leathery from the sun. As they descended the
Sierra Nevadas into California's Central Valley, they got their
first real sense of the vastness and variety of the North
American continent. Quite frankly, it put Obsidia's Trans-
migrational Steppes to shame. Earth, for all its warts and
blemishes, was a planet of endless surprises and noteworthy
attractions, that much could not be denied. So what if its
population was defined by a tendency toward paranoia,

revenge, and poor grammar? Wasn't it Edison Barnstable who famously declared in his *Allegories, Parables and Other Mumblings*, "What do you want, it should make sense, too?"

Jaxson pulled up at a roadside diner just outside Grass Valley, where he checked his gas, map, and bearings. He had his usual struggle with numbers—formulas on Earth being no less convoluted than those on Obsidia. After a long moment spent calculating gas mileage or distance or something to do with speed divided by time, he pointed to a low-slung building that looked like it had been prefabricated and dropped off on the side of the road almost by mistake. "Let's have a bite in there," he said.

Marta-2 glanced over at the mostly empty cafe. There were a couple of truck drivers, two teenagers on a date, and a scantily dressed woman who sat alone in a red, vinyl booth staring out the window. "What's the occasion?" said Marta-2, not used to the luxury of actually sitting at a table and eating with utensils.

"We have to talk."

"Okay," she said, wondering what Jaxson could possibly have to talk about at this stage of the journey. He'd been uncharacteristically quiet ever since the detectives pulled the plug on the experiment—and on him—and was mostly a passive listener rather than the charming conversationalist she'd come to know during his running monologue through space. A bright lime-green neon sign lit up the parking area with a modern Garamond typeface that flashed out *Rosebud Diner* every 20 seconds. Each flash was followed by the sizzling sound of a swarm of beetles, moths and fireflies that fried themselves on the hot neon tubes and landed in a smoking heap on the ground.

Marta-2 followed Jaxson inside to a snug booth with a Formica table that was bolted to the floor. They squeezed their aching bodies along some plastic slipcovers and settled into matching foam cushions. Each table had a chrome napkin dispenser, salt and pepper shakers, and a menu holder with a laminated list of specials, none of which apparently ever changed since they were sealed tight. The diner was unusually expensive—Chicken Salad Plate for 60¢, Golden Brown Waffles for 30¢, Tuna Fish Sandwich for 35¢— but Jaxson didn't much care since his generous credit line was far from running out. He settled on the Stuffed Red Ripe Tomato, which came with Creamy Cottage Cheese and French Dressing, while Marta-2 went for the Terrace Special Fruit Cocktail Bowl with an Assortment of Fruits, Chilled Just Right and Served on a Bed of Crisp Lettuce with a Large Dip of Creamy Cottage Cheese, a Roll and Butter.

A mopey waitress sauntered over, took their order, and returned to her shadowy spot behind the counter, where she all but disappeared. Jaxson sat there quietly, waiting for his food, collecting his thoughts. "Do you know where we are?" he finally said.

"Grass Valley, I think? Isn't that what the sign said?"

"The name isn't important. If we drive one more mile, do you know what happens?"

"Our kidneys calcify?"

"Well, that too, but if we drive one more mile, we can't get back to the rocket ship in time to leave."

"I figured we must be getting close."

"We're there. We've reached the point of no return. If we keep going, it doesn't matter what we do, there's no way back."

Marta-2 stared at the abstract design of the Formica table. It was almost like staring into space with its endless dots and swirls of stars and galaxies. She'd been gone from home for so long, she didn't even know how to measure the time anymore. It was pointless to count in Obsidian months and years since they had no relationship to time on Earth. Earth days were confusing enough in themselves, what with the sun rising and falling at different times each day. As if Earth weren't complicated enough already! All she knew was that she wasn't getting any younger, no matter which planet's calendar pages were flipping by. "Well," she finally said, "what do you think?"

"I think we should go back."

"Why is that?"

"Because even if we get to the coast and we find Nick and I somehow regain my essence, we'll still be trapped on this planet. Is it worth it? If we wind up losing our freedom in the process, what have we really got?"

"We'd have each other."

The waitress arrived with rolls and butter, then slipped silently back to her post. Jaxson cut a roll in half and held it in his hand for a long moment. "Listen, Marta," he finally said, "you need to understand something. You and me, we're not really an item, if you know what I mean. You're a good friend—probably the best friend I ever had—but as for something else, you know, a future, well, I don't really see any possibilities."

"I see."

"You've risked everything for me. I don't know why you did it, but I can't let you ruin your whole life over this."

"Let me understand something. You'd give up your essence in order to regain your freedom, is that what you're saying? You're willing to leave behind everything that makes you what you are in order to return to a home you wouldn't even recognize?"

"Home is home."

"Home is where you make your bed."

The Stuffed Tomato and Fruit Cocktail arrived with all the enthusiasm the waitress could muster, which was none. She slid them across the table, grunted out something that sounded like "enjoyyermeal" and shuffled back toward her spot behind the counter.

Jaxson scooped out some cottage cheese, savored it a moment, and let it slide down his throat as if it were fine

Halacian eel. "We need to make a decision," he said.

"You know what I think."

"Are you sure you understand the implications of this? If we don't turn back now, it's final. There's no going back."

"Nothing is final. You never know what tomorrow brings."

"I know that tomorrow brings the aphelion. At 5 P.M. there's going to be a little blip of light in the western sky and that will be that. The Pulsar-7 will vanish into thin air and we'll be left on Earth staring into a plate of cottage cheese."

Marta-2 tried her fruit cocktail. It was a splendid medley of peaches, apricots, grapes, and melons. "You know something?" she said. "They weren't kidding. It *is* chilled just right."

"Is that your answer?"

"That's my answer."

"Okay, then," said Jaxson, biting into his juicy ripe tomato. "Let the record show that on July 12, 1947, Ship Observer Jaxson Epsilon and Molecular Biologist Marta-2 made the dumbest decision of their lives."

"Cheers," said Marta-2, raising her glass of water in a toast.

"Cheers," said Jaxson.

Chapter 30

"Men trip not on mountains;
they trip on molehills."
—Chinese Proverb

The Nebraska sky was clear, the wind was calm, and the desert was at peace with itself. It was Saturday night— the calm before the storm, the silence before the dawn, the day before tomorrow. A little puff of a cloud circled the plateau and hugged the mesa as the sky yawned its goodnight. Beneath it, the Pulsar-7 had miraculously been put back together and was ready for takeoff. The wings were locked, the holes were patched, and the engine parts were matched up so that the gears jibed, the cylinders compressed and the pistons passed muster, or whatever it is that engines do when they're not causing trouble. For this, the crew had Teller to thank, since the Chief Engineer had singlehandedly put the three dimensional mechanical puzzle back together, a testament to his fortitude, his devotion, and, most importantly, his ever-present fear of re-re-re-deanimation.

Now, with the hustle and bustle behind them, a strange calm overtook the rocket ship. All of the interpersonal conflicts were put on hold, the petty jealousies and irritations and perceived slights to be revisited at some later time. The crew was a team again, a well-oiled unit that was fully capable of banding together and taking on the dangers of lift-off and the rigors of flight. It was, in fact, a rare time of personal reflection, an opportunity for each of them to spend a few hours remembering what they were doing on Earth in the first place. It was a chance to contemplate what had brought them to this point in their lives, what made them take such outsized risks for such unknown rewards. Was it fame? Was it fortune? Or was it something darker, some desire to escape the straightjacket of everyday life?

Captain Hieronymus Wambold sat in his operating quarters, staring at his hands. They were wrinkled, chafed, and covered with liver spots. He hardly recognized them. These were the hands that once held the delicate fingers of a shy young lady, the hands that soothed a baby's bottom, the hands that caressed a dying mother. Now they were deformed by arthritis, the fingers grown crooked, the knuckles malformed, the veins bulging. Wambold finally looked up and caught his reflection in a mirror. My God, he really had grown old! His eyes looked tired, with drooping lids and a kind of glassy semi-opaque surface glossing over the corneas. His nose was longer than he remembered—the nose and the chin keep growing even after the rest of the face have called it quits—and his skin was red and blotchy. There were new wrinkles everywhere, circling under his eyes, etched into his forehead, and splayed out from the corners of his mouth. "Well, old man, what have you got to say for yourself?" he said.

Even that was a sign of old age—talking to yourself—and for the first time it occurred to Wambold that Teller was right. He was at the end of the line, his career as an illustrious captain was drawing to a close, and he was about to be shuffled off somewhere where he wouldn't embarrass anyone too much or cause too much trouble. This was to be his reward for a lifetime of bravery and service beyond the call of duty. He'd be a footnote in some space exploration journal, there'd be a plaque or two gathering dust in some space museum, and before you knew it, there'd be nothing left but the temperature scale named in his honor, and the truth is, even that would one day be changed when someone bolder and braver flew through a meteor shower at –18° Wambold.

The Captain unfolded his flight logs and holographic charts and plotted course. It would be an initial thrust out of Earth's orbit, a midcourse correction, and then a straight shot to the orbiting judicial station—the Court of Last Resort—located at the gateway to the Outlying Penal Stations. There he would give his testimony and some smart lawyer would twist his words and get him all confused and make him backtrack, and that would be that, the fine end to a fine career. Wambold glanced back at the mirror, studied his slightly bent visage, shrugged his shoulders, and went back to plotting the end of his final journey.

Across from the Captain's quarters, down the hall, up a flight of stairs, and next to the primary ventilation system, Oblivia gazed out the portal of her living quarters. It was hard to say what she saw, since she didn't put things together the way other people did. Where other people saw an arm and a leg and a head and ascertained that they'd encountered a fellow human being, Oblivia was as likely to see a giant erector set flailing through a jungle of bouffant hairdos. For Oblivia the sum of the parts didn't equal a whole, but rather they were arbitrary pieces to be mixed and matched as only she saw fit. For Oblivia trees could talk, rocks could dance, and rivers could wrap their fingers around you and tickle you until you wet your pantsuit. Which is what was happening at that very moment. Wet pantsuit or not, Oblivia was nobody's fool. She had her own form of cognitive function which let her know that something was up, like *really* up, as in it's time to blow this dusty burg and hit the celestial highway.

She therefore did her own preparations, which consisted of arranging and rearranging the items in her travel bag, a collection of things she'd picked up on Earth that would be useful on the long flight home: liver pate remoulade, a corn-cob pipe, a McDonald's wrapper, a dance ticket, a canceled stamp from the free port of Danzig, Poland, a postcard of Isadora Duncan, a 78 rpm recording of Gene Autry singing *Back in the Saddle Again*, a roll of exposed film, a piece of asbestos roofing, a chest x-ray, a nylon hairnet, a sprig of weeping willow, a faceplate from a motel light switch, a Dairy Queen napkin, a strand of speaker wire, a rear view mirror, a book of Aleister Crowley's poetry, a still-blinking stop light from a railroad crossing, a bag of marshmallows, a bottle of expired snake oil, a street map of Tuscaloosa, Alabama, a porcupine quill, an armadillo foot, a trumpet mute, a can of athlete's foot powder, a bag of assorted rubber bands, a rectal thermometer, an application to Swarthmore College, an alabaster Virgin Mary, a ping pong paddle, a guide book to Grand Teton National Park, a dollars to yen conversion chart, a peach blossom petal, a potato peeler, a collection of Dear Abby advice columns, a Greyhound bus schedule, a Three Musketeers candy bar, a Betty Boop comic book, a plastic sword and scabbard, and a fake Van Dyke mustache and goatee, adhesive glue included.

Put together, the items created a dynamic world of their own, a world of great possibilities and endless intrigue. It was a world as only Oblivia knew it, but it made far more sense to her than Raleigh's quest or Wambold's legacy or Teller's plan of escape. That's because Oblivia understood something that no one else comprehended—*in everything is everything else*—and that's all anyone really needs to know.

Stashed away in his inner sanctum, Raleigh had barely left his chambers since his near-death experience in the gopher hole. He tried calming his mind and entering even deeper into the meditative state he'd been practicing ever since leaving Obsidia. He saw his crisis in the desert as a test of his entire belief system and instinctively bore down even farther into the cracks and crevices of his inner consciousness. He could almost see his brain waves flattening out as his thought patterns became quieter and the internal chatter of his mind hushed to a mere whisper. This was what it was all about, seeking an empty mind that would intersect with the eternal void and unify into the glorious nothingness of the time/space continuum.

And yet, in the self-fulfilling quietude of oneminded mindlessness, there arose again a purple-tinged shred of doubt. It wove its way through the tight-knitted fabric of his mind and burst into his consciousness like an unwelcome visitor come to upend his peaceful life. "What if you are nothing but a navigator who doesn't know where he's going?" said the shred.

The words cut deep. Raleigh was no fan of irony and the idea that he was leading himself astray didn't sit well at all. "But, but—" he said impotently.

"Raleigh, me boy," said the shred, "the brain is made up of two machines, one on the right side, the other on the left. Half your brain allows you to function in everyday life, while the other half is running at triple speed and shooting ideas around like shotgun pellets. You're trying to shut down the chatter, but what you're really doing is turning off the entire machinery of the left brain. It's like inducing a hemorrhage. My good man, the chatter is what makes us individuals. It's the source of our brilliance and creativity."

A glimmer of light coursed through Raleigh's vacant stare. "What exactly are you saying?"

"Don't meditate. It makes you stupid."

Raleigh nearly fell out of his lotus position. His legs cramped up and his chakras closed tight as a drum. His breathing became forced and his heartbeat irregular. His underarms began sweating and his feet itched. And then,

Raleigh both woke up and fell asleep into the deepest slumber he'd ever known. He dreamt of fireworks and orchestras and women dancing on high wires. His brain swooned and he took a wild leap from a flying trapeze. There was no net. He just kept flying and flying through the air, not knowing if he would ever land. Which was better? To land without a net or never land at all? Now, *that* was a question worth pondering.

Across the ship and up the stairs to the liminal level, Marta-1 was in a particularly contemplative mood. No, make that mode, for that surely is what it was—a mode—a way of thinking, a way of putting things together that accentuated what was important and negated what wasn't. It was definitely a mode. Although it wouldn't be entirely incorrect to say that she was in a mood as well. Mood, mode, it didn't really matter, since they were two sides of the same human operating system. And that, ladies and scientists, was the point of this whole exercise. Marta-1 was on her way to attaining every behavioral psychologist's greatest dream: eliminating the person and having only the behavior to deal with. Patients were always getting in the way of their cures and were an endless source of trouble. Behavior, on the other hand, was pure and direct. It had a beginning and an end and it could be measured. On the eve of her departure, Marta-1 reflected on what she had learned about the behavior of a certain detective who, for the sake of professional courtesy, shall remain unidentified.

Bitch! Bitch, bitch, bitch! Two-timing, lying, conniving cunt of a bitch! You built me up and tore me down! Oh, the sweet-talking and promises of all the tomorrows to come. The walks on the beach, the nights before the fireplace, the long lemon baths and massages in beds of red-yellow roses. The sweet smell of your breath on the tiny hairs of my neck, the feel of your tongue in my ear, the tingle of your fingers on my breasts. What stories you wove! You and me forever, you and me living the life of luxury on a paradise island in the sky, you and me blazing trails and climbing mountains and diving to the depths of oceans of love.

Nothing was left now but the sting of regret, the aching of the heart separated from its soul, the yearning of the skin stripped of its skeleton. Come to my room again in the middle of the night? Oh, yes, please, please, please, please just try it.

Teller sat perfectly still in his individual preservation module, or indie-prod as he referred to it, staring into the highly polished palimonium wallboard that served as his shaving mirror, bulletin board, and room divider. He liked what he saw—a man square of jaw, steely of stare, and tight of stomach. While the rest of the crew pondered their place in the larger scheme of things, Teller saw it for the waste of time that it was. He was a man of action and no amount of reason and deliberation was going to get in his way. He realized long ago that thinking only leads to more thinking whereas action leads to results. That was him, a results-oriented, finely-tuned, rock-solid pragmatist living in a watery world of what-ifs and why-nots.

Not that Teller was totally immune from internal conflict. There was one issue that gnawed at him day and night, something that made him question if he wasn't being played for the biggest fool of them all. He'd been the good soldier while selflessly putting the Pulsar-7 back together in one piece but what, exactly, was to be his reward? To be transported directly to the Court of Last Resort where he alone would face the music? Because that was going to be the result, no matter what anyone said. When push came to shove, he'd be shoved right off the cliff by the Captain's lackeys, ingrates that they were. Talk about building the gallows for your own execution! Why didn't they ask him to tie the rope and pull the lever as well?

Teller nonetheless prepared for the day of reckoning. He folded his socks and underwear with military precision while leaving a terrible mess of shaving cream, toothpaste, and shampoo that dribbled all over the place. That was Teller in a nutshell, two sides of an unsteady personality coexisting uneasily. He was predictably unpredictable, a bundle of nerves about to become unbundled, a firecracker ready to crack, a torpedo about to careen completely off-course.

Across the mesa, the Sprite 2000 settled into the horizon, silhouetted against the sky like a dwarf tree tucked in for the night. The cold fusion chamber was powered down and the ship glowed eerily as it gathered a bank of energy through its freeze-dried cellanators. The wafer-thin disks gathered layer upon layer of crystalline ice pellets which multiplied, regenerated and finally accumulated into the three-dimensional vivaforms that had powered space travel for a generation. It was an old technology but it was safe, clean, and didn't cost an arm and a leg.

Inside the space transport, Kalamata was fast asleep, the coming aphelion a minor blip on her social calendar. She dreamt of all the places she still had to go, the people to meet, the conquests to conquer. That was the beauty of her job as a roving detective. There was no need to stay in any one place too long. No messy good-byes. No regrets. No surprises. Life was just a bowl of cherries and she was picking the tastiest ones of all.

Loquacious was more circumspect, checking the space transport one last time for any information leaks, data inconsistencies, or statistical malfunctions. He was anxious to get off this malodorous planet and bring his quarry in for review. In the old days, he would've been called a bounty hunter, but somebody or other decided that bounties were unseemly and made the profession a salaried position. Fair enough, said Loquacious. Give me a ship, a schiller, and social security. Done and done, said the officers of the court, and that was that, even-steven, over and out.

Loquacious checked his personal belongings and decided to eliminate the excess baggage. He liked to travel light and was pretty sure he wouldn't be needing the currency converter, the magnetic chess set, or the book of Chinese proverbs, which turned out to be completely useless:

HAVE A MOUTH AS SHARP AS A DAGGER,
BUT A HEART AS SOFT AS TOFU.

TO TALK MUCH AND ARRIVE NOWHERE IS THE
SAME AS CLIMBING A TREE TO CATCH A FISH.

DO NOT REMOVE A FLY FROM A FRIEND'S
FOREHEAD WITH A HATCHET.

Huh? What the hell did that even mean? You could tell a lot about a people from their musings and this was more than he needed to know. Earth, like a 100-year-old bowl of hot and sour soup, was not his cup of tea. He got the rest of his things in order and secured them in his locker. Everything else was there: the duffel bags, the dead aliens, the tubes and fittings of the dream machine—

Except that the tubes and the fittings were slightly different than he remembered them. Weren't the tubes green and the fittings yellow? Or the joints blue and the latches orange? Something wasn't right. Loquacious felt the ribbed texture of the tubes, then unzipped the backpack, reached inside, and grabbed a big handful of fluffy goose down. "So-o-o," he said, giving vent to a full ten syllables worth of accusation, aggravation, and recrimination.

The detective pulled his hat low over his forehead, shimmied down the escape hatch of the Sprite 2000, jaunted across the mesa, climbed the polyprotopulsium ladder of the Pulsar-7, knocked on the door, and waited. A moment later Captain Wambold answered, wearing a sleeping cap that made him look as old and tired as a night clerk at a rest home. Loquacious immediately grabbed the old man around his neck and gave him a three-fingered squeeze of disapprobrium. Wambold lurched back, fell to his knees, and wobbled unsteadily to his feet. "A handshake would've been sufficient," he said, choking out the words.

"Do you know why I'm here?"

"I can guess."

"Gather your crew."

"Is that really necessary?"

"I'm getting ready, Captain. To blow."

The frazzled crew stood outside the Rejuvenation Chamber, staring at the *Occupied* sign on the door. "How many of you knew about this?" said Loquacious, studying their faces with the seriousness of a war interrogator.

"None of them had anything to do with it," said Wambold. "This was all my doing."

"Is that right? Just you, Captain? Well, then, why don't you tell me. If I were to open this door, what do you think I would find?"

"Not much."

"No, not much at all," said Loquacious, as he reached over, turned a truman valve 180°, and swung open the heavy terrafoil portal. Inside, the chamber glowed a cool phosphorescent blue which made it look even emptier than it really was, which was utterly and completely. "Well, look here," he said with mock surprise, "it appears not to be occupied after all. Two of your crew members seem to be missing. Would you like to tell me where they are, Captain?"

"It's hard to say."

"Is it? Try."

"Well, they could be in Denver. Or on the way back. Or somewhere else altogether. They could be anywhere a man goes to look for his essence."

Loquacious narrowed his eyes and turned his head like an owl. "I don't like metaphors, Captain. I take metaphors and strip them down to simple similes and then I let them wallow in their own juices like halibut steeped in rancid fennel mayonnaise."

"I wouldn't let him speak to you like that, Captain," said Marta-1.

"Me, either," said Raleigh.

"Ditto," said Teller.

"Oh? And what are you going to do about it?" said Loquacious as he pulled out his schiller and rolled it around in his hand.

Raleigh retreated. Teller went pale. Marta-1 held her tongue. Oblivia, however, thinking there was an air raid or a blitzkrieg or an alien invasion, screamed. It was a scream that came from the bottom of a skyscraper in London, rose through the elevator shaft, blasted out through the broadcast antenna, and traveled halfway around the world to their little mesa in Nebraska. The scream landed with the force of a grenade that shattered the wall, shook the floor, and cracked the glass. Loquacious got caught in a sonic back draft that nearly turned him upside down. The air pushed him seven ways to Sunday, which was exactly six ways more than Teller needed to grab the detective's schiller, buckle his knees, and spin him right around into the Rejuvenation Chamber, where he locked him up as tight as a tom-tom on Thanksgiving Eve.

"Teller! What are you doing?" said Wambold.

"I'm giving him a taste of his own medicine!"

"You'll do no such thing! You have no idea how dangerous

it is in there."

"Actually, I do," said Teller as he reached over and turned on the on/off switch. There was a churning sound from inside the chamber, a yell, the pounding of fists on the door, then total silence.

"Stand down, Teller!"

"Not this time, Captain," said Teller, aiming the schiller directly at Wambold's head. "I've got the detective just where I want him. As soon as his partner shows up, she can join him."

"I'm warning you, Chief Engineer. Return to your station!"

"I'm taking over, Captain. We'll lift off when I say we lift off. We'll plot course for where I say we plot course."

"Are you mad? I won't have it!"

"This day was coming, just like I told you," said Teller. Over the hushed silence of the crew, he reached over and pulled the Captain's insignia off his epaulets, then pointed him to his quarters. "Sorry, old man. You're relieved of your post."

Wambold turned from Raleigh to Marta-1 to Oblivia, but no one could meet his stare. Try as he might, his body slumped and his shoulders sagged as he tried to muster whatever dignity was left to him. Finally, he turned and walked off alone down the corridor. His footsteps echoed along the cold metal hallway, fainter and fainter, until they finally dissipated in the cool, quiet night.

Chapter 31

*"Ain't nobody here
but us chickens."*
—Louis Jordan

A rooster crowed at the break of dawn and Esmeralda's eyes popped open like an eggshell being beaten by a mallet. She glanced around Abe Kurlansky's bare-bones bedroom and wondered if she was back in the Joliet lock-up after a night of too much fun. There was a bed, a chest of drawers, a kerosene lamp perched atop an egg crate, a desk salvaged from a 19th century schoolhouse, a painting of a rabbi staring down from a mountaintop, and a Ukrainian wedding shawl with the embroidered image of a man, a woman and a chicken, Cyrillic good luck wishes included. The rooster crowed again, and then once more, as Esmeralda slowly came to terms with the idea that she was indeed in Petaluma, California, that she had taken possession of a broken-down chicken ranch, that Nick was sound asleep next to her, and that life had thrown her a curveball which was about to plunk her straight on the noggin.

In between the rooster crows, Esmeralda heard an incessant knocking on the door which she assumed was the head chicken coming to complain about the food or the toilet or the exercise yard. Just like in Joliet. Then she remembered that chickens don't have knuckles—or even hands, for that matter—which led her finally to get up and find out what was making such a racket. She snuck a look through the curtains to see a young wisp of a girl standing outside with a basket and a bonnet, and wondered if it was some kind of joke. Had she been magically transported to the pages of a Grimm Brothers fairytale? Was a wolf going to jump down the chimney and eat her alive? "What do you want?" Esmeralda finally grumbled through the door.

"Miss Kurlansky? Is that you?" came a sweet young voice. "It's Marlene Steinberg from down the road."

"What can I do for you?"

"Mr. Norris sent me over to show you the ropes."

"Ropes? What ropes? I don't remember hearing anything about ropes."

"Well, um, the chickens, you know?"

"The chickens?" said Esmeralda, suddenly tasting something terribly bitter in her mouth. It was the taste of bitter disappointment mixed in with the bitter truth of her bitter end. She was hardly in a mood to think about chickens and as for ropes the only rope she wanted was one to string over that big tree outside so she could hang herself before the sun got too high in the sky. "How about you come back later, okay? Maybe tomorrow or the next day or something."

"But, Miss Kurlansky, it's already awfully late. The sun's been up for almost ten minutes."

Ten *minutes?* Esmeralda didn't even know there was such a time of day much less how to get up and greet it. She bit her lip and opened the door. Marlene stood there just about as pert and pretty as a 15-year-old country girl could be. She was full of life and full of hope and eager to greet the day. She was like Little Red Riding Hood on uppers.

"Call me Esmeralda. Miss Kurlansky was my aunt."

"Hi, I'm Marlene."

"Yeah, I caught that. Now, what's this about Morris?"

"Well, I've been watching over things ever since Mr. Kurlansky passed away. You know, taking care of his flock and all. There's lots of stuff to do, of course."

"Of course," said Esmeralda, having no idea what one would do with a chicken other than roast it, bake it, or fry it.

"So, I guess we should just get started in the coops and kind've go from there."

Esmeralda started to laugh. "You're serious about this, aren't you? You actually think I'm going to go into a chicken coop with you? I haven't even had my coffee yet. I haven't brushed my teeth. I'm not even dressed."

"Yeah, you'd better put on some sturdy shoes. You don't want to step in the poop with those nice flats on."

"Poop?" said Esmeralda, her smile freezing on her face like an old metal etching plate gone cracked and withered. She walked out onto the porch and looked around the Kurlansky spread for the first time. There were five acres—that's what the deed said—and they apparently stretched from a fence up on a ridge over to a pond in the flatlands to a little scrub of dirt in the woods. There was the usual stuff you might expect on a farm—some trees and bushes and junk and crud—and a half dozen low-lying wooden huts that led out to some more fenced-in areas and then some more junk and crud and whatever.

"Shall we?" said Marlene.

"Yeah... yeah," said Esmeralda, following the girl around the side of the house to one of the coops. It was a long shed with a sloping roof, a series of glazed windows along its southern exposure, some vertical ventilation slats, a door just big enough for a chicken to run through, a plank leading down to the ground, and a fenced-in pen. On the other side of the shed was a larger door which Marlene unlatched and opened. "Whoo-ee," said Esmeralda as she caught a whiff of ammonia-soaked air.

"Probably needs cleaning," said Marlene, taking a deep breath. "Not everyday, of course—"

"I should hope not," said Esmeralda.

"Every *other* day." Esmeralda followed Marlene into the coop where 300 birds looked up in unison to check out the new chick on the block. They gave her the eye, which actually multiplied into one huge beady eye that stared right into her soul and saw her for the greenhorn she was. Unimpressed, they turned away to attend to more important business, that being the hunting and pecking of whatever could be hunted or pecked. "So, these are the chickens."

"You don't say."

"You've got your Rhode Island Reds and your Barred Rocks and those black and silver ones over there are Silver Laced Winedottes, and then there are the Brown Leghorns and the—"

"Okay," said Esmeralda, already worn out. "That's enough for today. We don't need to overdo it."

"Well, Miss Kurlansky—"

"Esmeralda."

"Esmeralda, I think we should just go on a bit more. I won't be able to come by too often and it's already getting late and—"

"Okay, okay. You showed me the chickens. What else is there?"

"There's the eggs."

"I was afraid of that."

"Now, these are pretty good layers. They'll give you an egg every day or two. You see those chickens over there with the white earlobes?"

Esmeralda glanced over at some birds with feathers and beaks and maybe a foot or two. As for other body parts, it was hard to say. The whole bunch of them could've been put together on an assembly line. "They've got ears?"

"Well, sure, otherwise they couldn't... well, anyway, the ones with the white earlobes, they give you white eggs. The ones with the colored lobes, they give you—"

"Colored eggs?"

"Actually, brown eggs. That's pretty much the range. White and brown."

"This is complicated."

Marlene led Esmeralda to a side of the shed that was warm, dark and moist. There was a series of nesting boxes lined up, each strewn with straw and wood shavings. "This is where they mostly lay. I mean, you'll find eggs pretty much anywhere, but this is the main area. You never really know when they're going to lay, so you just need to come in throughout the day and take a look around." Marlene did a quick once-over and pointed to a nesting box in the corner. "See, there's one. Why don't you just take it?"

"Where's the shovel?"

"No, no, just with your hand."

"I won't catch anything?"

"It's a lot more likely the chickens will catch something from us."

"I'm not exactly sure what you mean by *that*, sister," she said as she scrunched up her nose and plucked the egg out of the nest. "Hey, it's warm."

"Farm fresh."

"That's all there's to it?"

"Yeah, the gathering is the fun part. Except when they're fertilized, that is."

Esmeralda thought back to all those days she missed in biology class or health and hygiene or whatever it was they were trying to instill in her young, fertile mind. "Listen, honey, this may come as a big surprise to you, but I've got no idea what you're talking about."

"When they're fertilized, they'll hatch into chicks if you let them, so the hens roost on the eggs and they're not all that happy if you try to steal them away."

"Screw 'em. Whose farm is this?"

"I'd recommend a pair of real thick gloves and you might

want to be careful that they don't peck your eyes out."

"You're kidding, right?" said Esmeralda, laughing nervously.

Marlene smiled back at her and continued over to the feeding area. "Now here, you want to give them their food and water. This is real important, since chickens die pretty fast without food."

Esmeralda ran her hand through a bucket of corn meal. "Let me ask you something. What's a kid like you doing out here in the sticks? I mean, you seem pretty sharp to me and you got a pretty face under that bonnet thing you're wearing."

"I was born here. My parents came out from New York about 20 years ago with a bunch of people who wanted to work the land and have a community together."

"You don't say. You're Jewish, are you?"

"Most of us are. Jewish egg farmers. Pretty crazy, huh?"

"Real crazy. I don't get it."

Marlene mixed marigold flower petals and grit into the cornmeal, then poured it into the feeders. "I'm not sure I do, either, but they just wanted a place they could call their own and work cooperatively, you know, like a kibbutz or something. It's pretty cool, except for all the arguing, of course."

"I thought it was only my family that argued."

"Jews argue. It's in our blood. Anyway, there's a big to-do about politics all the time, since some of the families are pretty left-wing and others are less so and there's this fear about that Senator McCarthy making waves that gets everybody nervous."

"You just lost me, sweetheart."

"I know. What a bore, right? Anyway, you'll see. It's a pretty nice community."

"Oh, I won't be around long, you can be sure of that. Me and the great outdoors don't go well together. Put me in the countryside, my palms start to itch."

"Ever try aloe vera gel with green clay, wheat germ, lemon

juice and dried nettles?" said Marlene.

"That works, does it?"

"Takes away the itch and leaves your skin silk and smooth."

"You don't say."

Marlene plucked a few more eggs out of the nests, placed them in her basket, and led Esmeralda back to the door. "Ready to see the granary?"

Esmeralda tottered. "Oh, God, you can't be serious. There's more?"

"Oh, sure, we're just getting started."

Esmeralda sank into a pile of hay and flailed her arms like a petulant child. "I won't go! You can't make me!"

"Really, Esmeralda, it's not so bad once you get used to it."

Esmeralda looked around in a panic, weighing her new-found burden of responsibilities. "Gypsies don't own things! We steal!"

"—people will give you plenty of help—"

She threw her head back and screamed to the sky or the ceiling or whatever it was that was above her. "Oh, mama, why have you forsaken me?"

"You'll see, Esmeralda, you'll see."

Downtown Petaluma was mostly closed on Sunday morning. Pedroni Delicatessen, Antler's Pharmacy, Arcade Barber Shop, Nielsen Furniture Company, Linch Jewelry, Carithers Department Store, and J.C. Penney were taking their day of rest, not to mention the big poultry suppliers, the grain and feed stores, the feed mills, the hatcheries, the dairy co-ops, and the brooder supply stores. That left the Jewish businesses—Holtzman's Department Store, Feldman's Hardware, The Purity Food Store—which drew a smattering of customers, then closed at noon in order to picnic with their families along the beaches of the Russian River.

Jaxson guided his Harley down Petaluma Boulevard and pulled up in front of Levin's Kosher Deli. He and Marta-2 studied some unfamiliar writing that drifted from right to left across the window, then entered. Inside was a counter, a couple of tables, and Ira Levin, a middle-aged man in an apron and matching T-shirt. "What can I get you?" he said with a tired voice.

"We're looking for someone," said Jaxson.

"So, what do you want I should do, give you a medal?" said Levin. "Half the world is looking for someone. The other half is trying to get away from the ones who's looking for 'em. Me, I try to stay out of it."

"It's just some friends," said Jaxson. "We're not out to arrest anybody or anything like that."

"If you were such hot friends, how come you don't know where they are? Me, I tell my friends to come visit, they know where to find me."

"Perhaps if we ordered something?" said Marta-2, studying the menu board posted above the counter and trying another tact.

"Sure, order, don't order, what, it's going to change the world?"

"These, um, blintzes, can you tell me what they are?"

"What are you, from Mars?"

"No-no," said Jaxson quickly. "We're from Earth, just like you."

"Mazel tov. So what, you want I should give you the recipe? Maybe you'd like to come into the kitchen and write down the whole thing? I'm sure grandma Leah wouldn't mind I should give away the family secrets."

"I was just curious what it was—"

"Take my word for it, you'll like it. You don't like, there's something wrong with you, not the blintzes."

"Yes, well, I'll have the blintzes then."

"Wonderful. I'll buy General Motors. What about you?"

he said to Jaxson.

"I'll have the borst."

Levin looked at him out of the corner of his eye, like Jaxson was maybe messing with him. "We don't have anything called borst," he said with exaggerated patience. "We have *borscht*. Best borscht this side of the Mississippi River. All right, I exaggerate. Best borscht this side of the Petaluma River. Go ahead, sue me. Are you gonna ask me the recipe for that, too? Maybe I should just give you the keys to the place and leave right now? Is that what you want? God should cut out my tongue. Imagine, a coupla strangers come into a restaurant, the guy gives them the key to place," said Levin, laughing under his breath. "It's funny, don't you think?"

"It's very funny," said Jaxson, eager to agree. "So, our friends, they should be at the Kurlansky ranch."

"Oy, the Kurlansky ranch," said Levin as he scribbled the order on a pad and pinned it on a rack for the cook to see. "Abe Kurlansky, he should rest with the angels. A harder working man you never met. Up with the roosters, down with the owls. Now, *there's* a man they should give a medal."

"So, you knew him?"

"What am I, talking out of my hat? Sure I knew him. If I didn't know him, would I be giving out medals? Abe Kurlansky was a very important member of the community. He was treasurer of the Jewish Community Center, a job they should give to a grave digger if you ask me, so much trouble. Somebody should ask me to be treasurer, I'd run after him with a pitchfork."

"Do you think you could give us directions to his place?"

"What, now I'm a travel guide? I make blintzes, not maps. Which are almost ready, by the way," he said to Marta-2. "You want sour cream or apple sauce?"

"The sour cream sounds good," she said.

"Sure, it's good. What do you think, I'm gonna give you bad sour cream? It makes no sense. You give somebody bad sour cream, what are the odds they come back again?"

"Not good, I suppose."

"That's right, not good. People can say what they want about Ira Levin, but bad sour cream? Never!"

"So, about those directions—"

"Don't worry about the directions. A guy like you, you have bigger things to worry about. Like that jacket. What is it, beaver or something?"

"It's a motorcycle jacket."

"You don't say. You couldn't get me on one of those things for a million bucks. It's not good for the kishkes, you can be sure of that."

"Do those come with sour cream, too?" said Marta-2.

Levin's eyes danced with delight. "Kishkes with sour cream? That's a good one!" he hooted. "Here, eat," he said, taking the plates from the open counter. "You finish all your food, maybe I'll tell you how to get out to Kurlansky."

"That's very kind of you."

"Kind, shmind. I'm closing soon. How else am I gonna get you out of here?"

Nick awoke to an empty bed, a couple of flies buzzing around his head, and air so heavy it felt like prickly gabardine. The whole room seemed like it was wrapped in the pocket of an old moth-eaten coat. It smelled of must and musk, as if a deer's head had been drenched with aftershave and left to decay in the sun. He hadn't slept well, his dreams having been intermittent and scattered even more than usual. He awoke with a particular feeling of unease and a kind of general anxiety that he couldn't identify. He'd felt that way ever since waking up in Denver the other day—a little on edge, a little suspicious, a little raw of nerve.

Nick stretched his arms, glanced around at his new surroundings and wondered where Esmeralda was. It wasn't like her to be the first one out of bed in the morning and he tried to imagine her outside gathering a bowl of wild strawberries or cutting a bouquet of fresh flowers or picking a basket of plums. He quickly snapped out of that particular delusion of grandeur and decided he'd be satisfied if she'd simply not taken the car and split for Mexico.

Nick got up, pulled on his shirt and pants, and noticed the rabbi staring at him. He felt immediately guilty, like he'd been woefully immodest or unconscionably noisy or wildly irresponsible or hadn't studied enough, and slinked off to the kitchen. It was a simple room with a bank of windows that let in too much light and not enough air. There was a sturdy farmer's table and four mismatched chairs, some exposed shelves with three pots, two pans and a set of dishes, a nearly empty spice rack, a cracked and discolored porcelain sink, a dripping faucet, an old coal stove, a tiny refrigerator, and a combination set of drawers, counter top, and dish drying rack. So this is what a country ranch house looks like, thought Nick. Hmm. Very Interesting. Sort of. It's kind of like a regular house only without all the stuff.

He heard a shuffling sound on the porch, followed by the yanking open and slamming closed of the screen door. Esmeralda appeared with a bucket in one hand, an ammonia-soaked rag in the other, and the glazed eyes of a shell-shocked soldier. She looked disturbed, like maybe she'd left her soul in some foxhole, only the chickens had the run of this foxhole and that was nature in its most unnatural state. "Is breakfast ready?" said Nick.

"*Is breakfast ready?*" said Esmeralda, as she dropped the rag to the floor and pulled an egg from the bucket. "How do you like your eggs?" she said as she wound up like Eddie Lopat and fired it straight at Nick's head. "Over easy?"

Nick ducked as the egg smashed into a gooey mess against the wall behind him. "Hey! Take it easy!" he yelled.

Esmeralda picked up another egg and flung it wildly at

him. "How about soft boiled?" she screamed, then tossed another and another. "Poached?... Scrambled?... Maybe I could make you a nice Denver Omelette and feed it to you in bed?"

"C'mon, Esmeralda... I didn't mean anything..."

Esmeralda dropped the bucket and collapsed into a chair. "Do you know where we are, Nick?" she said, choking out the words between a torrent of tears. "An egg ranch! Did you know that eggs come from chickens? I didn't. I thought that eggs came from yokes. They're running wild out there—Red Rovers or Silver Bullets or Yellow Bellies or whatever the hell they call them—and do you know what you do with those chickens? You feed them. You water them. You pet them. You talk to them. You sing them lullabies. And then maybe, just maybe, they decide to poop out an egg or two and then what, you're supposed to sing their praises to the lord? Not me, Nick, not on your life. Some neighbor girl was here this morning. I offered to sell her the farm for 50 bucks. You know what she said? She said, no thanks. She's saving up for an accordion."

"The farm is worth a little more than 50 bucks. Abe's truck out there is worth at least 25 on its own."

"You know whose fault this is, Nick?"

"Yeah, yours."

"No, Nick, it's all *your* fault. Whoever heard of robbing a poker game disguised as a ghost? What were you thinking? No wonder Montgomery sent those goons after us. You played him for a fool and if there's one thing you don't do, it's play a dummy for a fool. Montgomery called our bluff and chased us halfway into the ocean and now all we've got to show for it is a broken-down ranch, six hen houses, and 2000 squawking chickens."

"Es, you're not completely making sense. Maybe you should take a deep breath and count to ten or something and then think about what you're saying."

"Is that right? You want me to count to ten? Okay, I'll

count to ten." She reached down into the bucket, grabbed an egg and tossed it at Nick's feet. "One..."

Nick jumped away like a cowboy being forced to dance by a crazed gunslinger. "Damn it, Esmeralda—"

"Two..." said Esmeralda, flinging an egg at his knees.

"Look, if you don't stop it, I'm getting the hell out of here—"

"Three..."

Nick grabbed the car keys off the table. "I'm warning you, I'll leave—"

"Promises, promises..."

"Okay, then, that's it. I'm getting out of here. I need a break. I'm going to San Francisco and see if I can find somebody sane to talk to."

"Somebody sane? In San Francisco? That's a good one."

"It can't be any worse than here. I need to listen to some music and clear my head."

"You want to clear your head?" said Esmeralda as she reached for more ammunition and fired away. "Go out to one of those hen houses and take a deep breath. That'll clear your sinuses right out."

"That's it, Es. See you later."

"Don't hurry back!"

"I won't!"

Chapter 32

"Who looks outside, dreams;
who looks inside, awakes."
—Carl Jung

Maybe it was the heat. Maybe it was the humidity. Maybe it was the cool ocean breeze. Whatever it was, it caused Jaxson's essence to awaken from its dormant state and clank around inside Nick's brain like a hyperkinetic pinball. It was Jaxson compressed and condensed into everything that gave him his Jaxsonness, an uncontrollable force in an ungovernable world that stumbled around with the grace of a blind man in a maze. Jaxson's essence knocked over a couple of stray synapses and loose neurons, then poked around in the outer cortex, seeing what trouble it could get itself into. Being disembodied, Jaxson's essence couldn't really do any physical damage, but like a bull in a china shop, it was a good idea to hang onto the cups and saucers anyway. Nick's emotional state, on the other hand, was fair game—what was that about consciousness hating a void?—and Jaxson was just the one to get in there and stir the pot.

Stir it he did, taking a few memories here, a pinch of paprika there, some raw uncooked feelings, and a couple of half-baked ideas and mixing them into a potent broth that seeped right through the windows of the Hudson Commodore. The taste of buffalo stew tickled Nick's tongue as he escaped the harsh Sonoma sun for the cooler breezes of Marin County and the blanket of fog that was San Francisco. It took him a moment to identify the tangy smell of buffalo meat and a moment longer to connect it to the outdoor stage of the Oneida Indian Nation, the halfhearted dance of the warriors, the tired chant of the medicine woman, and the proffered potion of the young squaw. He was transported back to his childhood in Wisconsin, and he could almost smell the pine trees in the air. He was floating again above the dancers, glancing at his parents in the stands, imagining his future, and he suddenly saw it—it came with such remarkable ease!—all he had to do was let his mind wander and take its own course above the pounding of the tom-toms, the shuffling of the moccasins, and the crackling of the bonfire, and now he was here, in his preordained destination, his future had been written in the wind, he had escaped his stunted childhood, he had escaped the foxhole in Italy, he had escaped the shabby clubs of Chicago, his mind was nearly clear of its nightmare, and he had finally arrived where he was always meant to be.

He got off the Golden Gate Bridge, took Bay Street to Columbus Avenue, and turned into a wall of fog as thick as minestrone soup. The sun disappeared, the wind kicked up, and the city took on the shadowy look of a black and white movie. Nick crossed Broadway, parked at the edge of Chinatown, pushed his collar up against the wind, and headed down Jackson Street. Even though it was early afternoon, the clubs and bars seemed less visible than a few nights earlier when streetlights and neon illuminated the neighborhood. He searched the street until the fog cleared enough for him to make out the letters of a half-finished sign. It drew him through a doorway and down some stairs to a basement club that appeared to be just waking up.

The hungry i had a smattering of customers, most of

whom were still drunk from the night before and hadn't managed to make it home. They looked like they had fallen down the stairs the moment the place opened in the morning, gravity being the great alcoholic equalizer, and maybe that was Big Daddy Nord's plan all along: build your club below ground and they will come. One way or another. Upright or in a ball. A couple of guys with two-day beards were propped up against the bar, while several others were bent over in chairs or passed out on the tables. The tables were tiny, especially when viewed against the barren landscape of a nearly empty club, and it seemed impossible that they could actually accommodate a guy and his girl, much less a party of four. Even now everything seemed jammed together—the tables, the chairs, the drinks, the drunks— even the bar and the stairway seemed too close together, like you might reach for the cigarette machine and find your hand in the ladies' room.

A young comedian was onstage, looking like he'd just arrived there straight out of college. He wore a V-neck sweater, had a newspaper folded under his arm, and flashed a sly grin that made him look wise beyond his years. *"Have you seen the Joe McCarthy jacket?"* he said. *"It's like the Eisenhower jacket only it's got an extra flap that fits over the mouth."*

A couple of grizzled customers hooted and somebody booed and that was all the young guy needed to dig in and make himself comfortable. He responded with a torrent of caustic words that resonated off the brick walls of the club like a machine gun volley. *"Joe McCarthy doesn't question what you say so much as your right to say it,"* he said, pushing a little further, as if challenging the drunks to a debate.

The plain brick walls were an odd touch, like you were outside the dump instead of right in its belly, and a single pin of light accentuated the feeling of having entered somewhere raw and a little dangerous. Big Daddy Nord's hulking body didn't help matters much, his six-foot seven-inch frame enough to intimidate any but the most recalcitrant drunk. "What'll it be?" he said.

"A Pabst Blue Ribbon," said Nick.

Big Daddy angled a glass under the tap and pulled the arm like it was a slot machine. "Don't I know you?" he said.

"We met the other night. You were painting the sign."

"Sure, sure, that's right. The harmonica player. Where's your dame?"

"Home with the chickens."

"That right? She didn't seem like the domestic type," said Big Daddy, chuckling under his breath while wiping down the bar. "So, you're probably here for the jam session. As you can see—"

Nick glanced at the comedian on the otherwise empty stage. "There's been a change of plans?"

"Not at all. The boys are just a little late today. Which is to be expected. It's a blues jam, nobody figures to be on time." Before Big Daddy could get the words out, there was the thud of something falling, the clang of metal on metal, and some indistinct swearing from the stairway. "See what I mean?"

Nick looked over to see a guy trying to maneuver a drum set down the narrow staircase. He was weighed down with snares, toms, cymbals, and a big bass drum that barely fit through the doorway. "Should I give him a hand?"

"Hell no, you never want to help the drummer. That's part of his job, lugging those skins all over the place. Don't give him any ideas. You offer him a hand, he'll start expecting it."

"Sure, I get you, gotta keep those drummers in their place," said Nick, playing along.

Big Daddy picked up a rag and dried a couple of glasses. "Tell you what. Just hang loose and I'll put you on the list. The rest of these mopes will fall by anytime now. Then we'll see what's what. Maybe I'll find a slot for you. Maybe not. Depends on what kind of mood I'm in."

"Fair enough."

"You can pull up a barstool or grab a table or flop in the green room backstage if you want. I'll call you when we're ready."

Nick turned back to the stage, where the novice comedian continued his rant to an unlistening audience. Nick had never really seen a comedian before, except for some clowns back at the Flame Club who squeezed out a few laughs from the audience. They had to. It was laugh, or else. But this guy was actually pretty funny: *"For a while,"* he said cannily, *"every time the Russians threw an American in jail, the Un-American Activities Committee would retaliate by throwing an American in jail, too—"*

The Petaluma sun held its own tortures. It waited until it was directly overhead in the sky, then opened the doors to its interior oven and blasted down a wave of heat that would've withered the grapes right off their vines, if only the Kurlansky ranch had any grapes, that is. Esmeralda lay on the bed, too hot to move, too distraught to care anymore. Let the sun bake her to a crisp, it didn't matter, maybe that girl down the road would come over and turn her so that she'd brown on both sides, and then they could serve her to the chickens, Baked Esmeralda, good to the last bite, finally good for something even if only as chicken feed, let them pluck her from head to toe and hang her skeleton as a scarecrow to warn other dreamers of their impending doom, oh, black crow, where were you now in her moment of greatest need, were you soaring in the cool breeze of the ocean, were you rising to the currents of the jet stream, were you circling the Alaskan gulfs, were you eyeing the Oregon streams, were you diving the Baja cliffs, come, black crow, swoop down and save this poor Gypsy girl from a life of trouble and turmoil, return her to her ancestral home deep in the blue Bulgarian sky, take her on your wing and fly her to a place of cool, unhurried, eternal freedom.

The screen door creaked in the kitchen and Esmeralda's eyes popped open. He's back already! So soon! He can't live without me! I knew it! I'll make him crawl! I'll make him squirm! She pushed her way through the heavy Saharan air and went to greet her Invisible Man. He'll need bandages, all right—

"Esmeralda?" said Marta-2 through the screen mesh. "Is that you?"

"Huh?" said Esmeralda, not sure if she was hallucinating from the heat or seeing a mirage or doing whatever it was one did when going crazy on a chicken ranch.

"It's us, Jaxson and Marta. We've been looking all over for you!"

"Marta? Jaxson?" said Esmeralda, still wondering if her brain was pulling a fast one on her. Something didn't add up, that was for sure, and even if things rarely added up in Esmeralda's world, this was outside all known boundaries and a few unknown ones, too. "What are you doing here?"

"You won't believe what we've been through! The deserts! The mountains! The delis!"

"How did you find me?" said Esmeralda.

"Well, I remembered the name of the town, and then I remembered the name of your cousin, and then... um, think we could come in?" said Marta-2.

"Sure, sure," said Esmeralda, opening the door. She barely recognized the weather-beaten bikers decked out in black leather, boots, and shades. "Man, look at you," she said. "When we first picked you up on that road, I thought you were missionaries."

Jaxson and Marta-2 laughed nervously. "Yeah, that's a good one," said Jaxson, anxiously glancing around the farmhouse. "So, where's Nick?"

"He'll be back sometime or other. We had a little disagreement."

"Disagreement?"

"Fight."

Jaxson and Marta-2 exchanged worried looks. "The thing is," said Marta-2, "we kind've need to find him soon—"

"Real soon," interjected Jaxson.

"Sure, sure," said Esmeralda, as she went to fill a tea kettle with water. The faucet wheezed, clanked and knocked, then dribbled a few drops from the tap. "So, you remember that story I told you about acres of wine and money growing on trees and living the life of Riley? Well, I hope you didn't come out here to help me share my fortune, because the whole thing turned out to be a crock of hooey! The only wine around here is some of that Mogen David stuff they use for holidays and two sips of that and you'll understand why Jews are never alcoholics. No, this cousin of mine pulled a real fast one. He decided to punish me good and proper. And why, you might ask? I never even met the guy! What could I have done to piss him off so bad? Usually, it takes at least a day or two before I've worn out my welcome, but this guy got me— how do they say it?—*preemptively*. Oh, yeah, he nailed me real good. You see, my dear cousin Abe dropped 2000 chickens in my lap and now he's up there laughing himself blue in the face with the rest of my accursed family."

Jaxson and Marta-2 listened to Esmeralda's story politely, trying to move her along. The instant she finished, Marta-2 jumped in. "So, about Nick," she said, "we really need to find him. Jaxson left something with him back in Denver—"

"Is that right? Nick didn't say anything."

"Well, no, he wouldn't have."

"So, it's a big rusheroo, is it? It figures, doesn't it? The one time Nick goes somewhere on his own is the one time somebody comes looking for him. Anyway, he said something about going to a club in San Francisco. I suppose I could give you directions, but I don't know if you'd ever find it." Esmeralda saw the disappointment on their faces, then shrugged. "Well, what the hell, I guess I could come along."

"Would you?" said Marta-2 with a sigh of relief.

"Sure, sure, not that you'll ever get me on that motorcycle of yours."

"How about that truck out there?"

"That old thing? I don't even know if it runs."

"Let me give it a try," said Jaxson, already heading outside for the old Dodge Pickup. He gave the handle a couple of good tugs before the door creaked open on rusted hinges. Marta-2 and Esmeralda followed right after him and slid onto the front seat. A cloud of dust stirred from the patchwork of broken springs and torn upholstery, then settled onto the dashboard. Jaxson turned the key, pumped the gas, and got the engine to cough intermittently to a start. It wheezed and shuddered much like Esmeralda imagined old Abe in his final days. Jaxson engaged the clutch, released the brake, and cautiously edged forward. A rooster crowed from the henhouse.

"Let's go before they get any ideas," said Esmeralda.

"What kind of ideas?" said Marta-2.

"How should I know?" said Esmeralda. "They're chickens. The damn things might follow us to town. They think I'm their mother or something." The engine backfired, another rooster crowed, and the Dodge bounced its way down the dirt road as 2000 chickens flapped their wings good-bye. "Can you imagine?"

Chapter 33

"... where the electron behaves
and misbehaves as it will..."
—D. H. Lawrence

Kalamata Quayle awoke late as usual on Sunday. Sunday was her day of rest, a day to pamper herself, write in her diary, catch up on correspondence, paint her toenails, and read a cheap novel. Today, of course, wasn't just any Sunday. Today was the day of reckoning, the day of departure, the day of the aphelion, and she was well aware that her leisurely activities would have to be cut short. She'd been on Earth too long already and was experiencing the dry throat, clicking jaw, and eye tics common to visitors when pushed beyond their limits. For those wired tight as a drum, three days on one planet was all they could take. Now, only five hours remained for her on this wretched rock, thanks be to whomever the Earthlings thanked at a moment like this. Those stone statues on Easter Island would do, she figured, tipping her sombrero south by southeast to where the turtles migrate. Kalamata painted her nails a luscious Cinnamon Satin, applied a coat of sparkle, then went off to see what her partner was up to.

Loquacious was nowhere to be found. He wasn't in the lounging area of the Sprite 2000, nor was he in the trepidation theater, beneath the ship overhang, or anywhere outside on the surrounding mesa. Kalamata next checked the decks, corridors and individual quarters of the Pulsar-7, but got nothing but cold shoulders and icy stares when inquiring as to the detective's whereabouts. The best she could get was a vague response from Captain Wambold, who said he hadn't seen Landry in 12 hours. That's when she began to worry in earnest. Detective Landry, after all, wasn't one to simply disappear without a trace, especially not mere hours before the aphelion. She had no choice but to play her final card, consequences be damned. Kalamata put on a pretty face, went to her favorite informer, and tried to talk sweet. "Hey, Toots, any idea where the head Dick is?"

Marta-1 tossed those words around every which way until they nearly exploded in her brain. "How dare you come here?" she finally exclaimed. "Where were you last night? And the night before? You just used me! You used me and tossed me aside like an old rag!"

"You forget something, angel. I'm a detective first, last, and always. My bags are packed, my passport is stamped, and my tickets are punched. I'm off at a moment's notice to the next adventure, wherever it might take me. I take no prisoners and leave no trace, I'm a free agent gumshoe in a galaxy where there's only bad guys, worse women, and unimaginable danger. What did you think, that I was going to take you with me?"

"Well, no—"

"Of course not, you'd wilt like the delicate rose you are. I could never live with myself, could I? Of course not. Now, tell me, where's Detective Landry?"

"I can't!" said Marta-1. "Don't make me tell you!"

"Sorry, sweetheart, but you've got to. For the memory of our unspoken love."

Marta-1 collapsed against the wall. She felt a hurt and a pang and an ache. Her lips moved as if on their own accord, unlocking untold secrets of the heart. "He's in the Rejuvenation Chamber," she said, choking out the words. "God knows what condition he's in."

"Thanks, angel face," said Kalamata as she gently squeezed Marta-1's hand. "I'll put in a good word for you with the judge."

"Caution! System in Use!" warned a halotronic messaging device that hovered just outside the Rejuvenation Chamber. It was there for good reason, too, since no one really knew exactly what would happen when the electrons from a living, breathing being were pulled and stretched into configurations completely beyond anyone's imagination. It had long been suspected that it was the electron—the simplest, most basic particle in the physicists' toolbox—which lay at the heart of human invigoration. Morphose Spillane's Theory of Rejuvenation arose from the idea that if one could revitalize a living being's molecular structure to a predictable orbital state, one could reestablish the vitality of the mechanism. While the protons and neutrons cooperated, the electron was another story. The problem of the electron was not the complexity of its orbit, but rather its inherent unruliness. The electron was the wild child of the subatomic world, flying off on tangents that left observers dizzy. Whatever machinery engineers devised to measure the path of the electron, the machinery itself invariably influenced its movement, making it impossible to predict its course. For decades, one inconsequential theory after another was offered to chart the precise movement of the electron, and every one of them failed. Then, one day, Periwinkle Wastewater had an idea. Her Principle of Complete Collapse posited that the reason no one had been able to chart the orbit of the electron was because there *was* no orbit of the electron. It moved willy-nilly, completely independent of rhyme or reason, and was in a perpetually free-ranging quest to upset the apple cart. The whole point of the electron was to act as a counter-balance to all of the predictable attributes of the protons, neutrons, and various other boring particles that inhabited the atom. The electron was the bête noir of physics, the rebel, the anarchist, the one ungovernable element in an otherwise predictable universe.

This led Wastewater to take accepted theory and twist it inside out. She turned left instead of right, then turned left again. Forget predictable orbital states. What was needed was to goose those electrons into even *higher* states of unpredictability, an idea which she based upon her own observations that it was better to give a drug addict all the drugs he could endure rather than cut off his supply. Freedom was always better than constriction, even it led to the occasional overdose. If it was the electron's nature to rebel, why not create a special environment where not only would all hell break loose, but it would be encouraged to do so? The Rejuvenation Chamber was just such a place, an electron de-inhibitor that not only allowed but promoted subatomic subterfuge. The whole key to revitalizing the body was to create enough disorder to shake it out of its torpor. "Let the electron spin itself silly," said Wastewater. "Let it bounce off the walls, flip its lid, and delve into total chaos. Then we'll see who's who and what's what."

The who in this case was Loquacious Landry and the what was anybody's guess. After a night in the chamber, Landry felt both better and worse, happier and sadder, and stronger and weaker as his electrons did a jitterbug that pulled him every which way and no way at all. His skull expanded to the size of an elliptical orbitron, then spun around like a washing machine stuck on rinse. His brain was washed, dried, and washed again, then left out to dry on a clothesline that stretched to infinity. Loquacious entered a truly rarified zone. He had a choice—expand or contract, live or die, thrive or wither—and he rose to the challenge like any good detective would do. *Give me liberty or give me that other thing, but give it to me straight, sister, and don't spare the mustard.*

"Detective Landry!" said Kalamata as she swung open the door to the chamber. "Are you all right?"

"Never felt better!" said Loquacious as he kangarooed out into the corridor. "I've never been. So refreshed."

"You had me worried there," said Kalamata as she lit up a Lucky Strike, blew a pretzel smoke ring, and tossed the expired match on the carpet. "Nobody knows what those electrons can do."

"It's like anything else, baby cakes," said Loquacious, taking a deep breath of fresh air, savoring it like fine wine, then slowly exhaling. "You've just got to show them who's boss."

"Glad to see you taking charge, Detective."

"Oh, I took charge all right. Positive charge, negative charge, and every charge in between. So, just a few questions," said Loquacious with a faraway, unfocused gaze. "What planet are we on? What day is it? And who are you again?"

"Detective Landry!" said Kalamata, suddenly alarmed. "Snap out of it! It's the day of the aphelion! We've got to get out of here in a matter of hours or we're doomed!"

"Right... right..." said Loquacious as he slowly pieced together the fragments of information from his jumbled memory. "There was a smart-ass engineer, an old captain, two missing crew members—"

"You can forget all about those two. They're long gone."

"Correction. They might be gone, but not for long. I'm going after them."

Kalamata studied his face and measured his intent. The numbers came up all skewed and wobbly. "That's completely out of the question. There's no time."

"Time is a rubber band. Sometimes you pull it, sometimes you give it a snap."

"Meaning?"

"We've been charged with bringing back seven prisoners. What do you think the Court of Last Resort would say if we come up two short?"

"But you'll never find them on such short notice! We'll be trapped on Earth!"

"No, *I'll* be trapped on Earth. You're not going anywhere. I'm leaving you here. In charge. When the aphelion hits, you'll pilot this ship into the outer stratosphere. I'll do everything I can to meet up with you. In orbit."

"Now, wait just a minute—"

"No, you wait. You see, I've got an ace. In the hole. The escaped prisoners took the Rev-It-Up® retrieval system with them, which is all I need to zero in. On them. Once I'm within the quantic dispersion range, my signals will lock in on the dream machine and I'll put that little buggy of ours on automatic pilot. There's really nothing. To it."

"Then let me come with you—"

"Impossible. There's barely room for three of us to return, much less four."

"This is highly irregular—"

"Screw regulations," said Loquacious as he turned back to the Rejuvenation Chamber and gave the door a vicious kick closed. "Sometimes you've just gotta grab the bull by the balls."

"That's for sure—"

A millisecond after Landry's foot touched the door of the unit, he felt something in the core of his being, as if a dial inside his brain had been tuned to a new radio station. He jiggled his arms to and fro as if to shake off some excess electricity, then clapped his hands together to get the feeling back in his fingers. They were cold and discolored and numb to the touch, but slowly they came alive—first the tips, then the pads, then the knuckles and then the joints—and then, quite uncontrollably, his fingers began snapping to a beat. It

was a lazy, crazy beat that flowed to the flight of his electrons. Those irrepressible freeloaders had taken off again on
some irreducible impulse that struck their fancy, and now
they were flying every which way and every way at once.
They were a big bang of utter disorder erupting inside his
cranium and headed for ports unknown. They were explorers
seeking new horizons. They were surveyors of new coastlines
and cartographers of lost continents. They were the finger-
popping, hand-jiving new generation of electrons on the
loose, and as the energy coursed through Loquacious's arms
and down his spine and into his legs, he fell to his knees,
spread his arms wide like a Broadway showman, and chan-
neled Frankie Laine right off the weekly Hit Parade:

All of me, why not take all of me?
Can't you see I'm no good without you.
Take my lips, I want to lose them,
Take my arms, I'll never use them.

Kalamata stared at him as if she were seeing a ghost, a
vision, and a nightmare all wrapped up in one. She wasn't
sure if she should applaud him, shoot him, or perhaps join
him in dance. "Um, Detective? Are you okay?"

Loquacious shook himself to his feet and made a quick
recovery. "Like I said, Detective, I've never felt better." He
checked his time zone regulator and headed for the polyprotopulsium ladder, as if nothing at all had happened. "Help
me strap in, Miss Quayle. It's time I earned my salary."

Kalamata followed Loquacious to the Sprite 2000, where
he adjusted some dials, checked the gravity flow chart, and
turned off the air intake valves. "Good luck, Detective," she
said as Loquacious flicked a switch, flashed her a thumb's up,
and disappeared into the Western sky. Kalamata straightened
her nylons, applied a fresh coat of lipstick, and headed back
to the Pulsar-7. It was several hours before liftoff on a lazy

Sunday afternoon and there were still a few things that required her attention. As for the detective, he was far, far gone and not even Morphose Spillane knew if he was ever coming back.

Chapter 34

"Fais de ta vie un rêve,
et d'un rêve, une réalité."
—Antoine de Saint Exupéry

Abe Kurlansky's Dodge Pickup coughed and wheezed its way through the streets of San Francisco. The back of the truck was loaded down with egg crates and wire cages and every time it hit a bump, the whole thing creaked and groaned like it would break into a hundred pieces. The noise was the perfect counterpoint to the flurry of chicken feathers that blew every which way in the breeze, leaving a trail as if to announce that Ma and Pa Kettle had just hit town. Esmeralda was embarrassed beyond words— San Francisco was a sophisticated city, after all—and she expected to arrive in style, not on the back of a turnip truck. When they got to North Beach, she sank a bit lower in the seat, mortified by the possibility that one of those fancy broads in a cocktail lounge might catch a glimpse of the bumpkin on the covered wagon. Jaxson found a spot on Jackson and struggled to park. Having snoozed through trigonometry, the concept of angling the tires, wheels, bumpers and fenders was completely beyond him. Marta-2 jumped out of the truck and guided him in. "Turn the wheel left, a little more, okay, a little more, no, *left,* Jaxson, *left,* all right, now straighten it out—"

Jaxson finally found the curb and turned off the ignition. The engine, with typical Kurlansky stubbornness, continued turning over until it finally had enough and conked out on its own accord. Jaxson hobbled out of one door, Esmeralda slinked out of the other, and they were nearly free of the smell of the barn when a crooked man with a cane stopped them on the street. "Hey, there—*Miss?*—how much for a dozen eggs?" he said.

"What? What's that?" said Esmeralda.

"Eggs. Isn't that what it says?" he said, pointing his cane at the door of the Dodge. Beneath the window were the remnants of a sun-faded sign:

FRESH EGGS

KURLANSKY FARMS

PETALUMA, CALIFORNIA

"What do I look like to you?" said Esmeralda. "A country girl who just came into the big city for a Sunday hoe-down?"

"No need for that kind of attitude, Miss. Nobody wants to buy eggs from a sour puss."

"A *sour* puss?" said Esmeralda, turning on him with wild eyes. "I'm a cocktail waitress, got it? I provide decent company and good conversation. I know which way is up, which way is down, and which way's the quickest way out of town. So if it's an omelet you want, I suggest you beat it yourself... as in buzz off!"

"That's very valuable advice," said the man, his voice dripping with sarcasm as he hobbled off down the street.

"Yeah," said Esmeralda, calling after him, "that and two bits will get you a fancy spread at the lunch counter."

Jaxson and Marta-2 observed Esmeralda's blowup and exchanged nervous glances. "So, about that club—"

"Follow me. Oh, and one more thing. If you see Nick, don't tell him it was my idea to come looking for him. Tell him you had to beg me to come and that I still didn't want to and then you got down on your hands and knees and finally, out of the goodness of my heart—"

"Got it."

Esmeralda led Jaxson and Marta-2 across the street to the hungry i. There were a couple of people hanging around outside, looking like they weren't quite sure what the place was or whether or not to go in. Esmeralda pushed past them like a San Francisco old-timer and knowingly pointed out the sign. "Guy's an old friend of mine."

The sound of jangling guitars drifted up from the basement, and when Jaxson opened the door the bass and drums nearly punched him in the guts. The music was loud, the club was packed, and the three of them could barely push their way inside. Onstage, the band was cutting loose on a 12-bar blues. The guitarist played high on the neck and held out a long soulful note just like Robert Johnson or Lonnie Johnson or even Blind Willie Johnson, for that matter, and then came the turnaround and he played the refrain and started all over again. The bass player stood there solid as a rock and with just about as much expression. Nothing on his body moved except for his fingers, his hands, and the big toe on his right foot. Meanwhile, the drummer was all over the place—arms flying, head nodding, his big bluesy bottom bouncing on a stool that looked like it might give way at any moment.

The audience seeped in through the door, the windows, the air shafts, and the keyholes. They were packed in wall to wall and front to back, dancing, drinking, and shucking to the jive, of which there was an endless supply. Big Daddy Nord made sure of that—the jive was so thick you could almost touch it. It was knee-deep and waist high. It was hanging off the ceiling and oozing down the walls. It was floating above the bar and buried beneath the sink. There was jive everywhere you looked and if you didn't grab it quick it just might take you by the shoulders and toss you out onto the street.

Esmeralda took a quick look-see. She searched for Nick on the dance floor, behind the juke box, and under the pool table, all to no avail. Finally, she pushed her way to the front of the bar and gave Big Daddy the big hello. "What's buzzin', cousin?" she said.

"What's kickin', chicken?" said Big Daddy with an exaggerated wink.

"I'm looking for my man, although I'd take an offer on a trade-in."

Big Daddy poured some beers as customers yelled out their orders over the din. "He's paying his dues in the Green Room," he called to her.

"You don't say. And how much exactly is that setting us back?"

"Anybody wants to play, I make them wait until I'm good and ready," said Big Daddy, "and then I make 'em wait a little longer. Don't ask me why. I had a difficult childhood."

"Didn't we all?" said Esmeralda.

Big Daddy wiped down the bar and poured another order of drinks while trying to talk to Esmeralda over the music. "There were a couple of guys looking for you. I told them to check back later."

"Were they writer types, all jazzed up on life?"

"Hard to say. Said they knew you from back there somewhere."

"Sure, sure, that's what they all say. I'm unforgettable."

Another wave of customers pushed in toward the bar. "I owe you one for helping me out with the sign," said Big Daddy. "Let me clear away some riff-raff from one of the tables and get you sitting pretty."

"That would be swell. Bring me three glasses and a pitcher of beer and we'll call it even."

Esmeralda met Jaxson and Marta-2 at a table in the center of the club. "Nick's backstage," she said. "He'll be making his grand entrance any time now."

Jaxson glanced at his wristtop. It was exactly two hours before the aphelion. "Okay," he said. "I'm just going to take a look around."

"Me, too," said Marta-2, following him around a couple of crowded tables to the side of the club.

"Cheers," said Esmeralda as she lined up the three glasses and settled in with her pitcher of beer.

The Green Room wasn't much to look at. There was a burgundy velvet sofa that looked like it had been pilfered out of some 19th century bordello and had all the rips, smears and stains to prove it; a love seat big enough to hold two average-sized romantics or one Big Daddy Nord; a coffee table that wobbled on three and a half legs and was propped up by a battered copy of W.H. Auden's *The Age of Anxiety;* several oversized pillows of such questionable provenance that even the floor recoiled at their presence; a window well that looked up at the back alley and turned away out of sheer boredom; and an assortment of microphone stands, speaker cables, guitar cases, and burned-out amplifier tubes.

The music shook the windows, the floor, and the brick walls, and Nick wondered if he was about to be buried alive in a pile of rubble. He figured it would be the fitting and proper ending to the short and magnificent life of a harmonica player who found love, loss, and five acres of poultry products at the end of the rainbow. When the door to the hallway creaked open, he saw a couple in black motorcycle jackets and shades slipping into the room. "Am I on?" said Nick, reaching for his box of harmonicas.

"You're on, all right," said Jaxson, pulling off his sunglasses. "You're on top of our list of places to go and people to see. Nice to see you, Nick!"

Nick looked at Jaxson as if he'd seen a ghost. Actually, he *wished* he'd seen a ghost. A ghost you can talk to, maybe reason with—who knows, maybe you can make a bargain about your soul or something and get him out of your hair— but Jaxson was a whole other problem. Who was this guy he picked up on the highway not once, but *twice*, this guy who got under his skin, irritated his bowels, and made his palms sweat, this guy who was guaranteed to say the wrong thing at the wrong time, bounce a pool ball off your testicles, and come off as some kind of literary savant? Jaxson was becoming Nick's new recurring nightmare and this was one he couldn't shake, bake, or wake up from. "What in God's name are you doing here?"

"We missed you, Nick," said Marta-2. "We never got a chance to say a proper goodbye in Denver. We were rudely called away on important business."

"I'll bet," said Nick, trying to imagine what important business these two could have. "So, what brings you here?"

"Esmeralda. She's out front in the club keeping our table warm."

"Esmeralda, you say?"

"We caught up with her on that nice ranch of hers. We got to talking and one thing led to another and then the chickens started making a fuss and, well, here we are."

"Yeah, so you are."

Marta-2 nervously edged closer to Nick, then reached into her backpack and pulled out a small canister. "I'm really sorry, Nick," she said as she spun around and sprayed a dose of Somatime Mist into his face. "This will only take a few minutes."

Nick was out cold before his head hit the cushion. Marta-2 made sure he was comfortable, then immediately emptied her backpack and began setting up the Rev-It-Up® retrieval system. Jaxson, meanwhile, locked the door and cleared some room on the coffee table. "Let's be quick," he said, "they could call him onstage any minute now."

Marta-2 connected a jumble of tubes and gaskets from

the dream machine to the Thetamax monitor system, then fit together all of the modular pieces, gauges, and meters. She attached electrodes to Nick's temples, modules to his fingertips, and pulsation anipodes to his toes, then moved on to Jaxson. "Okay, I'm ready," she said as she snapped open a vacuum-sealed pouch and pulled out the Eisenberg gloves.

Jaxson stretched his fingers and felt the oddly familiar transmutational material adapting to the curves and crevices of his hands. Almost instantly, the gloves formed a nearly transparent second skin whose microscopic sensors began mapping his physiognomy. "Comfortable as cotton, warm as wool," he said, trying to cover his nervousness with nonchalance.

"This is it, then," said Marta-2 as she moved a finger above a switch on the machine.

"I guess it is," said Jaxson, a brief moment of doubt clouding his mind. It occurred to him that he could still back out and save himself from the crazy-dangerous journey that lie ahead of him. All he had to do was pull off the gloves, snip a few wires, and leave well enough alone. "Let's do it," he finally said, tossing his better judgment to the wind.

"Good luck," said Marta-2 as she flicked the switch. Within seconds a soft glow emanated from his hands and feet, a pastel aura that moved from violet to rose to lavender, then shimmered just millimeters above his skin.

Jaxson began to feel tired and felt his head nodding slightly. Then, like clockwork, he saw himself staring back from the corner of the monitor. It was him, all right—Jaxson Epsilon, the ghost in the machine. Now, all he had to do was find his essence and get the hell out of there. "I'm going in," he said, as he surveyed the outer regions of the external auditory canal and took his first uncertain steps.

"Okay, Jaxson," said Marta-2, "fingers crossed."

"Fingers crossed."

The Sprite 2000 circled Denver, dipped over Reno, swung up to Portland, buzzed Los Angeles, backtracked to Seattle, and hovered for a full three seconds over Sacramento. Loquacious Landry didn't much care if some rancher in northern California reported suspicious lights in the sky or claimed to have seen a strange object doing Crazy-8s, Loopty-Loops or Upside-Down Flippity-Flops while going at least 50,000 miles an hour. The army would send out a couple of flunkies, the news networks would interview a drunk deputy, and some government bigwig would talk about weather balloons, optical illusions, or cracks in the atmosphere.

All Loquacious knew was that there were 93 minutes until the aphelion and time was fleeting. Oh, and that the Game of the Week was on at that very minute and he was missing the Chicago Cubs take on the St. Louis Cardinals for first place in the National League. His RCA television was completely useless at higher altitudes since the networks were barely able to put out a signal that covered a city, much less the sky. Instead, he occupied himself with the dials on his splashboard, watching the scanner for incoming signals that might indicate the presence of unusual activity, whether it be *Gillette Cavalcade of Sports*, *Meet the Press*, or something actually important.

The scanner was deader than a doornail except for a little blip over Los Angeles which proved to be nothing but an electric razor that fell into a swimming pool and fried a movie producer. Upon approaching San Francisco for the third time, however, there was a flurry of activity in the upper lambda ranges, which indicated a high probability of the kind of propulsive magnetic waves that a dream machine would generate. Loquacious watched the concentric circles on the scanner increase in amplitude, then zeroed in on the source of the streaming. As he guided his space transport toward the center of the city, the scanner locked in on a high priority target and its Instant Data Readout indicated a densely populated area known for its Irish Coffee, Italian Sausage, and Cantonese Dim Sum.

Loquacious hovered over a thick blanket of fog, the Sprite 2000 invisible to all but a few high-flying birds. He located a back alley behind the hungry i that was filled with garbage cans, debris bins, and empty beer kegs and decided to put down. Broad daylight or not, he figured to be safe so long as nobody picked up the trash in the next couple of minutes. As he settled in for a landing, the scanner almost blew out from too much wave-form activity. Something was going on, that was for sure, and Loquacious could almost reach out and grab it. He opened the hatch of the transport, dropped a mesh ladder to the ground, and climbed down. Just across the alley he could hear the blaring music that kids all over the universe were crazy about these days. It was just a bunch of noise to him and he held his ears against the jumble of screeching strings, squeaking reeds and clanging cymbals. Give him a nice cicada orchestra, a foot rub, and a mint frenzy any day.

Loquacious inspected an old brick building where a window well exposed an entryway into the basement. An iron grate was bolted over the window, a silly little contrivance that would hardly prove to be an obstacle to a Grade Four detective from the future. Loquacious pulled out his Fitz-All Toolset, located an old-fashioned Phillips head driver, and unscrewed the bolts. Within seconds, he had the grating off and the window removed. He took a quick glance around, lowered a flexirope, shimmied down along the inner wall, and landed as silently as a cat burglar in a mouse hole.

Loquacious checked his wrist timer and edged along the wall. There were still 75 minutes until the aphelion, which was all the time he needed to make an arrest, read the riot act, mess up a few hairdos, and get his charges on the way to their day in court. Justice served is justice well-done, Loquacious liked to say, unless you like your justice rare and bloody in the middle, in which case he was prepared to turn up the heat, get out the frying pan, and let 'er rip.

Detective Landry turned a corner in the basement and was astonished to find Jaxson and Marta-2 all wired up and plugged into the very same Earthling they'd procured in Denver. Talk about nerve! They were so engrossed in their subterfuge they didn't even notice he was there. Something about seeing the same cast of characters set Loquacious off even more than usual. It was bad enough that they were committing the same crime, but with the same guy? It was like robbing the same bank twice, or burning down the same house, or shooting the same stoolie. Where was the honor in *that?*

It was time to put an end to this nonsense once and for all. Loquacious was beset by a mix of emotions, all of them bad. First there was the anger of seeing his orders being so blatantly and willfully disobeyed. Then there was the disgust at seeing an Earthling being used as a guinea pig when everyone knew that a warthog would do just as well. Then there was that damn music which was pushing him right over the edge—those same 12 bars, over and over—it was enough to drive a man to murder. Then there was the pure unadulterated rage of seeing Jaxson in two places at once, once on the chair and once on the monitor, a double dose of profound displeasure, and then it all began to build—the rage, the music, the disgust—until Detective Landry had what he later would refer to as a short-term psychotic meltdown in which he pulled off his shirt, picked up a steel bar, and charged at Jaxson like an aboriginal headhunter hopped up on fermented bug juice. Loquacious swung that bar—oh God, did he swing that bar—around and around in a circle it went—like a helicopter propeller unleashed from its casing, like a giant mosquito gone wild with malaria, like a samurai sword seeking its scabbard—it took on its own thoughts and its own personality, it cried out for blood, for revenge, for payback, for respect, and whether it was Loqua-cious or his subconscious or the iron bar itself that was in control of the moment, the damn thing zeroed in on its target, its mind made up. There was no stopping it now, not with Jaxson's head looming large. Who could accuse him of improper behavior? It would be called an accident, or an aberration, or a one-time failure to exercise caution—who really cares anymore?—but whatever it was, the moment had come, now was now, then was then, and never the twain shall meet, and with that Loquacious smashed not Jaxson, who, after all, was the perfect target, but rather the Thetamax monitor, breaking it into a hundred shards of very expensive, state-of-the-art debris. "Damn Jaxson Epsilon and his essence!" he bellowed like a crazy man. "Now let's see! Whose dream! Is whose!"

Chapter 35

"The sky is falling!
The sky is falling!"
—Chicken Little

Detective Quayle was ready to boogie. The scene on Earth had gotten stale, the relationships sticky, and the entertainment dubious. Kalamata, never the most even-tempered of mood in the best of times, was not only feeling stale, sticky and dubious, but she was getting downright testy as well. Her throat was dry, her lips were cracked, and she was developing little patches of eczema on her hands and feet. It was, therefore, with a sigh of relief and a jolt of adrenal fluids that she received an urgent message on her Filibuster 500:

MISSION COMPLETE. PRISONERS IN HAND.
MEET YOU ON THE OTHER SIDE OF THE MOON.

Ah, what sweet music to her ears! Even if the message was sent to the obtrusive chirping of a cicada orchestra that could rattle anyone's nerves and set the teeth to chatter. Detective Landry's choice of background music was a joke throughout the force, something akin to the old geezers on Earth who listened to Lawrence Welk while polishing their dentures. This, though, was no time for recriminations or indulging old peeves. Because when all was said and done, Detective Landry, bless his pointy little head, could be counted on to make right what was wrong and deliver the goods as promised. The man could plunge head first into a field of rotting sarsaparilla and come out smelling like a root beer float.

Now, with the aphelion less than an hour away, it was time to set course for outer Earth orbit. There, she'd rendezvous with Landry, drink a toast to the archangel of prison guards, head for the Court of Last Resort, and disappear into one of its shady dive bars. The very idea made her giddy. "Attention, my merry little band of dream thieves," she said, gathering the crew together. "It's time to take the road less traveled. Also known as the road to salvation, the high road, the low road, and the road to the other side of here. In other words, we're fleeing this planet and we're fleeing fast."

Teller perked up from his spot behind the control panel. "Not so fast there, Detective," he said. "Maybe you didn't hear. I assumed control of this ship. We'll go when *I* say we go and we'll go *where* I say we go. Isn't that right, Captain?"

Wambold glanced up from Teller's old spot in the Chief Engineer's Section. He looked utterly defeated and old beyond his years. "I'm afraid so. I have relinquished control of the ship as per Title XII of the Captain's Code, which states—"

"I'm well aware of what it states," said Kalamata. "Fortunately, Section VIII of the Outernational Tribunal contravenes Title XII and establishes that—"

"That may be," said Raleigh, "but Subsection IX of the Treaty of Gur states unequivocally that—"

"Enough!" said Teller, grabbing his schiller from beneath the control board and taking aim. "We're leaving all right, but not to any damn courtroom. I've got a nice desert hideaway picked out in an asteroid belt nobody will ever find."

Kalamata, strangely unperturbed, stared at her fingernails. "Um, Teller," she said, "can you help me with my polish? I seem to have missed a spot."

"I don't think you know who you're dealing with," said Teller, his face reddening.

"Oh?" said Kalamata. "What are you going to do, shoot me?"

"If I have to."

"Then go right ahead."

"Don't push me, Detective—"

Kalamata looked at him with total disregard. "Just as I expected," she said dismissively. "No guts."

Teller had no choice but to fire. At least that's what he would tell the Court of Last Resort 12 days later when they pulled his sorry carcass onto the witness stand and threw every book in the judicial library at him. But for now, he did what came naturally, which was to react without thinking. He aimed at Kalamata's smug kisser and let her have it. The schiller made a little popping sound, like a toaster trying to shoot out a piece of thick sourdough, then fell quiet.

"Thanks, Toots," said Kalamata, blowing a kiss to Marta-1 and grabbing the weapon out of Teller's hands.

"Anytime," said Marta-1 as she pulled a file of papers that had been curled up and shoved into the barrel of the gun.

"A file?" said Teller. "I was done in by a two-bit paper file?"

"It's not just any file," said Marta-1. "This is a Skørsgåård Personnel Profile I've been keeping on you since the day we left. Your behavior is so far off the charts, it makes me blush."

"And that's saying something," said Kalamata. "All right, Captain Wambold, you're back in charge. Prepare for lift-off."

Wambold's face brightened and he straightened to his usual commanding presence. "As ordered," he said, saluting smartly. He moved to his old position at the Control Post and lovingly rubbed his hands along the cold metal walls, the pneumatic convo tubes, and the duracast command stool. "Crew, proceed to your duty stations," he said. "As for you, Teller, take your usual post. I'll deal with you later."

The crew sprung into action. Even Teller. Everyone had trained for this a thousand times and they moved automatically to the required tasks. Raleigh set the coordinates and reconfigured the flight plan. Marta-1 secured the laboratory and lock-down chamber. Teller tested the thruster engines and shut-off valves. Wambold filled in the day charts and mission papers. Oblivia wiped down the windows.

Kalamata proceeded to Jaxson's observation quarters and strapped herself in. Everything in his bunk space was just as he'd left it. The chromium pillow, cold-fusion blanket, and fluoroscopic nightlight were all there, as was his Observation Log, with its stiff spine and blank pages. Kalamata glanced through it, mystified as to what the Ship's Observer actually did on this mission—

"Captain!" said Oblivia with rare urgency. She pointed to the edge of the mesa where two U.S. Army jeeps were headed right their way across the rocky precipice. They were the same jeeps she'd seen parked outside Fort Sedgwick.

"Roswell Air Base," said the Captain, reading the stencils on the doors.

Teller came running over with a crazed look in his eyes. "Captain, permission to address command," he said as beads of sweat poured from his forehead.

"Granted."

"I think we should just zap them, sir."

"Zap who?"

"The Earthlings. A couple of laser bursts will show them who's who."

"Are you crazy, Teller? We'll do no such thing."

"They're after the body bags. Do you know what they'll do when they find them? We'll never get off this planet!" Teller looked out the observation port in a panic, then turned back to see Wambold dusting off the control board and fumbling with a series of switches. "Let's get the show on the road, old man! C'mon, it's time for lift-off!"

"We'll lift off when I say we lift off," said Wambold. "Right now, it's far too dangerous. Our exhaust fumes could incinerate them."

"Are you kidding?" screamed Teller. "Let's go!"

"Stand down, Teller!"

"Not this time, Captain!" said Teller as he raced for the laser tubes and stood above them with his finger poised. "Now, count down for lift-off!"

"Not on your life."

"I'm warning you, Captain."

"Return to your station, Chief Engineer!"

The jeeps slowly approached and cautiously circled the perimeter of the spaceship. Once they entered the ship's defensive zone, red warning lights strobed across the bridge. Teller knew it would only be a matter of seconds before the protective barriers engaged and the deflective shields deployed, and then they'd be forced to just sit there. He did what came naturally. He followed his instincts. He fired the lasers. A bright yellow trail of light burst out from the nose of the Pulsar-7 and engulfed the jeeps. There was a poof, a pop, and then nothing. The vehicles were instantly vaporized.

The crew recoiled in shock. Teller's insubordination in deep space was one thing, but to contravene an order while docked in a neutral port was unthinkable. "Teller," said Captain Wambold over the hushed silence, "you are relieved of your post."

The rest of the crew quietly took their positions as the captain checked his final readings. "All set, sir," said Raleigh, as he confirmed the navigation charts.

"Ready," said Marta-1.

"Ditto," said Oblivia.

"Prepare for lift-off," said Wambold as he stared at the empty mesa with a hollow look and an empty feeling in his stomach.

Kalamata tightened her seatbelt and watched the crew

with a mix of admiration and horror. There was a slight vibration of metal and an almost intangible feeling of thrust as the Pulsar-7 lifted off and headed for outer Earth orbit. Kalamata couldn't even imagine what she'd tell Detective Landry about this. Maybe nothing. This was a report better left unwritten.

Detective Landry had his own report to write. He figured he might goose his up a bit with a few superlatives like brilliant, brave, and heroic. This was the part of the mission he liked best, the quiet aftermath when he could savor a job well done. Now it was just a matter of escorting his prisoners out onto the street, into the space transport, and off into the wild blue yonder. It was enough to make him want to sing, but he scotched that idea good and quick. No, the singing was definitely out of order, now and forever.

Loquacious kicked some broken glass under the carpet, straightened the table, and hastily fluffed the pillows on the sofa. He checked to see that Nick was still breathing, then gathered his prisoners and led them out of the Green Room. They edged along the hallway past the Gents room, where two guys were lurking in the shadows. That seemed to be a favorite pastime of Earthlings—they were great lurkers. It was a planet of oglers, Peeping Toms, and Lookie-Loos whom he wouldn't miss for a minute.

Marta-2 looked downcast as she inched her way forward into the club. The whole mission had become a disaster and she felt she was to blame. Jaxson, for his part, didn't show much emotion one way or the other. He was still in a quasisomnescent state of Conscious Hibernation™ and was as much in his own world as the one before him. "Detective," said Marta-2 as they headed through the club, "our friend is waiting for us at a table. Can I say goodbye?"

Loquacious checked his wrist timer and saw they had an

extra minute or two before things got really hot. "Make it fast," he said, narrowing his eyes and squinting through the darkness. "A handshake will do. Got it?"

"Got it."

The mirror inside the Gents room was distorted, chipped around the edges, and hadn't been cleaned in ages. Still, a guy could gaze into it and get a sense of what he looked like. He could see if his hair was parted straight, if he had any lipstick on his collar, and if there was any spinach stuck between his teeth. Or, in Ray's case, he could see if his lip was swollen beyond recognition, if his eyelids were pink and puffy, and if his ears were big as cauliflowers. In this case, the answer was yes, yes, and yes. Which was kind of comforting in a strange sort of way. He liked scaring the crap out of people and had gotten used to looking like he'd just walked off the screen of a Saturday afternoon creature feature. It had been two days since he and Dirk got out of the hospital and he was feeling his sense of purpose returning full bore. It was time to pollinate a certain flower, put the old stinger in somebody's ass, and get a taste of sweet revenge.

Out front, Dirk kept an eye on things. His hands were bandaged and his head was swollen like a surgical balloon but that didn't keep him from zeroing in on a certain dame at a certain table. Esmeralda was there all right, all dolled up and knocking back the juice just like in the old days. Did she really think that she and her bozo boyfriend could show up at a blues jam and not attract attention? It was truly amazing, the nerve of some people. The joint was plenty crowded, with a thick layer of cigarette smoke hanging like a cloud over Mount Fuji. Onstage, a piano player was tickling the keys, the guitarist was thwacking the strings, and the drummer was bouncing his sticks right off the skins. The band was tight and getting tighter, as pitchers of beer kept making their way to the stage and coming back emptier than the collection plate at a Gypsy wedding.

Which brought Dirk back to Esmeralda. He saw the three people from the hallway moving through the crowd, then watched as the broad in the motorcycle jacket hugged Esmeralda and gave her the big goodbye. This was the perfect time to make his move. He motioned to Ray, who slipped out of the Gents room real catlike and moseyed on over to the other side of the room. Dirk signaled Ray by tapping his nose with his forefinger, Ray responded with a little pull of his earlobe, and the game was on. They approached from two sides and before Esmeralda knew what hit her, she was the luncheon meat in their ham-fisted sandwich. "Hey, doll, we've been looking all over for you," said Ray.

"Hey, boys," said Esmeralda, swallowing hard. "Nice to see you."

"Let's go," said Dirk as he grabbed one arm, Ray grabbed the other, and they lifted her right out of her seat. "We got a hole needs filling. With you."

"Okay, boys, no need to get rough."

"Esmeralda?" said Marta-2, turning back to her friend. "Are you okay?"

"Sure, sure," said Esmeralda as Ray grabbed her tightly around the wrist and pulled her away. "I've got everything under control."

"Doesn't look that way to me," said Marta-2.

"Keep your nose out of it, sister," said Ray.

Loquacious didn't much like the tone in Ray's voice. He saw a bit of himself in Ray—the tightly wound core, the sagging shoulders, the tired face—but mostly he saw the shadows that coursed over his eyes and down along his cheeks. He knew those shadows—they came from within. They were the shadows a half-closed blind had cast across his soul, and that surely was what the two of them shared—

their insides were dark, hidden and closed to the world. Loquacious and Ray were from opposite sides of the universe and on opposite sides of the law—the cop and the robber, the hunter and the hunted—but they were cut from the same piece of cloth. If Loquacious had to look in a mirror, let it be now. He'd had it with these Earthlings. They needed to be taught a lesson and he was just the guy to teach them. "No need," he said. "For that kind of language."

"Oh?" said Ray, wondering if he had heard right. "You got a problem, buddy?"

"As a matter of fact, I do," said Loquacious. He pulled his schiller out of his pocket, just to give them a scare. Let them get a glance of some unknown future, a future in which the good guys had the guns and the bad guys got the wrong end of the stick.

"Hey, look, Ray," said Dirk. "Flash Gordon."

Ray got a glance at what he took to be a crummy piece of junk. The thing seemed to be made of cheap plastic and didn't even have a proper trigger. What, was this guy playing them for a couple of rubes? "Where'd you get that, buddy, some toy shop?"

"Toy shop?" said Loquacious. "Do you think this is a game?"

Ray shot Dirk a look. Dirk shot Ray a look. They both shot Loquacious a look. "Well, gee," said Ray, "I really don't know—"

Before Loquacious knew what hit him, Ray tackled his shoulders, Dirk clipped his ankles, and the schiller went flying into the air. "Run!" yelled Esmeralda, although to whom she was yelling was anyone's guess. If anyone should be running it was her, and run she did, behind the bar and into a crawl space beneath the taps.

Jaxson and Marta-2 took their cue and disappeared up the stairs and out the door. "Where to?" said Jaxson.

"Follow me," said Marta-2.

By the time Ray, Dirk, and Loquacious regained their balance, the schiller was in Dirk's hand. He twirled it around like a prop out of some b-movie. "I'll take that," said Loquacious, moving carefully toward Dirk.

"Oh, yeah?" said Dirk, playing keep-away. He held the schiller above his head and behind his back. When Loquacious finally grabbed for it, Dirk squeezed something or other. It wasn't a trigger really, but more of a gel-like scanner that reacted to his subconscious intentions. The schiller fired.

Onstage, the rock-solid bass player became animated for a brief, unforgettable moment. The ray from the schiller struck his sizable midsection and deconstructed his body parts into a cubist pile of skin and bones. He teetered momentarily, then collapsed onto the floor like a quivering catfish pulled from the bayou. It would be an hour or so before he would reanimate. When his various extremities finally reassembled, the band would still be playing, the beer would still be flowing, and the audience would swear that he never missed a beat.

Ray and Dirk split faster than paramecium on a Petrie dish. When Dirk discovered what a powerful weapon he had in his hand, he did the only reasonable thing: he fired again. This time it was out on the street, about a block from the hungry i, where a policeman was walking down the sidewalk, real big and tough-like, swinging his nightstick in a tight little circle, looking for somebody's skull to clobber. "Hey, copper," said Dirk, "you got change for a three-dollar bill?"

"What are you, some kind of wise guy?" said the cop.

"Yeah, real wise," said Dirk, firing the schiller and leaving the guy in a blue pile of police parts. This was the way Dirk liked to see cops, real twisted and all shook up.

"Lemme see that," said Ray, grabbing the weapon from Dirk and holding it gingerly in the palm of his hand. He aimed it at a brand new Packard that was parked across the street and took a shot. Blotto.

"Whoa," said Dirk, looking at the now-empty parking space. "This'll come in handy during rush hour."

"Real handy," said Ray, turning back and looking toward the club. He saw that the guy in the fedora was headed their way. "Let's get moving. God knows what else that guy has in his bag of tricks."

The fact is, Loquacious didn't have a bag of tricks. What he did have was a world of trouble. To return to the Court of Last Resort with two missing prisoners was one thing, but to return without his schiller would be unthinkable. A detective never gives up his weapon—that was true the universe over—but especially not to primitive Earthlings who would be sure to use it indiscriminately. If anybody was going to shoot up the place, it would be him, damn it, not a couple of smart-ass palookas.

There were 17 minutes left until the aphelion. Seventeen minutes to find Ray and Dirk, 17 minutes to recover the schiller, 17 minutes to recapture Jaxson and Marta-2, and 17 minutes to get the hell out of Earth orbit. A lesser man would panic. He'd curl up in a ball and bemoan his fate and curse his childhood and blame his father for not loving him enough and admonish his mother for loving him too much, on and on until he completely fell apart. But that was not Detective Loquacious Landry, not here, not now, not ever.

Loquacious took a deep breath of the cold, foggy air. It was invigorating and held a taste of the ocean, a tinge of the mountains, and a touch of the evil that only the coming darkness could disguise. He looked up and down the street— at the long-legged broads on their way to secret assignations, at the poker-faced patsies looking to get taken for a ride, at the goons in the shadows and the gobs lurking in alleyways. He made a beeline due west, because that's what a detective does—he goes west. East is for sissies. He crossed Columbus Avenue and found himself in the pagoda-shrouded streets of Chinatown where even the shadows had shadows. They elon-gated across the street and up along the buildings and down the endless alleys. You could get stuck in those shadows. They were like flypaper. Always keep one foot in the light and one in the dark—that was Landry's motto— otherwise you might get sucked down into some deep dark pit of regret.

Shadows or sunshine, Dirk couldn't help himself. He shot up a newspaper stand, a dim sum parlor, and a ginseng shop just because he could. So, this was Chinatown. He'd heard plenty about it even if Alcatraz had always been at the top of his list of places to see in San Francisco. Al Capone had been holed up there until just a few months ago and it was a site of pilgrimage for any self-respecting hood from Chicago. He also wanted to visit Room 1219 of the St. Francis Hotel, where Fatty Arbuckle got popped for messing with that underage tart, not to mention the room where Emperor Norton died, the room where Warren Harding died, and the room where the Maltese Falcon disappeared, even if that was only a movie.

Loquacious followed the smell of singed newspaper, charred dim sum, and burned ginseng roots, and found himself closing in on his prey. Ray and Dirk were sure to make a mistake and they made their first misstep on Powell Street, where a cable car was blocking traffic. They tried to go around, but people were getting on and getting off, moving in and out of the shadows, in and out of the fog. There were more people now, people in gray suits and black hats. A funeral procession passed by and Loquacious got all mingled up with a casket and some flowers and a photo of the deceased, and then an eerie gong echoed through the misty air. There were ten minutes now—no time to waste—and that's when he saw them. Ray and Dirk were walking briskly down the street, weaving in and out between the crowds of shoppers, passengers, and mourners. Loquacious lost them for a second, then caught sight of them again as they slipped into a cable car barn. The barn was a place he'd read about in his travel guide and it intrigued him. Imagine, a spot where giant underground cables scraped and growled beneath the streets as they pulled those goofy little cable cars halfway to the stars.

Loquacious followed Ray and Dirk inside, listening for the intermittent echo of their footsteps as they edged their way along the tracks. Half of the barn was piled floor to ceiling with wheels, gears, brakes and other spare parts, while the other half was inhabited by a giant turbine that spooled the cable through a series of pulleys. Beneath the mechanism was a tunnel which housed the steel wires that stretched out beneath the streets of the city. The pounding of the turbine and the shriek of the cable against the casings set off a deafening cacophony of sound. Ray and Dirk could barely think for the noise, which was just fine with Loquacious. His jaunt through Chinatown had at last inspired a use for his book of proverbs. *"The greatest conqueror is he who overcomes the enemy without a blow,"* he called out over the clamor.

"Huh?" said Dirk, "Who said that?"

"I don't know," said Ray, nervously glancing around the barn at an observation tower, a catwalk, and a maze of ladders.

Dirk heard something amidst the clatter of the machinery. He turned with a start, fired the schiller, and vaporized a pile of brake pads. Then he saw a shadow on the wall. He fired again and a stack of spare seats went up in a poof of smoke. Seconds later, a door creaked in the wind. Dirk shot out a panel of windows along the wall.

Loquacious climbed up a ladder and grabbed a steel ring that swung from the catwalk. The ring was attached to a rope, the rope was attached to a pulley, and the pulley was attached to the giant turbine. He took a deep breath, took a running start, and flew through the air like a trapeze artist. There was no net. There was no safe landing. There was only Ray, Dirk, and a schiller pointed directly at his head. He had no choice. There were a mere ten minutes left before the aphelion.

Chapter 36

"If the dream is a translation of waking life,
waking life is also a translation of the dream."
—René Magritte

Marta-2 had a plan. It was a crazy plan, almost impossible to pull off in the few minutes allotted to her and Jaxson by their propitious escape, but sometimes you take what's given and hope for the best. She had ten minutes to perform a miracle, and that meant there was no time to measure parameters, formulate probabilities, or calculate consequences. She had to find the Sprite 2000, retrieve a crucial piece of equipment, return to the Green Room, get Jaxson back inside the dream machine, recover his essence, and return to the spaceship before the aphelion of the sun. It would be the perfect test case to study the human organism's ability to navigate a maze of obstacles if only she weren't the organism and their very survival the obstacle.

Marta-2's thoughts pinballed back and forth at light speed. In moments of greatest stress, the brain doesn't exactly focus, it *expands,* and that's what was happening to her at that moment. Her brain was expanding to include a giant basketful of notions and images that had at one time or another flown through her mind. It didn't matter that half of those thoughts were completely inappropriate to the situation. Was this really the moment to be thinking about roasted potato peals, her favorite cartoon character as a child, or how many eyelets were in her surfies? Probably not.

As Marta-2 and Jaxson searched for any sign of the Sprite 2000, the late afternoon fog settled over San Francisco like a thick white quilt dropping from the sky. There was a certain comfort in that fog, as the impenetrable haze that separated the streets from the trees and the windows from the doors was also the thing that brought them together. The fog was what they all had in common—the shared mystery of what might lie around the next corner, what dangers lie in wait, what the night might bring. Jaxson and Marta-2 searched the rooftops of low-lying buildings, the courtyards of neighboring apartments, and a vacant lot near the hungry i. Then, as the seconds ticked away, the fog cleared just enough for them to see the alleyway behind the club. A glimmer of hope at last! They hurried past a couple of parked cars, a cluster of garbage cans, and a pile of construction materials to find the space transport nestled between two buildings.

Marta-2 reached for the mesh ladder while Jaxson took up position beneath the exhaust fans. When she came up a few inches short, he boosted her on his shoulders and hoisted her to the bottom rung. Oh god, oh god, oh god, she thought to herself, what was she doing climbing this ladder, twisting open this hatch, and pulling herself inside? Was she becoming the misbehaving floozy from one of Jaxson's blues songs? Were they going to send her up the river to some country shack where the sun don't shine? Marta-2 slid down the entry tube and took a quick look around the interior of the spacecraft. It was just as she expected, a stripped down law enforcement model with one important addition: the RCA television set that Loquacious had nabbed from Fort Sedgwick. The unit was so primitive it was laughable, but this was no time for jokes. Marta-2 examined the miniscule 10-inch screen, which was surrounded by a refrigerator-sized console. When she tried disassembling the unit, she discovered she'd have to go around from the back, no easy task considering that the console weighed a good 300 pounds. The scientist in her determined she'd have to get it at least a foot away from the wall, then apply truby's torque theory to elevate the manifold, release the joist joints, and partition the flyover valves. She reached for the Fitz-all Toolset that was standard issue on all Sprite-2000s only to discover it was gone. Unbelievable! Her brain began expanding again, throwing a useless hodgepodge of algebraic hypotheses, geometrical theorems, and differential equations into the mix. She was so overloaded with information that her brain was ready to fizzle when she saw a quote from some Earthling come scrolling across her field of vision:

> *"Always make things as simple*
> *as possible... but no simpler."*
> —*Albert Einstein*

This Einstein guy was definitely onto something. Why complicate simple Earthling problems with complex Obsidian solutions? Marta-2 tossed aside her torque theory, reached inside the console, and undid a couple of screws. Simple, indeed. Thirty seconds later, she had the RCA monitor in her backpack and was out the door.

Jaxson and Marta-2 made their way across the alleyway to the back of the hungry i. They could hear the music pounding out of the club and felt a shaking of the walls. A pane of glass clanged to the beat of the drums and Marta-2 noticed some broken shards lying around the window well. Taking a closer look, she could see that the whole thing had been broken out and there was just enough room to slip inside. "That must be how Landry got in," she said. Sure enough, as she lowered herself into the well, she found the detective's flexirope still attached to the wall. "Let's go," she said as she shimmied down the rope. Jaxson followed, careful not to smash the monitor onto the floor below.

Once on solid ground, they followed Landry's footprints across the dusty floor. The music was louder now and they could feel the reverberation of the guitar and the thump-thump-thump of the bass as they got closer to the Green Room. After trudging down a back hallway, they pushed open a door and found themselves face to face with Nick. He was just as they'd left him, sound asleep, with the bundle of wires and electrodes still attached to his forehead. The Rev-It-Up® retrieval system was also there, minus its screen, of course, which lie in a hundred pieces on the floor.

Marta-2 pulled the monitor from her backpack and performed a feat of prestidigitation that would've impressed Houdini. She swapped coils, connected hoses, rewired transistors, and rerouted circuits with a sleight of hand so fast it appeared to Jaxson like a big blur. By the time she was done, the dream machine looked like it had been through a tornado, with wires hanging everywhere and extra parts lying all over the place, but the screen was intact and that's all that mattered.

Jaxson picked up a spare knob and showed it to her. "Do we need this?" he said.

"I sure hope not," she replied as she took a deep breath, turned on the power, and waited. The ancient cathode tube had to "warm-up" before a flurry of "snow" appeared on the screen. Marta-2 wondered for a moment how the Earthlings had even managed to survive this long. Was there really a time when technology operated at such a primitive level? Finally, there was a little hum and a crackling sound, as if the monitor was waking up from a long night's sleep. Never before had Marta-2 been so happy to see a cluster of white pixilation projections flash before her eyes.

Without saying a word, Jaxson sat down next to her on

the velvet sofa and faced the coffee table. Marta-2 adjusted a few dials, reset the meters, flicked a switch, and watched for any changes to his physiognomy. Like clockwork, a pastel glow arose from his Eisenberg gloves and a second later, Jaxson's image appeared at the corner of the RCA monitor. He was back at the entrance to Nick's external auditory canal.

The inside of Nick's skull was becoming almost familiar and Jaxson wasted no time maneuvering down the well-trod pathway to the tympanic membrane. After taking a brief moment to get his bearings at the opening to the inner ear, he passed through the moveable gateway, then proceeded along the malleus, incus, and stapes. From there he headed along the outer walls of the Eustachian tube, arrived at the cochlea, and entered the eighth cranial nerve. After negotiating a complicated series of twists and turns, he approached the outer surface of Nick's cerebral cortex.

Marta-2 followed Jaxson's journey on the monitor. "Okay," she said, "I have you located just above the median of the Sylvian fissure. You need to adjust your path 2° toward the lateral, then cross the Sagittal plane to the medial temporal lobe. She watched as Jaxson moved along the neural tissues until he reached the doorway to the limbic system. Surrounding it was the familiar maze of tunnels that led inside. "Can you identify the opening you took last time?" said Marta-2.

"I don't know," said Jaxson as he looked around the folds of the trans-occipital sulcus. "They all look the same to me."

"Jaxson, I want you to close your eyes, take a deep breath, and pick the right one. I know you can do it."

"Yeah, okay," said Jaxson, trying to clear his mind. He blinked a few times, put out his arms as if they were dowsing rods, and headed directly for a particular fissure. To the untrained eye it looked exactly like any of the others, but to Jaxson it had a certain vibration that only a harmonica player could hear. "I'm going in," he said, as he examined the opening, then shimmied down the channel to the hippocampus.

Marta-2 followed his progress on the monitor as Jaxson traversed the cracks and crevices of Nick's limbic system. "We don't have much time," she said. "Your essence is in there somewhere and, well—"

"Yeah, I know. *It's there but not there. It's me but not me.* How will I know when I find it?"

"You'll just know."

Jaxson maneuvered through the upper cortex like an intruder inspecting a socialite's summer home. He ducked in one room after another, hoping not to get caught with the silverware. As for his essence, it was apparently fast asleep in some remote bedroom of Nick's bohemian pad. It figured that he'd have to descend into the basement since nothing, as he reminded himself, ever came easily in the life of Jaxson Epsilon. He braced himself, then headed for the lower cortex, the darkest corner of the brain and the home of anxiety, despair, and nightmares extraordinaire. Great. Just what he needed.

The lower cortex was thick with ganglia and nerve cells. It was like walking through an equatorial jungle, all damp and moist and humid, only this jungle was pitch black with the occasional sliver of light that only made things *worse*. It occurred to Marta-2 that when poking around a snake pit, sometimes it's better not to see the snakes. "Anything?" she said, nervously checking the time.

"No, nothing," he said as he moved from one unwelcoming inner sanctum to the next. It felt like the fires of hell were about to erupt. He almost welcomed them. If it all had to end right here, at least let it be fast, hot, and easy to dance to—

There was a flicker. At first Jaxson thought it was a momentary flash from his embedded video camera, but this flickering was different. It was sustained and sharper in definition and seemed to be generating its own power. At the same instant, Marta-2 heard a rustling from Nick's chair and glanced over to see that his eyelids were flickering. As he entered the REM state, the inner walls of Nick's hippocampus lit up with a powerful burst of electrical energy. The remnants of his recurring nightmare were strobing across his cranium and it was as if Jaxson's jungle had burst apart at its seams. He was trapped in a thunderous hurricane as Nick's neurons and synapses flashed like angry bolts of lightning.

The pounding torment of Nick's dream sent shock waves through his brain and cast Jaxson adrift in a sea of roiling cranial fluids. He was battered from one bundle of nerve cells to another, each of them burning with enough electrical energy to knock him senseless. He swam through a murky pond in the amygdala and came up gasping for air. Reaching out blindly, he grabbed for a maze of synaptic threads and was caught like a fly in a spider's web. The more he struggled to free himself, the more tightly wrapped he became. A voice echoed in his ear: "Jaxson, please," said Marta-2. "There's no time left."

"I know," he said, trying desperately to break free. All around him, bursts of black lightning erupted on the horizons of Nick's brain. Jaxson felt like he was being attacked on all sides—by warplanes, by heavy armor, by artillery shells—but mostly he was being attacked by Nick's dream itself. An artillery barrage exploded with such force that the entire interior wall of Nick's cranium lit up. There was an eruption of total chaos. Nick's neurons retreated, his synaptic threads withdrew, and his connecting tissues recoiled for a brief second.

In that instant, Jaxson's body nearly flew out of the web. He hadn't been expelled with such force since they tossed him out of middle school for behavior unbecoming a child. As he broke free of the synaptic maze, he felt a wondrous jolt to his inner core. His pulse increased, his heart pounded, and his spine tingled as his essence magically—*no, gloriously!*—reappeared from the fog and reunited with his body. He felt whole again, as if some missing part of his psyche had returned from a long trip abroad. Even now, in his most desperate moment, the old Jaxson emerged from the deepest level of Nick's lower cortex. "Did you hear the one about the guy who walks into a bar with a duck on his head?" he said with total seriousness.

"I must've missed that one," said Marta-2, staring into the monitor.

"The bartender looks up and says, *Where'd you get that ape?* The guy says, *This isn't an ape, it's a duck.* The bartender says, *I was TALKING to the duck.*"

"Welcome back, Jaxson."

Loquacious Landry had his own duck problem, as in sitting duck, except for the fact that he wasn't sitting at all, no, he was flying through the air with a schiller lined up right between his eyes. Dirk would've fired immediately were it not for his remembering something about "don't shoot until you see the whites of their eyes." That was probably sensible advice except that Loquacious didn't actually *have* whites in his eyes—they were more like purple polka dots set against flaming pink stripes—and that was because his electrons, bless their unruly souls, were flying off on tangents off of even *bigger* tangents, an unusual electrical phenomenon that Morphose Spillane once referred to as $tangents^2$ although that might have been more hyperbole than mathematical certainty. The additional electrical activity was further enhanced by the steel ring of the pulley system that the detective was holding. The ring was a veritable race track of electron activity and acted as a perfect half-wave dipole antenna which pulled in the local Top 40 hits. When Loquacious landed on his knees on the cable car platform, he was in perfect position to channel Woody Guthrie's new protest song, which was fast rising up the charts:

This land is your land, this land is my land
From California, to the New York Island
From the redwood forest, to the gulf stream waters
This land was made for you and me.

"I should've known," said Ray, watching him with utter contempt. "The guy's a communist."

"And this must be one of those new Russian weapons Senator McCarthy's been talking about," said Dirk, holding the schiller at arm's length. "This explains everything."

Loquacious dropped the steel ring to the platform floor, shook off his electron charge, and got to his feet. Maybe he'd sit back someday and think about his impromptu performance in the cable car barn. Then again, maybe he wouldn't. The future was hard to predict. But right now was right now and if there was one thing he knew, it was that time was fleeting. "Earthlings," he intoned with a stentorian voice that sounded like it echoed from a mountaintop. "You've had your fun, but I'll take that now," he said, reaching out for the weapon.

Ray and Dirk couldn't help but notice the Godlike quality of Landry's voice. It was downright off-putting. *"Earthlings?"* said Dirk. "You hear that, Ray? These commies got a lot of nerve, like they think they're superior or something."

"Real superior," said Ray, his voice dripping with sarcasm. "What did you have for lunch today, buddy, boiled cabbage or boiled beets?"

Loquacious truly couldn't wait to get off this planet. The whole place was a rip-off, from the taxi drivers to the motel clerks to the gas station attendants, and he'd had it up to here. And by here, he meant *here,* as in the back of his hand, which he slapped across Dirk's arm so quickly that Dirk didn't even know what hit him. But hit him he did, on the pressure point of his upper arm, the nerve nexus of his lower leg and the ancillary axiom of his middle neck, and then he moved on to Ray, unleashing a barrage of judicial chops that landed the tough guy in a pile of pain and suffering that the best Chicago lawyer couldn't alleviate. The schiller predictably wound up in the detective's hand. As it was always meant. To be. Loquacious checked his wrist tingler/time zone regulator and saw there were only three minutes until the aphelion. There was no time to waste. He pulled Ray and Dirk to their feet and motioned his new prisoners to get a move on. "Come with me," he said. "You'll have to do."

"Have to do what?" said Ray.

"Move!" said Loquacious, motioning them along the cable car platform. Having seen firsthand the effects of the schiller, they moved spritely, not wishing to become the latest victims of communist technology.

The three of them walked briskly beneath the catwalks, ladders, and pulleys, then passed the giant turbine that was pumping its pistons and cylinders with a steady, clanking beat. They hurried past the bins of spare parts that were piled halfway to the ceiling, hustled up a staircase two steps at a time, and finally returned to the street.

A taxi was parked at the corner. Loquacious shoved Ray and Dirk inside and shouted out directions. "The hungry i and make it snappy," he said to the driver.

"That's only two blocks from here," complained the cabbie.

Loquacious shoved the schiller into the driver's ear and a $100 bill into his hand. "Step on it!"

"You got it, buddy."

Jaxson crawled through the cracks and crevices of Nick's lower cortex, looking for an opening that would lead to the hippocampus. Just get out of there, he told himself, get out of Nick's brain, get out of the Green Room, get out before the aphelion. Another explosive charge from Nick's nightmare briefly illuminated the ceiling of the lower cortex and Jaxson saw an escape channel at last. It was part of the maze of fissures that led to the medial temporal lobe and whether it was the exact one he'd traversed before didn't matter anymore. It was a way out, of that he was certain.

"Please, Jaxson," said Marta-2, as she checked the time. There were less than 40 seconds left. "You've got to hurry."

Jaxson moved up along some neural tissue to the entrance of the tunnel, then looked back one last time. Nick's dream was exploding all around him on every surface of his brain. It was like being in a theater in which every wall was a projection screen—be it the lobby, the balcony, or the restrooms—and no one could get away. There was a terrible onslaught of dirt and mud and noise as the German tank headed directly for Nick's head. He was trapped outside his foxhole, his leg was bleeding profusely, and he couldn't move a muscle. The blood was red-black, the sky was red-black, and the rain was red-black. His fingers dug into the mud as the steel tracks of the tank churned ever closer. He felt the earth give way, the twigs and branches of a tree brushing his face, the first touch of crushing metal on his forehead—

"I can't leave," said Jaxson.

Marta-2 spoke quickly and firmly. "Jaxson, listen to me. You have to get out of there immediately. There's not a second to waste."

"I can't leave him like this. He's going to relive this nightmare forever."

"You can't change what happened to Nick in the war!"

"No, but I might be able to change what happens in his dreams."

Marta-2 glanced at her watch. There were 26 seconds left.

The Yellow Cab screeched to a halt in the alleyway outside the club. Loquacious pushed Ray and Dirk out of the back seat and slammed the door. "Hey, your change!" yelled the driver.

"Keep it," said Loquacious as he ran across the alley.

"You bet, buddy!" said the driver. He was so hypnotized by the size of the bill, he didn't even notice the space transport parked just across the way.

Ray and Dirk noticed, though. Especially when they stood right beneath the intake valves and adjustable wing louvers. "What the—"

Loquacious checked his watch one last time, then glanced around the alley for any sign of Jaxson and Marta-2. He gave up any hope of finding them. He knew this was going to go down as one of his biggest failures ever, made only somewhat more palatable by the fact that he'd have seven prisoners after all, even if two of them were going to take some real explaining. "Okay, let's go," he said to Ray and Dirk, as he motioned them up the mesh ladder to the hatch above.

"Go?" said Dirk. "What do you mean, go?"

"Moscow," whispered Ray to Dirk, knowingly.

Marta-2 stared at the monitor, unable to move a muscle. There was no time left. If Jaxson didn't come out immediately, they would be trapped on Earth forever. "Jaxson," she said with a hollow voice, "this is our last chance."

"Not for you," said Jaxson. "You've got just enough time to get to the spaceship."

"Jaxson, please!"

"Go quickly!" he said. "Get out!"

Marta-2 felt a wave of dread unlike anything she'd ever known. He was right, if course. She had to leave. She decided to leave behind the monitor and the main switch and the power system. She'd take the primary unit and the hoses and the meters—*no! He'll need that!*—and then she dropped a bundle of wires on the floor in a moment of pure panic. She

reached down for the bundle, saw her reflection in the
monitor, and barely recognized the woman staring back at
her. Who was this disheveled creature in the black motorcycle jacket, boots, sunglasses, and torn dress? Surely not the
molecular biologist whose greatest dream had been a
tenured position at some respectable scientific institute.
Strange, what these days on Earth had wrought. She may not
have fully recognized the woman in the monitor, but she
wanted to get to know her better.

Marta-2 could feel every hair on her head and every cell
on her body and every drop of blood in her veins. Her life
was exploding right before her eyes. The past and the present
and the future all combined in a kind of thick stew that
poured open-ended into a vast ocean. The water changed
color from blue to red to green. A giant wave passed over her,
and then, without warning, everything was quiet. She felt
such remarkable calm it reminded her of her mother's womb.
There was a warm breeze and the smell of jasmine in the air.
A touch of mist hung in the sky. "Sorry, Jaxson, I can't do that."

"Listen to me. You have to go!"

"I'm afraid not," said Marta-2 as she sat back down and
fiddled with one of the dials. "If you're staying, I'm staying."

Loquacious, Ray, and Dirk strapped themselves inside the
space transport. Loquacious set the coordinates and counted
down. There were less than ten seconds until the aphelion of
the sun. "Five... four... three... two... one..."

The Sprite 2000 lifted off with barely a sound and headed
for outer orbit. For Loquacious, there would be the rendezvous with Pulsar-7, the usual chit-chat, a bit of extra paper-
work, and then a jaunt into deep space. He looked forward to
the next chapter of his life as an interstellar keeper of the
peace. It beat selling medical supplies any day of the week.
Especially if it was on a planet far away from this one.

As for Ray and Dirk, they would never be heard from again, except as a footnote of some inquisitive Earthlings who years later would investigate the strange goings-on in the summer of 1947. The two guys from the south side of Chicago would forever be known as Earth's first case of alien abduction. It would, alas, not be the last.

Chapter 37

So there I was, trapped inside Nick's brain by nothing but my own stubbornness. It's true, I could've left right then and there, saved Marta-2 from a completely unknown future, and escaped Earth by the skin of my teeth. That's what a sensible person would've done, but I left my sense, along with my thermies, my swimsuit, and my Hawaiian shirts on the Pulsar-7, and that ride was long gone. In fact, it wouldn't be much longer before the spaceship left outer Earth orbit, at which point our remote machinery would stop functioning altogether and I'd never get out of this synaptic jungle. It behooved me to move quickly and decisively, two qualities for which I was not well-known. If I had anything on my side, it was that I was whole again and in control of all of my senses, even if they were nothing more at this moment than a shimmering entity on Marta-2's 10-inch RCA TV screen.

The ones and zeroes of Nick's dream flew by as the tank bore down on the foxhole. The terrifying scene was projected on one screen after another as I moved through the nooks and crannies of Nick's lower cortex. I felt like I could almost jump into the dream itself, as if I could enter the movie through the movie screen. That's what I needed to do, jump in there and make a few directorial changes. Didn't the Eisenberg Paradox say that the material and immaterial nature of a body's mass are identical yet opposite aspects of the same phenomenon? For the first time, it almost made sense. What could be more material than a tank rolling through a field yet more immaterial than a dream that was just passing through the ether?

Which is another way of saying that what I had to do to enter Nick's dream was to *enter* Nick's dream. The way in was right before my eyes, those two sets of vision I had been granted which allowed me to simultaneously see one image from two different perspectives. One was from my view inside Nick's brain, the other from my view outside the monitor. Putting the two sets of eyes together gave me a stereoscopic effect that may not exactly have been a look into the fourth or fifth dimension, but it sure as hell gave me something more than the three dimensions I'd been saddled with all these years. It was all I needed to make that last simple leap.

And leap I did. I grabbed those ones and zeroes by the balls and gave them a good squeeze. It felt good, actually, the first time I had a real connection with science. I took those digits and flipped them on their sides and crunched them upside down and the next thing I knew, I was flying through a whole new part of Nick's lower cortex. This was deeper and darker than anywhere I'd been before and I felt like a caterpillar twisting and crawling through some kind of primeval forest. I began falling—I was falling through a tunnel, I was falling through a womb, I was falling through a birth canal— and when I came out I was in the bottom of a foxhole on a muddy mountaintop in the war-ravaged Italian countryside. The color had been drained out of the ground until there was nothing left but a red-black hue cast upon the surroundings. I looked down and saw that I was wearing khaki pants and

black boots and a shirt with the insignia of a flying crow, like
I was in an army division of wild birds that would peck their
way to victory or dive-bomb with impunity or claw their way
to the top branch or whatever it was that soldiers did when
they lost their minds, but there I was and it was as ugly a
sight as I'd ever seen, mud and blood and body parts, bullets
flying by, bombs dropping from the sky, grenades exploding
a few feet away, I'll tell you, no wonder those guys get a little
goofy, you'd have to be crazy not to fall apart when everything around you is total madness, and then I started
thinking that *I* was going to have nightmares if I didn't move
things along—like that's all I needed—so I crawled up a
broken piece of a ladder and grabbed the roots of a bush and
the branch of a tree and pulled myself to level ground and
that's when I saw it, I mean, you talk about the horrors of
war and the chaos, let me tell you, nothing describes what
was going on, guys were running this way and that, who
knew if they were enemies or friends, their uniforms blended
into one piece of tattered material and they were running
and shooting and stabbing with their bayonets and this was
the end of the line for most of them, they weren't coming
back, no, this was going to be the final thing they saw,
imagine, dying with this on your mind, this was going to be
their final picture of life on Earth, what a terrible, terrible
way to go, and Nick was right in the middle of it, he was face
down in the mud and couldn't move, his leg was caked in a
pool of blood and his knee was cut open right to the bone, I
could see cartilage and pus and an invasion of maggots
already crawling into the wound, and then I saw the steel
tracks of a tank headed right for him, the thing was churning
up dirt and mud and tossing bodies into the air, and there
was no getting away, no, it was too big and fast and unrelenting, and the only thing that made any sense at all was to grab
Nick by his good leg and pull him back into the foxhole, and
that's what I did, I pulled him with all of my strength out of

the mud and along the field and into the pit and as we went tumbling down the foxhole, the tank passed over us—I could see the wheels and the gears and the churning underbelly of this monstrous beast—and we were saved only by how big it was, its tracks dipped into the crevice then leveled even to the ground as it charged on, and when it finally passed, we were buried in dirt and grease and oil, the smell of metal hung in the air, and that's when our eyes met, me and Nick, soldier to soldier, musician to musician, and I wasn't sure if I was saving his life or he was saving mine, we just looked at each other as the fields and hills and mountains disappeared around us and at that moment I understood something— something important—I understood the difference between zero and nothing.

"Ah, now we're getting somewhere," said my inner reporter, who chose this, of all times, to make his reappearance. I had become a pretty important character in my own story and he wasn't going to let slip the chance to get deep into the who-what-when-where-why of the situation. Great. Was this really the moment I had to face my other self as a crack reporter on a newspaper that didn't even exist? This other Jaxson Epsilon looked totally ridiculous, having gotten himself all decked out in war correspondent garb, but this was his once in a lifetime opportunity to cover a real battle. Obsidia had ended warfare centuries ago and there was no way he was going to miss the chance to wear a helmet, carry ration packets and, best of all, don a 16-pocket vest in which he could stash film canisters, notepads, and God knows what other "critical necessities."

I remembered what Marta-2 had told me—*nothing is nothing, but zero is the flip side of one*—and now it finally made sense. I had entered Nick's dream, a world which existed in the billions of digital files that were stored inside his brain, and in the digital world zero is the converse of one. In the real, physical world, zero is a number, a part of an endless sequence, but in the world deep inside our brains, zero is one of the poles on the light switch which lets us turn on our dreams.

"If zero is the flip side of one, then what's nothing?" said the reporter. He'd wiped grease across his forehead, had a cigarette hanging from his lower lip, and looked like he'd just stormed the beaches of Normandy. The guy was possibly taking his job just a bit too seriously.

"Nothing is the absence of anything," I said, as I glanced outside the foxhole. "There's nothing worth saving on that battlefield, nothing worth remembering, and nothing worth rebuilding."

The reporter shuddered as he looked around. "It's like we're at the dead center of the universe."

"It's the place from which everything is created and every-thing destroyed."

"And dream energy—?"

"—is all those ones and zeroes we're pulling out of the files in the brain."

The reporter took a deep drag of his cigarette and let the smoke filter up through his nostrils. "Doesn't it seem strange to you that Nick dreams night after night about being crushed by a tank when that never even happened? We know he makes it all the way to California two years after the war, right? He obviously didn't die."

"Nick isn't reliving what actually happened. He's reliving his greatest fear of what *could've* happened. That's why he wakes up in a sweat every night and why he can't sleep. The doctors call it shell shock."

"Poor guy, he's gonna wind up on some psychiatrist's couch for the next ten years spinning in circles."

"Not if I can help it. These twentieth century shrinks are new to the game. They haven't figured out what works and what doesn't. They think that if they can get a guy to relive his trauma and face up to his fears, they'll be able to change his behavior, but they're barking up the wrong tree. Give them another 50 years and they'll realize that none of this helps anybody overcome his problems. Their patients might understand why they're having nightmares, but they'll still keep having them. No, what Nick needed was a new ending to his dream."

The reporter glanced at Nick and watched him staring up at the sky. "And now he's got it."

"Got your story?"

"Aces," said the reporter as he flipped his notebook closed.

"Catch you on the flip side," I said, as the reporter disappeared into the fog of war. And now that crow was back, that goddamn crazy black crow which kept showing up at all the wrong moments, and he was pecking at the ones and zeroes of Nick's dream, grabbing them in his beak, and flying off to some unseen nest. Was he building a new nightmare for some other poor slob to fall into? Not this time, crow, I'll take those, and I grabbed the whole damn bunch of them and sucked them out of Nick's brain and into the receptacle of the dream machine, where they would marinate and stew in their own juices. Let somebody else compact, destabilize, strip, sterilize, varnish, and reanimate them. Nick's dream wouldn't be seen again except maybe one day in some power terminal on Obsidia where it would light up an afterhours club on the Rue de Reverie.

"Jaxson, please," said Marta-2, interrupting my own reverie. "They'll be leaving outer orbit any time now. You've got to go."

It was time to get out. Nick's lower cortex was a nice place to visit and all, but I wouldn't want to live there. No, my days of intercranial exploration were over and not a minute too soon. Once I had the final ones and zeros of the nightmare all gathered up, I rode them right out of there like Hopalong Cassidy on the range. That whole area of the lower cortex is so unfriendly to either man or beast that I simply took the first way out I could find. There was a light at the end of a tunnel and I figured, yeah, that'll do, so in I went and the next thing I knew I felt myself floating, which, in my experience, can't be all bad, so I gave in to gravity or lack thereof and floated right the hell out of that primordial pit of dread and trepidation into the much friendlier confines of Nick's upper cortex.

Never before did I think I'd feel relieved to be tangled in synaptic threads and cranial fluids, but after what I'd just been through it was like a day at the beach. The rest of the journey was a breeze which I could've done with my eyes closed. In fact, that's exactly what I did, I closed my eyes just to see if I could get through Nick's cochlea without looking. I slid down the auditory nerve canal, hung a left, and flew down that vestibule like a bobsled on a ski slope. That's when I smashed head-first into Nick's tympanic membrane and almost knocked myself silly.

"Jaxson!" yelled Marta-2. "What the hell are you doing?"

"Nothing, nothing," I said, opening my eyes to see that the malleus and incus were vibrating sharply to her voice. Being in no mood for a scolding, I played the rest of the journey straight. I passed through the eardrum and moved along the tissue and cartilage of the outer pathway. The music got louder. Strangely enough, I thought I got a whiff of Pabst Blue Ribbon. And then—

I was back at the coffee table. The me on the monitor flickered a few times, then faded out. My Eisenberg gloves transformed from violet to aubergine to natural. Marta-2 popped the wires off my forehead, hands and feet, and looked deeply into my eyes like she was studying a pickled frog in a beaker. "Welcome back," she said.

"Yeah, yeah," I said, "long time, no see."

There was a knock on the door of the Green Room. "Nick Blake," said Big Daddy Nord from the hallway, "you're up."

Marta-2 and I shot each other quick glances. She reached over and pulled the plugs off Nick, but his head flopped back against the bordello sofa. He was still under the effects of Somatime. "How much longer before it wears off?" I said.

"Hard to say," said Marta-2. "Could be five minutes. Could be ten."

"Hmm," I said. I walked over and checked him out up close. He was out all right, like a ten watt bulb in a five watt socket. As I stood up, I caught sight of something shiny in his shirt pocket. I reached inside to find a Marine Band Harmonica in the key of D, which just happened to be my favorite. Hmm... did I dare?

The stage was wet with sweat and packed from one brick wall to the other with musicians, instruments, amplifiers, and empty pitchers of beer. The guitarist was off on some 12-bar solo which stretched to 24, 36, and 108, if I was counting right. But nobody was counting, it was every man for himself and the band against the world. This was no polite group of chamber musicians—these were afternoon blues cats who made up the rules on the spot—and it was survival of the fittest. You want to play? Sure, jump right in, but it better be good, baby, you've got one run through the changes and then it's goodbye, sucker, back to the woodshed. Unless, that is, you blow some riff that makes the bass player blink and gets the drummer to sit a little straighter and makes the piano play chords and gets the guitar to turn down the volume. Okay, let's see what you have inside, maybe you got lucky and hit a couple of clean notes, but clean is clean and dirty is dirty and this is the blues, baby, we're gonna hang you out to dry. Let's take it from the top, but don't even think of playing the same riff—not here, not on this stage—there's no time for messing around. If you've got something you want to say, then go ahead, tell us your story, we'll listen until you start

repeating yourself, but then it's the hook, rook, and don't be
coming back for more.

The black crow flies on Sunday
You hear what I say
The black crow flies on Sunday
Not just any day
You better look out people
Black crow comin' this way.

The crowd pushed closer to the stage and Big Daddy Nord
looked up from behind the bar. He took a couple of steps
forward, like he finally realized that I wasn't who he thought
I was, but then he figured what the hell, one guy's as good as
the other, and poured another round. Esmeralda snuck a
look from the far corner, saw that the coast was clear, and
took her seat at the table. A minute later Nick joined her and
stared up at me on the stage. A hundred different emotions
passed between us and I probably couldn't explain a single
one. Our eyes met and for a brief second it was as if we were
back in the foxhole, me and Nick, staring at each other
again. It was that same look, like we understood something
even if neither of us had any idea what it was. Nick nodded
his head. I nodded mine. The band hit the turnaround.

The fellas played a boogie and I felt like I was on a train
flying down the tracks, clackety-clackety-clack, the steel
wheels churned against the iron rails with an incessant beat,
over and over it repeated, the wheels, the tracks, the clacks, it
kept going and going, pushing on and on, and it was as if I
was crossing the prairie again, we were rolling and tumbling,
destination nowhere and headed there fast, we were chasing
gophers around the bend, throwing open the windows and
doors, feeling the wind blowing off the plains, that's right,
this train is gonna blow its whistle all night long, so grab on,
people, we're gonna ride this train to the end of the line.

Ten thousand miles from nowhere
Twenty light years from home
I'm ten thousand miles from nowhere
And twenty light years from home
Won't somebody help me
I got nowhere to call my own

The guitar was playing sevenths, the bass was slapping back, the piano was comping minor chords, and the drum was pushing track. Oh, the nightlife, baby, there's nothing like it. There was a commotion at the back of the club, three guys fighting to buy a drink for some sweet young thing, and now I was feeling it deep inside, I cupped my hands around the harmonica and growled into the microphone like a banshee in a meteor storm. Oh, she was a real looker, all right, black motorcycle jacket, shades, boots, swinging her hips to the beat like she was born to boogie. Oh, yeah, baby, I got my eyes on you, I really do, and then the crowd cleared just enough for me to get a closer look and I saw her for the first time.

Oh, baby, baby
How could I have been so blind?
Hey, sweet angel,
Was I right out of my mind?
This must be the first time I saw you
Cause you're lookin' mighty fine.

Was this really the same woman who'd been pressed against my back halfway across America? Some slick cat whispered into her ear, another guy flashed a sapphire ring, and I felt my larynx open like a giant wind tunnel. I hit a note that I didn't know existed. It blasted from the bottom of my toes, up my legs, through my spine, and right out the top of my head. The guitarist looked over at me like I was a six-piece horn section and I returned his gaze by pushing that note right through the roof, that's right, it tore a hole in the ceiling and kept going and going until it blasted clear into outer space. Marta-2 looked up at the stage, our eyes met, and something melted. That's right, Chicken Little, the sky is falling, and I'm the guy with a broom in my hand and a song in my heart. I got your number, baby, you got mine, and let's just see something try to come between us.

A clock above the bar stopped ticking at 5:30 and I figured the end must be coming near. I froze this perfect moment in time, this is what it's all been leading to, the saline wash, the orphanage, the job on the twentieth floor, the long flight to nowhere, the unrequited love, the crash landing, the broken collarbone, the 3:10 to Denver, the backseat of the Hudson, the guy at Western Union, the breakfast at McVittie's, the writer in the pool hall, the Rainbow Ballroom, the dream machine, the disaster in the motel room, the taxi to Fort Sedgwick, the BFMC, the point of no return, the ranch in Petaluma, the ride across the bridge, it all led to this moment on the stage of the hungry i, the moment I played with a real, live American blues band, this moment that forever will read 5:30 in my mind, the moment my dream came true, the moment I understood why I was on Earth.

Chapter 38

*"Sorrow compressed my heart, and I felt I would
die, and then . . . Well, then I woke up."*
—Fyodor Dostoyevsky

A rooster leaned back its head, cleared its craw, and belted out a wake-up call that bounced off the ceiling, angled out the window, swung around the barn, rebounded against a tree, drilled into the ground, shot up from a well, and set in motion a weathervane in the shape of—what else?—a rooster. As it spun in the wind, the weathervane clanged its tin body against a metal base, sent a piercing clamor up its spine, and let out a terrible screech that awoke anyone living north of the horse stables on Spring Hill Road or west of the grazing cows on Guglielmetti Road. If the rooster didn't wake you, the weathervane did.

For Nick, the incessant crowing of the rooster had become almost comforting in the month he'd been on the Kurlansky ranch. Predictability had its own benefits and there was something about waking up every morning at the crack of dawn that gave him a fresh perspective. Six weeks ago he was living in a dump in Chicago, his girlfriend was in a world of trouble, and he was kept awake by a recurring nightmare that threatened to drive him crazy. Now, his biggest problem was deciding which coop needed cleaning, how much alfalfa to mix in with the cornmeal, and whether or not to go into town for supplies. There was something about life on a farm that complemented the life of a blues musician. Everything was right in front of you—the emotions, the conflicts, the rawness—and you didn't have to run through a million hoops to figure out what it meant. Every day on the ranch actually meant something, rather than the days and weeks all blending into one another as they did back in the city. No, Tuesday was definitely Tuesday and that meant something to Nick, even if he couldn't put his finger on what exactly it was.

Esmeralda, on the other hand, knew exactly what to say when the rooster crowed again and awoke her from a deep sleep. "Son of a bitch," she groaned, but she said it with a certain lack of conviction, like it was more from habit than anything else. Esmeralda needed to complain—it was built into her DNA—but her grumbling didn't have its usual bite. She simply uttered a few oaths and blasphemes, then went about her business of getting up and tending to her brood. She was, after all, the mother hen to 2000 unruly chickens, all of whom depended on her good will and better intentions to get through the day. Nobody had ever depended on Esmeralda before and this burden of responsibility did strange things to her psyche: it cut it down to size. For the first time, Esmeralda saw herself as part of something bigger, a mere cog in a natural order that was based on the sun and the moon, not upon the number of drinks she could ring up on a bar tab. The fact is, Esmeralda needed the chickens as much as they needed her. When she looked into their eyes, she recognized something as black and beady as her own. It was disconcerting to see something of yourself in a chicken, and she couldn't help wondering what it meant. What was behind those eyes? What mysteries might they foretell? What lessons were to be learned? Life, death, chickens, eggs—around and around it went.

Marta-2 also awoke to the rooster's crow, which was even

louder in the guest bedroom down the hall. She was intrigued by the correlation of the rooster's call to the onset of daylight and was calculating what variables, if any, influenced its timbre, amplitude, and duration in relationship to the temperature, humidity, and wind speed. When Esmeralda offered Marta-2 and Jaxson a room on the ranch, they jumped at the chance. What better place to begin their new lives as free-spirited explorers of a mostly uncharted planet? From here they planned a tour of the far corners of Earth, investigating the hidden valleys of South America, the desert oases of North Africa, and the mountain retreats of central Asia. Not that Marta-2 had completely fallen into the old habits that had left her on the social bubble back in Obsidia. There was, after all, lipstick and nylons, as Esmeralda had taught her, not to mention lace and lingerie. No, the day might be devoted to scientific exploration, but the night was reserved for a whole other kind of investigation. And by that, she wasn't referring to harmonica lessons.

Jaxson was the only one who didn't awaken to the rooster's crow. That's because he was already awake, having spent the night dismantling the Harley-Davidson and trying to put it back together. The Knucklehead was a primitive contraption and yet there was something, well, *perfect* about the way it all fit together. Even a sci-phobe like Jaxson couldn't fail to be impressed by the efficiency of design and the economy of construction. With 1210 cubic centimeters, 48 horsepower, dry-sump oil recirculation, and a twin-cylinder flathead engine, it was one classy chassis, brother, and that ain't no jive. Jaxson had to pinch himself. It was hard to believe that his life had taken such a crazy turn and he could only imagine what his pals back on Obsidia would think if they could see him now. He thought back to the Friday night film festivals and the record club where he traded blues albums and the vintage clothing store where he gave up a week's salary for a pair of triple-pleated rayon pants. Now he was on

Earth itself, not as a tourist but as a harmonica-slinging front man, ready to take center stage at the drop of a boogie.

Jaxson headed into the kitchen, where the rest of the gang was already having breakfast. Esmeralda had traded in her paisley shawls and fringed blouses for a simple apron and a plain scarf that was wrapped around her head like a babushka. From behind the stove, she looked like somebody's grandmother. "So?" she said to Jaxson. "What'll it be? A chicken liver omelette or maybe some nice latkes with sour cream?"

"The latkes sound like a gas."

"Listen, my latkes, you're lucky they shouldn't *give* you gas."

"Mrs. Bernstein from down the road showed us how to make them the other day," said Marta-2. "A very sweet lady from the old country, isn't that right, Esmeralda?"

"Yeah, the old country. Like this is so new and modern."

"Admit it," said Marta-2, gently ribbing her. "You're starting to like it out here."

"Like-shmike. *Vos art es mich?*"

Marta-2 was momentarily lost, her Yiddish to Obsidian dictionary being sadly lacking. "It's hard keeping up with all the new expressions," she said.

"You talk to too many people around here, your verbs and nouns get all turned around," said Esmeralda. She grated some onions and potatoes, mixed them with flour and salt, added an egg still warm from the nest, and scooped a couple of patties onto cousin Abe's cast iron skillet. "I'm lucky I even speak English anymore."

"So, what's the plan today?" said Nick.

"I was thinking we could fix up the nesting area in the back coop," said Jaxson.

"Speaking of which, I ran some numbers," said Marta-2. "You've been averaging 835 eggs per day which, at 2.7¢ per egg on the wholesale market comes out to $22.54 per day.

From that, of course, you must subtract the cost of production including feed, medicine, transportation and all other incidentals, which I have calculated to total $18.12 per day, leaving a pre-tax profit of $4.42 per day."

"Gypsies don't pay taxes," said Nick.

"No, but Jews do," said Esmeralda.

"Anyway, after making a few calculations, I've determined that it would be optimally beneficial for you to increase the flock by 663 chickens, thereby requiring either the expansion of the present quarters or the construction of a seventh coop, preferably on land facing the pond and providing a southern exposure to the sun."

"And who's going to build that coop?" said Esmeralda.

"Well, you've got two strapping young men here quite capable of undertaking the project."

Nick quickly jumped up from the table. "Okay, I've got to go to town."

"Me, too," said Jaxson. "I just remembered I need some new carburetor gaskets."

"What about your latkes?" said Esmeralda.

"Latkes?" said Jaxson. "Who's got time for latkes?"

The Kurlansky Farms pickup truck bounced along Jewell Road, missing one pothole only to hit the next. "That was a close call," said Nick as he downshifted gears.

"Too close," said Jaxson. He was hanging his right arm out the window, cowboy-style, like maybe he could lasso a stray calf or grab a can of beer off a fence post.

"You know anything about carpentry?"

"I know enough to stay as far away as possible. You?"

"Same thing," said Nick. "A musician has to protect his hands. Bang yourself in the thumb, the next thing you know you're playing harmonica with your feet."

"Exactly." They drove along in silence through the rolling

hills of western Sonoma County. The fact is, there simply wasn't as much to talk about in the country, and if there was, it could be handled in a few words rather than a whole explication. "It's nice out here," said Jaxson.

"Real nice," said Nick.

"Esmeralda seems to like it more each day."

"She likes it fine. I think that once she got some dirt between her toes, her mind stopped spinning so fast and she could actually think something through."

"And you?"

"I sleep better, that's for sure."

"Yeah," said Jaxson. "I can see that."

They drove on silently along Spring Hill Road until they came upon the outskirts of town. A few buildings dotted the landscape—a creamery, a hatchery, a pottery—and the traffic built slightly as they headed down Western Avenue. "Esmeralda and I have been talking," said Nick.

"Oh?" said Jaxson, glancing at Nick out of the corner of his eye while waiting for the other shoe to drop. That's what usually happened when someone began a sentence so ambiguously. So-and-so has been talking, such-and-such is not acceptable, and this-and-that simply will not do. That would invariably be followed with a stern warning, a strict fine, or outright expulsion. In other words, pack your bags and don't let the screen door hit you on the way out.

"We appreciate everything you and Marta have done for us on the ranch," said Nick. "I just wanted you to know that."

"It's nothing."

"Yeah, well, we were thinking maybe we should kind of formalize things. Make you partners or something."

"Partners?" said Jaxson, surprised. "What, the four of us?"

"Two plus two."

Jaxson was touched. He felt a sense of camaraderie he'd never imagined possible with an Earthling and didn't know what to say. "That's a really nice offer, Nick, but—"

"You'll think it over?"

"Yeah. Of course."

Esmeralda was kicking back in the kitchen, doing absolutely nothing, when there was a knock on the door. She opened it to find five middle-aged women in assorted shapes and sizes lined up across the porch. "Miss Kurlansky?" said a short, squat woman with hair as black as Esmeralda's and twice as long. "I'm Mrs. Stern from down the road."

Esmeralda didn't like the looks of it. She was outnumbered and outmuscled. These were country women, the kind that take no guff and give no quarter. They looked like a lynch mob, like maybe somebody was spreading rumors about the new hussy in town and now they'd come with the tar and feathers. For what? Winking at that old man in the hardware store? Flashing a little shoulder to the guy at the deli. Puh-lease. "Look, ladies, I can explain—"

"You didn't forget, did you?"

"Forget?"

"The challah? Mrs. Bernstein said you'd be expecting us."

The *challah?* Of course she'd forgotten. Who remembers an offer to come by and show you how to make bread for the holidays? Better the tar and feathers. "No, no, of course I didn't forget," said Esmeralda as she reluctantly showed the ladies in.

"So, we'll get started," said Mrs. Stern. "We'll need some flour, a little salt, some eggs—"

Mrs. Feinstein, who was also from down the road, ran her finger over the counter and glanced around the kitchen approvingly. "You keep a clean kitchen. That says a lot about a person."

"We don't really have much to get dirty."

"Whatever you need, you can borrow. What else are neighbors for?"

"That's very nice—"

"So, tell us," said Mrs. Schwartzbaum, who was, of course, from down the road, "why don't we ever see you at the Jewish Center in town? Every night there's an event."

"Well, to tell you the truth," said Esmeralda, treading carefully, "I'm not all that big on religion."

"Religion?" laughed Mrs. Schwartzbaum. "Who is? Hardly anybody in Petaluma follows that stuff. I think even the rabbi is an atheist."

"Agnostic," said Mrs. Stern.

"Atheist, agnostic, what's the difference? It's like corned beef and pastrami. It's all in the way you slice it."

"I didn't realize—"

"No, no, tonight is bridge night, tomorrow is poker—"

"Poker?" said Esmeralda, her eyes lighting up. "I play a little poker."

"Listen to her," said Mrs. Plotkin, who wasn't from down the road, but *was* from across the field. "A real card shark, if you ask me."

"So, are we going to make bread or talk all day?" said Mrs. Stern.

"We'll do like always," said Mrs. Danoff, who was from down the road of some other field altogether. "We'll do both."

The ladies rolled up their sleeves and dug in. "Did you hear about Mrs. Cohen down the road?" said Mrs. Plotkin. "Her daughter is dating an Italian boy."

"Get out!" said another. "Tell us more."

"Well, I was walking in town the other night—"

Esmeralda felt strangely at ease. Gossip was good for the kishkes, or whatever it is they say. She had absolutely nothing in common with these women, but there was an unexplained familiarity that allowed her to let down her guard and open her home to them. Maybe it really did have something to do with genetics, that part of her which knew when to kvetch, when to argue, and when to bat her eyes. Somehow or other, Esmeralda found herself embracing her inner Jew just as her inner Jew was embracing her. God knows where this all would lead.

Nick waited in the Dodge while Jaxson stood in line at the Post Office. The back of the truck was piled high with 50-pound bags from Parker & Gordon Grain & Feed. It still amazed Nick that filling the troughs with bags of cornmeal would lead eventually to eggs on the table and meat in the oven. Nature was a real gas, all right. He thought about what Muddy always used to say, that it didn't matter what came first, the chicken or the egg. What mattered was the wing or the thigh, the cornmeal batter or the hot sauce, the fricassee or the jambalaya. Muddy knew what Muddy knew.

Jaxson came out of the Post Office holding a letter in his hand. He got into the truck and swung the creaky door closed. Nick glanced over to see some crazy-looking, undecipherable stamps plastered across the envelope. "Letter from home," said Jaxson, matter-of-factly. The fact of the matter was that there was nothing at all matter of fact about that letter. Not so much because of where it came from, but rather from whom it came. As Nick pulled out onto the road and headed back to the ranch, Jaxson opened the letter and began to read:

JUST A QUICK NOTE TO LET YOU KNOW THAT WE GOT BACK TO OBSIDIA SAFE AND SOUND. THE COURT OF LAST RESORT WAS QUITE TRYING, AS THEY SAY. THERE WERE ALL SORTS OF QUESTIONS AND NOT TOO MANY ANSWERS, BUT IN THE END WE WERE ALL GIVEN SUSPENDED SENTENCES. EXCEPT FOR CHIEF ENGINEER TELLER, THAT IS. HE WAS GIVEN THREE LIFE SENTENCES, ONE FOR EACH OF THE PILOTS HE KILLED, PLUS AN ADDITIONAL TERM

FOR INSUBORDINATION BEYOND THE CALL OF DUTY. HE ACTUALLY THOUGHT THAT WAS A GOOD THING. ANYWAY, TELLER WAS TAKEN AWAY AND THROWN INTO AN IMPENETRABLE PRISON FROM WHICH... HE IMMEDIATELY ESCAPED! HE WASN'T THERE MORE THAN TWO NIGHTS BEFORE HE SLIPPED THROUGH THE DOOR AND LEFT A CRYPTIC NOTE THAT NO-BODY UNDERSTOOD. IT WAS SIGNED HARRY HOU-DINI. DETECTIVE LANDRY WAS ASSIGNED TO THE CASE AND WAS LAST SEEN CROSSING THE QUANTIC DIVIDE IN HIS SPACE TRANSPORT TO SOME UN-CHARTED GALACTIC ISLAND. HE SAID HE WOULDN'T REST. UNTIL JUSTICE. WAS DONE. DETECTIVE QUAYLE ELECTED TO STAY BEHIND AND RECHARGE HER BATTERIES, WHATEVER THAT MEANS. SHE LEFT A DO NOT DISTURB SIGN ON HER DOOR, WHICH SEEMED ODD SINCE THE DOOR WAS ALWAYS WIDE OPEN. CAPTAIN WAMBOLD WAS RELIEVED OF HIS DUTIES AND PUT OUT TO PASTURE IN A SPACIOUS HABLUM FIELD WHERE HE CAN PUTTER AROUND TO HIS HEART'S CONTENT. HE'S ALSO SIGNED A CON-TRACT WITH ST. MARTIN'S PRESS TO WRITE HIS MEMOIRS. THE NEWSPAPERS SAY IT WAS "A VERY NICE DEAL." CHIEF NAVIGATOR RALEIGH HAS QUIT THE FORCE, PUT ALL OF HIS POSSESSIONS IN A BACK-PACK, AND GONE OFF IN SEARCH OF THE PERFECT WAVE. LET'S HOPE HE FINDS IT BEFORE IT FINDS HIM. MARTA-1 HAS RETURNED TO HER PSYCHOLOGY LABORATORY, WHERE SHE IS RESEARCHING THE BE-HAVIOR MODIFICATION OF MICE AND TSETSE FLIES. SHE'S ALSO PLANNING A VACATION AT AN EXCLU-SIVE SPA WITH A FEW GIRLS FROM WORK. NO GUYS ALLOWED. THERE WERE TWO OTHER DEFENDANTS WHOM NOBODY HAD EVER SEEN BEFORE. ONE HAD A FACE LIKE A FRYING PAN AND THE OTHER WAS

SHAPED LIKE A SALAMI. THEY WERE LAST SEEN WORKING AS SHORT ORDER CHEFS AT A DINER IN THE OUTER REALMS. AS FOR ME, I'VE GOTTEN A JOB AS A LATE NIGHT DJ ON AN OLDIES STATION. PRETTY CRAZY, HUH? I'VE STILL GOT MY DANCING SHOES. YOU'LL BE HAPPY TO KNOW, BY THE WAY, THAT THE LIGHTS ARE ON AND BURNING BRIGHT. CIAO FOR NOW, OBLIVIA.

Jaxson folded up the letter and tucked it into his shirt pocket. He glanced out the window at the passing fields, where a flock of sheep moseyed down to a narrow glen, a couple of cows stood passively under the shade of an oak tree, and a goat nibbled on a patch of grass. "Everything okay?" said Nick.

"Couldn't be better," said Jaxson.

And so it was.

Saturday morning, the rooster crowed as usual, showing as little respect for the Sabbath as everybody else in Petaluma. Nick and Esmeralda rolled into the kitchen bright and early, surprised to see that Jaxson and Marta-2 were already up. Marta-2 was working on a big stack of pancakes and Jaxson was brewing his incomparable *coffee supreme,* which consisted of ground coffee beans, filtered water, and a dash of marigold leaf to give the morning that special golden glow. "What's the occasion?" said Nick.

"Well," said Jaxson after a moment, "we have something to tell you."

"The chickens are all dead?" said Esmeralda, hopefully.

"Afraid not," said Marta-2. "I just checked in on them."

"Well, what then?" said Nick.

Jaxson pointed outside to the Harley where the saddlebags were all packed up, along with sleeping rolls and a tool kit.

"Oh, I see," said Nick.

"We were going to tell you the other night," said Marta-2 after a moment, "but, well, you know how it is."

"Sure, sure," said Esmeralda, "easy come, easy go."

"I've never been very good at goodbyes," said Marta-2. "I mean, what do you say to somebody? Thanks? Good luck? Much obliged? It all seems so empty."

Nick pulled out a chair and leaned against the table. "So, where you headed?"

"South Dakota," said Jaxson. "A little town called Sturgis."

"Never heard of it."

"There's a motorcycle rally in the Black Hills that sounds too good to miss. We've got some friends there."

"Friends, huh?" said Esmeralda. "What kind of friends?"

"Nobody like you, that's for sure," said Marta-2.

"And then what?" said Nick.

"We're going to check out the highways and byways of this great country," said Jaxson. He looked out upon the horizon like Gary Cooper on the range, head raised high, eyes clear, voice strong. "Wherever there's a roadhouse open late on a Friday night, that's where you'll find us. Wherever there's a poolhall with a sucker willing to place a bet, that's where you'll find us. Wherever there's a two-lane blacktop with a Burma Shave sign, that's where you'll find us."

Esmeralda paid him no mind. She poured some hot water into a cup and stirred in a spoonful of tea leaves. "Well, don't expect us to bail you out," she harrumphed.

"Who knows?" said Marta-2. "Maybe we'll miss the smell of ammonia and the flapping of wings. There's a lot to be said for life on a chicken ranch."

"I wouldn't trade this for anything," said Esmeralda. "I like putting my head down each night on something I can call my own." Jaxson and Marta-2 took a last look around the ranch house and headed for the door. Nick followed them outside while Esmeralda lingered in the kitchen for a moment. She poured the tea out of the cup until there was nothing left but a residue of leaves, then raised the cup a few inches and spun it three times in a circle. Two lines of leaves formed an arrow that pointed straight up. Was it to the ceiling? The attic? The sky? She couldn't tell.

Outside, the motorcycle was all gassed up and ready to go. Jaxson had on his jacket, boots, and shades, and Marta-2 was already curled into the small of his back. "You know which direction you're going?" said Nick.

"We'll figure it out along the way," said Jaxson as he kicked the starter pedal a few times. On the third try the engine turned over with that classic Harley roar. He revved the engine, then put the bike in gear and slowly pulled out along the dirt path.

"Well, hold on then," said Esmeralda, who appeared on the porch, then went over and handed them a fresh loaf of challah. "You've always got a home here, don't ever forget that."

"We won't," said Marta-2, who teared up a bit as she gave Esmeralda a warm hug. Jaxson touched fingertips with Nick in the latest hipster hand jive, then gave the bike some gas. They drove slowly down the bumpy path, then turned one last time to wave to them from the road. And with that they disappeared into the sunrise.

From high in the sky, a familiar black crow circled the ranch and watched as Nick and Esmeralda waved to their friends. The Harley got smaller and smaller until it became nothing but a fond memory that blended into the landscape. The crow caught an updraft and soared higher into the atmosphere, where he could see the curve of the horizon. The sky was clear and glistened with the first rays of the morning sun. There was a wisp of a cloud, a reflection from the ocean, and something way out in the northern sky that formed a striking geometric pattern. To the crow, it looked like a giant peacock whose tail flashed a thousand eyes.

Maybe that's what it was, a giant peacock with all kinds of crazy transmitters and flashing lights and the insignia of Reverie Energy scrawled beneath its wings.

The crow turned tail and fled south, where the skies were clear, the waters were blue, and his dreams were safe from pilfering. The Earthlings, already mired in paranoia brought about by two world wars, were about to discover what happens when a planet falls into a deep sleep, devoid of its dreams. Would it lead to the mass psychosis of which the Obsidian scientists had warned? The crow decided not to wait around to find out. He turned back for one last look, dipped his wings, and flapped a little faster. The Earthlings would have to deal with this particular invasion on their own.

Appendix A

Omaha Steak

HEAT SKILLET TO MEDIUM-HIGH. MIX TOGETHER 4 TSP. SALT, 2 TSP. GROUND BLACK PEPPER, 1 TSP. ONION POWDER, 1 TSP. GARLIC POWDER, 1 TSP. CAYENNE PEPPER, ½ TSP. CORIANDER, ½ TSP. TURMERIC. COAT STEAKS WITH SEASONING ON BOTH SIDES. SEAR STEAKS ON BOTH SIDES FOR ABOUT 30 SECONDS EACH. LOWER HEAT SLIGHTLY. ADD OLIVE OIL TO PAN. COOK STEAKS 4 MINUTES ON EACH SIDE, PRESSING DOWN AS NECESSARY. REMOVE FROM HEAT AND LET SIT FOR 5 MINUTES. SERVE.

Appendix B

Denver Omelette

HEAT AN 8 INCH SKILLET OVER MODERATE HEAT. BEAT 3-4 EGGS, SALT AND PEPPER IN MIXING BOWL. ADD 1 TSP. BUTTER AND ½ TSP. OIL TO PAN UNTIL SIZZLING. ADD ¼ CUP DICED COOKED HAM, 2 TBS. DICED GREEN PEPPERS, AND 2 TBS. SLICED RED ONION TO PAN. SAUTÉ FOR TWO MINUTES. WHIP EGGS AND POUR INTO PAN UNTIL EGGS BEGIN TO COOK AROUND THE EDGES. LIFT EDGES WITH SPATULA AND TIP PAN TO ALLOW LIQUID TO RUN. ADD ½ OUNCE GRATED CHEDDAR CHEESE. COVER UNTIL CHEESE IS MELTED. FOLD OMELETTE, DIVIDE, AND SLIDE ONTO PLATE. SERVE.

Appendix C

Mormon Funeral Potatoes

GREASE 9X13 BAKING DISH AND PREHEAT OVEN TO 350. IN LARGE BOWL COMBINE 2 CANS CREAM OF CHICKEN SOUP, 2 CUPS SOUR CREAM, 1½ CUP GRATED CHEDDAR CHEESE, ½ CUP CHOPPED ONIONS, AND ½ CUP OF MELTED BUTTER. GENTLY FOLD 32 OUNCES OF FROZEN, SHREDDED HASH BROWNS INTO MIXTURE. POUR MIXTURE INTO PAN. COMBINE 2 CUPS FINELY CRUSHED CORN FLAKES AND 2 TBS. OF MELTED BUTTER AND SPRINKLE ON TOP OF POTATO MIXTURE. BAKE FOR 30 MINUTES. SERVES 12 MOURNERS.